Also by Jennifer Hartmann

Adult Romance from Bloom
Still Beating
Lotus
June First

Catch the Sun

JENNIFER HARTMANN

Bloom books

Published by Bloom Books, an imprint of Sourcebooks
P.O. Box 4410, Naperville, Illinois 60567-4410
(630) 961-3900
sourcebooks.com

Cataloging-in-Publication data is on file with the Library of Congress

Printed and bound in the United States of America.
SB 10 9 8 7 6 5 4 3 2 1

To those who have weathered life's harsh-
est storms and sought its silver linings,
And to those still seeking their sun,
This one's for you.

CONTENT WARNING

This book contains murder, blood/violence, some sexual content, bullying, alcoholism, depictions of chronic illness, attempted assault, underage drinking, guns, and is suitable for readers ages 16+.

"The nicest thing about the rain is that it always stops. Eventually."

—EEYORE

Prologue

ELLA

RED.

    All I see is red.

I burst into the bedroom, my wild gaze landing on my brother. "What did you do?" I sob, breathless and horrified. "What did you *do*, Jonah?"

He sits stone-still on the edge of my bed, staring at nothing, his eyes hollow and bloodshot. Red splatters stain his T-shirt, and his red-slicked hands are balled up in his lap.

"Jonah!"

His chin lifts in slow motion, pupils dilated as his attention settles on me. "Ella…" My name is a choked whisper, a plea. A torn-up love letter.

My head swings back and forth as I fist my hair, tears pouring down my cheeks.

"I'd do anything for you," he says. "You're my whole goddamn world and have been since the moment Mom brought you home from the hospital." His thick Adam's apple rolls, working in his throat. "She set you in my arms, a tiny bundle of pink. My baby sister. My purpose."

I can't stop shaking.

Why did he…?

How could he…?

He stands, grabbing me by the biceps and hauling me to his red-stained chest. Stroking my hair back, he whispers in my ear, "If there ever comes a day when we can't be together, keep me in your heart. I'll stay there forever."

"No," I croak. "J-Jonah… Why, why, *why*…?" My voice dies out on a horrible wail, my forehead slamming to the center of his chest.

Pain.

I'm crippled by it, drowning in it.

It's all I feel. All I know.

"Remember the good times, okay? Not this. Anything but this." Heartbeats pound as his hands hold my hair back. "We're on that bridge under a Nashville sky, a pile of sticks at our feet. You and me, Ella. Just you and me. We're riding horses until sunset, drinking lemonade by hay bales, and telling stories by the fire, untouchable. Think of me that way. Always," he grits out. "Promise me, Piglet."

I can't promise him that.

All I see is red.

It's everywhere.

Sirens flicker red and blue outside the window. More red. Even Mom's sedan is red as it flies into the driveway, the door hanging open as she stumbles out of it and races into the house. I know what's coming next. I try to brace myself for it. Try to prepare.

I can't do that, either.

Mom's scream tears through the house as she stalls in the threshold of my room, her hand sliding down the doorframe as she drops to her knees.

"What have you *done*?" she bellows. Howls. Dies inside.

Jonah glances at our mother with devastation in his eyes before looking back at me.

His cheeks are flushed red.

"I love you both so much. Believe that." He presses a hard kiss to the top of my head, squeezing me tight. "Take care of Mom."

I don't believe it.

If he loved us, he never would have done what he did. It's unfathomable.

I yank myself free of his arms, pivot around, gag, then vomit on my bedroom floor. I'm hunched over, sobbing and retching, when police officers storm the bedroom and whiz past me.

Jonah doesn't fight.

His hands fly up with surrender as he's read his rights, the voices fusing with our mother's painful moans.

I watch as he's hauled away in handcuffs while Mom lies boneless on my bedroom floor. She grabs at my brother's ankle, forcing an officer to peel her fingers away from him before they disappear down the hallway, out of sight.

Gone.

As my mother disintegrates a few feet away, I sink to the floor, collapsing near my bed, trembling in the aftermath of my hell.

I stare dazedly out the window, numb, just as the sun peeks through the clouds and bathes the sky in happy golden light.

But there is no sun in my sky.

No light.

No warmth.

All I see is red…

"HOW TO CATCH THE SUN"

STEP ONE:

Chase the Horizon

The pursuit begins.

Chapter 1

ELLA

AGE 7

THERE'S A POPSICLE IN MY MOUTH.

Orange.

It's my favorite flavor *and* my favorite color. But that's not what makes it the best Popsicle in the whole world. No, it's the best Popsicle because my best friend, Max, is eating one right beside me.

Smiling, I kick my feet back and forth on the swing as one sticky hand curls around the chain and we both sway in opposite time. Max's twin brother, McKay, plays in the sandpit across the playground, digging plastic shovels and toy tractors into the sand and making zoomy sounds. McKay's Popsicle is purple, but orange is way better.

It's a perfect summer morning. The sun is extra bright and the blue sky is striped with clouds. I imagine hopping from one to another, my sneakers sinking in the mounds of fluff.

"Think we'll get married one day like my mom and dad?" Max wonders aloud, straightening his legs out, then bending his knees as he moves back and forth on the swing.

"Sure," I say with a firm nod.

"That would be cool, right? McKay could live with us, too."

"I love that idea." I smile at him, watching his mop of brown hair stick straight up when he pushes forward on the swing. "When should we get married?"

"I dunno," he says. "When we're older, I guess."

"Your parents are kind of old. I don't want to wait that long."

"We can be younger. Maybe in a couple of years."

"Okay."

McKay makes a loud noise and jabs his violet-stained Popsicle stick into the sand. I giggle before glancing over at Max. "You're lucky you still live with your brother," I tell him. "I miss mine."

I miss Jonah so much.

Mom too.

But especially Jonah.

He's four years older than me and my greatest protector. One time, he pushed a little kid off a play set because the bully was throwing rocks at me down below and making me cry. The boy broke his ankle and Jonah got in really big trouble. But he did it for me, so that makes him the best big brother in the whole world. We used to pretend we were Winnie the Pooh characters and the woods behind our horse farm were the Hundred Acre Wood, just like in the storybook.

I love stories. I love books.

I love Jonah.

"My brother is a pain sometimes," Max replies. He watches his brother for a moment before swiveling toward me, his dark eyebrows lifting. "You like me more than McKay, right?"

"Yeah." My lips pucker as I think about it. "You're nicer to me and I like your dimples."

"We look the same," he reminds me.

"He doesn't have dimples."

This seems to satisfy him, and he swings as high as he can one more time before hopping off and dropping to the wood chips. "Come on. Let's go explore."

We discard our Popsicle sticks in a trash can and I follow Max to the tree line to search the ground for treasures. Jonah and I used to look for treasure, too—back when I still lived in Nashville last summer. Back when Mom and Dad were together and we were a happy family. I'm not sure why Dad took me away, and why Jonah stayed behind with Mom, but they said it was because of the divorce. Whatever that means. I guess that's what happens when moms and dads don't love each other anymore.

It's not fair that Jonah and I had to get a divorce, too. He was my best friend. *Until Max.*

My shoes crunch along sticks and green leaves as we explore the trail. "My brother wrote me a letter yesterday," I tell Max, crouching down to stare at a weird-looking caterpillar with stripes.

"Yeah? What did it say?"

"I couldn't read all the words, but Dad read it to me and said Jonah missed me a lot, and he told me about the horses back on the farm. I used to love the horses. Phoenix was my favorite." I nibble my lip. "Jonah also said he'd beat up any boys who were mean to me. He's my protector."

His nose screws up. "You should tell him that I'm here now. I'll protect you."

I smile as wide as the sunny sky.

"Does he write you a lot of letters?" Max continues, bending beside me and sticking out his hand to the bug. The funny caterpillar slithers over his finger, then moves to his knuckles.

"Yep. Every week there's a new letter."

"That's cool." Studying the strange insect, Max relocates it to a nearby branch and we watch as it crawls onto a bright-green leaf. "I bet this little guy will be a butterfly soon. Maybe one of those zebra butterflies."

"Those are my favorite."

"Hey, we should find a clearing in the woods and make it our own special hideaway. Dad can help me build a bench for us to sit and read books together. We can talk about our day at school and watch the butterflies flutter by. It'll be our secret hiding spot."

I think that's the best idea ever. Bobbing my head eagerly, I point to a small clearing covered in a canopy of treetops. "Over there is a good spot."

"Let's go."

We spend the next hour in our new secret spot, sitting cross-legged across from each other and telling magical stories. Stories about swinging on vines and drinking water from fresh streams. Eating berries, swimming in lakes, and dancing under a summer sun. Then when night falls, we'll stare up at the stars instead.

Before we head back to the park, Max holds something out to me. "Look what I found, Ella. It's pretty cool. Do you like it?" He stretches out his palm to show me a shiny white stone.

My eyes light up. It *is* pretty cool. "I love this. Maybe I'll start a rock collection," I say, plucking the stone from his hand and plopping it in the pocket of my tangerine romper.

"And whenever you look at this one, you can think of me."

Max sends me a goofy smile that shoots a tickle to my heart. Almost like fluttery butterfly wings.

As we exit the woods, I spot Dad's silver car waiting for us on the side of the street. He's checking his watch and looking around the playground for me.

Ugh.

I don't want to leave yet. The late August sun is glowing and warm, and it's one of the last days of summer before school starts up again. We're going into second grade. "My dad is here," I mumble. "Guess I gotta go."

Max makes a sour face. "Let's meet back here tomorrow after lunch. I'll tell my dad about the bench. I bet we can carve it up real fast."

"Okay. I can't wait." Sighing, I trudge toward the edge of the playground, saying goodbye to McKay as I pass him.

"Bye, Ella," he says back, his face smudged with sand and dirt.

Dad picks me up in his shiny car.

When I buckle my seat belt and roll the window down to wave goodbye to my friends, Max runs toward me at the speed of light. I learned about light speed in a book once. It's fast.

Almost as fast as Max.

"Ella, wait!" he calls out to me, winded when he reaches the window. "I got this for you."

I look at what's tucked inside his fist, and my heart soars all the way up to the sun-streaked sky. It's a beautiful orange flower. The prettiest flower I've ever seen. "Wow, thanks!"

When he smiles, his dimples pop even more than my eyes. "It made me think of you."

"Really?"

"Yeah. It's bright like the sun," he says, glancing skyward. "And the sun is bright like you."

Dad glances at me over his shoulder. "Time to go, Ella. Say goodbye to your friend."

I bring the flower to my nose and inhale deeply, my eyelashes fluttering over the neon-orange petals. "Bye, Max."

"I'll see you tomorrow?" The car begins to move, and Max runs to catch up with it. He runs faster and faster, almost at the same speed, almost *catching* it.

I hang out the window and smile at him just as the car jerks forward, too fast for Max to keep up with any longer. "I'll see you tomorrow!" I yell back.

Max disappears out of sight when we round the corner and I slump down in my seat, the flower twirling between my fingers. Then I whisper to myself, "And every day after that."

———

Dad drives me away in his shiny car. We leave Juniper Falls and head back to Nashville that night, suitcases and boxes stuffed to the ceiling in the back seat. He lets me sit up front, even though the police might give him a ticket. He says it's a special trip, and because it's special, I get to sit up front and eat a whole bag of gummy bears. I save the orange ones for last because they're my favorite.

By the time we pull into my old driveway on the horse farm, my stomach feels sick.

But not because of the candy.

I think it's because, deep down, something tells me I'll never see Max again.

Mom and Jonah run down the long driveway and tackle me with hugs and tears. My brother spins me around in circles, my hair swinging behind me as I hold on tight.

I'm happy to see them—I am. But I'm sad, too.

As I walk toward the big ranch house and look around at all the horses, my belly suddenly pinches with a tight knot. I whirl around to Dad who is yelling at Mom about something. "Dad!" I call out, tears sprouting in my eyes.

His shoulders slump when he turns to look at me, his gaze dull and tired. "What's wrong?"

"I forgot my stone. The one I picked up at the playground today with Max."

"It's just a stone, Ella. You can find another one."

"But…that one was special. Max found it for me." My bottom lip wobbles as the tears burn. "We have to go back and get it. Please, Dad."

He smiles but it doesn't reach his eyes. "I'll mail it to you, kiddo."

Puffing out a sad sigh, I turn around and walk away, dragging my suitcase behind me. When I make it to the front of the house, I stop and look down at the orange flower still tucked inside my hand.

It's already dying.

And my father never does mail me that stone.

Chapter 2

ELLA

THERE'S A DICK IN MY MOUTH.

Not a real one, of course. It's a drawing of a hairy penis scribbled with Sharpie onto a photograph of me singing karaoke one summer, my mouth wide open, making it the perfect picture to use when depicting a phallic-shaped object jutting between my lips.

Groaning under my breath, I make a mental note to lock down my Facebook account.

Maybe I should delete it.

I snatch the photo off my locker and pick at the tape before crumbling it into an angry wad and stuffing it in my back pocket.

Classmates snicker behind me. Snide whispers float through the hallways, causing my stomach to pitch. I glance down at the cream-and-tan linoleum tiles and blow out a breath.

Ella Sunbury: the weird new girl, who went from riches to rags. The sister of a murderer. The broken teenager who was forced from her pretty house made of bricks and shingles and shlepped over three hours away to the small town of Juniper Falls, where everyone judges her.

Where everyone hates her.

That's what people see when they look at me. That's what they think they know based on news reports, rumor mills, and gossip trains.

And I suppose they're not wrong—I'm all of those things.

But those things are not all I am.

I stretch a piece of chewing gum from between my teeth and twist it around my index finger until the digit is woven with neon-yellow ribbon. Students shuffle past me, muttering nasty comments under their breath.

"She was probably his accomplice."

"I bet she bought him the gun with her million-dollar weekly allowance."

"Maybe we shouldn't piss her off. First-degree murder runs in the family, after all…"

Before I can make a hasty retreat to my next class, someone bumps into me from behind, and I nearly topple forward, no thanks to the extra weight on my back from the dozens of books stuffed into my orange Vera Bradley book bag that I couldn't bear to sell in the auction.

I catch myself on my locker door with an *oomph*.

"Sorry," a voice says, snatching my elbow to keep me steady.

That's all he says, but his hand feels like a hot laser on my skin. Hot enough to leave a future scar. My eyes flick up and meet a familiar shade of clear blue as I recoil, readjusting my bag strap over my shoulder. "No biggie," I mutter. When his hand falls away from me, I take a step back and scratch at the itchy heat left behind.

He doesn't linger; he just stares at me for a stuttered heartbeat, then rejoins his brother who must've bumped him into me.

The Manning brothers.

Max and McKay.

A decade ago, Max became my best friend during a memorable year here in Juniper Falls—the town where my parents first met as teenagers. That was until my father abruptly whisked me away without allowing me to say goodbye. Now, it feels like a lifetime has passed, and I realize that Max is no longer the same person he was back then.

Just like I'm not the same girl who told him I'd marry him one day as I sucked on a tangy orange Popsicle and stared up at the puffy clouds with sunbeams in my heart.

These days, he acts like I don't exist. I'm sure he saw that news story of me, where I made a fool of myself on national television, and now he's grateful we lost contact over the years.

Associating with me would make him a social pariah, too.

I inch my dark beanie down my forehead and glance over at the two brothers now conversing against a row of blue lockers across from me.

"You should come tomorrow," McKay says, shoulder wedged up against a locker door, his back to me. "Bring that chick. Libby."

"I'm good," Max replies. He fiddles with a pack of cigarettes, pulling one out, then pushing it back into the box. "Doesn't interest me."

"You need to get laid, man. You've been a real asshole lately."

My nose scrunches up. Neither of the Manning brothers have said much to me since I arrived back in Juniper Falls—a small community in Tellico Plains, Tennessee—four months ago. Truth be told, I wouldn't be disappointed if they both dropped off the face of the earth. The only person who's shown me an ounce of real kindness since my mom and I moved here is Brynn Fisher.

She just so happens to be dating McKay, which is probably why the brothers haven't outright tormented me like everybody else in this school.

Ancient schoolyard magic be damned.

I tuck my hair behind my ear, my sandal squeaking along the linoleum when I shift my backpack onto my other shoulder.

When Max glances up at me, I realize I'm eavesdropping like a snoop. He doesn't say anything and just furrows his espresso-brown eyebrows together, probably irritated by my existence, while McKay prattles on about beer and Libby's tits.

Then Max blinks and looks down at the grubby tile, which is evidently more enticing than my face.

As fate would have it, the Manning brothers aren't just my schoolmates—they're also my neighbors. They live across the street from the little ranch home my grandmother purchased for us this past May, after Mom drained her bank accounts close to dry paying for my brother's legal bills.

Sometimes I'll see Max outside, mowing the front lawn.

Smoking near his pickup truck.

Careening out of the gravel driveway with shrieky tires as he inevitably takes off into the night to find trouble.

On occasion, he'll glance across the street at me while I'm sitting on the wooden porch in a beat-up folding chair, reading a novel or bookbinding. The eye contact never lasts long, and it's often followed by a pitying headshake or a squinty-eyed scowl.

He doesn't like what I've become.

The feeling is mutual.

Mom used to tell me to go over there and reattempt to make friends with them, even though they are not at all approachable. I told her she should make friends with their father first and then I would consider it. That was the end of the conversation. She hasn't brought it up since.

I swallow down the grit in my throat and move away from the wall lined with lockers. The choked-down emotions are making me thirsty, so I decide to grab a Dr Pepper from a nearby vending machine before heading to English class.

The hallways are mostly cleared out, save for a few stragglers jogging past me with their noses in their cell phones. Everyone is a blur of monochrome. Everything looks desaturated. It feels like I'm moving in slow motion while faceless bodies rush past me like an old VCR tape that's being fast-forwarded to the good part.

But there is no good part in my movie.

There's only this vending machine staring back at me, filled with overpriced snacks.

Sifting through my pockets for spare change, I blink myself back to color and real time. The crumpled photograph falls to the floor when I yank out a handful of dollar bills, and I can't help but cringe as I lean over to snatch it up.

I'm midbend when a voice blares, "Just leave it. Your maid can come by and pick it up for you."

I'm pretty sure the voice and steroid-infected body belong to a football douche named Andy, but I might be wrong. It could be Randy. All I know is that he was blowing spitballs at my head last period and he smells like an off-putting combination of man sweat and butterscotch pudding from the cafeteria.

"Fresh out of maids," I shoot back. "But the position is open if you're interested."

"Yeah, right. It'll take a fucking saint to clean up your brand of mess." His buddies saunter alongside him, trying to cover up their laughter with coughs and dramatic throat-clearing.

Potential-Andy pauses then, his biceps twitching beneath the hacked-off sleeves of his white gym T-shirt. Brown-black eyes trail me from toes to top, the expression he wears brimming with distaste, as if I'm some kind of lower being. Nothing but pond scum or chewed-up taffy wedged into the sole of his shoe that he can't scrape off.

He averts his attention to the photograph and a smirk blooms. "Is that your locker decor? It was so tasteful."

"Was that a gift from you?" I glance boredly at my tangerine-chipped fingernails. "Charming."

"You're flattering yourself if you think I spend my time scouring the internet for pictures of you, Sunbury."

"I guess I overestimated your ability to multitask. Figured you'd find some time in between Googling yourself and browsing low-budget porn sites."

Popping a finger in the air, he perks up like he's had a light-bulb moment. "Speaking of, wasn't that you I saw in that video of—"

"Let's go, Andy. She's weird," a gum-snapping brunette says, giving his ribs a pinch.

Confirmed-Andy sends me a wink before he jogs into one of the bustling classrooms and out of sight.

I can't help the internal flinch as his words pierce through my armor, but I try to brush it off, grabbing the photograph off the tile and throwing it in a nearby trash can.

I'm about to twist back around to the vending machine when a bright-blond ponytail and a pink sundress zooms by. Brynn Fisher catapults herself into McKay's arms with a squeal, and the two of them stumble back as her boyfriend catches her by the thighs and they kiss hotly in front of us, making a scene.

I fidget in place. I've never been kissed like that before, and I idly wonder what it would feel like.

Scratch that: I've never been kissed at all, period.

Double scratch that: I don't care.

After smothering him with repetitive kisses, Brynn slides back down onto her white sneakers and reaches for the backpack she dropped at her feet. When she pops up, she throws a beaming grin in my direction. "Hey, Ella!"

She's the bubble gum to my black licorice.

I drag the beanie off my head and smooth down my hair, startled by her use of my first name. Everyone calls me *Sunbury*, or *new girl*, or *Whatever-her-name-is*. And those are the kinder variations. "Hey," I murmur, lifting my hand in a half-hearted greeting.

"Are you coming to the bonfire out by the bluffs tomorrow tonight?"

I'm fairly certain I missed that invitation. "Wasn't planning on it. Everyone thinks I'm a loser, so that will probably make things awkward."

"You're not a loser."

"The entire school thinks I'm a loser, Brynn. According to this town, I will die a loser. My tombstone is going to say, 'She was a loser. And she lost.'" I shrug, feigning indifference, even though my heart wilts a little. "It's fine."

"That's so dramatic," Brynn replies through a laugh. "Screw them. I think you're cool."

A soft smile stretches on my lips just as the bell rings.

Brynn hauls her book bag over her shoulder as she skips toward me. "It starts at eight. I can pick you up if you need a ride." Before she runs off to class, she pulls a gel-tipped pen out of her ponytail, reaches for my wrist, and scribbles seven numbers onto the underside of my forearm. "Add my number to your phone. Text me any time!"

I'm so taken aback by the gesture, by the token of friendship, that a response jumbles on my tongue and all I do is nod.

Her smile brightens twofold before she whips around, her hair following like a tail of pale honey, and she drags McKay with her down the hallway.

Max doesn't look at me as he shoves the pack of cigarettes into his pocket, grabs an armful of textbooks, and trudges behind them.

While the rest of the students disperse from the halls, I peer down at the writing etched onto my skin in violet ink. I tilt my arm from side to side as the numbers shimmer with glittery specks under the fluorescent lights.

A friend.

I haven't had one of those in over a year. Not since everyone abandoned me after the news broke about Jonah. My mother, Candice Sunbury, owned a well-loved equestrian farm and was a highly respected horseback guide before the entire Nashville area put my family under the proverbial microscope and dragged our name through the mud. And yet, that was nothing compared to what we went through in those subsequent months.

Vandalism. Threats.

Even violence.

I had to carry pepper spray in my book bag as I walked the school hallways during the remainder of my sophomore year, after a friend-turned-enemy shoved me down on the school's running track so hard, I dislocated my ankle.

We didn't press charges. Mom was too busy trying to bail Jonah out of jail to worry about a busted ankle.

And that was fine by me. The last thing I wanted was more negative attention.

Sighing, I drop my arm and make my way over to the vending machine to retrieve the Dr Pepper as I try to shove the barrage of bittersweet memories aside.

Sliding a few dollar bills into the machine, I make my selection and glance at the wall clock, already knowing I'll be late to class. Not a big deal—I'm sure no one will even notice.

I watch as the soda can jerks forward and prepares to fall.

But then it comes to a stop, making a grinding sound and jamming before it can slide loose.

Of course it does.

I kick the machine a few times, begging for the can to wriggle from its entrapment. I smack it with my hand. I even growl at it, hoping it will sense my rage and slither free with fear.

Nothing.

Great. Even the Dr Pepper loathes to be associated with me.

Closing my eyes, I press my palms and forehead to the glass face and inhale a long, tired breath before blowing it out with a miserable groan.

I make a quick stop at the water fountain before plodding to my next class.

———————

Monster.

It's a book written by Walter Dean Myers that we're reading for English class, and it's exactly how I feel when people look at me these days.

Even my teacher, Mrs. Caulfield, has punitive action in her beady eyes as she wields a metaphorical gavel and aims it right at me. My thoughts scatter, and I imagine her adorned in a judicial robe while slamming the gavel down on her desk as stacks of assignments go flying.

"Guilty on all charges," she announces to the classroom.

Everyone claps and cheers as I'm handcuffed and hauled away in an orange jumpsuit.

Fair enough; I love the color orange and the sentence is valid.

I'm guilty.

I'm guilty for not believing in his innocence like Mom does.

I'm guilty for still loving him, despite it all.

Most of all, I'm guilty for not loving him hard enough to keep him from pulling that trigger. He must not have felt the strength of my heart or known how much I'd miss him. He made a choice that night and it wasn't us.

He didn't choose us, and sometimes I feel like that's *my* fault.

"Miss Sunbury."

My chin is propped up on my hand as I stare blankly to the left, my mind still padlocked in a jail cell. I don't hear Mrs. Caulfield right away. I also don't realize I'm staring directly at Max Manning with a smidgen of drool dribbling from the corner of my mouth.

"Miss Sunbury," she repeats, louder this time. "I've been told that Mr. Manning is quite the catch here at Juniper High, but that is what Instagram is for. Please be respectful and ogle on your own time, during after-school hours."

Everyone laughs.

I straighten at my desk and start frantically swiping at my chin. My mortified eyes meet with crystalline blue across the classroom and my face heats to an inferno level, mimicking my own personal hell. "Sorry," I fluster, inching up on my elbows. "I spaced."

Max continues to watch me from his adjacent seat, leaning back against the sepia plastic chair, both hands twirling a pencil around in aimless circles. His jeans are ripped, his hair is dark. He's tall and lean, towering well over six feet and a head above the guy seated behind him. A tattoo made of black ink ropes around his right bicep and his skin is bronzed from the Tennessee sun.

He runs a lot, remains unattainable and mysterious, and has perfected the smolder. I'd say he stands out among the rest of the uninspiring student body… except he has that same look everyone has when they stare at me.

The look of pity because I'm washed-up and unworthy.

The look of annoyance because I don't belong in this town or at this school.

The look of revulsion because my blood swims with the same blood as Jonah Sunbury's.

At the end of the day, Max is still one of them.

I dart my gaze away and focus on Mrs. Caulfield, who is now half-sitting on the edge of her meticulously organized desk. Her flaxen-blond hair is sprinkled with silver and tied up in a harsh twist, enhancing the narrow peak of her head. She's a *missus* instead of a *miss*, which means someone liked her enough to marry her. Good for her, because I sure don't. She's the one teacher who's been a jerk to me, and if I didn't want to draw more negative attention than I already have, I'd probably report her to the school board.

"You know, Miss Sunbury," the teacher drawls, one of her tawny eyebrows lifting with mock consideration. "The literature we're currently reading has some striking parallels to your own personal history."

Her words hit me like a silver bullet to the chest.

My throat closes up. Oxygen is hard to catch.

Shifting in the squeaky chair, I part my lips and release a soundless whisper. All I do is shake my head, feeling all eyes on me. Feeling the judgment, the persecution, the slew of gavels hammering down on particleboard desks.

Guilty, guilty, guilty.

I brave another quick glance in Max's direction, unsurprised to find he's still boring holes into me. Boring holes into *my* holes. I bet he wishes that if he glowers at me long enough, my cracks and gaps will stretch so wide that there will be nothing left of me.

Poof.

Sometimes I wish that, too. Especially right now.

I'm sure Max regrets ever being friends with me in the first place.

I clear the misery from my throat and find my voice, looking back at Mrs. Caulfield. "I wouldn't know," I lie. "We've only just started reading."

True enough, but I know exactly what the book is about. The blurb is on the back.

"Yes, well, has anything stood out to you thus far?" she probes, and I can almost hear the smirk on her face. "Anything you'd like to discuss and share with the class, while pulling from your own real-life experiences?"

"Not really. That's personal."

"It made national news. Your brother's trial was publicly broadcast."

My chest tightens to the point of near suffocation.

This is ridiculous. It's cruel and invasive.

Heart galloping with indignation, I start stuffing books and pencils into my bag, then zip it up as I prepare to bolt. "That's what Instagram is for," I fling back, using her own words against her. "Please be respectful and meddle on your own time, during after-school hours."

Gasps ring out all around me as I push up from my chair and haul my backpack over one shoulder. I don't spare the teacher another glance, but I do catch Max's eyes for a split second before I storm out of the classroom.

He's still staring at me.

Still watching.

Only this time, I swear the ghost of a smile flickers on his lips.

As I race out the door, knowing I'll be headed for detention after school, I jog toward the far end of the hallway, where the vending machine still taunts me with that elusive Dr Pepper. It's basically holding it hostage and the notion manages to heighten my anger to an unhealthy level.

I want that soda.

It's mine, I paid for it, I want it.

Mostly, I want to be mad at something other than Jonah for once.

A snarling sound fizzes in the back of my throat as I stomp forward and stare down the machine. I kick it again. Bang on it with both hands, then turn my hands into furious fists and pound some more.

It doesn't move.

Doesn't budge.

I'm pretty sure I hear it laughing, but that could be my own inner voice.

With a final knock with my sandal to the base, I shout, "Fuck you, Dr Pepper!"

My words echo through the empty hallways, ricocheting off the walls and immortalizing themselves in the ugly blue lockers and even uglier tile. I'm embarrassingly close to tears when—

Thwap!

A yelp flies past my lips.

I jump back when a fist whips by me and slams against the front of the vending machine. My heart leaps, and I glance up with wide eyes, watching as the can of Dr Pepper wobbles free and drops into the dispensing slot.

Plop.

I lift my chin.

My gaze locks with Max Manning's.

He doesn't say anything. Doesn't smile, blink, or even breathe. He just stares at me for a heavy beat, his chocolate-dark hair falling over his forehead, his pale-blue eyes blank and unreadable.

Then he takes a step backward.

Turns around.

And disappears down the hallway.

Chapter 3
ELLA

"HOW WAS SCHOOL?"

My mother's back is to me as she leans over her computer desk, furiously typing something into a search engine. All she does is work, even though she hasn't nailed down a job yet. Lord knows what she does all day, but it seems to keep her busy.

I drop my backpack by the front door and toe out of my sandals, inhaling a deep breath. The house smells like sugarcane and citrus zest. "So much fun. I learned a lot. Made out with a boy under the bleachers right after I was nominated for queen of the Fall Fling. Then I chased a lifelong dream and joined the cheer squad."

She falters, twisting around in her rolling chair. "Really?"

Flashing her my teeth, I wave my invisible pom-poms in the air, wondering if perhaps I should have joined the drama club. My acting skills seem to be remarkably decent, according to the spark of hope shimmering in my mother's gaze.

But her face falls when I cock my head and give her that "Have you lost it?" look. The one she's all too familiar with. The one that has become my entire personality at this point.

Mom sighs, plucking her wire-rimmed glasses off the bridge of her nose and leaning back. The chair swivels from side to side as two gray-green eyes narrow in my direction. "Ella."

"Mom."

"How was school?" she repeats.

We maintain eye contact for a drumbeat before I pick my bag back up and shuffle past her down the short hallway toward my bedroom without a word. She doesn't need to know that I had detention today, after calling out a teacher on her bullshit. She probably wouldn't care.

"Ella!" Mom hollers after me.

I'm too tired to respond.

Tired of pretending to be happy.

Tired of trying to acclimate to a world that is constantly against me.

Tired of waiting for a little bit of good luck to fall into our laps.

Most of all, I'm tired of missing my big brother while simultaneously hating him for what he did. Loving and hating somebody at the same time has got to be the most exhausting thing in this world.

I waltz into my bedroom and toss my backpack to the floor, then close the door behind me. I don't slam it because I'm not angry.

I'm just tired.

Since I don't hear my mother's footsteps closing in, I plop down in the middle of my room and stare at the faded orange book bag resting between my ankles.

My heart rate kicks up.

When I was eight years old, I asked for one of those Doodle Bears for Christmas. I recall tearing apart silver and gold wrapping paper that glinted like tinsel underneath the grand chandelier in our living room, begging for just *one* of those boxes to be a Doodle Bear. But that didn't happen. My uncle told me I was spoiled when I exploded into tears beside the multicolored tree and collapsed among a plethora of pricey electronics.

I didn't feel spoiled; I just felt like Santa had forgotten about me.

Jonah found me crying in my bedroom later that night. He was only twelve at the time, but he was wise. There was a time when I thought he was the smartest person in the whole world.

I don't think that anymore…but, at one time, I did.

I remember the way he pulled my brand-new Vera Bradley book bag out of the closet, clutching a Sharpie in his hand, and tossed it on the mattress beside me. The bag was orange, which has always been my favorite color.

"It's not a Doodle Bear, but it'll work," he told me, flicking his copper bangs out of his eyes with a lopsided grin. "Sometimes we just need to improvise."

I didn't know what that word meant, but I nodded anyway.

He uncapped the marker and proceeded to doodle on the burnt-orange fabric. My smile was wide and whimsical as I watched him draw Winnie the Pooh onto the front zipper pocket, along with a cartoon heart on the bear's chest.

It became a tradition after that.

Every day, Jonah would draw a new picture or scrawl a silly word onto my backpack. It's now covered in random images, quotes, doodles, and symbols.

This backpack is my most prized possession. It's the only thing I have left of the boy I used to know.

I'm picking at the zipper slider when my dark cloud of solitude is interrupted by the whoosh of the bedroom door swinging open. Mom spots me seated in the center of the room and props a shoulder against the doorframe, eyeing me with her signature look of motherly worry.

I shoot her a glance before returning my attention to the backpack.

"I made that citrus cake you love," she states.

"Orange or lemon?" I pull to a stand and start flitting around the small bedroom, tidying aimlessly, pretending to be a normal teenager preparing for a normal afternoon of post-school activities.

"Orange."

"Aww, shucks, you know me so well."

She pauses. "Do I?"

My feet slow to a stop and my hand stalls midreach for a book dangling precariously over my bookshelf ledge. There's a fluttery feeling in my chest, but it feels more like an ache. A dull throbbing. I pan my gaze over to my cantaloupe-stained walls and the slew of posters and art pieces taped to the plaster.

Horses. Nature. Stevie Nicks.

An abstract canvas of a citrus tree that Jonah bought for me on my fourteenth birthday.

It was the year before everything changed. A precious memory trapped in time. Jonah had led me into my bedroom, his hands over my eyes like a make-shift blindfold as he muttered, "You needed a color pop in this room."

It was true. At the time, my walls were stark white, making the gift he bought and hung on the far wall even more striking and vibrant.

"Happy birthday," he said, uncovering my eyes.

I squealed with joy, my gaze aimed at the bright canvas, just as it is right now. "Oh, I love it! It's like you plucked a slice of sunshine and hung it on my wall."

"Can't have you living in this drab, sterile room. That's not you."

I nudged him with my elbow. "It's perfect. You always find a way of bringing a little color into my life."

"That's what big brothers are for. Besides, fruit trees are badass. They weather all those storms and still manage to produce the sweetest fruits." He shot me a little smirk. "Hey, that's not a terrible analogy for life."

"Maintain the resilience of a citrus tree," I said, bobbing my head up and down. "Noted."

Jonah's smile softened as he pulled me into a side hug. "Exactly."

I rub at my chest with the heel of my palm to soothe the obnoxious pang, then pivot toward my mother, her question still teasing the silence. "You know me as well as I know myself," I tell her. My voice is shaky. It seems the throbbing sensation has made its way from my heart to my words. "Undetermined."

My mother's eyes mist as she drinks in my pain. She sees it, feels it, hears it loud and clear. Inhaling a tapered breath, Mom straightens from the doorframe and folds both arms across her flowery blouse. "I'm trying," she says. "I'm really trying to make a better life for you, Ella."

I purse my lips and study my fingernails. They could use a fresh paint. "'Better' is subjective."

"No, it's not. Better is always *better*."

"Can you go back in time and change the past?" I whisper, still avoiding eye contact. "Can you take that gun out of his hand before he—"

"Don't." Her own voice cracks, and it's more than an ache. More than a throbbing. It sounds like a massacre just took place inside of her. "Don't you dare finish that sentence."

It's true that I wasn't angry before.

But now I am.

I hate, I hate, I *hate* that I'm not allowed to talk about it. My brother is sitting on death row for murdering two people, and it's real, and it happened, and it's my goddamn reality, but I need to pretend that it was nothing more than a bad dream.

Mom still believes he's innocent, and I'm envious of her. I wish I could believe that. I wish I could simmer in denial and imagine a version of my brother that wasn't covered in the blood of two innocent people.

Bile burns my throat. Nausea churns in my gut.

I want to pound my fists against the wall until my knuckles crack and bleed. I want to scream until my throat is shredded, raw, and blistered. Until I can't speak.

If I can't speak, I can't lie.

And if I can't lie, I won't have to live in this awful purgatory, caught between my mother's nonacceptance and my own devastation.

I see the instant regret on her face, but I don't want her apologies or back-pedaling, so I change the subject. "School was fine. We're reading a book called *Monster*. It's interesting," I explain. Drumming my fingertips along the top of my hand-me-down desk, I glance out the window when I hear the guttural rev of a lawn mower being started.

Max.

He's shirtless, angry-eyed, and already slicked with sweat from the ninety-degree heat.

I pull my attention away from the window and continue speaking. "My math teacher cuts his sandwiches into four pieces, instead of in halves. It's really weird," I tell my mother. "And this girl in P.E. had her period while we were running laps today. Our gym uniform is white." I drag my index finger along the desktop, resting it on the leather cover of a book I bound myself. "And…I miss the horses," I finish quietly. "I miss Phoenix."

I miss everything.

I don't say that part. In fact, I don't tell her anything of real importance. My day sucked, thanks to Andy, Mrs. Caulfield, and Dr Pepper. But telling her that won't change anything; it will only make her day suck, too.

When I swivel toward the window again, I watch as Max dumps an entire bottle of drinking water over his head and shakes his mop of wet hair like a dog in the rain. I'm sure the gesture would cause ovaries around the world to abruptly fertilize, but luckily, mine are immune.

I move away from the window and collapse back down to my butt in the center of the bedroom, tugging my backpack toward me with the heels of my feet.

Mom's eyes follow my movements, filling with a look I recognize. She's about to say something sentimental and I'm not going to appreciate it.

"Who knows, Ella…maybe you'll find happiness here," she murmurs, a wistfulness tingeing her words. "I fell in love here once. Maybe you will, too."

I freeze.

I fiddle with a keychain on my book bag as my eyes skip away from my mother's to focus on the beige carpeting beneath me. This town is where Mom and Dad first met. It's the town my father brought me to during the separation, and now it's the town I'm forced to call home.

When I don't respond, Mom finally releases a sigh. She sighs with sadness, with regret, with knowing. The wistfulness is long gone.

She knows I'll never fall in love. Not after what happened with Dad.

Not after what happened with Jonah.

Sitting cross-legged on my floor, I listen to her footsteps retreat into the hallway as the door softly closes.

Click.

Only then do I glance up, my eyes watering with trapped emotion.

One week before the murders, my brother told me something that has remained lodged in the back of my mind like a pesky headache I can't seem to shake.

He said, "Ella, listen to me, and listen good." His sage-green eyes glittered with affection as he pressed a hand to my shoulder and squeezed. "I don't know much, but I do know this: love conquers all. Love conquers *everything*. If you're ever feeling low—and I mean, rock-bottom *low*—remember that, okay? Remember that I love you. Always. And you'll get through it."

Love conquers all.

I'd heard the saying before, but I never gave it much thought. It bled into all the other cliché quotes out there, like, "*Take the road less traveled,*" or "*Life is a journey, not a destination.*"

Insipid words for thirsty minds.

Turns out, he was right—love *does* conquer all. But I don't think he understood what those words truly meant at the time.

Love conquers your common sense, your good reasoning, your sound logic.

Love conquers your heart until it's a mangled, stomped-on, barely beating organ.

Love conquers your carefully assembled dreams and puts them in the hands of someone else.

Love conquers.

Consumes.

Kills.

In my opinion, love is life's most skilled assassin. And that's because it hides in plain sight, well versed in camouflage and deception. It wears the face of that one person you would die for on the front line as you bleed out in the dirt, whispering *their* name on your final breath.

No.

I will not go out like that.

I will never fall in love. Falling leaves you with broken bones and shattered pieces. Falling leaves you in ruins. And if you're really unlucky, falling leaves you dead.

I don't want to be conquered.

I don't want to be overthrown.

I refuse, I refuse, I *refuse…*

I refuse to be victim of love again.

Chapter 4

MAX

A VASE SHATTERS AGAINST THE WALL BEHIND ME, MISSING MY HEAD BY LESS than an inch.

I scratch at the tickle left behind by the near-hit before jumping into action and rushing into the bedroom. Dad stumbles toward the bed, leaning heavily on his cane.

"You're a goddamn whore, Carol Ann!" he shouts at nobody.

He's slurring so badly, it would be difficult to understand him if the words weren't so familiar.

I step forward with a cautious gait like he's a rabid animal prepared to pounce—which isn't the worst analogy when he tries to drink himself into a coma.

My eyes track him as he tugs at his thinning hair. He's aged. Dad had us later in life—making him recently sixty—but even still, he looks like he's been dead for years, recently dredged up from a crud-laden coffin. Yellowing sclerae and blackened fingernails add to the zombie persona.

Finding my voice, I swallow hard and take another step closer. "Dad, it's me. It's Max. You should lie down."

He swings his head back and forth, still fisting his hair from the roots while muttering gibberish under his breath.

"Dad—"

"Where is she?" he demands, looking up suddenly, his sick eyes darting around the room. "She's with Rick, I know it. Tell her she's dead. I'll kill her myself."

"Mom's been gone for five years."

"She's with Rick." His face turns crimson, the veins in his neck popping. "That backstabbing bitch!"

Glass shatters when he chucks an empty bottle of whiskey at the far wall. He doesn't throw it in my direction this time, but I still jump back on instinct and almost trip over a booze-stained rug. I watch with hopelessness as he starts tearing apart the bedroom as if he's looking for something…but what he's really looking for walked out on him half a decade ago and never came back.

I shout for backup over my shoulder. "McKay!" I'm confident he put his earbuds in and can't hear me. He'd already be in here by now, considering Dad is on a rampage and it's a damn miracle the neighbors haven't sent the cops over for a welfare check. "McKay…fuck!" I storm out of the room, and sure enough, I find my brother lying on the couch with an arm draped over his eyes, two wires dangling from his ears.

Anger burns me. I can't blame my brother for blocking out the destruction going on a few feet away, but I can blame him for leaving me to deal with it all on my own.

Not like that's anything new.

I stomp toward him and yank a wire from his right ear. "Asshole. Get up."

He opens one eye, then the other, irritation shimmering back at me. "I'm listening to a podcast. True crime." Throwing his arm back over his eyes to erase the image of me looming over him, he finishes with, "It's riveting."

I pluck the earbud from his other ear with double the force and fling both across the room until he's glaring up at me. "You're about to be living a true crime if you don't help me calm Dad the fuck down. He's going to kill himself."

"Well, it's just a matter of time, anyway."

My heart stutters. "How can you say that?"

This has him lifting off the couch and scrubbing both hands over his face, elbows planted on his knees. He swipes at his hair, the same chocolate-brown

CATCH THE SUN

color as mine, only longer. His hangs at his shoulders, where mine is a tousled mess on top but shorter in the back.

McKay closes his eyes for a beat, flinching when it sounds like the dresser gets flipped upside down in the adjoining room.

He pretends he doesn't care.

But I know better.

My twin brother has simply grown content in the role of useless bystander, knowing damn well I'm here to keep the house from going up in flames.

Steepling his hands together, he finally looks up at me with something other than aggravation. "He needs help, Max. Actual help. We can't keep doing this."

"You think I don't know that?"

Crash.

Bang.

"*Whore!*"

My throat rolls with despair. "Just help me get him into bed. Once he sleeps it off, he'll be fine. I'll get rid of the liquor he managed to get his hands on."

"Solid plan," he grumbles. "You're such a genius."

No—I'm not a fucking genius. If I were a genius, I'd have come up with a better strategy by now, instead of the following endless charade:

Keep Dad sober.

Keep Dad alive.

Keep myself alive.

Go to school and learn about pointless shit like potato batteries and long division, instead of important things like the above-mentioned points.

Repeat.

The thing is, he wasn't always like this.

Once upon a time, we were a picture-perfect family living that idyllic, rural lifestyle in southeastern Tennessee. We had bonfires. We swam in lakes and washed dirt off our skin under waterfalls after endless afternoons of hiking and exploring. We fished, we laughed, we roasted hot dogs on tree branches over firepits, and we ate s'mores until our bellies ached.

Then the accident happened.

Seven years ago, my father worked as a machine operator at a local factory

33

and was responsible for operating heavy industrial equipment. On that shitty, fateful day, Dad was maneuvering a large hydraulic press used for shaping metal components, and due to a misjudgment in timing, the press came down unexpectedly, resulting in a severe crush injury. Despite the emergency stop being activated, the damage was done. The force exerted by the press caused significant trauma to his spine, resulting in a spinal cord injury that nearly paralyzed him from the waist down. He used a wheelchair for the better part of a year, while he took to the bottle to ease his pain and self-loathing.

Mom couldn't deal, so she had an affair with a coworker named Rick.

Then she left.

She left all of us with nothing but a note that said: "*I'm sorry.*"

We haven't heard from her since and that's fine by me. I want nothing to do with a woman who was so quick to walk out on her family, leaving two young boys behind.

McKay took Mom's abandonment the hardest, leaving me to step up to the plate. At twelve years old, I became a caregiver. The head of the household.

And to be fair, Dad isn't always like this. Some days, I see glimmers of the man who raised me right for twelve golden years, who showed me how to build and fix things, who took me camping under the stars, and who taught me that the most important thing in the world is family. For better, or for worse. Always.

Dad is my "for worse."

My father is not a bad person. He's a flawed person who needs somebody willing to put in the effort to bring him back to his former self. He's a run-down house with peeling paint, cracked tiles, and faulty appliances, where the inspector tells you that it needs some work, but at least the bones are good.

When another crashing sound rattles the walls, McKay finally pops up from the couch with an exasperated sigh and sweeps past me, beelining toward our father's bedroom.

I follow.

We both enter the room, but it's me who Dad looks at, his chest heaving, shoulders sagged and hunched over. He stares at me with drunk-glazed eyes, hobbling in place, a look of absolute defeat etched all over his face. "She left me," he murmurs, bottom lip quivering. "And I miss her...so much."

McKay is not at all moved. "She left all of us. Not just you," he states firmly.

Dad's gaze is still locked on me. Something tortured gleams within the shadows and desaturated blue. A shade of blue that was once ocean-strong.

And it breaks my fucking heart.

"It's okay, Dad." Even though McKay shoots me a deadly look that screams, "*It's not okay, you dipshit,*" I step forward and lead my father toward the bed. "Let's clean up this mess and get you to bed. We can talk later."

"I d'wanna talk," Dad slurs, stumbling along and holding on to my arm. "We've got that barbecue tonight. Jefferson'll be here soon. Gotta make my brisket."

Jefferson was an old coworker. Haven't seen the guy in years. "I've got the brisket covered. Don't worry about it." I help Dad slide into bed and pick up a pile of wadded-up blankets from the floor, draping them over my father's shivering, weakened body. He curls his knees to his chest and latches on to a downy pillow like it's his only lifeline.

I'm about to turn away when he stops me.

"Maxwell," he murmurs, face partially buried in the pillow.

I glance down at him. "Yeah?"

"You're a wonderful son." His eyes close and he's passed out within seconds.

There's a ball of brimstone in my throat when I lift my eyes to McKay. My brother remains silent, his stance rigid as he ignores the inadvertent dismissal and focuses on a blue jay perched on a tree branch outside the window. Then he pivots and stomps away, heading back to the living room.

I flick both hands through my damp hair, still slick from a water-bottle cooldown while mowing the lawn. When I exit the bedroom, McKay is plucking his earbuds off the living room floor and returning to his can't-be-bothered position on the couch.

He collapses with a long breath. "You should go to the bonfire tomorrow night," he tells me, avoiding the prior exchange like a skilled tactician sidestepping a minefield. "You're still young and stupid. You should do what I do and enjoy life while you can."

"What, and watch other people get drunk and belligerent?" I counter, crossing my arms over a sleeveless heather-gray tee. "I've had my fill. Thanks."

"Bring a girl and get your dick wet. It's a great distraction." He smirks at me. "Libby would climb you like a tree if you'd let her. Or…what about that red-head across the street you used to hang out with when we were kids?" Collapsing onto a sofa cushion, he spreads his arms across the back of the couch. "She got hot, I'll give her that. Weird but hot. Great tits."

"I don't give a shit about her tits."

"That's your problem. You have no hobbies, no interests, no sex life. Your entire existence is holed up in this cesspit with a depressed alcoholic who doesn't appreciate a single thing you do for him."

My teeth grind together but I don't acknowledge the barb.

Our father isn't the only one who doesn't appreciate me.

McKay has no fucking concept of the fact that I'm doing all of this so *he* can live the life he wants *me* to live. He doesn't realize that we both can't have that life. One of us has to hold down the fort. One of us has to sacrifice, so all three of us can survive.

And that person just so happens to be me.

I brush off the bonfire invitation and slip into my beat-up running shoes. "I'll think about it," I mutter, catching the shrug he sends me before lying back down and closing his eyes.

I take a moment to savor the silence.

Dad is quiet.

McKay is quiet.

But my mind is still restless, so I do what I always do when I need to find true peace:

I run.

———

It's mid-September and the weather is a scorching ninety degrees. The lemony fragrance of bloodroot wafts underneath my nose while a shaft of sunlight breaks through the cloud cover.

It's the perfect Friday afternoon for being anywhere but there.

Sticks and branches crunch underneath my shoes as I make my way down the wooded trail toward Tellico Lake. I'm eager to be in the water, to erase the decay off my skin. McKay used to come with me, back when we were younger. We'd race to the lake together after Dad worked himself up into a whiskey-induced meltdown, and we'd pretend we were plotting our grand escape out of this town. For a few hours, we'd hide underneath the lake's surface, counting those blissful seconds of freedom while we held our breath.

No sound, no sight, no stale taste of agony and broken dreams on our tongues.

It was just…quiet.

Peaceful.

I'm not sure when McKay stopped coming with me. I can't pinpoint the exact year or date, but eventually he found other outlets to keep him sane.

Schoolwork. Basketball. Girls.

Brynn has been the best thing that's ever happened to him and I'm thankful for that. But for me, a relationship just isn't in the cards. Girls, friendships, connections—they all take up too much emotional capacity, and I don't have room for the added burdens.

Besides, how could I ever invite a girl over? Our house is small, hardly nine-hundred square feet, and my father's demons are vast. My responsibilities are widespread. Brynn has never even come by, and while McKay is content with the arrangement, I wouldn't be.

A relationship is not feasible.

My fists clench as my speed kicks up and I leave a cloud of dirt and dust in my wake. The lake water sparkles on the other side of the tree line, calling to me, serving as one of the only things in life I can actually count on. Nature soothes me. I have a secret spot in a clearing a few yards from the water's edge, tucked within a canopy of moss-covered branches that embrace each other like old friends. It's where I go to relax, to decompress. To get away from it all.

After stripping down to my boxers, I take a dunk in the lake, floating on my back for a few minutes and staring up at the pillowy clouds.

It's not long before I'm restless again.

I need a cigarette.

The legal age to buy tobacco in Tennessee is twenty-one, so my neighbor, Chevy, scores me a pack every now and then when he has the extra cash. Sometimes I'll find them tucked inside a bag of groceries he'll leave on our front stoop. It's not even an actual patio, just a block of cement. Kind of like our house is barely a house—it's an unfinished product of a washed-away dream.

Pulling my jeans back on, I fish out a cigarette and light up, watching as the sun dips lower in the sky and sets the treetops aglow.

I'm inhaling a long drag when a flash of orange catches my attention in my peripheral. Glancing up, I spot a girl in a carrot-colored romper leaning over the bridge, her arms folded on the rail as she stares down into the water.

Auburn hair, long and thick.

Pale skin.

Sad jade eyes.

Ella Sunbury.

Ropes of red-brown hair dance across her face while she hangs over the edge, unaware of my presence. Her attention is on the water as it flows downstream. She leans over farther, then farther, and my heart skips, wondering if she's contemplating climbing over and jumping in. Maybe she wants to wash her entire life away. For a beat, I find her painfully relatable as I watch her hair float and undulate amid the early-autumn breeze. I've stood on that exact bridge before, in that same position, transfixed by the running river water and praying it would take pity on me and haul me away from here.

She lifts up then, shoving the hair out of her face.

The breeze goes still.

And so do I.

Her head tilts toward me and our eyes meet across the embankment. Recognition flickers to life. Ella straightens and stiffens, her fingers curling around the railing.

She doesn't smile and neither do I.

I don't wave and neither does she.

We just stare at each other as the sun lights her up and causes her hair to shimmer like a vibrant flame. Memories burst to life. Golden, long-ago memories of watching her smile at me in the schoolyard on the first day of first grade with a Winnie the Pooh storybook splayed in her lap, and thinking with my whole heart that she'd be mine one day.

Stupid.

Silly, stupid childhood fantasies.

I swallow, my throat tightening as smoke curls around me and drifts skyward. My breath stalls. I wonder why I'm staring at her and I wonder why I can't seem to pull away.

But I don't have to wonder for long.

She blinks, glancing back down at the water and breaking the palpable tether as dishwater-gray clouds roll in, blotting out the sunshine.

Another beat passes before she sends me a final, sharp glance across the ridge with an expression that screams, "*Fuck you, Dr Pepper.*"

And then she walks away.

I toss the still-smoking cigarette to the ground, stomping it out with the toe of my shoe as I watch her saunter away in a cloud of volatile orange.

I smile.

Chapter 5

ELLA

SEPTEMBER ROLLS BY, AND I'M GRATEFUL THE HEAT WAVE HAS PASSED AS I trudge through dry dirt and crisp leaves, making my way to a little clearing partially hidden from the walkable trails. A canopy of sun-kissed branches and greenery blocks out most of the sunlight, providing an added sense of seclusion to the small hideaway I remember discovering with Max years ago.

I toss my backpack into a pile of brushwood and take a seat on a rustic-looking bench. It appears to be hand-carved, which causes my heart to skip. I remember him telling me on that final day that he wanted to build us a bench.

No.

Highly doubtful. I was gone by sunset and he never saw me again.

With my luck, this is probably the meeting place for some weird cult, where they do rituals involving baby goats and virgin blood.

I sift through my book bag and pull out a spiral-bound notebook and a black pen. Mom went to work today. She scored a job as a receptionist at Delores' Hair Salon and will be working five days a week until something better comes along. The owner's name is actually Anne, so I'm still scratching my head at the business moniker. Regardless, Anne seems nice and I can appreciate a good mystery.

Lifting my ankles to a cross-legged position on the bench, I flip open my notebook and land on a blank page. My ballpoint pen glides across the lined paper in little swoops as I begin to write.

> *Dear Jonah,*
>
> *I hate you.*

I draw a line through the first sentence and try again, lowering my pen right underneath those three words and starting over.

> *Sorry. That was a bleak opening, even though it's true sometimes. There are days I hate you and there are days I love you. Then there are days when I feel both of those things at the same time. Those are the hardest days. Those are the days I scream into my pillow until my vocal cords are swollen and raw, and I lash out at Mom, and I refuse to eat because eating makes my stomach hurt even more than it normally does.*
> *Anyway, this is depressing, so I'll stop writing now.*
> *I just wanted you to know that I really do love you. I love you so much.*
> *And that's what makes me hate you.*
>
> > *Ella*

This is beyond emo.

I rip out the page and crumple it into a tight ball, stuffing it into my open book bag. Maybe I should try again. I can lie this time. I can tell him that life is going really well and we're doing okay without him. People like liars. People enjoy fairy tales because they always end with a satisfying conclusion, tied up in a little pink bow with a happily-ever-after. I'm not sure why the bow is pink, but pink is a happy color. Seems fitting.

I forgo my black pen and exchange it for a hot-pink pen.

This is better. I will lie to him with pink ink and fairy-tale words.

I'm about to start another letter when I hear footsteps approaching from the bordering trail. Branches crunch under swiftly moving feet. Sticks and loose leaves rustle as the footfalls inch closer. I hold my breath. A vision of a cloaked figure with a dagger glinting in the sunlight flashes across my mind. The dagger has the word *virgin* etched into the blade, and a helpless goat bleats in the far-off distance.

This is it; I'm a goner.

The sunshade of green foliage is pulled back, revealing the intruder.

I freeze.

I blink up at the familiar face as he blinks down at me. We stare at each other. Nobody moves. Nobody speaks.

Max.

Max Manning towers before me in faded blue jeans and a damp T-shirt stuck to his chest. His hair is a slow-drying mess of dark waves over his eyes, and his white sneakers are worn and smudged with dirt.

More importantly, he looks furious. My existence has provoked him.

Sighing, I glance back down at my barren note page and pretend he's not there. If I avoid things long enough, they tend to go away. This worked against me that one time Mom bought me a betta fish, but generally, the results are favorable.

"What are you doing here?" he demands, stepping farther into the clearing.

It doesn't seem to be working this time. "Taking a bath." I start doodling at the top of the page, drawing a dubious picture of a sun.

Silence infects the space between us, but his presence is loud and commanding. I can almost see the flare of his nostrils and the twitch of his eye, even though my gaze is fixed on the sun design that has somehow morphed into a flower. I turn the sunrays into petals and add a long stem.

Finally, he says, "This is my spot."

"I don't see your name written anywhere."

"You're sitting on it."

Frowning, I inch my butt off the bench and peer down at the mahogany wood, narrowing my eyes at the jagged little letters carved on the top.

Manning, 2013

Well then.

Resituating on the bench, I fill my cheeks with air and let out a breath. "Sorry, I didn't think to check for ownership. Do you have the official deed?"

"I'm serious. I come here when I want to be alone."

"You can still be alone."

I spare him a glance, noting the way he folds his arms across his chest as a strand of brown hair curls over his left eyebrow like a corkscrew. His cheeks are flushed from the Saturday sun, adding more color to his already bronzed skin, and his arms are well defined, the muscles twitching with suppressed wrath. They're nice arms. If I had a thing for arms, I'd consider his top tier.

And I understand why girls fall all over themselves when he sweeps through the hallways, leaving them in a cloud of mint, pine, and shunned infatuation. I have twenty-twenty vision. Max Manning is good-looking, a ten across the board. If I ran purely on hormones, I could become bewitched. Thankfully, I run on trauma, black coffee, and sarcasm, so his compelling man-body and enigmatic blue eyes are wasted on me.

Max's gaze flits around the scenic space before settling back on me. "I can't be alone if you're here. I'm sure there are plenty of other places you can mope."

Feigning outrage, I let out a huff and hold up three fingers. "First of all, you can absolutely be alone. We can be alone together. Loneliness is nothing but a state of mind." I lower my index finger. "Secondly, I wasn't moping. I was brooding." I lower my ring finger, leaving only my middle finger pointed toward the cloudless sky.

I don't verbalize the third point because I'm already making it.

Slanting his eyes at me, Max rolls his jaw, scratches the back of his neck, then proceeds to plop down against a thickly trunked tree. "Fine."

This surprises me. I definitely expected him to scram.

He draws his knees up to his chest and drops the crown of his head to the deep-brown bark. Our eyes snag for a split second before I clear my throat and avert my attention back to the blank pages of my notebook.

I chew on the end of the pen, brainstorming my letter. My letter of lies.

Perhaps I should tell Jonah I found a boyfriend here in Juniper Falls—a boy who lives in the forest and swings from vines, who eats fresh berries from fertile bushes and drinks water from streams. My brother was always eager for me to fall in love and to experience that soul-aching tug that happens when heartstrings tangle and knot. If he wanted anything for me, it would be that.

It would be love.

Removing the pen from between my teeth, I begin to scribble down my fiction story.

Dear Jonah,

Today I fell in love with a boy who

"Question for you."

Max's voice tears through my myth-in-the-making before I can fully develop the plot. Releasing a sigh, I flick my pen against the notepad. "Sure."

"What's the difference between moping and brooding?"

Our eyes meet again. "Brooding is dark and mysterious, where moping makes me think of Eeyore from Winnie the Pooh," I explain, as if this is a tried-and-true fact. "Nobody wants to be Eeyore."

I watch his expression shift from curiosity to perplexity. In my experience, aversion usually follows, but if that's what he's feeling, he hides it well. All he does is nod like he finds the answer acceptable. This is the part where I should go back to conjuring up silly daydreams for Jonah, but, for some reason, the silence is feeling heavier than normal. It's making me itchy, so I keep the conversation going. "You know, my mother has encouraged me to make friends," I announce, observing the way his head tilts and his foot taps at the tall grass. "Want to be friends again?"

"No."

I am unfazed by his rejection.

"Good. I was hoping you'd say that." I return my attention to the notebook. "I'll tell her I tried." He doesn't say anything, but I sense his eyes on me for a solid minute, so I eventually glance back up as I smear a glob of ink into the pad of my thumb. "What?"

"You didn't try very hard."

He's not smiling, per se, but his tone of voice has my own lips twitching as if they want to. I don't, though—*nope*. Slapping the notebook shut, I purse my lips together to keep them from doing something unreasonable. "Did you want me to try harder?"

He shrugs as he drags the sole of his sneaker along a patch of loose dirt. "I'll admit, I'm curious."

A challenge.

I can't back down now.

Blinking slowly, I study him sitting propped up against the mature basswood tree across from me. He breaks eye contact to stare out at the lake while the sun glimmers down on the water and lights it up like diamonds. "I guess I could fill you in on all of my good qualities," I tell him. "There aren't many, but there might be enough to lure you into some kind of makeshift friendship."

"Oh yeah?" He's still focused on the glittery water.

"Maybe." With a dramatic clear of my throat, I attempt to enchant him. "I have very few hobbies, so I'm readily available for friendship dates. I'm also excellent at arm wrestling, for whenever boredom strikes. When I was six, I planted my orange crayons in the garden, thinking they'd grow into carrots. That's not a quality, by the way…just a random fact you didn't ask for." I slide my tongue along my bottom lip as his attention falls back to me, his brows pinched together with what looks like concern. "Oh, and I'm shockingly good at catching things. All things. Especially when their trajectory is abrupt and terrifying. It comes in handy if you're ever about to drop your casserole dish or if you're in need of a goalkeeper."

He blinks at me with a deadpan expression as a symphony of crickets serenades us from the shrubs.

Then it happens so fast.

His hand flies up and hurls a small stone in my direction before another meaningless word can pass through my lips.

Just as quickly, my own hand raises with the suddenness of a trap-door spider lunging for its prey. I catch the stone with a *thwack*, my palm encompassing the rock.

It's pure instinct.

Max isn't slow-clapping, but he might as well be. "Nice reflexes," he says, his eyes appearing two shades darker when the sun sneaks behind the clouds. "I'm impressed."

"Shit." I sigh. "I took it too far. Now you're in love."

A beat.

A breath.

And then his lips curl up, revealing a pair of deep-set dimples I haven't seen in ten years.

Oh my God—he's actually smiling and it feels contagious.

I really did take it too far.

I promptly look away and start rummaging through my backpack to find the orange I brought along. It's better if I keep my mouth distracted before any smiling lines are crossed. After discarding the smooth white stone, I peel back the skin of my fruit and pluck off a pulpy piece, tossing it into my mouth. "What?" I inquire as I chew, still feeling his stare.

"You're wearing orange, your backpack is orange, and you're eating an orange," he notes.

"Congratulations! You have eyes."

"I just mean…it's a happy color. Sunny and warm, like you used to be." Thoughtful consideration twinkles in his gaze as he gives me an additional once-over. "I feel like black fits your personality better these days."

Juice dribbles down my chin and I swipe it away with the back of my hand. "That's fair."

"That doesn't offend you?"

"Nope. Being offended by something somebody says implies you care about what that person thinks of you. Which I don't." Clearing my throat, I add, "No offense."

"Mmm."

We blink at each other.

Max Manning still watches me, even after another long silence stretches and my face reverts back to its typical state of scowling. I reopen the notebook. The words on the page muddle together and my legs feel like I've come down with a spontaneous case of restless leg syndrome. I uncross them, letting them dangle over the side of the bench, and then cross them again. My pen taps repetitively against the paper. I sigh a few times for no reason. I think it's because I'm aware of him. On a regular day, I take shutting out other people to a professional level. It's a blissful skill to possess. In fact, I should have mentioned it to him.

I guess I'm realizing that I don't feel lonely right now and I don't know why.

This makes me scowl harder.

"Are you going to that bonfire tonight?" Max pulls to a stand, swiping dirt and grass blades off his blue jeans as he towers over me.

"No," I reply, lifting only my eyes. Lifting my entire head makes it seem like I care more than I do. "Are you?"

Now it definitely seems like I care. *Dammit.*

"No," he says.

"Cool."

We stare at each other.

No one moves. No one speaks.

Eventually, he sends me a quick nod and retreats from the little hideaway without another word, leaving a lingering cloud of pine needles and mint behind.

My heart is beating faster than usual. It's not a gallop, more like a traipse. But it's a noticeable quickening.

I rub at my chest.

And for some preposterous reason, the echo of our unspoken words reaches my ears as I watch him disappear into the woods.

See you there.

Chapter 6
ELLA

I HAVE NO GOOD REASON FOR BEING HERE, ASIDE FROM THE FACT THAT MOM had an emotional breakdown over dinner tonight. She made a chicken casserole. It was semi-burnt and tasted like sawdust, so I thought I understood why she was crying. My eyes were watering, too, if I'm being honest.

But then she sobbed into her napkin and blurted out, "This was the last meal I cooked for him."

My fork clattered to the kitchen table. My hands trembled. The overcooked chunks of chicken settled in the pit of my stomach like acidic bricks.

I had to get out of there.

Around 7:00 p.m. I text the phone number Brynn scribbled on my arm, having added it into my contacts before I showered the night before.

Me: Hey, it's Ella. I'm thinking about going to that bonfire tonight, but I'm still on the fence. Convince me with three words.

Brynn: I'll be there! :)

Me: Sold. My social skills need work, just a fair warning.

Brynn: That's what beer is for! Need a ride?

Me: I'm not far. I'll walk. See you soon.

Brynn: Can't wait!

She's an exclamation-point girl.

I edit her name in my phone contacts to "Brynn!" before throwing a hoodie over my tank top and stepping into a pair of dark-wash jeans. I study my reflection in the mirror. My hair is freshly blow-dried, falling in long, thick waves over my shoulders, and my eyes don't look as tired and tortured as they usually do. After applying a coat of black mascara, a layer of lip gloss, and pinching my cheeks that are already stained pink with a touch of nerves, I call out a goodbye to my mother, who managed to collect herself and is watching *Grey's Anatomy* reruns in the living room.

She waves at me from the couch, her voice still hoarse. "Don't stay out too late. I'm going to wait up for you."

"Please don't."

"I can't sleep, anyway. And I worry about you."

I'm not sure I buy that last part, but all I do is shuffle to the front door, snagging my purse off the wall hook. "Okay. Bye."

Twenty minutes later, I'm stalking down the grassy hill toward the bluffs where firelight flickers in the distance and laughter drowns out my anxious heartbeats. The temperature has fallen to a crisp fifty-eight degrees, so I'm grateful I grabbed my hoodie. But as I get closer to the gathering, I notice that all the other girls are wearing crop tops, spaghetti straps, and cute dresses. The intoxicated whoops and cheers of fellow classmates have me wanting to disintegrate into the grass blades or, at the very least, walk back in the opposite direction. But before I can debate my next move, Brynn! is prancing over to me.

It's a legitimate prance. She looks like a unicorn with her high ponytail and pink-and-white sundress, swooping in to carry me away to her storybook world of wonders.

Also known as this shitty bonfire with a bunch of idiots I don't like.

"Ella!"

I freeze in place. I'm the deer in headlights to her majestic unicorn. "Hey."

"You made it! I didn't think you'd show." She slides her arm through mine, infecting me with glitter and watermelon-scented body mist. "Come on. I'll introduce you to everyone."

I allow her to pull me forward, my feet stumbling to keep up with her prancing. "I'm pretty sure everyone knows who I am. And they'd rather they didn't."

"Don't be such a Debbie Downer."

"Okay." I try again. "I'm a sparkling spitfire with an ungodly knack for adventure and fun."

"That's the spirit!"

We make our way to a circle of wooden benches around the firepit as tendrils of smoke obscure the horrified expressions I'm certain are staring back at me. The laughter dies down instantly.

I murdered the fun.

Brynn! seems unbothered by the silence that washes over the group and proceeds to link our fingers together like we share an intimate bond—like she didn't give me her phone number a mere twenty-four hours ago. As she offers up an animated introduction, her palm squeezes mine, and the kindness is appreciated. I force a smile and lift my unoccupied hand with a wave.

Soot bites at my eyes, ashes at my throat. I'm so out of my comfort zone, I've forgotten what it feels like to be comfortable. Back in Nashville, I had friends. I had a social life. I wasn't a unicorn like Brynn!, but I knew who I was and I felt a sense of belonging and community. People smiled at me in the hallways and invited me to bonfires and boat rides out on Percy Priest Lake.

Right now, even my own hoodie is trying to suffocate me.

I scratch at my collarbone, shifting from one foot to the other. "Hi."

Pathetic.

Nobody says anything, which I suppose is a tiny miracle considering the alternative. They simply go back to talking among themselves like I'm invisible.

Brynn! drags me around the back of a bench toward the waterline, where two figures are silhouetted, conversing with each other. I can already tell that one of them is Max Manning by the stretch of his shoulders and the tousling of his hair as pale moonlight hugs him. McKay stands beside him with a beer in hand, his profile strikingly similar to Max's, only with longer hair that teases his shoulders.

"I want to introduce you to McKay, my boyfriend," Brynn! says to me, still dragging me along by the hand. "And his brother, Max. I think they live by you."

"They do. Across the street," I confirm. "And I already know them. I lived here with my dad for a year, back when we were in first grade. We went to school together."

Her eyes ping open as we trek forward. "Wow! I didn't know that. I didn't move here until I was in junior high. We'll definitely need to get together and watch a movie or something." She pauses, looking away. "At my house, anyway. I'm not allowed at McKay's house. I guess his dad is kind of a mess."

"Oh, really?" I immediately sympathize with Mr. Manning since "mess" is almost always code for *misunderstood*.

She shrugs. "I wouldn't know. McKay never talks about him."

"How long have you two been dating?"

"Six months."

Six months is a long time to have never met the parents—but, then again, what do I know about dating? Nothing. I know nothing.

Nodding, I follow beside her as she releases my palm. "I've seen you two in the hallways together," I say. "You really like him."

She lights up like a moonbeam, flipping her long ponytail over her shoulder. "I think I love him, Ella. Is that weird?" Shaking her head, she waves a hand in the air as if to erase the question. "Don't answer that. I already know you'll think it's weird. You have anti-love eyes."

"What? I do?" I blink repeatedly like I'm trying to see my own eyes. "I think people call that resting bitch face."

Her nose scrunches up. "That's just a classless term for girls who wear their pain in their eyes. I always hated that phrase." Then she grabs me by the shoulders and halts me in place before we reach the base of the hill. "What do you see when you look at me?"

Glitter. Everywhere.

Aside from that...

We stand face-to-face as starlight reflects off the lake and illuminates her shimmery hazel gaze. I tilt my head and reply with the first thing that comes to mind. "You're compassionate and fun-loving. A good friend to everybody," I tell her. "You have Christopher Robin eyes."

She squints, processing the response. "Who?"

"A character from Winnie the Pooh."

"Oh…" Those pretty, kind eyes twinkle as a bright smile follows. "That sounds like a compliment."

"It is."

"Well, thank you."

"Hey, Brynn!" McKay hollers from a few feet away. "What's the holdup?"

Lowering her hands from my shoulders, she smooths out the baby hairs frizzing along her hairline, then picks up her pace, still grinning wide. "Coming!"

Max turns toward us when we approach, his focus sliding over to me and holding tight. His lips twitch with the barest smile and I'm not sure what to make of it. It appears he's not disappointed to see me, even though I was kind of a jerk to him earlier at the clearing.

I don't say anything and duck my head, erasing his smile from my mind because it shouldn't have been there in the first place.

When I lift my eyes, it's gone. Perhaps I imagined it.

"Hello, lover!" Brynn! squeals, leaving my side to wrap her arms around McKay. "I didn't realize you used to know Ella. She's my new friend."

How easily the title has been bestowed upon us.

No wariness, no indecision.

Only: *"I think you're cool. Here's my number. Now we're friends."*

It's almost like Max and me when we were bright-eyed first graders, scoping out our future lifelong friendships on the first day of school.

McKay gives me a once-over. His eyes are the hue of midnight against the nighttime backdrop, but I know from catching them in the school hallways that they are only a shade darker than Max's. Still blue, still piercing, but a little less light. Shaggy dark hair frames his face, landing at his broad shoulders, and while his bone structure is similar to Max's, McKay has a wider nose and zero trace of dimples. He smiles a lot more than Max, so I've noted their absence.

Puckering his lips, he debates his next move. I'm certain he thinks I'm less compelling than his reheated leftovers from last week, but his girlfriend likes me.

A conundrum.

"Yeah, hey," he opts for, extending a hand. "I remember you."

"Cool," is my lame reply. I accept the handshake but my attention pans over to Max, who is glaring at our clasped palms. Clearing my throat, I pull free. "How's it going?" I ask Max.

"Fine. I didn't think you'd show," he replies.

"Me neither. Mom got all emotional over a chicken casserole so the bonfire suddenly became more appealing." I chuckle awkwardly but no one else does.

My knack for honesty is not at all charming and always misplaced.

"Chicken has that effect on me, too," Brynn! eventually pipes up. "That's why I'm a vegan. Did you know eight billion chickens are slaughtered each year by the food industry?" She visibly shudders. "No, thanks. I'll have no part of that."

McKay nudges her with his elbow. "Nobody is perfect, baby."

"Ugh. You're lucky you're adorable and well muscled."

They start making out until kissing sounds mingle with raucous laughter from the bonfire. Max glances at me again, his hands stuffed in the pockets of his jeans. I watch as he teeters on the heels of his worn-out sneakers, looking like he's about to say something. Curiosity dances in his eyes, swirling with intensity. I'm not sure why he's always looking at me like that, like he wants to know more, wants to learn more, wants to dig deeper than what I offer on the surface. Most people see right through me, but I'm pretty sure he just…*sees* me.

I'm not sure how I feel about that.

McKay interrupts, drawing back from Brynn!'s watermelon kisses and swiping at the balm left behind. "Max, help me grab the coolers from the truck. I need a beer," he says.

Max blinks, tearing his attention from me with a hint of irritation. "Yeah, fine." With a drawn-out sigh, he sifts through his pockets and pulls out a pack of cigarettes before shoving the box back in. He follows McKay up the hill made of sand and dying grass, sneaking a final glance at me over his shoulder, then disappearing over the peak.

Brynn! trails behind them, her skips eager, hair bouncing. "Be right back!" she calls out to me.

I nod, tugging the sleeves of my hoodie down over my palms. "I'll be here," I whisper to the night. Lake water ripples and laps beneath the starlight, a picture of tranquility. It looks so peaceful, so unburdened. Envy spools and coils in my chest because…

I want that. I want that more than anything.

Peace.

Just one peaceful moment. Lots of people get thousands of peaceful moments and all I want is one.

Just. One.

As I exhale deeply, my hand instinctively slides into my back pocket, wrapping around a polished white stone. It's the same one Max tossed at me earlier today—the one that brought back memories of the small stone he handed me just before my father drove me over two hundred miles away, leaving him behind on a sunny playground, expecting to see me the next day.

I give it a squeeze before looking back out over the water as the moon offers a glimmer of contentment to the graphite sky.

I'm not sure why I brought it.

I'm not sure why I kept it in the first place.

Flames crackle and glow as I sit by myself on one of the wooden benches with my hands folded in my lap. Brynn! and McKay are snuggled up near the water, kissing and giggling by the light of the moon. Well, she is giggling. McKay is scrolling through his phone.

Music blasts from someone's Spotify playlist, serenading us with The Arctic Monkeys' best song, "Do I Wanna Know." I like the band but prefer classics like Fleetwood Mac and The Eagles, because they remind me of blissful family road trips before Dad cheated on Mom with my first-grade teacher and Jonah committed two counts of murder in the first degree.

I knock my knees together and fold in my lips, feeling antsy. Out of place.

Max wandered over to the bonfire a few minutes ago and is seated on the bench across from me, his face going in and out of focus as fire spits and smoke billows. I've caught him staring at me a few times and I wonder what he sees right now. What he feels when he looks at me. Disenchantment would be my guess, with pity taking second place.

Andy is seated beside him, chugging down his fifth beer and acting loud and moronic. He's living up to the football player stereotype just as effortlessly as I've been embracing my title of tragic outcast, so I can't really judge him.

I watch as Max reaches into the cooler beside him before I pull my eyes away and redirect my attention to my hands fisted tightly in my lap. I circle my thumbs, zeroing in on my still-chipped nail polish. One of these days, I'll feel motivated enough to repaint them.

I'm so immersed in my fingernails that I fail to notice Max has left Andy's side and is now taking a seat to my left. It's a small bench, so our shoulders brush. Warmth seeps through the thick sleeve of my hoodie as his scent wafts around me, something like burnt wood and peppermint gum.

I glance up just as a dewy can of Dr Pepper is tossed at me.

I catch it one-handed.

And then my heart does a weird loop-di-loop thing.

Partly because I'm not expecting it, but mostly because I'm shocked that he remembers the kind of soda I like and that I wield superhuman reflexes. People have a knack for being oblivious to trivial details. They often miss the essence of what others are saying or doing because they're too preoccupied with their own bullshit. Your favorite things only matter to them if they genuinely care enough to listen and see you for who you are.

Max was paying attention to my bullshit.

I curl my fingers around the ice-cold beverage. "Thanks," I say, blinking over at him. He's clasping a red plastic cup that's likely filled with flat beer. "That was nice of you."

"We're friends again, aren't we?" He takes a sip from his cup, eyes pinned on me over the rim. "Friends do nice things."

I watch his throat bob as he swallows a gulp, then swing my gaze back up. "You rejected my attempt to rekindle our long-lost friendship. You seemed repulsed by the very prospect."

"That was before you won me over with promises of an arm-wrestling competition."

A laugh falls out of me, unexpectedly. Untethered and unplanned. It's like he poked a tiny pinhole in my balloon of sorrow and some of the sadness leaked out. "That was what sold you, huh?"

"Yes. Your arms look small and breakable, so my curiosity was piqued. Still is."

I glance at one of my arms. Once upon a time, I was more filled out. Athletic and defined. I was even sporting a little tummy from laughter-lit nights of pigging out on pizza bagels with Jonah, or shoveling popcorn and sweet snacks in my mouth with friends during giggle-infused sleepovers. I miss my tummy. It meant I was living. It meant I was enjoying life and all of the highly caloric wonders that came with it.

Now I'm feeble and petite. Withered. My breasts are full and my hips are wide—*child-bearing hips*, according to Grandma Shirley—but my arms are gangly, my belly sunken-in. To be honest, I'm not sure how I'd perform in an arm-wrestling match these days. Max may be supremely let down.

Not wanting to disappoint him prematurely, I lift my arm and pump my fist, flexing with conviction. "We can give it a go if you'd like."

He shakes his head at the offer. "You mentioned it's for when boredom strikes." Twirling the red cup between both hands, he chews on his bottom lip for a beat before glancing up at me, his blue eyes reflecting the orange flames. "I'm not bored."

The look he sends me has me squirming for unknown reasons. He's not bored because he's at a bonfire with his friends. It has nothing to do with me.

Obviously.

I scratch at the back of my hand as my legs start to bob up and down, toes digging into the sandpit. My undiagnosed case of restless leg syndrome is acting up again. "That's fine." I shrug and sip my soda. "I didn't want to hold your hand, anyway."

"Why? I have nice hands."

I peer over at them. He's right; they're really nice hands. Just as nice as his arms, which do not affect me. "They're okay," I lie. "What are you doing here, anyway?"

"Taking a bath."

My mouth snaps shut when his answer sinks in.

That's…

That was my line.

Max looks blasé as he sips from his red cup and stares into the blaze of fire-light. He's managed to render me speechless, which is rare and unprecedented. I don't think I like it. Swallowing, I fumble for something smart and witty to say but come up as empty as my cold, black heart.

I pop open the tab on my can of Dr Pepper and start to chug. It fizzes on my tongue, bringing it back to life. "So, are you actually friends with these guys?" I flick my hand up and wave it around, referencing Andy and his cringey followers.

Before Max can respond, Andy interrupts with a roar of laughter as he slaps a buddy on the back with a *thwap*. "Dude. You're so hard up for a lay, you were playing Bloody Mary in the bathroom, hoping that bitch would show up so you could get some."

"Shut the fuck up," some blond guy says while putting my scowling abilities to shame.

I groan inwardly. If Max says yes, any friendship potential will shrivel on the spot.

"Nope," Max mutters, shifting on the bench until his denim-clad thigh kisses mine. "I only have one friend and she's still in the preliminary stage."

"Preliminary?"

"Mm-hmm." He nods, squinting into the fire. "I need to make up for my knee-jerk rejection that had nothing to do with her and had everything to do with my own isolated tendencies."

Something tells me he's serious. He wants to be friends.

I have no idea what to say, so I say nothing. I see Max staring at me in my periphery, waiting for a response. For a confirmation or a handshake. A friend-ship bracelet.

Maybe a binding blood oath.

All I offer is a weird noise. "Ohm."

Awesome. My brain couldn't decide between *oh* and *um*. I fill my cheeks with air and blow out a slow breath, tapping my feet in opposite time and becoming supremely interested in a tiny insect crawling along the toe of my faux-suede boot.

He's still staring and it's making me fidgety.

I spare him a glance and watch as a smile stretches on his lips, his eyes twinkling against the flames.

Why is he smiling at me? Why is he twinkling?

I'm feeling hot all of a sudden. From the fire.

I curl my fingers around the hem of my hoodie and pull it over my head with both arms. I smooth my hair back down and readjust the straps of my navy tank top, catching the way Max's eyes flick to my chest for half a second before he looks away and takes another sip from his cup.

When I peer across the firepit, I spot Andy leering at me. His gaze rolls down my body and hovers on my cleavage. He doesn't break away like Max did and instead licks a dollop of beer—or drool—off his bottom lip before capturing it with his teeth and making a hissing sound.

Then he makes a derogatory comment, to nobody's surprise. "I didn't think you had any redeeming qualities, Sunbury, but you're making quite the case for yourself with those titties."

Max flies up from the bench and hurls his drink in Andy's face.

"The fuck, Manning!"

"Have some respect, you piece of shit." Max returns to his place beside me, tossing the empty cup in the fire as the plastic curls and chars.

My cheeks burn. My heart teeters.

I sit there stunned, my hands raised, palms forward, as my chest heaves with a quick burst of adrenaline.

That was…unexpected.

Andy rumbles with laughter as he shakes the moisture out of his T-shirt and slides his tongue along his chin to taste the stray droplets. "Water," he mocks. "Fucking pussy."

Max stands again, glancing down at my wide-eyed expression. "Want to go for a walk?"

"No. What? Okay," I ramble through the mood whiplash. I squeeze my can of soda and pull up from the bench, then start walking hurriedly in front of him toward the water's edge. I hear his footsteps following, a whoosh of kicked-up sand and rustling grass blades as I toss the Dr Pepper into a recycling can. "So, um, why are we walking?"

"I'm walking," he says. "You're sprinting."

I slow my gait and watch as he sidles up beside me with his hands tucked in his pockets. Biceps lined in blue veins tick and stretch under the moon's glow. He's not wearing a sweatshirt or hoodie and his sleeves are cut off at the shoulders.

"You're sizing me up for that arm-wrestling match, aren't you?"

He caught me staring at his arms. My face burns hotter, so I decide to pivot. "What was that back there?"

He shrugs with nonchalance. "Andy Sandwell made a disrespectful comment toward you and I reacted accordingly."

"You didn't have to do that. I don't need someone to rescue me."

He's silent for a beat as we traipse toward the lake. Moonlight paints a shimmering path across the water like a mirror speckled with stardust. "Nobody ever really needs rescuing," he says, our footsteps slowing. "But it feels nice sometimes."

I glance around, wondering where Brynn! and McKay ran off to. I let his response roll off me, not knowing how to process it or what to say. Max keeps doing that. He keeps tying my tongue into knots and zapping my words to ash. I'm not used to it.

"Why did you want to take a walk with me?" I ask again, picking at the frayed hem of my tank top. "According to everyone ever, I'm pretty off-putting."

There's another long pause as the breeze coasts off the water and causes my hair to whip around my face. Then Max says softly, "Remove the term 'off-putting' and I'll agree with you there."

My brain rewinds and I almost choke. A heavy lump lodges in the center of my throat as I flit my gaze over to his. "You…think I'm pretty?"

We come to a stop at the edge of the lake where soggy sand meets water. "Yeah. Sure." He acts like the admission is no big deal.

I gape at him, mouth unhinged. "Are you flirting with me?"

"You tell me. I've never flirted with anyone before, so I wouldn't know."

The lump swells, threatening to overtake my response, but I manage to croak out, "Sounded like you were flirting."

"Then I guess I was. Does that bother you?"

"Yes. I mean…not really." I shake my head, blinking rapidly. "But yes."

A smirk spreads, carving out those signature dimples. Every time they appear, it feels as though a little secret has been shared, turning an ordinary moment into something more intimate, more personal. "Which is it?" he wonders. "Am I allowed to flirt with you or not?"

I swallow hard, swiping my clammy palms down my thighs.

I don't do intimate. I don't do personal.

Max watches me, eager for my reply, his starry eyes scanning my face for a reaction. Something inside me melts a little. I think it's my heart. Goopy pieces start to drip, making a slow slide down my chest and depositing in my belly with a warm plunk.

This is probably the part where I'm supposed to smile back at him, or say something flirty, or ask what he's doing tomorrow so we can make plans.

But in true Ella fashion, I ditch him like a coward.

Backing away, I stutter through a goodbye and offer a quick wave. "Sorry but I gotta go. Curfew. Mom will be worried. Bye." I catch the way he blinks with confusion, his brows furrowing in disappointment, before I spin around and sprint from the bluffs.

I run the whole way home.

Chapter 7

MAX

E VERY DAY OVER THE NEXT FEW WEEKS, ELLA WALKS THREE MILES INTO TOWN after school, clad in a black beanie and her orange backpack, only to return hours later looking exhausted, defeated, and burned out. She's hardly spoken a word to me since the bonfire, but I heard from McKay—who heard from Brynn—that she's been picking up résumés and applying for jobs.

Today, I've attempted to make her trek into town somewhat more palatable.

Why?

Still undetermined.

Maybe I'm reminiscing about the little girl I used to know and wondering if she's still in there somewhere. Or maybe I've faced so many challenges in life that I've become prone to seeking them out. Ella is a puzzle. She's a jigsaw with missing pieces, and the more time I spend with her, the more I feel like I'm finding new fragments. Is she still that girl with the megawatt smile and infectious laugh who found joy in books and butterflies? Or have life's hardships snuffed out her light?

I've gotten glimmers.

And that leads me to believe the old Ella hasn't faded entirely.

I'm pulling weeds from the vegetable garden in the front yard when I catch her stepping out her screen door and onto the cedar porch. The porch takes up the whole length of the house, which is made up of plain taupe siding and dark shutters. It's a ranch-style home like mine, only it's in much better shape. Our house is half-built, partially finished, and full of angry ghosts.

Ella's sneakers clap along the wooden planks as she jogs down the four steps that lead to a patchy front lawn. I pretend to be absorbed in weed-pulling and dirt-sifting, but my chin lifts as my gaze trails her from underneath my Grizzlies ball cap. She doesn't notice anything at first, too focused on the clouds hovering in a meltwater-blue sky as both hands grip the straps of her book bag.

Then she falters, doing a double take. She comes to an abrupt stop, her head canting right, and she just stands there, still as a pillar, her back to me. The moment she swivels around, I duck my head and return my attention to the garden bed. My heartbeat kicks up when I hear gravel crunch beneath the soles of her shoes. Shoes that are now headed in my direction.

"Max."

I feign indifference, not bothering to glance up. "Hey, Ella."

"Do you know who put that bicycle on my property?"

I hide my smile, swiping the back of my forearm across my mouth to erase the beads of sweat as I fall back on my haunches. "No. Probably Chevy."

Ella turns to stare across the way at Chevy's property strewn with mechanical chaos. Old cars, in varying stages of disrepair, are scattered across the lot, the bodies faded and weather-beaten. Engines are disemboweled, with tires stacked in leaning towers, and tables are cluttered with tools and grease stains. She frowns thoughtfully before panning her gaze back to me. I stare up at her, wiping my hands down the front of my dirt-dappled cargo pants.

"Hmm," she murmurs. "That was really nice of him."

"He's a good guy," I say, nodding my agreement. "Not everyone in this town is out to make your life miserable."

We hold our stare and I hope she catches my hidden meaning.

I'll admit, her abrupt departure from the bonfire left me feeling a bit… stung. I thought I had high walls, but if I have walls, Ella has concrete fortresses, complete with a drawbridge and a moat teeming with metaphorical monsters to keep people at bay.

And that's oddly compelling.

She clears her throat, tugging her beanie farther down her forehead. Her fingernails are painted a sun-kissed orange, contrasting with her rain-cloud personality. "Yeah. I guess." Kicking at some loose stones, she begins to back away. "Well, tell him I said thank you…if you see him before I do."

"Sure. Will do."

She turns toward her yard, where the bicycle is leaning against the wood railing of her front porch. It's ruby red, freshly cleaned with air-filled tires, and perfectly functional. It's been buried in our one-car garage for years, so I figured someone could get some use out of it.

As she trudges back toward the house with a slew of book-bag key chains shimmying behind her, I draw to a stand and call out to her. "Ella."

She pauses, peering at me over her shoulder. "Yeah?"

"We could, uh…" I scratch the back of my neck, unsure of what I even want to say. But I want to say something. "We could catch a movie tomorrow if you want."

Her stare is blank and unblinking, almost as if she has no idea what movies are.

"At the movie theater. You know, that establishment off Richter Avenue that has the giant projectors and smells like buttered popcorn and—"

"I know what movies are." She looks completely unamused. "I'm busy. Sorry."

"Maybe another time."

"I'm busy forever." Two jade-green eyes narrow at me, her head tilting with suspicion. "Wait. Are you flirting with me again?"

I sniff, folding my arms. "Definitely not."

"Okay." The word is drawn out and her eyes are squinty and searching. "But you still want to be friends?"

"Sure. Why not?"

Her eyebrows arc up. "I could make a list. Do you like lists? I love lists."

"Go for it. I'm intrigued." My arms flex and I don't miss the way her focus flicks to my muscles for a beat before she blinks back to my face. Smirking, I add, "While you're at it, add an evaluation of my biceps to that list. I'd love to know how they rate."

Color stains her pretty pale cheeks as her eyes flare. Then she whips around, hair flying with her from underneath the beanie, and storms away. "Goodbye, Max."

"See ya." I send a two-finger salute to her back before returning to my position beside the garden.

Ella flies by on her new bike moments later, just as the rickety screen door snaps shut behind me. When I turn, I spot my father leaning forward on his cane with two sunspotted hands as he stares at the cloud of dust Ella's tires left behind. "Hey, Dad."

He looks better today. Sober. Moving around.

Relief sweeps through me as I take in his too-big corduroy pants and half-tucked flannel. My father is no less gaunt and frail, but his eyes hold a semblance of a spark as he glances my way.

It's a good day. I live for these good days.

"She seems like a nice girl," he notes, tipping his head toward the gravel road, his thin hair fluttering when a breeze rolls through.

"'Nice' isn't the word I'd use. More like…moody. Unapproachable."

Obnoxiously intriguing.

"Huh." Dad takes a wobbly step forward, then peers up at the sky of blue and patchy white. "Your mother…she was a slippery one, too. Hard to catch. Harder to hold."

I stiffen at the reference to my mother. "I'm not interested in Ella like that."

I'm not.

Sure, maybe I was trying to get a rise out of her at the bonfire last weekend—and yeah, of course I think she's pretty. She is. She's that piece of fine china perched on the top shelf, out of reach, for display only. Dusty and shadowed. Breakable. People stare at it, curious and admiring, but they don't dare touch it.

But I'm not *interested* in her.

Not like that.

Romance is out of the question for me, and considering her reaction to my harmless flirting, she's very much on the same page.

Works out.

"I never see you with any girls, Maxwell," Dad says to me, expression clouding. "Your brother has a girlfriend. You're just as good-looking and like-able. I want that for you."

"I'm fine. I stay busy." Readjusting my baseball cap, I wave a hand through the air, showcasing the fruits of my labor.

My father takes another slow step forward and glances at the vegetable garden thriving with snap beans, turnips, and kale. The tiny spark in his eyes evaporates. Glancing around, he blinks a few times as he fully takes in the glowing green grass, well-manicured chrysanthemums, and de-weeded flower beds, like he's seeing it all for the first time. "Max…" Emotion has his throat bobbing, his balance teetering. "This is too much, Son. I feel…" He almost chokes. "I feel like I've failed you."

I frown, pulling off my cap and swiping the disheveled hair off my forehead. "You haven't. I enjoy doing this."

"You should be enjoying your youth. Nights out with friends, boat rides on the lake, camping, girls."

"That's McKay's scene. I'm good."

His head swings back and forth as he zones out and stares dazedly at the front of the house with a weary sigh. "We never finished," he says softly. "It's one of my greatest regrets."

My teeth clench, my molars grinding together as I follow his gaze.

Years ago, shortly before the accident and Mom's subsequent abandonment without a backward glance, me, Dad, and McKay started building this house from the ground up. It was supposed to be our family project, a labor of love. We'd spend weekends working on it—sawing, hammering, and laughing under the warm sun. The foundation was laid with bricks and mortar but also with hopes, dreams, and visions of a picturesque future. The idea was to create not just a house but a *home*.

Now, the half-built structure is nothing more than a shell of what it was meant to be, much like our family. Each beam, each unfinished room, holds a fractured dream. A sad memory. While the house stands unfinished, it isn't entirely unlivable. We managed to get the roof up before everything fell apart, and the walls, although unpainted and raw, provide a solid barrier against the elements. A layer of sturdy plastic sheeting tacked up on the inside of the frames doubles as both insulation and a way to keep out wind and rain.

The house's bones are solid. The floorboards may creak underfoot, and the plumbing might groan in protest, but the lights come on and the water runs hot and cold. Chevy and I rigged up a wood-burning stove that not only suffices for cooking but also throws out enough heat to keep the chill at bay during the colder months. The unglazed windows were temporarily patched up with clear, durable plastic that let in light and kept out the weather. We've made it habitable with quick fixes—a Band-Aid on a wound that runs deep.

I cast a sideways glance at Dad, his face etched with lines of burden and regret. I feel his sorrow. Feel his pain. Physically, he'll never be able to finish this house, and McKay has no interest. That leaves me. And without the financial means or an extra pair of hands to help me, the house will likely remain a lost cause. I've accepted that, so I do what I can by keeping the landscaping maintained and making sure the vegetables stay ripe and healthy.

McKay says I'm polishing shit.

I say I'm tending to hope.

Dad glances skyward, squinting at the sun, still shaking his head like the burning beacon has personally affronted him somehow. Seemingly zoned out, he mutters, "I guess I'll get the boat ready. Find me the fishing nets, will you?"

I must have misheard him. "What?"

"The nets. I…" Lifting a hand to his hairline to blot out the sunrays, he frowns, confused. Then he blinks repeatedly before turning to look at me. "A nap sounds good. I'll leave you to it."

He hobbles back inside and the screen door claps shut once again.

My brows pinch together. Seeing Dad out of sorts and not making sense isn't anything new, but he seemed coherent enough. Sober. I suppose when you've grappled with alcoholism for close to a decade, a few screws are bound to come loose.

Drawing in a long breath, I look up toward the yellow sun and let the warmth wash over me. It's a beautiful October afternoon, yard work is done, Dad is detoxing, and Ella doesn't have to walk six miles. I'm not sure what McKay is up to, but he's probably getting laid. All is well.

For now.

I rinse off with the watering hose, tighten the laces on my shoes, and head toward the lake for my daily run.

Chapter 8

ELLA

I WAKE UP EXTRA EARLY ON MONDAY MORNING AND PLOP DOWN AT MY DESK for a bookbinding session before school. It's been a few weeks since I've enjoyed my favorite hobby, thanks to stress, job hunting, homework, and period cramps. I've always loved reading, so I took up bookbinding when I was a preteen after taking a lesson on it in a junior high art class. It was a way to immerse myself deeper in the world of literature. The feel of the paper, the rhythm of the stitch, the intricacy of the folds…it's meditative.

My workstation is a little universe of its own: a trove of tools, threads, crafts, and papers. Sometimes I create my own books, using cream-colored sheets that stack together neatly, their edges aligned, and then fold them in half to create what will become the book's signatures. And then I start stitching, which is my favorite part. It's like therapy, in addition to my *real* therapy in the form of monthly in-person sessions with the school counselor.

When I'm not creating a whole new book for scrapbooking or journaling purposes, I'm designing covers for my favorite novels. It's my personal take on the world the author brought to life. I always purchase two copies of my favorite books—one to honor the original cover design, and the second to piece together my own cover concept using leather, cardstock, and textured cloths. My favorite work to date is my rendition of the Winnie the Pooh collection that Jonah helped me create a few years ago. It's always been our favorite story. I'm his Piglet and he's my Pooh Bear.

Well...*was*.

As I reach for my awl, my cell phone vibrates from atop the desk and a familiar name pops up.

Brynn!: Good morning! McKay and I are ditching school today to go tubing at Big Bear! Want to come? 👀

I consider it.

The sun is extra bright today, the sky clear and cloudless. It's going to be a perfect seventy-degree day and I'm confident my classes will be bleak and stormy. On the other hand, my mother doesn't need the added anxiety of her daughter ditching school. She's barely holding it together. Another casserole meltdown sounds as enticing as a root canal performed by a blindfolded dentist using a rusty spoon.

I text her back.

Me: Thanks for the offer, but I'll pass. Maybe next weekend.
Brynn!: No worries! See you tomorrow!

The message is followed up by eleven emojis of happy suns, pink hearts, and a bento box filled with sushi. A finger slip, I'm assuming. After I spend another half hour on a little scrapbook, I take a quick shower, blow-dry my hair, and apply a coat of mascara before slipping into a pair of jeans and a faded sweatshirt.

When I hear the guttural roar of a truck revving to life outside my window, I traipse across the bedroom and push back my peach drapes. Max is smoking beside his truck. He's leaning against the bed with a ball cap concealing his eyes and his feet are crossed at the ankles, his muscly arms bronzed with a post-summer glow.

Stupid arms.

It's his fault I'm always noticing them, considering he's prone to wearing sleeveless tops. Winter can't come soon enough. Out of sight, out of mind.

I crack my window halfway and lean out over the ledge, inhaling the early-morning breeze filled with dew-kissed grass and earthy soil. I've been trying to avoid Max since the bonfire, which is kind of a dick move, I realize. I also realize it was *me* who broached the friendship topic in the first place, so I can't blame him for making an effort.

But then he called me pretty.

He…*flirted*.

And my anti-romance instincts flared like a well-shaken can of Dr Pepper on a hot day. Unpredictable and abrupt, leaving a messy aftermath that no one really wants to clean up. Dramatic, I suppose. But my defenses are nothing if not stubborn and thorough.

Max pops his head up then, spotting me dangling out my half-open window. He pulls the cap off his head and runs his fingers through his hair, taming the coffee-brown locks. I don't move away when our eyes meet across both yards. I don't smile or wave either, but I don't want to be too much of an asshole.

Max stares at me for a few beats before glancing down and kicking at the loose gravel in his driveway.

And when he lifts his eyes one more time, a small smile shines back at me.

At first, I want to slam the window shut and run away. I want to glare at him for no reason just because it's easier that way.

But then the bonfire flashes through my mind. The Dr Pepper he brought for me. The way he defended my honor when Andy acted like a cretin. The way his blue eyes shimmered with fire and moonlight as he looked at me with something other than disgust. It was nice to feel like my existence mattered to him in some way. I wasn't a burden or a waste of space. I wasn't an outsider.

He saw that same little girl on a playground from long ago.

Most of all, he saw me as something other than Jonah Sunbury's sister.

So I smile back, hesitantly, softly. It's not a full-fledged grin, but it's a real smile. It's effort.

It counts.

Then I inch away from the window and finish getting ready for school, doing my best to ignore the tickle in my chest.

I'm midchew when I hear it.

The grating, awful sound of my own voice. Sobbing. Begging. Choking through a waterfall of love-drenched tears.

"H-he's not a b-bad person, I swear. He's good. It was a misunderstanding. Please, please. Believe him. He's my big brother… You have to believe he's innocent."

The corn bread turns to rocks in my mouth. Dry, hard, bitter lumps. Crumbs flutter from my parted lips as my stomach drops out of me like a boulder.

I feel sick. I might actually puke.

"Look at this loser defending a monster," a voice sneers from the adjacent table, belonging to some no-name girl. Students swarm to watch the video and the cafeteria morphs into a prison cell.

Bars close me in. Guards pace back and forth, eyeing me with revulsion.

Guilty.

For a few seconds, I pretend to ignore the commotion going on beside me. Pretend I'm blissfully unaware of my pain being laid out on display and mocked by my senior class. Sitting alone like I always do, I attempt to chew the corn-bread gravel in my mouth and swallow it, hoping it doesn't sever anything vital as it slogs down my throat.

"Hey! Sunbury."

I pull my beanie down over my ears. Maybe everyone will think I have earbuds in and they'll give up. There's no fun in tormenting someone if the victim is oblivious.

The act is up sooner than I'd like.

My beanie is yanked off my head and tossed to the dirty linoleum.

"Hey!" I jump up from the bench. "Don't touch me, you pig."

One of Andy's football buddies—Heath—stares back at me. Under the brassy cafeteria lights, his hair looks like the sickly shade of a jaundiced sun on a smoggy day and his eyes are one shade darker than vile. He shoves his cell phone in my face, flaunting the media footage of my desperate appeal.

I realize sticking up for a murderer on national television was a grave error on my part, but it's hard to apologize for grief. Grief does what it wants when it wants to. I was hardly sixteen years old; a devastated, confused child whose life was just blown apart by a semiautomatic shotgun.

I shove Heath's arm out of my face and storm past him and the gaggle of sniveling girls beside him.

He grabs me by the back of the shirt.

My eyes bulge with shock that he had the nerve to put his hands on me. "What the hell? I said, 'Don't *touch* me.'"

Heath sniffs, letting me go. "You don't belong in our school. I'm surprised they even enrolled you here, considering how you've sided yourself with the devil himself."

"He's my brother," I spit out through clenched teeth. "I was scared and grieving. Leave me alone."

"Look at you in your fancy clothes, crying tears of sympathy for that murderer." The no-name girl points at the video.

Heath rewinds the footage.

With my jaw clenched tight and more tears burning, I glance at the phone screen. I'm all dressed up in a nine-hundred-dollar pantsuit, my hair teased and curled, my lips slicked in bright-pink gloss. My eyes are bloodshot, lips quivering with loss. Mom stands beside me, holding on to me with one arm, her face buried in my shoulder as she breaks apart on camera.

Nausea coils in my gut. Bile crawls up my throat.

I won't cry. I won't cry.

"I've suffered enough," I croak out, looking around at the assortment of hateful eyes on me. At the cliques and snickering groups of classmates. My judges and jurors. "My brother is serving his sentence and so am I."

"What about that girl he slaughtered? And the guy she was fucking?" someone from the crowd blares. "They're in the ground and you're walking free."

"I didn't do anything."

"You're breathing my air and I don't fucking like it." Heath steps toward the table behind us and snatches my backpack from the bench. Shoving at me, he taunts, "Don't forget your doodle bag."

My cheeks are burning with the fire of a trillion suns and my oxygen is compromised with an edging panic attack. Everyone around me snickers and points. Heath smirks before flitting his hand in the air as if to shoo me away.

I spin around and book it from the cafeteria. From the school. From everything.

My legs carry me through the main doors and out into the balmy air. Sunshine beats down on me, doing little to brighten my spirits. I should have gone tubing.

I've hardly made it across the field when I hear footsteps coming up behind me. It's probably Heath or Andy or No-Name Girl here to put me out of my misery.

And a hopeless, jaded part of me might just let them. I wonder if I'd even fight back.

"Ella! Wait up."

My stomach pitches.

It's Max.

For some reason, the sound of his voice angers me. He's chasing after me instead of running me out, and that doesn't make any sense. I whip around to face him, tears streaking down my cheeks despite my valiant effort to keep them contained. "*What*," I seethe at him.

I sound furious, rageful, unhinged. He doesn't deserve my wrath, but I didn't deserve to lose everything days before my sixteenth birthday. Nothing is fair because there is no "fair" in this world. It's an illusion. We're sold the belief that there's an order, a balance, but life has shown me time and time again that it doesn't work that way.

Max stops just short of me, looking wounded. "Whoa. What happened?"

I narrow my eyes. "I didn't think there was room for interpretation."

"I was coming out of the library and saw you running down the hallway."

"Well, sorry to hear you missed the entertainment. I'm sure you'll get the recap soon. In fact, I'm confident someone documented it and you'll get to see it firsthand. Probably on a billboard somewhere."

He shakes his head. "Did someone hurt you?"

I swallow then turn around to stalk away. "Doesn't matter. I gotta go."

"Ella."

"Leave me alone, Max. I don't want to be your friend. I don't want you to rescue me. Just stay away from me before I taint your precious reputation."

He's blocking my escape before I make it three steps. "You think I give a shit about my reputation?"

I shrug. "Don't know, don't care. I don't want to know anything about you, to be honest. I just want to be left alone." My chest tightens. I'm not sure I actually mean that, but it's better this way. Max is a decent person and he doesn't need to be associated with the school's waste.

Max stiffens in front of me, shoving his hands in his pockets. He glances down at his shoes for a beat before lifting his eyes to mine. "You don't deserve whatever happened back there."

"That doesn't mean it didn't happen. And your pity isn't going to change anything."

"It's not pity," he says. "I'm just trying to be your friend again. Should I stop trying?"

I take a moment to study his face. His icy-blue eyes that somehow look warm. His tousle of brown hair that looks as soft as the expression he wears. I blink. Max sounds genuine and the concept is foreign to me. Brynn! wants to be my friend, too, but I wonder if she means it. I wonder if she could handle everything that comes along with being associated with me. I bet she'd cower under the pressure, the gossip, the sneers and side-eyes. I bet Max would, too.

I look away, sniffling as I swipe at the traitorous tearstains dampening my cheeks. "You know that brother I used to tell you about? The one who wrote me letters?" I ask him. "That's Jonah Sunbury. As in the convicted murderer sitting on death row."

"I know," Max replies. "I saw parts of the trial on TV."

Curling my fingers into fists, I meet his eyes again. "I'm sure you did. But let me tell you about it from my perspective. From his grieving little sister's point of view."

He goes quiet, licks his lips, and answers with a small nod.

"Jonah fell in love with a beautiful girl named Erin. She was outgoing and bubbly, always kind to me. Treated me like a sibling because she was an only child. She was the daughter of that famous actor, Peter Kingston. I'm sure you've seen his action movies. Erin was his prized possession. A budding actress herself, bound for stardom. Their family had fame, fortune, everything you could ever wish for." I swallow, catching my breath. "We had money, too. My mother owned an equestrian ranch on the outskirts of Nashville called Sunbury Farms. Erin took up horseback riding lessons and that's how she met Jonah. It was love at first sight, as they say." Bitterness drenches my words. I hate that phrase; it's utter bullshit. "Anyway, I'll spare you all the gooey details, but their whirlwind romance turned tragic one day when, supposedly, Jonah caught her cheating on him with one of her costars in some made-for-TV movie. Tyler Mack. Sounds like a movie all in itself, huh?"

His throat works as he stares at me, hanging on to every word. "Ella…"

"They say he killed them in cold blood, Max. According to the evidence, my sweet, loving brother fucking *snapped*. And it wasn't a spur-of-the-moment snap; it was a weeklong lethal breakage. Premeditated, they called it. He took a shotgun from our mother's safe. Stalked her for a few days. And then he broke down the door of her high-rise condominium and shot her in the face. He shot Tyler in the back of the head as Tyler was trying to give CPR to what was left of her mouth. Then he shot them both again, just to be sure they were dead…"

Finally, I snap my mouth shut, not wanting to say anymore. He gets the picture. I've painted it well enough, and truthfully, there is no palette, no color spectrum, no tools or canvases that could ever fully depict the world I live in, day in and day out.

"Do you think he did it?" he asks softly.

More tears leak out as my stomach lurches with a new wave of nausea. "I didn't…at first. He was my big brother. My greatest protector. But I saw him covered in their blood. He said he was trying to help them, but…the evidence…" I fold both arms across my abdomen to keep myself from heaving on the spot and finish with, "Yes. I think he did it."

Max ducks his head and nods, letting out a long breath.

"And yes…I think you should stop trying to be my friend again."

When I try to move past him, still swiping at my treacherous wet eyes with the sleeve of my sweatshirt, Max stops me one more time.

"I made you a list."

I freeze. My throat rolls as his words register and I slowly turn around to face him. "A list?"

"Yeah. You said you love lists, so I made one for you."

I'm staring blankly at him as he reaches into the back pocket of his tapered jeans and pulls out a folded-up piece of notebook paper.

He hands it to me.

I pluck it from between his fingers.

Then I watch his mouth flicker with the saddest smile before he turns and walks away.

More tears pool to the surface because I wasn't expecting the gesture. I'm never expecting anything from anybody, and Max continues to surprise me.

Swallowing hard, I unfold the white lined paper and read over his words, scribbled in black ink.

Why We Should Be Friends

1. I want to be.
2. I have a hunch you secretly want that, too.

—Max

P.S. Shouldn't everything in life be that simple?

Holding back some kind of cry-laugh sound caught in my throat, I sniff, rubbing away mascara streaks from my cheeks as Max saunters back into the school, never once looking back.

Then I tuck the note inside my front pocket.

Right beside the smooth white stone.

Chapter 9
MAX

McKay is running with me today.

It's rare that I'm able to pull him away from Brynn or his busy social commitments, so I savor the hour we share running down winding roads, alongside creeks, and through dense tree lines carved with walking paths. When we're breathless and parched, we take a break and sit side by side on a gnarly-looking log and gaze out at the lake through leafy branches.

McKay pulls a water bottle out of his backpack, then hands one to me. After chugging down the whole thing in a few swallows, he lets out a sigh and stares at the ground between his feet. "This is nice," he says. "It's been a while."

"Too long," I agree.

"Sorry, I just… I've needed to do my own thing, you know? Nothing personal."

It sure feels personal when you're on the receiving end of someone's cold shoulder. Still, I say flippantly, "I get it."

"I know I've been distant lately. That shithole of a house is depressing and spending time with you reminds me of…" He blinks a few times, and his voice trails off.

My jaw tics as my eyes remain firmly fixed on the gleaming lake. "I remind you that Mom didn't love us enough to stay, Dad has more issues than *People* magazine's entire publication history, and our dream house is one strong wind away from becoming a pile of kindling. Glad that's clarified."

"I didn't mean it like that."

"You did." I gulp a few sips of water and they burn on the way down. "It's fine."

"Max, c'mon. You've always been the golden child. Even when Mom—" He blows out a breath and ruffles his shaggy hair. "Mom and Dad always preferred you."

"*Preferred* me?"

"Yeah. Mom would take *you* to run all the errands and go on happy, whole-some lunch dates. Dad would take *you* fishing because I didn't know how to swim until I was nine. *You* were the one he sat down with and talked construction and building-code crap. I'm the odd one out. Always have been and you know it."

"That's bullshit. It was an even playing field growing up."

"Ask Dad," he shoots back. "I dare you. Ask him in confidence which son he likes better and you'll see exactly what I'm talking about."

Anger filters through me, hot like the sun on my skin. "Well, you only have yourself to blame for that now. I'm the one keeping him safe and sober. I'm the one cleaning up his puke and piss when he drinks himself nearly to death. I'm the one who keeps the place clean, cooks, and does your fucking laundry. Don't try to act like the helpless victim, McKay."

His eyes radiate fury for a heartbeat before he blinks it away. Sighing, he shakes his head and kicks at a jagged rock. "Fine. You're right."

"I know I'm right." I glance at him. "Besides, your life isn't that bad. You have an awesome girlfriend. Brynn loves the shit out of you. Your grades are good, basketball keeps you busy, and you're less than a year away from gradu-ating and getting out of this town."

His lips thin. "I guess."

"Am I wrong?"

"I mean…grades don't matter in the long run, basketball can only take me so far, and I have no real plans after graduation. I don't know what I want to do with my life," he says bleakly. "Brynn is a nice distraction, but she's going to Florida State."

I frown. "She got in already?"

"She will. She's smart as hell and she wants to pursue criminal justice."

Nodding, I swallow down the rest of my water and squeeze the empty bottle in my hand. "Good for her. You could follow her."

An indifferent shrug is his reply.

I'm not sure what I was expecting out of this impromptu bonding session, but I was hopeful it wasn't going to turn into this. I miss the relationship we used to have. I miss my twin brother who always had my back, who followed me around like I was king, and who never once looked at me with bitter, resentful eyes.

I hate what we've become.

Swiping my palms down my shorts, I turn to him, taking in his slumped shoulders and hollow expression. "If it makes you feel any better, I don't have the option of leaving after graduation. As long as Dad's alive, I'll be here."

A hint of sympathy glimmers back at me. "It doesn't have to be like that. We could get out of here together. Travel, start up a business, get an apartment. Lay roots in a big city with bright lights and excitement on every corner." Hope seeps into his words. "We could do anything, Max. See the whole fucking world if we want to. Just like we used to talk about."

I swallow. "And Dad?"

"Dad's made his bed."

"He was nearly paralyzed in a freak accident."

"And then he turned to booze instead of his family to help him through it," McKay counters. "There's assisted living housing, programs that can—"

"No." I cut him off. "There's no fucking way can we afford that."

The hope fades, tinting his eyes to that familiar bitter gray. He stuffs his empty water bottle into his backpack. "Can't say I didn't try." Before he stands from the log, he falters, his attention snagging on something above us and slightly to the left. "Is that Ella?"

I follow his stare. Sure enough, Ella is perched on the bridge again, her long hair glowing an electrifying shade of red beneath the sunlight. It matches the bike I gave her, the one currently leaning against the guardrail. I'm glad she's getting use out of it.

For a moment, I empathize with her. She has a brother, too; one who's changed, one she can no longer reach. I can see the weight of that burden in her eyes, the same heavy burden that I carry for McKay. It's a different kind of struggle, but I can't help but relate to it, anyway.

Ella is staring down at the water with two sticks in her hands. I gaze at her for a few seconds, watching the way she aligns the sticks side by side, hesitates, then lets them go. They splash into the water and she moves to the other side of the railing, her back to us. "Yeah, that's her," I say.

"Brynn heard from Madi what happened yesterday at lunch, so she snitched to Principal Walker. Heath has detention all week."

"Good. He's a prick."

"I heard a rumor that Caulfield is also catching heat for some comments she made to Ella in class." McKay pauses. "You see that video? When Ella was crying to the reporters?"

My defenses flare. "Her brother had just murdered two people. I'd be crying, too."

He doesn't say anything.

Part of me wonders if McKay is Team Everyone Else and thinks Ella is no better than her brother. And that's shit. The poor girl hardly stood a chance after her name was smeared by the media and that video of her, at her lowest moment in life, was made a mockery of all across the internet. Only seventeen years old and she's already a villain who committed no crime other than harboring undying love for someone who did a really bad thing.

Kids our age are fucking sheep.

Society is a cesspit.

The human race is on a downward spiral, and I'll be damned if I contribute to the charade with a pitchfork mentality. If we're all heading for the same cliff edge, I'd rather take the scenic route.

McKay pops up from the log, pulling his backpack over one shoulder. He glances up at the bridge again as Ella reaches for more sticks piled near her feet. "You got a thing for her?" he wonders, nodding toward the bridge. "Like you used to when we were little? I remember you were always saying stuff about getting married."

My brows pull together. "No. We were just kids. It was dumb."

"I saw you two acting all chummy at the bonfire."

"So? She's cool. She's funny and smart." I swallow, following his stare. "Maybe she just needs a friend."

He shakes his head. "Leave the kumbaya shit to Brynn. She's good at that."

"Maybe I want to be her friend."

It's true.

I avoided Ella at first because there hadn't been any room in my life for new friendships or connections. It's not that I cared about her media interview. I didn't care about her reputation, or mine.

I just wanted to be left alone.

But…I don't think I want that anymore.

McKay shoots me a baffled glance, blinking a few times before nodding slowly. "All right, then. Good luck with that. I'm going to head home and check on Dad."

I scrape my teeth together as I watch him retreat. "Check on Dad" is code for "sit on my ass and listen to podcasts until Max gets home to check on Dad." I mutter a goodbye he doesn't hear, then look back up at the bridge. Ella's back is to me again and she's staring down into the water, half-draped over the shoddy railing. Curiosity has me standing, and a burning fascination to get to know this girl again has me moving to join her.

I make my way up the ravine until I'm within earshot. The bridge creaks beneath my weight, causing her to whip around with a look in her eyes that wages war.

My hands fly up, palms forward. "I come in peace."

She relaxes a little when recognition settles in. Ella gives me a once-over, as if checking for hidden weapons, before lifting up from the railing. "Peace," she murmurs. "An unattainable concept as elusive as a rainbow's end. Always within sight, yet perpetually out of reach."

"That's grim."

"That's life." Looking me over one more time, she stalks back over to the opposite side of the bridge and plucks two sticks from her stockpile. "Are you here to give me another list?"

I stuff my hands in my pockets as I study her. I have no idea what she's doing, but she looks focused. Ella bends over the guardrail, carefully extends both arms, and drops the thin branches into the lake. Then she rushes over to watch them swim downstream. "I can if you want me to."

"Sure," she answers, sounding uninterested.

I fumble for something to say that might change that. "Okay. This list will be titled, 'Things We Should Do Together Now That We're Friends.'"

Ella scoffs and shakes her head, attention still pinned on the running river water.

"One: Skip stones across the lake. You've been throwing sticks, but I bet I can teach you to make stones skim the surface. I'm a pro."

She glances over at me, curiosity flickering in her eyes.

Progress.

"Two: Stargaze. There's an open field not too far from here that's perfect for a clear night. My dad used to take me there when I was a kid and we'd try to count the stars." I hold up a third finger. "Three: Attend a local music festival. Tagline unnecessary."

I pause, searching her face for a reaction, and see a flash of consideration.

Something has her interest piqued.

"And four…" I clear my throat and take a tentative step toward her. "Go to the Fall Fling."

Her expression sours quicker than milk left out on a hot summer's day.

I should have stopped at three.

"Fall Fling?" she echoes, her voice dripping with as much enthusiasm as a cat offered a bath. "Somehow I've led you to believe that I enjoy dancing, social gatherings, and wearing dresses. I'm sorry for that."

"What do you enjoy these days? Do you still love books, butterflies, and orange Popsicles?"

"Nice try." She glances back down at the water, though her resolve seems shaken. "And for the record, I never agreed to being friends."

The Fall Fling was a stretch, I know. I had no intention of going either, but I also had no intention of going to that bonfire. She made it better.

She made it fun.

I continue to step forward until I'm close enough to get a whiff of citrus and honeysuckles. Ella looks up at me as I approach, her wide green eyes panning to my face. I offer a smile to soften her steel. "I thought my list was effective. It wasn't as detailed as the bullet points you listed off back at the clearing the other day, but I felt good about it."

She blinks up at me before letting out a breath that sounds like surrender. "You're obnoxiously persistent," she mutters. "Skipping stones, huh?"

"Pro," I confirm.

"Jonah tried to teach me how to do that, but I could never get it. I didn't have the touch. Eventually, we started collecting sticks to toss over bridges." She holds up two knotty branches. "Pooh sticks."

I make a face. "Sounds gross."

Her lips twitch, a prelude to the laugh I'm desperate to hear. Ella doesn't really laugh and she hardly ever smiles. I've caught her smirking a few times but never a full-fledged grin. There were no dimples, no sparkling flash of teeth. Only a flicker of buried happiness clawing to the surface.

And maybe it's silly, but I'm determined to be the cause of that dimpled, toothy grin.

Real, genuine belly laughter would be a plus.

"It's from Winnie the Pooh," Ella explains. "Each person drops a stick over the upstream side of a bridge and the one whose stick first appears on the downstream side is the winner. My brother and I used to—" Looking away, she swallows. "I played it when I was a kid."

I glance at the two sticks in her hand. "But you're playing alone."

"Yeah. I guess I am."

"That's no fun."

Her head pops up, jade eyes narrowing. "It doesn't need to be fun," she says. "Fun is a privilege. Fun is the result of good, wholesome living." She pivots back to the bridge rail and stares down into the water, any trace of that would-be smile stolen by a sweet life gone sour. "I'm just trying to survive at this point."

Melancholy threatens the fragile moment, so I do my best to hang on to the levity still within reach. Extending a hand to her, I open my palm. "Can I play with you?"

Her eyes fixate on my hand before her gaze travels up the length of my arm and settles on my face.

My smile stretches, calling for hers.

"Okay." Ella doesn't smile, but she does hand me a stick. "We need to align them just right, then drop them at the same time."

"Got it." I move in right beside her until our shoulders brush together. Her tangerine top is a formfitting V-neck and her shorts are faded denim. Our hips bump. I look down at her, at the way her throat works, and at the way she stiffens slightly but doesn't inch away from me. The sun still bathes her hair in a rosy glow, making it hard to concentrate on the simple task of releasing a stick. I clear my throat and lean over the guardrail, holding out my arm. "All right. Tell me when."

She mimics my stance, nose to water. "Okay…now."

We drop the sticks and watch them flutter to the stream below. The moment they break the surface with a small splash, Ella snatches my wrist and hauls me toward the opposite side of the bridge. Her fingers curl around me, and the feel of her dainty palm on my skin has me stumbling as I follow. We make it to the other side and peer over the rail, watching as both sticks emerge a few seconds later. They're neck and neck, side by side. I should probably keep watching to see which one prevails, but her hand is still loosely holding my wrist, so I look at her instead. Anticipation glitters in her eyes as she stares over the ledge. She squeezes me a little and I don't think she even realizes it.

I startle when she points down below with her free hand and announces, "I won."

Enthusiasm laces her tone.

Excitement skips across her face like a skillfully tossed stone across water.

I don't bother to look at the competing sticks. I'm too transfixed on her face as a smile blooms. I'm enchanted by that sun on her hair and how it softens her, warms her. Makes her look like she was made for it, just like I remember thinking it did that afternoon in the park.

I murmur gently, without thinking, "Nice job, Sunny."

She blinks a few times, registering the name. Finally, she lets go of my wrist and glances up at me. "Sunny?"

"Yeah." I scratch at my hair, wondering why the nickname spilled out of me, while also wondering why my internal thoughts have taken a sharp left turn onto Weird and Sappy Avenue. "Your last name is Sunbury," I explain with a shrug, glancing up at the light-streaked sky. "Besides...the sun turns your hair this ruby shade of red. It's kind of pretty."

Ella fidgets in place, seemingly allergic to compliments. Then she starts playing with her hair, letting the red-brown strands dance between her fingers. "I'm sure there are more fitting nicknames." She ponders them. "You could call me Monday. Nobody likes Mondays."

"I happen to like Mondays, but I'm a bit of a nonconformist."

Another tiny smile flickers as she peers up at me again through long, inky lashes. "Relatable."

"I guess we have something in common, after all."

At first I'm afraid she's going to shut down. Run away. Hop on her red bike and leave me in the dust, turning this budding friendship into a mere shadow that fades in the light of her swift retreat.

But all she says is, "Want to play another round?"

My heart gallops with the prospect of spending more time with her. With knowing that she's letting me in, even in this small, inconsequential way. Because I know it's not nothing—not for Ella. She's programmed herself to keep people out. I recognize the signs because I'm well trained in emotional evasion, as well. Like two sides of the same coin, we've both mastered the art of keeping the world at arm's length, turning solitude into our shield.

But her armor has slipped. Her shield is lowered.

I've breached her.

I make my way to the pile of sticks and pluck two more from the lessening mound. "All right, Sunny. Best out of ten. If I win, you have to go to the Fall Fling with me." Then I add, just to be safe, "As friends."

She purses her lips. "Not a chance."

"Fine. Go to a music festival with me this fall. My favorite band is playing in Knoxville." Again, I add, "As friends. We can invite Brynn and McKay and make it a group thing."

Contemplation twinkles in her eyes as she studies me, thinking on the terms. She relents with a sigh. "Deal."

I'm grinning ear to ear when I hand her a stick.

We spend the afternoon dropping sticks off the bridge, racing back and forth from rail to rail and watching as the water decides our fate. Each time we let go of our branches, Ella takes me by the wrist to pull me to the other side, almost like it's instinct—like I wouldn't know where to go without her hand to guide me—and every time, my skin tingles in the wake of her touch.

We play Pooh sticks until the sun dips lower and an hour has sailed by.

It's silly.

It's simple.

I think it's just what we need.

Ella manages to be the winner in every match, her sticks always edging out mine at the last second, prompting her arms to rise in victory as the sunshine blankets her in a new light.

She wins.

And yet, when I walk away from the bridge to go for a swim, with her easy smile ingrained in my mind…it feels like I've won it all.

———

I didn't mean to fall asleep.

My eyelids crack open, lashes fluttering with the telltale splashes of color from a setting sun. Pink, gold, orange.

Orange.

I immediately think of her.

I pull up on my elbows and my gaze snaps up to the bridge above me. Her bike is still there, leaning against the distressed salt-and-pepper railing. At least two hours have gone by since we dropped sticks over the bridge, but her bike is still there.

Problem is, I don't see Ella.

Voices sneak their way into my sleep-glazed mind as I sit up fully and scrub both hands over my face. I passed out after my swim while staring up at the sky and counting the clouds. Sometimes I take catnaps by the lake since sleep is often compromised by my father's night terrors.

But I slept too long today. Dad is going to be worried, assuming he's sober and coherent. McKay will come looking for me soon.

And Ella's bike is still on the bridge.

The voices carry over to me again when a breeze rolls through, bringing me back to reality. I glance around, left to right. The water's edge is lined with mature trees, but there's a short dock a few yards away where kids from school occasionally gather to drink and smoke joints.

Reaching for my discarded T-shirt, I throw it over my head and wince when the fabric makes contact with a flush of sunburn. I'm an idiot for drifting off in direct sunlight.

But the sunburn becomes the least of my worries when I hear a scream.

I jump to my feet, glancing back up at the bridge, then at the abandoned bicycle.

My heart fumbles, the beats erratic.

"*Let go of me!*"

I fucking fly.

Dirt and weeds kick up as I race through the brush, forcing branches and leaves out of my way. It's not a far run to the dock. The final trace of sunset highlights four figures wrestling at the ledge of the age-old pier. Andy and a few of his football buddies.

And Ella.

Ella.

They're tormenting her. Tossing her orange backpack back and forth to one another, over her head, just out of reach.

"Give it back!" she shouts, jumping up on her tiptoes to no avail.

I cup both hands around my mouth. "Hey!"

Heads twist in my direction. Andy sees me and laughs, sending me a hearty salute as I pick up my pace. Two more classmates are hovering at the entrance to the dock, looking gleefully entertained. Fucking animals. I dart forward, slipping a few times as I make my way down the sharp incline, and the back of my calf scrapes along a patch of thorny undergrowth. I don't care.

Andy hollers over to me as he watches me approach. "Come to enjoy the show, Manning?"

"Leave her the hell alone," I growl back.

Ella looks horrified. Tears stream down her sun-kissed cheeks, her hair in disarray. She spares me a glance before charging at Andy and clobbering him with both fists.

"You *asshole*." She pummels his back until he whirls around and picks her up, right underneath her rear.

I make it to the bottom of the ravine when the two football douches stop me, blocking my rescue attempt. Heath grabs me by the arm and his friend, Lisbon, snatches my other. Holding me back. Keeping me restrained.

Andy hauls Ella over his shoulder, her fists still pounding his lower back, her nails scratching, protests echoing through the stillness of dusk. Another guy chucks her book bag into the lake with a resounding splash. Ella shrieks. Andy stomps toward the edge of the pier, Ella squirming and flailing atop his bulky shoulder.

I try to fight my way out of the two-man hold, but they grip me tighter, their fingernails gouging my biceps. Motherfuckers. I'll kill them for this.

"Watch me take out the trash, Manning," Andy says, whistling as he stalks closer to the water. "This bitch doesn't belong here. You see her media interview, defending that sick fuck? She's no better than that scum. Good riddance."

Then he tosses her into the lake like she's a rag doll. A sack of rice.

A bag of trash.

Her scream pierces the woodlands.

Strangles my heart.

Andy swipes his hands together as if he's wiping them clean. "Time to cleanse this town of all the waste."

I'm snarling like a rabid dog, struggling against the two meatheads as I watch Ella break the surface and disappear into the murky lake. She'll pop back up any second and these bastards will let me go so I can dry her off and take her home. Then I'll crucify them. Somehow, some way. Don't know what I plan to do, but it won't be good. They'll be fucking sorry they ever laid a hand on her.

"Ella!" I call out as fat fingers bruise my skin.

Everyone is laughing except for me.

Everyone watches the water ripple and bubble in the space where she sank.

Everyone waits.

And waits.

I wait.

The seconds turn into a minute and fear stabs me like a pickax. Heath and Lisbon finally loosen their hold, their laughter fading when Ella doesn't resurface.

Is she drowning? Can she not swim?

Fuck!

I rip myself free, catching Andy's wary expression as he stares blankly out at the too-calm water. "I–I didn't know she couldn't swim…" he stutters. "I just wanted to… Shit…"

I fly past him and his friends, my sneakers untied and pounding the rickety wooden planks as I race toward the lake. Yanking my shoes off, I inhale a lungful of air. And without a second thought, I lunge forward when I reach the edge and dive in, feet first.

Cool water surrounds me, eating me up. Swallowing me. Kicking my feet, I force my eyes open through the gray murk and search for Ella. The world shimmers above, distorted and dreamlike as a wash of stillness fills me. Everything is muted, quiet, familiar.

I see her then, through the muddy wall of water, her hair floating around her in crimson-brown ribbons. She's a few feet away, so I swim and I swim, and she comes more into focus the closer I get.

Her eyes are open. Her arms are extended at her sides, lazy and levitating. She's staring at me, the slight flare of her gaze telling me she's not drowning. She's not.

She's choosing.

I can't help but stare at her. It feels like an eternal moment frozen in time as I watch her and she watches me, and something raw and painfully tantamount passes in the watery space between us. A common thread.

She looks peaceful. Ethereal.

Done.

My mind races to years past, remembering that I've been here before. McKay and I used to hold our breath and stare at each other beneath the lake's surface, just like this, a battle of wills and strong lungs. A competition of who could hold out the longest.

I always wondered who would give up first. Who would give in. Who would submit to the dregs and sink away forever. We were cowards, though. Just kids. We'd kick our feet when our oxygen verged on depletion, gliding back up to the fresh air and sunlight, and it never really felt like an accomplishment when we'd resurface. In a morbid way, it felt like there was no winner.

We both lost.

I'm snapped out of the reverie when Ella's eyes roll up, and I realize the moment is not eternal. It's not eternal, but it will be. *Fuck.* What am I doing, staring at her when I should be saving her? My instincts snap back on and I paddle forward, my chest aching, lungs stretched and bruised. She's running out of time, dying right before my eyes. She's giving in to the quiet moment and I refuse to let that happen.

I reach for her. I grab her by the front of her tangerine top and haul her skyward as my oxygen dwindles and I begin to see stars. She doesn't fight, doesn't swim. She's weightless and drifting. Unconscious, somewhere else. I propel myself up and up as this sad shell of a girl dangles beside me, and I wonder if she'll hate me for this…if my saving her will feel like a tragic loss.

We breach the surface and I inhale.

Big, deep, greedy breaths.

Ella hangs against me, boneless, lifeless. She's not breathing. She's not drinking in the warm autumn air as sustenance like I am.

No, no, no.

Dragging her over the ledge of the dock, I haul myself up and situate her on her back, straightening her legs and tipping her head back.

I fall to my knees beside her.

Everyone else is gone. They fled the scene.

I slam both clasped palms to her chest and pump, terror sluicing me as my wet bangs bounce in front of my eyes.

Breathe, breathe, breathe.

I'm shaking, desperate, frantic.

I keep pumping. Keep trying. Keep begging.

"Come on, Ella. Come on."

I bend down. I'm about to press my lips to hers, to give her fresh air and new life, but then she lurches up off the deck and gasps, her eyes pinging wide open.

Lake water pours out of her.

She rolls onto her side and retches, coughing up bile and mouthfuls of clear liquid.

She coughs and coughs, choking and spluttering, before returning to her back and inhaling more wheezy breaths. I push strands of knotted hair out of her eyes, stroking her forehead with the pad of my thumb. It's an intimate gesture, but saving someone's life is an intimate event. It doesn't seem out of place.

Ella draws in waterlogged breaths, her lungs purging, her body convulsing as it comes back to life. Her wet top clings to her curves as her hair fans out across the dock in soaked, dark tangles. I keep stroking her forehead, telling her she's okay, looming over her until her eyes deglaze and pan over to mine. She blinks up at me, her chest still heaving. Limbs quivering. Her lips part, searching for something to say.

I don't let her speak. I'm too afraid of what those words might be.

I hate you.

How dare you.

You should have let me drown.

Instead, I lean down and whisper softly in her ear, just as the sun disappears beyond the horizon and the sky's fire is snuffed out. "Hey, Sunny."

Chapter 10

ELLA

I THINK I HEAR...CHRISTMAS MUSIC.

Johnny Mathis.

He's crooning about snow and mistletoe, and for a moment I'm stolen by a childhood reverie—a warm haven of nostalgia, snickerdoodle cookies, and those little pine tree air fresheners for the car. My parents would never purchase a real tree because Jonah was allergic to pine needles. So, I'd improvise. I'd gather my allowance, ride my bike to the grocery store, and collect a respectable number of my favorite spruce-scented air fresheners. When I got home, I'd decorate the tree with them, dangling the strings from the plastic needles and inhaling the musty aroma of artificial pine.

Close enough.

Johnny Mathis used to serenade us throughout the month of December. Mom loved to play this shoddy, old VHS tape of Johnny aimlessly strolling through holiday backdrops with people in mortifying nineties Christmas sweaters. It was some kind of seasonal special that aired and it was beyond hokey, but she loved it. We loved it because Mom loved it, and...well, years later, I guess I love it, too. It reminds me of a happier time, sweet moments trapped inside of a magical snow globe.

My head starts to throb.

There's a roaring in my ears, chasing away the memories. Images of sitting by the fireplace with Mom's homemade Chex Mix and Jonah's chocolate-covered marshmallows are replaced with a burning in my lungs. My chest hurts. And it's not the usual ache of sadness this time. It's a physical fullness, a heaviness. Hot pressure strangles my ribs and climbs up my lungs. Johnny Mathis' effortless vibrato is drowned out and all of my senses soon follow.

My eyes fly open.

I lurch.

I heave.

I retch.

I breathe.

Water spurts out of my mouth with the violence of an angry tempest as I lift up off the dock and roll onto my side, my fingertips clawing the wooden planks, my throat on fire.

I think I almost drowned.

I think I wanted to.

I think I meant to.

Out of all the things to feel right now, I feel embarrassed. Someone is here with me. Someone saw me at my worst rock-bottom moment and plucked me off of the lake's floor.

Not just someone.

Max.

I slump onto my back as the memory of him watching me drift away in the deep water with a soul-wrenching look in his eyes seeps into my psyche. My lids flutter open as my head pounds and my lungs continue to work overtime. I don't know what to say.

He's a blur above me, a glowy haze.

God, I was so stupid…so reckless.

I should thank him. Apologize.

But he bends down before I can choke out words, his lips against my ear. "Hey, Sunny."

Emotion rushes through me. Tears sting my eyes. I almost died, but I don't think I actually want to die. Not now, not yet. I'm not ready for such frightening permanence. I need to change my life; I need a second chance to be better. Do better. I have to—

"Stay."

Max hovers over me, sweeping back my dripping wet hair and brushing his thumb against my forehead as my breaths finally begin to placate.

Stay, he says.

Just a single word.

I feel it more than I hear it.

A calming light infiltrates the black cloud swallowing my soul. The roaring in my ears dulls to a peaceful hum until Johnny Mathis is a distant echo once again, reminding me I'm still alive. There are more Christmases to be had.

I fade out, but I'm not gone.

I slip away…

But I'm still here.

———————

He carries me the whole way home.

Two miles.

One arm linked underneath my knees, the other cradled around my back, and my sopping orange bookbag dangling off one shoulder.

His breathing is labored, his footsteps heavy as they crunch along rocks and dirt. Cars zoom by. Streetlights glimmer. My eyelids flutter, exhaustion stealing me away.

He's warm and I'm cold.

He smells like lake water and earth and pine.

Max squeezes me a little tighter as I press my temple to his shoulder and close my eyes.

He holds me.

I let him.

Chapter 11
ELLA

PNEUMONIA.

That's what I get for thinking it would be easier to float away than to fight my way back to the surface. Truly, that's what it came down to. It's not that I actively wanted to die. It just felt…*easier* somehow. It was less work to allow the universe to have its way with me.

We'll call it laziness.

Now I'm suffering the consequences, bedridden at home after a three-day hospital visit where I was poked and prodded by a woman in scrubs who smelled like uncooked rice and wore her hair in a lopsided beehive. The good news is I'm out of school for two weeks. I'll take the win where I can.

Mom doesn't know all the gory details of my near-death experience, nor will she ever know. After Max carried me the two-mile trek home that evening, he stayed with me until my mother returned from work twenty minutes later. He told her I went swimming in the lake and my shoelaces tangled in the underwater vegetation.

Luckily, she was too blindsided with worry to question why I was wearing shoes while swimming.

A small oversight.

Everything inside of me yearned to call out Andy Sandwell and his meathead cronies, but the only thing I yearned for more was *peace*. And peace would never come if I began an uproar in Juniper Falls. I'm done with battles, done with unproductive wars that can't be won. Besides, Andy didn't intend to drown me. He's not a murderer like Jonah. It was my choice to lay down my sword.

I surrendered.

He won.

That's that.

Now I'm lying in bed five days into my at-home recovery when Brynn! breezes into my bedroom with bouncing pigtail braids and the brightest smile I've ever seen.

It's too bright. It hurts my eyes.

I pull the covers up over my face and hide.

"Ella!"

I groan into my blanket cocoon. "My lungs are filled with mucus. My body feels like I was on the losing side of a UFC match. My brain is as responsive as an AOL dial-up connection." I wheeze a little. "I smell like feet."

"AOL?"

"That's what Mom always says when I complain about the Wi-Fi connection."

The covers are whipped off me, revealing my lowly state. Brynn! winces when she drinks me in but recovers well. "These are from me and my dads."

"Dads?" I wonder, blinking slowly.

"Yep. I have two."

"Lucky. I don't even have one." My gaze trails over to a platter of chocolate-dipped fruit made up of pineapple stars and strawberries turned into heart-eyed emojis. "This is supersweet. Thanks."

"You're welcome!" She sets the plate down on my cluttered nightstand strewn with used tissues, antibiotics, and fifty-thousand water bottles, and plops down beside my legs. "I'd ask how you are, but you already gave me a detailed rundown."

"I'm sorry I smell like feet."

She sniffs me. "You don't. You actually smell like orange peels and sweat. It's not a terrible combination."

"I was eating an orange when my fever broke," I tell her. Finding my strength,

I inch up to a sitting position and lean back against the wooden headboard with a sigh. Air-dried tangles of hair fall across my face from my latest showering attempt, and I flick them aside to look at the beaming ball of sunshine perched next to me. Her posture is impeccable. Her hair is like mulberry silk. Her teeth are whiter than freshly fallen snow. She can't be human. "Thanks for visiting me. You didn't have to."

"I wanted to. I tried to come by yesterday, but your mom said you weren't ready for visitors yet."

True enough. Mom is using her vacation time to stay home with me while I recover. She's been adamant about me getting enough sleep, staying hydrated, and making sure I take my antibiotics at exactly the precise time to avoid a relapse. I'm grateful that our state medical insurance kicked in last month while we get back on our feet, so my hospital bills were fully covered. I have no idea what we would have done otherwise.

Guilt gnaws at me because I'm responsible. If only I had pushed my way to the surface, none of this would have happened. Mom has been a nervous wreck, thinking I'll croak in my sleep.

I force a weak smile. "How is school?" Not that I care, but it's the one thing we share in common.

"It's good. McKay officially asked me to the Fall Fling today." She beams. "Do you think you'll be well enough to go?"

"Probably."

"Yay!"

"Doesn't mean I'm going."

Her nose scrunches up. "Oh, you should! You can ride with us in McKay's truck. Technically, it's the family's truck, but it's so vintage. One of those classic models from the sixties; a Chevy, I think—" She notices my eyes have closed, so she taps me on the shoulder. "We can get ready together. I still need to pick out my dress."

"Pass," I mumble groggily.

"Come on...you should go with Max. Last year he went with a girl named Libby, but she was boring and had a weird fascination with pickling things. Onions, cucumbers, beets. Even pigs' feet. You're a lot more fun."

"That's arguable."

She sighs. "Max is really worried about you, by the way."

My eyes ping back open, one at a time. "He is?"

"Yup. There's a rumor going around that he saved your life, but he doesn't want to talk about it." Hesitating, she nibbles on her rosebud bottom lip and lifts her hazel eyes to me. "Is it true? Did he save you?"

I close my eyes again and flash back to the lake. The quiet lull. The stillness. The warped twinkling of orange and yellow sunlight rippling above the surface.

Max.

I think about the way he stared at me underwater, his brown hair floating around him like a halo of autumn leaves. Something told me he'd been there before, just like me. He knew what it was like to want to sink. And then he carried me all the way home without a single complaint, the warmth of his strong arms enough to extinguish the cold lake water threatening to freeze my bones.

Hey, Sunny.

Stay…

I won't deny that he saved me. Max Manning deserves full credit for bringing me back from the dead. "Yeah, it's true," I confess. "He saved me."

Tears glitter in her eyes as she clasps both hands to her chest. "Wow. That's something."

Turning my head, I stare up at the ugly popcorn ceiling. "I guess it is."

"Oh! That reminds me," she says, fishing through her romper pocket. "He said his dad was having some kind of episode, so he couldn't come over here with me…but he wanted me to give this to you. He'll try to visit you tomorrow if your mom is okay with it."

Brynn! holds out a folded-up piece of paper and my heart jumps. My fingers tremble as I reach for the note. "Thank you."

"No problem! I'll let you rest now. I just wanted to see how you were doing." She stands from the bed and gives her braids a tug. "Enjoy the fruit tray. The pineapple is my favorite."

I smile up at her—a real smile this time. "Tell your dads I say thank you. Maybe I can meet them sometime."

"Yes! They've already invited you over for fondue and charades. It's a thing."
Stepping away, she gives me an enthusiastic wave. "Take care, Ella."

"Bye."

After she skips out the door, leaving me in a cloud of candied sweetness, I shift on the bed and quickly open the note from Max. Familiar black ink stares back at me and I bite down on my lip.

Three Reasons You Should Always Swim to the Surface

1. Swimming is good exercise. It's the reason my arms look so good. (Don't deny it. I know you like my arms.)
2. The sun is above the surface. The sun suits you.
3. I'd miss you.

—Max

I'm interrupted by my mother bounding into the bedroom with a mug of hot tea, her hair in curlers, eyes bloodshot. I stuff the note underneath my pillow and flash her a semi-maniacal smile. "Hey, Mom."

"Your fever broke." She approaches with a sigh of relief and sets the neon-orange mug down beside my lava lamp. "How's that cough?"

"Phlegmy and grotesque."

Pressing the back of her hand to my forehead cased in cool sweat, she smiles softly. "You look a little better. Less flushed."

"Yep." My head drops to the headboard as I twist to face her. "I'm back to my standard complexion of ghostly and pale."

"Your friend is lovely, by the way… Brynn." Mom takes a seat beside me. "She dropped off some homework assignments for you to work on once you're over the hump."

I groan. "The anticipation is too much. You shouldn't overexcite me in my current state."

"Oh, Ella." Sighing, she presses her palm to the blanket wad that houses my legs. "You have no idea how thankful I am for Max. I can't imagine…" She blinks away a wall of tears. "The thought of you… I can't…"

Her voice cracks. She can't even get the words out.

Guilt comes soaring back to the surface as gavels slam down all around me.

I was so fucking selfish. I almost left her entirely alone. Childless and bereaved.

I don't reply.

I'm too afraid I'll confess my horrible sin and my sentence will be a slow death.

Regrouping, she clears the anguish from her throat and forces a smile. "Grandma Shirley sent you a nice card and a check for fifty dollars. I told her you were struggling to find a job and this infection is going to set you back."

Grandma Shirley is one of those stingy old ladies who has spent her entire life putting her money away. She's loaded. She claims she's being responsible, but she's turning eighty this year.

While she was helpful in our time of need, buying us a used car and purchasing us this little house after Mom went close to broke paying for Jonah's legal bills, she still gave us a lecture on how important it is to dig our way out of the hole on our own.

I tug the bedcovers up to my chin and make a humming noise. "Cool. Thanks."

"I'm headed back to the salon tomorrow," Mom continues. "Will you be okay on your own? Should I wait a few more days?"

"No, I'm fine. I think I'm through the worst of it." I look out the window when I hear some kind of crashing noise across the street. Nothing looks amiss at the Manning residence from the outside—but I know better than anyone that outward appearances can be deceiving. I blink back to my mother. "I'll call you if I need anything."

"All right." She gives my thigh a squeeze and stands from the mattress before hesitating briefly. "Oh, and Ella?"

I glance at her. "Yeah?"

Mom studies me for a beat, her eyes thinning with contemplation. Then she shakes her head full of pink curlers and asks through a frown, "Why on earth were you swimming with your shoes on?"

A tapping sound wakes me from the dead.

Tap, tap.

My eyes fly open and I'm met with darkness. Scrambling for my cell phone charging beside me, I see that it's a little after 10:00 p.m. I must've fallen asleep after my succulent feast of pea soup and year-old saltines. Yawning, I rub my eye sockets with the heels of both palms.

Then I hear it again.

Tap, tap, tap.

I glance over at my cracked window. A light breeze shimmies through, causing my peach drapes to dance with foreboding. Goose bumps prickle my skin, even though I'm sure it's nothing but an active tree branch. I've always been that "It's just the wind" type of person, where Jonah was more prone to worry and alarm—especially when it came to me.

I slither from my bedcovers and climb off the mattress, reaching for my lava lamp as I yank the cord from the wall and stomp over to my window with bare feet and a bleary-eyed scowl. I'm tired and sweat-soaked, and I'm either about to concuss an intruder with a vintage lighting fixture, or I'm going to give an unsuspecting tree branch a very bad night. Either way, I'm swinging.

Storming forward with little regard for self-preservation, I whip open the curtain and lift my arm to strike.

Max peers back at me through the glass pane, arms crossed.

Stare amused.

Eyebrows arched, visible even through the black of night.

"What the hell?" I bark at him, though I don't lower my arm. I haven't decided if I'm smacking him or not.

He circles a finger in the air, signaling for me to open the window wider.

No.

I'm absolutely not doing that.

"Max," I whisper-hiss. "Go home."

The window is partway open because it's prone to sticking, so he crouches down so I can hear him better. "Can I come in?"

"Does it look like you can come in?" I wave the lava lamp around with menace, adorned in my avocado onesie complete with a hood that features a stem and a leaf on top, which admittedly kind of cancels out the menace. "I'm sick and probably dying. Please leave."

"Aren't you curious why I'm here?"

"No. Bye."

"Are you going to turn me into guacamole?"

My eyes narrow with disdain. "Do not mock my avocado pajamas or I'll cough on you."

"Pneumonia is not contagious," he counters.

I glare at him because it's my only defense. *I knew that.*

He doesn't look like he's preparing to leave, so I finally drop my arm, my shoulders slumping with defeat. Fine. I guess I'm a little curious why he's here. Setting down the night-light, I bend over and widen the screenless window enough for him to climb through.

He grins victoriously as one long leg slides in, followed by the other.

This is weird.

There's a boy crawling through my window in the middle of the night while I reek of fever sweat and pea soup.

However, he did save my life, so I school my face into something less scathing. "There are doors for knocking. There are phones for calling and texting."

With both black-booted feet firmly planted on my beige carpet, Max straightens in front of me, his lips still stretched into a smirk. "There are also windows for climbing through when it's too late to knock and when I don't have your phone number for calling or texting." He crosses his arms and tilts his head, expression softening. "How are you feeling?"

He's standing far too close. He's tall and smothering, and he smells clean and earthy, just like he did when he carried me home from the lake. Even my congested nostrils aren't immune to his appealing man-smells. Swallowing, I dart my gaze away. "I'm fine. Doing better."

"I brought you something," he says. Circling an arm behind his back, he pulls an object out from the waistline of his jeans and hands it to me. Moonlight glimmers from the open window, spotlighting what looks to be a small pot. "I figured you'd be getting a lot of flowers, so I tried to think outside the box. A get-well-soon gift."

I refrain from glancing around the bedroom that's filled with an abundance of invisible flowers. Then I look back toward the item he's holding in the palm of his hand. It comes more into focus when I lean over and squint.

Oh my God.

It's an orange crayon sticking out of a pot of dirt.

I blink a thousand times before my eyes lift to his. "What is this?"

"One day, maybe, it'll grow into a carrot. I'm hopeful."

My mouth snaps closed. My chest squeezes. I can't stop blinking repetitively in time with my erratic heartbeats. "Do you remember every word that comes out of my mouth?"

"Yes." He shrugs. "I'm a good listener."

My traitorous hands are trembling as I reach out to accept the tiny terra-cotta pot. It must be the fever, because emotion slams into me and inhabits my eyes. I'm forced to keep blinking so he doesn't spot the evidence. "Um, thanks. This is…nice." It's really nice. It's thoughtful. Absurdly ridiculous, but thoughtful. "So, you climbed through my window at ten o'clock at night to give me a potted crayon?"

Smiling, Max steps away from me and begins to look around my bedroom. "Sure," he replies.

I reach for the lava lamp and race over to my nightstand, plugging it back in and turning it on. A muted fuchsia glow fills the room as I set down the pot, then swivel around to face him. "What if I slept naked?"

"Unlikely. You're way too guarded." He paces the room, perusing the poster-lined walls and bookshelves stuffed with novels and trinkets. "However, I do sleep naked if you were curious. I'll keep my window unlocked."

"Gross."

Pivoting, he throws me a grin. "I also wanted to check on you. Make sure you were okay."

"Yeah, I'm good. Thank you for the list, by the way."

"Of course." He nods, his blue eyes trailing me from toes to top. "I wanted to come by during the day, but my dad…he, uh, was having some issues."

I recall Brynn! mentioning that at the bonfire. My posture softens some more and I take a step toward him. "What's wrong with your dad?"

Clearing his throat, Max palms the back of his neck, looking like the subject makes him uncomfortable.

That's relatable, so I won't pry. "You don't have to answer—"

"He's an alcoholic," he says. "He suffered a debilitating injury years back and turned to booze to help him cope. Whiskey, mostly. He's a good person, but he needs a constant caregiver, especially when he gets his hands on liquor." Max sighs, looking as bone-weary as I feel. "Anyway…I like Stevie, too."

My brows furrow with confusion. "What?"

"Stevie Nicks." He waves a hand at my posters. "She's a legend."

"Oh. Yeah, she's awesome. I didn't peg you as a Fleetwood Mac fan," I admit. "I saw you as more of a death-metal, mosh-pit enthusiast. You're kind of dark and broody."

He smirks at me, eyes glittering almost violet in the dim fuchsia lighting. "But not mopey, right?"

"No." I shake my head and chew on my lip. "Not mopey."

"What's your favorite song by them?" he wonders, inching closer to me as I fidget near the edge of my bed.

"'Thrown Down.'"

"I don't know that one."

"It's on a later album called *Say You Will*. 2003," I explain.

"Hmm. I'll check it out."

My cheeks feel warmer, the closer he gets. I wonder if my fever is creeping in again. Max stops a few feet away from my bed, his gaze is fixed on my face. Something familiar flickers in his stare. For a moment, we're in the water again, an earnestness passing through the murky space between us. A bind. A common thread. I swallow again, my throat tight. "I don't think I ever thanked you properly…for saving my life," I tell him. "And for going back for my book bag and bike."

I'm not prone to being vulnerable and Max knows that. I don't think he's expecting the sincerity that bleeds into my words. There is no bite this time, no clipped tone or chewed-off edges.

I mean it. I'm so thankful.

He inhales a tapered breath. "You're welcome, Sunny."

My chest feels achy. I've come to loathe nicknames, aside from the ones Jonah used to call me. Piglet, mostly. And I'd call him Pooh Bear—or Pooh Stain when he was acting like a dweeb.

But lately, the nicknames that have been bestowed upon me have all been cruel and hurtful.

Princess.

Accomplice.

Scum, Waste, Garbage.

Even my last name sounds like an insult these days.

But…Sunny isn't so bad. In fact, nothing feels all that bad when Max is around. And I'm not sure if that's a good thing or a cause for concern.

Before I can reply, Max's gaze pans right and settles on what appears to be my nightstand. I watch his eyes narrow as he focuses on something. He blinks a few times before a small smile pulls and then he glances back at me.

I turn to face my nightstand, trying to find his source of interest. Wads of used tissues take up most of the space, along with fever reducer, water bottles, and the nasty bowl of half-eaten soup. It's dark green and crusty. Embarrassing. "Sorry about the mess." I wince. "You can judge all you want."

His smile only blooms. "You kept that stone I tossed at you. From the clearing."

When his words register, my eyes pop and my cheeks flame. "Oh, um…no. I didn't. I infected you with fever and now you're hallucinating." I race toward the nightstand and snatch up the stone left in plain sight, trying to hide what he's already discovered.

But it slips from my fingers and bounces off the table.

And in my frantic attempt to fetch it, my shoulder bumps the lava lamp and that, too, tips over, clattering against the wooden bedstand. "Crap."

Footsteps approach from the adjacent room.

My mother.

Shit.

Boy in my bedroom.

Shit!

Panic rips through me and I rush at Max with my eyes bugged out and arms flailing. "*Hide*," I hiss through my teeth.

He's still smiling.

I grab him by the upper arms, spin him around, and walk him backward toward my closet. Then I whip the door open and shove him inside as his eyes twinkle with amusement. For a moment, I'm keenly aware of my hands curled around his bare arms. Warm skin, hard muscle. Broad chest inches from mine. Dark closet.

Mom knocks. "Ella? Everything okay in there?"

I jump back and slam the closet shut before jogging over to deal with my mother. I'm so flustered I forget how doors work, so I push instead of pull, twice, before successfully yanking it open. "Hi, Mom. Whoa, it's late." I yawn with exaggeration. "Good night."

She catches the door before I close it in her face. "Are you okay? I thought I heard a crashing sound."

"I was exercising."

"Ella…it's ten thirty at night."

"There's never a bad time to make your cardiovascular health a priority."

Doubt glints in her gaze. She crosses her arms over a periwinkle nightgown "You must be feeling better?"

"I feel great." I stretch out my arms, then twist one behind my back like I'm preparing for a midnight run. "I slept all day, so now I'm awake. Sorry… I knocked over my lava lamp…while doing jumping jacks."

She glances at my chaotic nightstand and scrubs both hands over her face. "All right. Well, try to get some rest. I have melatonin if you need it."

I smile and nod. "Yep. Great. 'Night." When she backs away, I close the door and lock it, pressing my forehead to the wood and blowing out a breath. Rustling noises have me trudging over to the closet and swinging it back open.

Max arcs an eyebrow. "You hid me in here like I'm your dirty little secret."

"Yeah, well, the last thing I want right now is my mother's the-birds-and-the-bees spiel after she discovers a boy in my bedroom."

He plucks one of my old stuffed animals, which happens to be Tweety Bird, from an open box. "Fair enough. I wouldn't want to summon a parental lecture on avian and apian relationships."

Max tosses Tweety at me and I catch it with ease. "You should probably go now," I tell him, holding back a smile.

"Can I come by tomorrow?" He steps out of the closet and shuffles past me to the window.

"Why?"

"To see you."

"I look like death that has been put through a blender, microwaved, and then left out in the sun to rot."

Before he slips through the open window, he turns to face me. His eyes soften in the magenta haze. "You don't look like death, Sunny," he says. "You look like the opposite."

Glancing at my nightstand that houses the potted crayon and a little white stone, Max sends me a farewell nod, then draws a leg up and climbs out the window, leaving me alone in my quiet room.

I swallow, staring at the way the drapes flutter and sway in the night breeze as his figure disappears into the dark.

His presence lingers.

I can still feel his arms around me as he carried me home from the lake.

Shivering, I drink in a shaky breath and rub at my arms before stalking back to my bed. I pluck the stone from my bedside table and curl up under the blankets.

When the sun rises the next morning, it's still there, tucked inside my palm.

Chapter 12

ELLA

ANDY SANDWELL GLARES AT ME ACROSS THE CLASSROOM WITH TWO BRUISED black eyes.

I click the end of my ballpoint pen with my thumb, maintaining eye contact. I don't surrender this time. I won't give up. I have too much to live for—homemade guacamole, good books, legal adulthood right around the corner, the sweet victory of peeling an orange in one go, and Max's lists.

I realize that now.

I'm not sure why Andy has two black eyes, but I wouldn't be surprised if he accidentally ran into a brick wall. Flashing him a smile, I scribble something onto a blank notebook page and discreetly tilt it toward him:

I'd love a tutorial on that sexy smoky eye. Are you practicing for the dance?

He flips me off and I throw him a wink.

Beside me, a new student sits quietly, a boy who recently moved here from the Philippines while I was home fighting off a pesky lung infection. His name is Kai, a name as short and crisp as the black hair that hangs over his eyes like a veil. His locker is two down from mine. He's shy and reserved, but when he catches my note to Andy, he snorts a soft laugh.

A potential ally. Sweet.

Our algebra teacher paces the front of the classroom, rambling on about the thrill of factoring. He's waving his arms like a conductor in an orchestra.

His chalk-dusted hands create a cloud of academic enthusiasm that has failed to reach the majority of the class, who are either doodling on their textbooks or participating in undercover texting.

I flip to a blank page in my notebook and scrawl another note, then twist it in Kai's direction.

Mr. Barker's zest for parabolas and roots is bordering on manic.

He grins at me and scribbles something back.

I read it with a side-eye.

Nonsense. His excitement is contagious. Spoiler: I'm regretfully immune.

Holding back a chuckle, we continue the notebook conversation for a few more minutes until the bell rings and students scatter.

Kai stops me in the hallway, pushing his jet-black bangs out of his face. "Hey," he says, holding out his hand. "I'm Kai."

"Ella," I greet back, accepting the handshake. "This is probably the part where I should welcome you to Juniper High with shining hope and optimism, but I'm no liar. I hate it here."

"Have you lived here long?"

"Luckily, no. We just moved back to town a few months ago." I readjust my backpack, which took days to fully dry out on my front porch. Some of the doodles and designs are now nothing but droopy ink and smears of color. "Are Andy and his dumb friends giving you trouble?"

He shrugs. "Not really. They haven't acknowledged my existence. There's a really nice girl in my art class, though—Brynn Fisher." His honeyed cheeks pinken. "Have you met her?"

"Yep, she's cool. She was the only person who really gave me the time of day, aside from—"

"Sunny."

The rich baritone voice of Max Manning has me pivoting around in a full circle until our eyes meet. He's leaning against a wall of blue lockers with irises three shades lighter, and his arms are not visible today due to the faded black hoodie he's wearing. The hood is drawn up, also concealing the majority of his pecan-brown hair, save for a few stray locks that spill over his forehead in a casual sort of disarray.

Shoulder pressed to the locker, he flicks his attention to Kai and then me.

"Hey," I say, my voice still hoarse from bouts of dry coughing. "This is Kai. He just moved here."

Max gives him the smallest nod before returning his attention to me. "Meet me in the clearing after school today. You know the one."

"Oh." I fiddle with my backpack straps. "I was going to head into town after school. There's a coffee shop off Walnut Street that has a job opening."

He nods again. "I can drive you."

"Drive me?"

"Yeah, in my truck with wheels."

I blink, then shake my head. "Right. Um…sure. I guess I should refrain from biking until this cough clears up." On cue, my throat tickles and I start to cough.

Also on cue, some guy sweeps past me and smacks me on the back. "Lay off the deep-throating, Sunbury. You sound rough."

Max looks like he's about to fly at him, but the student scampers away like a frightened mouse as a barricade of football buddies and cheerleaders bursts out laughing and surrounds him on each side.

Embarrassment warms my cheeks while I watch them disappear around the corner. I'm not sure why. These idiots don't get under my skin—nobody does, really—but for whatever reason, I don't like the implication that I'm a floozy when Max is within earshot.

My gaze trails to Max, who has one taut hand pressed to the locker. His face is full of hard lines and edges and his blue eyes gleam with fire when he looks at me. It's then I notice his split bottom lip, the wound looking a few days old. I frown. I'm about to ask him about it when Brynn! skips into my line of sight, dragging McKay behind her by the shirtsleeve.

"Hey, guys!" She beams, dressed in a sun-yellow dress with white polka dots, a light denim jacket, and canvas sneakers. Her hair is braided and tied with pink ribbon, and it shimmers like a golden summer under the recessed lights.

She's the Barbie to my Monster High doll.

I almost forget Kai is hovering beside me when he inches forward and taps me on the shoulder. "Hey, it was nice officially meeting you. See you around."

I swivel to face him and note the smitten glow in his brown eyes as he peers at Brynn! through long, black lashes. Somebody has a crush. As he moves to retreat, I snatch him by a backpack strap. "Hold up. Let me formally introduce you to my sort-of friends—Brynn!, McKay, and Max."

He gulps.

Brynn! lights up, bobbing her head. "Hey! You're in one of my classes. Art, I think?"

"Yeah," he replies, hands stuffed in his pockets.

Max interrupts. "*Sort-of* friends?" he parrots, leveling me with an arched brow of mock outrage.

I give him a one-shoulder shrug but step forward and link my arm with his. "I suppose you've earned an upgrade. The crayon plant won me over."

Everyone goes quiet when our arms loosely hitch.

Why did I do that?

Now I'm entirely aware of how good he smells.

I don't know why I'm touching him. McKay clearly doesn't know why either as his gaze locks on our joined arms.

Max senses my pullback and tugs me closer by the elbow. "Is it a carrot yet?" he asks, gazing down at my red face and pop-eyed expression. I think he's teasing me, but his mouth doesn't lift and his eyes look heated and intense, instead of playful.

"The metamorphosis is beginning," I croak out. "It'll be ready for stew in no time."

Brynn! looks completely confused, but she goes with it. "I love stew."

Kai is lost. "I'm going to head to lunch now. Bye." He makes a hasty retreat without another word, and I immediately feel a kinship toward him.

With an overdramatic throat clear, I slide my arm from Max's and take a sizable step backward, almost bumping into another student. McKay is still eyeing me, and I can't really read him, so everything is awkward. "So," I mutter, drawing out the word. "Lunchtime. My favorite. I'm going to go find a quiet bathroom stall to dine in." Not waiting for a response, I whip around and book it in the opposite direction, paralleling Kai's escape.

It's not long before footsteps race to catch up. "You're not eating in the bathroom," Max says, walking beside me.

"I like reading the graffiti on the stalls while I eat. It's therapeutic. Did you know someone turned the second stall into a makeshift 'Dear Abby' column? They're giving advice on everything from forbidden love to biology homework. It's like a live-action, anonymous Reddit thread."

"Ella."

"I never see you eating in the cafeteria, so you can't judge me." It's true—I've never once seen him there. Brynn! and McKay are usually in their own little love bubble and I'm not one to intrude. She's invited me to sit with them a few times, but there's only so many kissing noises I can take while I'm trying to eat a turkey sandwich.

"I usually eat outside by the willow tree or hang out in the library," Max says. "Come join me."

I spare him a glance as my feet keep sprinting forward. "Just the two of us?"

"Sure."

"Because we're friends."

"Yes. The arm-link sealed it."

My face heats again. "Sorry. That was weird and intrusive."

"More or less than when I snuck through your bedroom window three times?"

My lips curl into a small smile and I bite down to repress it.

Following Max's evening visit, he stopped over two more times after school last week. Mom was at work and kept the front door locked, so he claimed the window was more convenient since I didn't need to get out of bed and walk down a short hallway to the foyer. Thoughtful, I guess. And some foreign part of me kind of enjoyed the little secret we shared.

The visits were fairly uneventful, but we listened to Fleetwood Mac playlists, talked about autumn plans, and I showed him some of the bookbinding work I'd been doing. We kept the conversations light—no talk of what happened at the lake, or of Jonah, or of his father and his tumultuous family situation. I appreciated the reprieve from my usual dark cloud of woe.

During the last visit, I had just battled through my final brush with fever and passed out on the bed while Max flipped through *The Bell Jar* by Sylvia Plath. It was a copy I'd created my own cover for and the leather-bound novel was decorated with a fig tree made of felt and fabric scraps, some of the figs ripe and vibrant, while some were rotting and shriveled.

When I awoke hours later, Max was gone, but the book was left open on my desk to a specific page. An orange Post-it note was stuck underneath a sentence, underlining the quote:

> **"I felt my lungs inflate with the onrush of scenery—air, mountains, trees, people. I thought, 'This is what it is to be happy.'"**

The gesture made me smile. It also made me wonder how long it took for him to find a quote he found worthy enough to highlight and leave out for me.

It had to have taken some time.

It had to have taken effort.

Max waltzes beside me now, his posture looser, arms swinging at his sides as he glances at me every few seconds while we wind in and out of distracted students.

The little smile still pulls at my lips like my favorite bookmark saving my place in a chapter I'm eager to get back to. "I didn't mind the visits," I admit. "Thanks for keeping me company."

He nods. "You can return the favor by keeping me company at lunch out by the willow tree."

The stubborn loner inside me itches to turn him down. Run away. Lock myself in a restroom stall and force down my dry turkey sandwich while I wait for the bell to ring. It's comfortable and safe. The notion is like a knobby finger poking at my side, over and over, until it's all I can feel.

Run.

But then Max slides his arm through mine, linking them together and tugging me closer as we move through the hallway.

He looks down at me, his expression soft. Eyes warm.

And suddenly…that becomes all I can feel.

I'm catching up on reading *Monster* while I wait for Max at the clearing after school. There's a passage toward the beginning of the book that has stayed with me since I read it:

"You need to predict without predicting."

It was in reference to the ending of a film. If you write your movie too predictably, the viewers will make up their minds before it's even over.

In a way, our lives are like a movie and the viewers are the people we surround ourselves with. Something tells me my movie is pretty damn predictable.

Sad girl is sad.

Sad girl moves to a new town where everyone hates her.

Sad girl succumbs to the torment and leads a sad, unremarkable life.

The end.

Perhaps my surrender when Andy threw me in the lake was a reckless attempt at a plot twist. Everyone predicted that I'd pop back up from the water and make my way to the dock. They thought I'd shake myself off and shout obscenities into the setting sun with a heaving chest and balled-up fists, and my miserable existence would carry on accordingly.

But I didn't do any of that.

I sank.

I surprised everybody by letting myself drown.

Take that, predictability.

After all, predictability is nothing but a thief of thrill.

As I pull my feet up onto the hand-carved bench, I watch the sun splash stripes of pale light across the clearing while tree branches create dancing shadows along the patches of grass and dirt. Footsteps rustle from a few feet away, the sound of boots against crunchy sticks pulling my chin up.

Max appears at the opening seconds later, and I curse my heart for whatever the hell it just did. Some kind of weird leaping thing.

Maybe I need to make an EKG appointment.

I snap the book closed and sit up straight. "Here I am, appeasing your ominous request to meet you at the clearing after school."

He's still wearing his hoodie, the sleeves rolled up. "Sorry it sounded ominous."

"Don't be. That's what sold me."

His lips twitch. "Come on. I want to show you something."

"Ooh, also ominous." I jump from the bench, ready and eager. "Sign me up."

A full-blown smile emerges and he ducks his head like he's trying to hide it. Damn, it's kind of cute. Especially when he pairs it with a hair ruffle while lifting only his eyes to me.

I swallow, banishing the thoughts.

Then I break away, bending to retrieve my backpack and stuffing the book inside before zipping the bag shut. A chilled breeze kisses my skin as a few sun-wrinkled leaves flutter down around us like autumn's version of snowflakes. Max stares at me for a beat while I situate my book bag over my shoulder. "What?" I probe.

He takes a tentative stride forward and extends a hand, plucking a golden-green leaf from my tangled mane of hair. He falters a little, his fingers falling away in slow motion. "Follow me," he says, turning around and walking away.

Instinct has me combing my own fingers through the hair he just touched before I jog after him. "Where are we going?"

"Mexico."

"I love chilaquiles." I look up at him as we move in tandem, taking in his pulled-back hood and dark sleeves pushed up past his elbows. Slate-gray jeans, worn and faded, encase two long legs, and his shoes are scuffed and mud-smeared as they kick up gravel beside me.

It's newly November and the weather has cooled. Tennessee offers a wide range of temperatures in the fall, from hot and humid to cool and crisp. Today is in the midfifties, which I think is perfect. My pale skin is unforgiving in the scorching sun and my preference for sweatshirts and cozy sweaters has always been inconvenient while living in this state. To be honest, I probably wouldn't love Mexico. Beaches are dirty and full of sweaty people and sand is nature's cruel version of glitter.

My dream is to move to the Upper Peninsula of Michigan one day, where summers are tame, winters are cold, and snow sparkles like diamonds.

When we approach the waterline of Tellico Lake, I already know what he brought me here for. "We're skipping stones, aren't we?"

"Did you bring the stone from your nightstand?"

Yes—it's in my back pocket. "No."

"That's fine. We'll find plenty." He veers toward the lake's edge and combs the ground for stones to skip. "You said your brother tried to teach you?"

My heart skitters. He brought up the topic of my brother so easily, like it wasn't a giant, unhinged elephant in the room charging toward us. Fidgeting in place, I nod. "He did try. He said it was like dancing—all about the rhythm and the glide." I shrug. "I'm a terrible dancer, so the outcome wasn't surprising. They all belly-flopped."

Crouched down, Max glances up at me for a split second. "Tell me about him."

"What?" I blink. "My brother?"

"Yeah."

"Um…" Smoothing back my hair that's capering in a cool breeze, I keep shifting from foot to foot, unsure how to respond. "I told you what happened."

He seems unfazed. "That's not what I want to know," he says, plucking a gray-tan stone from a patch of gravel and stroking it with the pad of his thumb. "Tell me about him before."

Before.

Nobody ever wants to know about the before. Nobody cares. They only want to know about the after…about the monster, not the man.

Monsters are interesting. Men are ordinary.

The man is the predictable narrative in the story, but the monster—

The monster is the thrilling plot twist that keeps you turning the pages.

Inhaling a breath of earthy air tinged with the distant smoke of bonfires, I crouch down beside Max and collect a few stones in my palm. "Jonah was my best friend," I confess. "He loved me. So much. There was a time when I was convinced he'd do anything for me, but it turns out…that wasn't the case." I peer over at Max, my voice softening. "All I ever wanted was to keep him by my side forever. And now, I'm not even allowed to touch him."

Max studies me, passing his stones from hand to hand as he listens.

I continue. "He was four years older than me, but that never put a damper on our bond. I think it made it stronger. He was wiser than me. He taught me things. He loved playing the guitar and reading really tedious literature that he'd try to explain to me. He enjoyed camping in the Smoky Mountains…oh, and he liked cooking the most complicated recipes in existence just to say he did it." I chuckle a little, the memories bursting to life like fireflies at dusk. "Jonah said that love conquered all and to always remember that he loved me when life got hard. Nothing else should matter when you have love like that. It was a stupid thing to say and all it made me do was resent love. It turns hearts into stone, men into monsters, and dreams into ash. It's not a fairy tale—it's a tall tale, shoved down our throats to keep us whimsical and yearning. But when the love goes rotten, so do we. People never stop to think about that. They don't consider who they might become in the wake of bad love, or how that poison will affect the ones who love *them*."

The words spill out of me and I'm forced to stop to catch my breath. Emotion seizes my chest, holding tight. I gaze out at the lake as my dreary words hover around us like sad little rain clouds.

When I brave a glance at Max, he's staring at me with a wrinkle between his brows. His expression is pinched and thoughtful. Worried, maybe—worried that my sanity is hanging by a cobwebby thread.

It is.

"Anyway," I mutter, exhaling a breath and drawing to a stand. I swipe the dirt and grit from my blue jeans, feeling silly for the depressing word vomit. "Sorry I got carried away. That's not what you asked."

"It's what I wanted to know." Max slowly rises to his feet, both fists filled with round, multicolored stones for skipping. "Come on. The water is perfect."

I shuffle behind him, my throat still stinging with leftover bitterness. Swallowing it down, I move in next to him as he looks out at the unburdened lake.

"Your brother was right about treating it like a dance," Max tells me, setting the collection of stones near his feet, save for one. The surface of the stone is grayish-white, weathered smooth by rain and time. "It's all in the rhythm."

"I have two left feet," I grumble. "And, apparently, two left hands."

Max weighs the small stone in his palm, popping it up and down a few times before situating it between his thumb and forefinger. "Watch this." His arm draws back, elbow bent, hand held just above shoulder level. Effortlessly, he steps forward and swings his arm in a low arc, releasing the stone with a flick of his wrist.

The stone leaves his hand and races over the water. It touches the surface, skips once, twice, three times and beyond, each hop leaving a succession of tiny ripples before it sinks with the inevitable pull of gravity.

I glance up at Max, my eyes wide and impressed. There's a big smile on my face. I can feel it. It blossomed as fluidly as Max's stone skipped.

He turns toward me, his gaze dipping to my mouth. To my smile. To the authentic joy painting my lips—a rare, rare thing. When his attention returns to my eyes, his own smile draws up to match mine. We stare at each other, smiling at the simple, basic concept of a stone dancing across water on a crisp autumn day.

There's a tightness between my ribs, so I press the heel of my palm to my rust-colored hoodie, rub at my chest, and look away. "Can I try?"

"Of course." Max sifts through more pebbles and plucks one from the pile. "I'll help you."

I refuse to look at him as he comes up behind me. I don't move, don't breathe, when the front of his chest presses to my spine and he wraps both arms around me like a gentle backward hug. My heart is doing more than leaping now. It's vaulting. Somersaults and cartwheels.

Gymnast shit.

"Like this," he says, his chin hovering above my shoulder, warm breath ghosting over my ear. His hand slides down my arm with a featherlight touch as he tucks a small stone in the center of my palm. His fingertips are calloused yet soft. Delicate as they graze against mine. The scent of pine needles, clean soap, and a trace of cigarette smoke curls around me. A compelling elixir.

With our arms overlapped, he guides them both upward to mimic the throw, his wrist flicking out at the end. "Feel the rhythm, Sunny."

We practice the motion a few times.

I try to focus.

I try to concentrate on my breaths and the instructions he gave me, all while he's pressed against my back, his body heat seeping through my hoodie.

Eventually, Max pulls away and gives me space to toss the stone. I feel his eyes on me, watching, waiting. I heave in a shaky breath, square my shoulders, and haul my arm back like he showed me. I let go of the stone and watch with anticipation as it glides through the air—

And immediately plops into the water like a boulder.

Epic fail.

I shake out my arms, groaning with self-deprecation. "I'm a natural."

Max chuckles and finds me another stone. "Not bad. You'll get it."

"Your unwavering belief in me will be your downfall."

"There are worse ways to go." He hands me a smooth pebble, slightly smaller than the last one. "Try again."

I do try again.

And again, and again.

Plop.

Plop.

Plop.

I'm not even mad about it. My inefficiency at stone skipping is truly hilarious.

I keep tossing stones until every splash of defeat has laughter stirring in my chest, bubbling to the surface. Max skips them beside me with elegance and finesse, while I double over with giggles and give up trying altogether. Now I'm just chucking rocks at the water to see how far I can throw them. The buoyancy in the air is contagious and Max laughs, too, until nearly an hour has passed us by and my arm starts to hurt from dozens of unproductive swings.

Eventually, our collection of stones reaches its end and Max turns to me as the sun dips lower in the sky. "Ready to head into town?" he asks. "Luck is clearly on your side today."

I jab him in the ribs with my elbow but my smile sticks. There's a happy glow shimmering around my heart and I feel brighter. Lighter. A little less buried.

I don't skip a single stone that afternoon.

Predictable.

But I realize as I traipse alongside Max to his truck, the sunset staining the sky apricot-orange—that wasn't the point.

The point was, that with every stone that left my hand and plunked into the water…the whole world fell away.

And that was something I did not predict.

Chapter 13

MAX

THE SOUND OF SPOONS CLANKING AGAINST CERAMIC BOWLS FILLS the tiny kitchen as McKay and I slurp down soup with week-old bread and tumblers filled with sink water. Dad is passed out on the couch behind us, one arm hanging over the edge while his hair sticks up in all directions and makes him look like a mad scientist who had an explosive day at the lab.

McKay glances up from his bowl every now and then, unsaid words dangling between each spoonful. When our eyes finally meet, he clears his throat, swiping at a drop of broth dribbling down his chin. "I invited Libby to the Fall Fling with us."

My spoon freezes midair and an undercooked carrot lodges in my throat. I frown at him. "Why?"

He shrugs. "She's a babe and you don't have a date."

"If I wanted to go with Libby, I would have asked her."

"Are you going with Ella?"

The carrot slogs down my throat like a piece of driftwood in a syrupy sea. "No." I sniff. "She turned me down."

Nodding, McKay continues to sip his soup. "We're swinging by Libby's after we pick up Brynn. I left some condoms on your nightstand."

"What the fuck, McKay?"

"Fine. Slide in bare, then. Brynn and I stopped using condoms last month. She's on the pill. It's a game-changer."

I push myself away from the table, the screeching chair legs enough to stir Dad awake long enough to mumble something about mustard. "I'm going for a run." The lone, bare light bulb swings overhead from the force of my escape while pink insulation pokes out from the unfinished wooden walls, taunting me as I move to the front of the house. It's not exactly the color pop one might find suggested on an interior design blog, and it only serves to make me move faster.

"I'll go with you." McKay stands and curves around the table to follow me.

"No."

"Yes."

"I'd rather go alone." He huffs behind me as I stalk to the foyer where I left my shoes. I glance over at Dad who is now sprawled out on his stomach, face smashed into a couch cushion. "Fuck you, by the way."

"What?" McKay scoffs, offended. "I think you mean, *you're welcome*."

"No. I mean, *fuck you*. I'm not going to the dance with Libby and I'm not having sex with Libby. Stay out of my business."

"She wants you, man, and she's cute as hell. Maybe if you got yourself a little action, you wouldn't be so edgy lately." McKay slips into his own sneakers and trails me out the front door.

I run ahead of him, my gaze skating briefly to Ella's ranch house across the street. She's sitting cross-legged on her front porch with a giant book in her lap and a spool of thread between her teeth. The image has me slowing my pace and hesitating at the edge of the driveway. Our eyes meet across the dirt road and I lift my hand with a wave.

She one-ups my wave, spits out the spindle woven with white, and cups both hands around her mouth. "Hey, Max!"

I'm grinning like a doofus when McKay comes up behind me and bumps my shoulder with his.

"Are we running?" he asks, sounding impatient.

I don't reply and instead jog across the street to Ella's front yard. "Hey," I say back to her. "Bookbinding?"

"Yup. I bought a copy of that book we're reading in English class. I'm enjoying it." Her eyes pan to my left.

McKay is standing beside me, toeing a mound of dirt. "Hey, Sunbury."

"Hi."

"Max and I were just discussing Fall Fling next week. I invited Libby. If you need a ride, we'd be happy to take you. There's space in the truck if you don't mind squishing in with the girls."

My blood boils. Every muscle locks as I roll my jaw and close my eyes. When I open them slowly, releasing a calming breath, the glimmer of that smile Ella was wearing has vanished.

Her eyes dim but she recovers well. "I'm not going, but thanks for offering. Have fun." She returns to her bookbinding process like we're not even there.

I'm not sure what to say. I've always hated going to the dumb dances, but McKay drags me along every year. Last Fall Fling was a total bust. I went with Libby, who was sweet but clingy, and she smelled like pickles. I had no intention of going this year until the idea of going with Ella actually sparked an interest.

The sound of her laughter at the lake the other day hasn't left my mind since it spilled out of her, all bare-boned joy and raw feeling. The echo of it lingers, inciting a yearning to be the one who makes her laugh like that again.

In a friendly way, of course.

Because I'm pretty sure we're friends now—*real* friends. And it's been a damn long time since I've had one of those.

I scrub a hand through my hair and watch as she tinkers with the thread and hums something under her breath. "Are you sure you don't want to go? McKay invited Libby. I'm not going with her." Something nags at me to clarify that. "Could be fun."

"Could be," she answers dismissively. When her head pops up, the smile is back. It doesn't reach her eyes, but it's there. "If one were to enjoy exaggerated balloon arches, a gymnasium that reeks of pit stains, and the dubious honor of sharing the dance floor with sweaty teenagers gyrating to overplayed eighties music while parent chaperones eyeball us like they're undercover agents waiting to make their move, it could certainly be fun."

So damn dramatic.

The corner of my mouth quirks up and I cross my arms. "We'll make it fun."

She hesitates.

She knows we will.

Still, Ella wrinkles her nose and lowers her eyes. "I'm good. I have a crap ton of homework to catch up on from my brush with death. Let me know how it goes."

Disappointment filters through me.

I'd do some pretty shady shit to see this girl dancing, head-thrown-back laughing, and all dolled up in a pretty dress, having the time of her life. Alas, I'll only sound like I'm begging at this point, so I retreat with dignity. "All right, Sunny. See you tomorrow."

"See ya." She doesn't glance up.

"Sunny?" McKay questions, parroting the nickname like it's something foul as he follows me out of Ella's front yard. "She's not into you, bro."

My teeth clench. "Thanks for your insight."

"Just telling you how I see it."

"It's not like that with Ella," I clip in, breaking into a lazy jog. "We're just friends."

"Yeah. Because she's not into you."

I pick up my pace, hopeful my brother will find something better to do so I can run in peace. Normally, I enjoy the rare bonding moments we share, running and hiking, swimming or camping, but lately his presence has only served as a dull thorn in my side. Not sharp enough to draw blood but irritating, nonetheless.

"I just worry about you, man," McKay carries on as we curve onto a busier street before heading toward the trails. "I don't want to see you get bogged down with that girl's drama."

I don't reply.

Ella isn't an added weight—she's a reprieve. Skipping stones with her at the lake felt just as soul-curing as drinking in the fresh Tennessee air. Her laughter was a remedy, not a hindrance. Her smile made me feel like I was flying high, just like how I feel when I'm running through lofty trees and bluebell shrubs, trying to get away from it all.

But I don't know how to tell him that without more questions.

And I definitely don't have answers to those questions.

"Oh, and don't forget," McKay adds, sprinting toward the opening of a running path. "Condoms are on your nightstand."

Shaking my head, I ignore the comment and we spend the rest of the run in silence, only listening to the slap of our soles against earth and the winded rhythm of our breaths.

I toss the condoms in the trash the second I get home.

Crash.

I shoot out of bed, my heart in a tailspin. Throwing my legs over the mattress, I attempt to hop into a pair of yesterday's jeans as Dad's agitated slurs reverberate through the small house. Belt hanging loose, I race out of my bedroom and turn the corner, bare-chested and blurry-eyed.

My father is pacing around in aimless circles near his bed frame, swinging his head back and forth as he spouts off something unintelligible. This is nothing new. Dad often has night terrors and it's the reason I don't sleep very well. McKay goes to bed with earbuds in, blissfully ignorant.

I've read up on night terrors, so I know that I need to approach with quiet caution. I do my best not to wake him. My tone is always soft and gentle, my words reassuring. Most of the time, I'm able to guide him back to bed without incident and he falls asleep with no memory of it come sunrise.

I don't smell liquor on his breath when I step forward, and that's a silver lining. "Dad. It's okay," I say in a low voice.

My father doesn't like the dark, so he sleeps with a table lamp on. Mom left him in the middle of the night when the sky was midnight blue and the moon was veiled by smog. He woke up alone, searching for her in the shadows to no avail. She was long gone, never to return.

Now the dark is a trigger, a reminder of what he's lost.

"Let's get you back to bed," I tell him.

"You're fucking my wife, Rick," he blares at me, wild eyes settled just beyond my shoulder. "I'll gut you with my fishing hook."

My skin prickles with foreboding. Part of me wonders if I should leave him be, but one time, he tried to bust through the window with a coffee mug, thinking the house was on fire. Sliced his hand open in three places.

He could get hurt. He could kill himself.

"Dad, it's fine. You're okay. It's me. Max—"

I don't expect what comes next.

It happens too fast.

As I take another step closer, my father snatches up the table lamp, leaps forward, and smashes the clay base against the side of my head. Before I can comprehend the strike, he's on me, tackling me to the bedroom floor with both hands wrapped around my neck like a thick-fingered noose.

Pain explodes behind my left temple.

Blood dribbles into my eye.

The back of my head slams against raw planks of wood as my own father tries to choke the life out of me.

I'm blindsided.

My father is feeble. I could easily overpower him. But my mind is a blur, my instincts caught between survival and love. Unconsciousness teases me, threatening to swallow me whole.

The room is dark now and I can hardly see the glazed eyes above me as he snarls and spits. "You monster," Dad growls, squeezing harder. "You ruined my goddamn life."

A light flickers on from the hallway. Footsteps pound against wood.

In my periphery, I see my brother appear in the doorway.

"Max! What the fuck…?" McKay charges forward, dropping to his knees beside us and reaching for Dad, yanking him up by the hair. "Get off him!"

The hands release me.

Hands belonging to my fucking father.

He's not thinking clearly. He's dreaming. He doesn't know who I am.

I collapse with strained breaths, drawing one knee up and massaging my throat. I'm vaguely aware of McKay dragging our father across the floor as a trace of light from the hallway illuminates my own personal hell. I pull myself up on my elbows as my head throbs, temple pulsing with agony.

Dad jolts with awareness and starts scrambling to the far wall the moment McKay lets him go. "What…what's happening…?"

McKay is livid, a menacing shadow looming over a tormented man. "You almost murdered your own son. That's what happened."

"No, I–I would never…" Dad's eyes widen through the dimly lit shadows as he shakes his head, scrubbing both hands over his haggard, whiskered face. "Maxwell."

I'm shell-shocked. I can hardly catch my breath as blood continues to ooze down the side of my face. I swallow, my throat too bruised to form words.

I can't be here.

A piercing panic stabs me and I need to get out. Run, flee. Never look back. Maybe McKay has been right all along. Maybe our father is truly beyond hope. I should start looking into programs and resources—not that we can afford anything, surviving solely on Dad's disability checks and Supplemental Security Income. We have just enough to get by each month.

I haven't gotten a job because I'm basically his full-time caregiver. With school and looking after him, I hardly have time for anything other than the small pockets of freedom I get while running or swimming—necessities that keep me sane and clearheaded, allowing my responsibilities to remain manageable.

Fuck.

I force myself up off the floor, rising to shaky legs. McKay is still vibrating with tension as he watches me stumble from the room.

"Max!" he calls after me. "Where the hell are you going?"

I don't answer him. He can deal with Dad for once.

I can't be here.

My balance is unsteady as I head to the foyer and look for my sneakers, my equilibrium teetering like a leaf clinging to a branch during a windstorm. I find a pair of shoes. Someone's shoes. Untied and one size too small, they manage to carry me out the door and into the cool night.

I stagger across the front lawn with a bloody gash on my head.

Confused and heartbroken.

Shivering with no shirt.

And two minutes later, I'm knocking on Ella's window.

Chapter 14

MAX

I DON'T KNOW WHY I CAME HERE.

Ella is probably going to give me another head wound with her lava lamp when she spots me shirtless outside her window in the dead of night, looking like a lost, wounded animal.

A few beats pass before I finally hear the creak of her footsteps approaching. I brace myself for impact as the curtains crack and Ella appears.

She blinks.

Freezes in place.

Clad only in a white tank and faded gray sleep shorts, she stares at me, registering my presence. Processing the state I'm in. Her complexion goes ashen as she stands there, scanning me from head to toe through the dusty pane, her eyes glassed over like she sees a ghost.

Maybe I am a ghost. It's possible my father killed me on his bedroom floor.

Hell—if that's the case, she should feel honored I'm here. There aren't many people I would care enough about to haunt in the afterlife. Ella Sunbury made the cut.

I stare right back at her, lost for words. Unsure what to say or how to explain myself.

Can ghosts talk?

The window draws up and she leans out, fingers curled around the sill. "Holy shit. What happened to you?"

My throat works through a painful swallow. I shake my head a little, and the slight motion causes a surge of pressure to swell behind my eyes. Dizziness claims me. I sway in place, almost tipping to the right, when Ella's hand snakes out, catching me by the wrist and squeezing.

Worried green eyes flare and dark brows bend as her thumb dusts across my skin. "Whoa... Hey, come inside." She gives me the smallest tug forward. "Come on. I'll wake up my mom and we'll take you to the hospital."

"No."

"Max...you're bleeding."

"No hospitals." I lift my free hand and touch two fingertips to my temple. To the slash near my hairline carved into me by my father's table lamp. My fingers come back sticky and wet. "I'll be fine," I murmur. "Can I...stay the night?"

It's a dumb question. Wildly inappropriate. We're still getting to know each other and I'm asking if I can have a sleepover in her bedroom. My eyes close briefly as I attempt to backtrack. "Sorry. I can just—"

"Get inside, will you?"

There's no hesitation, no indecision lacing her tone. I don't have it in me to question anything, so I accept the invitation and step forward, her hand still curled around my wrist. Her bedroom window is at ground level, making it easy enough to climb through, even with a probable concussion. Ella helps me inside, her warm hands sliding up my bare arms, steadying my shoulders and maintaining my footing while I place the soles of my mismatched shoes on her bedroom floor.

We linger for a moment as my eyes adjust to the darkened room, her palms gliding down to my biceps and her concerned expression coming more into focus with every passing second. When she steps away, it's a careful, slow-motion pullback so I don't collapse at her feet.

I keep myself upright and lean back against her wall. "Thanks. Sorry...I know it's late."

Ella moves around me and fetches her desk chair, dragging it over. "Sit." She then rushes to the nightstand and flips on the lava lamp until the room is blanketed in a purple-pink hue. "What the hell happened to you? Did you get into a fight?"

Taking a seat, I drop my head and link my fingers behind my neck. The gesture sends more pain rippling through me, but I shove it aside, fighting the waves. "My dad. He had a night terror…thought I was somebody else and tried to knock me out with a lamp."

"Oh my God." Ella rushes back toward me and immediately drops between my knees, resting her hands on both of my thighs like it's nothing. Like it's completely natural. "You can stay here as long as you need. Mom will be fine. I'll explain everything."

"No, I–I just need a night. Don't say anything to her. I'll leave in the morning," I rush the words out, too aware of her small hands squeezing my upper thighs. My belt is still loose, but she doesn't seem to care. "He's not a violent person. Something's not right. It's like he completely blacks out and doesn't even recognize me sometimes."

"Has he been to the doctor?"

I huff out what sounds like a laugh, though it's anything but. "No. I can't ever get him to go. McKay wants me to drop him off at some assisted living facility and never look back, but…I can't do that. He's my family."

She nods like she understands, and I think she does. Falling back on her haunches, she studies me, weighing her words. "You should go to the hospital. Get checked out. You probably have a concussion."

"Likely. But what am I supposed to say?" I counter, lifting my head and steepling my fingers to my chin. "My father assaulted me with a fucking table lamp? He'll get arrested. Spend the night in a jail cell. I can't do that to him."

"Max, you need to—"

"Did you go to the cops after Sandwell tossed you in the lake?" I throw back at her. We both know that some battles aren't worth pursuing.

The parallel registers in her eyes as she shakes her head. "No," she whispers.

Through the magenta haze, I watch her focus slip to my mouth, settling on the still-healing cut on my lower lip. Jagged and scabbing. She stares at it, putting two and two together.

"You gave Andy those black eyes, didn't you?"

I swallow. "He deserved worse."

Ella looks away, marinating in the implication before she glances back at me.

Then her hand lifts to my face. Tentative. Trembling slightly. I stiffen with anticipation and hold my breath as her fingertips inch closer and graze along my bottom lip.

So light. Barely there.

My eyelids flutter closed. I'm still holding my breath, my hands clenched to stones in my lap, when I feel her fingers travel upward and gently brush aside my blood-slick bangs. It feels intimate, in a way. There's a tenderness there, something unfamiliar yet strangely comforting and warm. Ella touches my temple, her careful fingers tracing the outline where my fresh wound pulses.

"I'll be right back."

The sound of her voice jars me back to reality. When I open my eyes, she's already on her feet, moving across the carpet to her bedroom door and slipping out silently. She returns moments later with an armful of bandages and a small white first-aid kit. The items clank against the quiet backdrop as she places them on the desk, revealing her haul of ointments, gauze, and a wet cloth.

My eyes track her through the dim light while she sifts through the pile and returns to her position in front of me, settling on her knees between my spread legs.

"I'm far from a nurse, but I used to tend to the horses on our farm," she tells me, reaching out to cleanse the wound with the moistened rag.

I wince at the contact but hold back a hiss.

"There was one horse, Phoenix, who loved getting into trouble. He was feisty, full of energy. He had this habit of scraping his flank against the barn wall and ended up with a nasty gash one day."

Ella is propped up on her knees, her porcelain face inches from mine. While her eyes are focused on the task, her mind is far away, lost in the memories of a Nashville horse ranch. My hands unclench as my body loosens, the warmth of her proximity melting my walls.

Or…maybe I have no walls.

Not with her.

She continues, her gaze flicking to me briefly, then returning to the cut. "I spent hours cleaning the wound. Dressing it. I put together this concoction of honey, fresh herbs, and bread to draw out any infection—a recipe Jonah gave me," she explains. "Phoenix hated it, at first. He didn't like people fussing over him. But eventually...he realized I was just trying to help. It's silly, but there was a time when that stubborn horse felt like my best friend." Soft melancholy infects her tone as she exchanges the burgundy rag for a tube of ointment. "The horses were more than animals to me. They were my family. When every god-awful human in that town shunned me, tormented me, ridiculed me, the horses were there. Phoenix never looked at me like I was a monster. I was just...Ella."

I'm silent and unmoving as I drink in her words, her past, her torn-away dreams. She dabs the ointment to my temple and the cream cools the sting of the wound, adding to the lift I feel at uncovering another piece of her. Swallowing, I keep my attention on her profile, memorizing the furrow of her brow as she concentrates, the bow of her lips as warm breaths beat against my skin.

Comfort.

That's what I'm feeling right now.

Sitting on this hard wooden chair without a shirt, bruised and battered, relying on this broken girl to fix me...

I feel remarkably at peace.

As she fiddles with a butterfly bandage, I inhale a breath and it's dangerously shaky on the way out. "You must really miss the horses."

She smiles. "I miss a lot of things."

"Do you think you'll ever ride again?"

"I hope so," she murmurs, applying the adhesive wings of the bandage to my skin with two steady hands. Moving in closer, she pauses to assess the series of tiny bridges across the cut. "I want to move to the Upper Peninsula of Michigan after graduation. Save up for an RV and hit the road. I don't need much. I'll find a quiet place to lay roots, and eventually I'll purchase a horse of my own. Maybe even my own horse farm. That would be my ultimate dream." When the butterfly bandage is secured, Ella covers it with a piece of gauze for protection. "And then I'll ride again."

"Why Michigan?" I wonder.

"I don't really know. I've just always wanted to live there," she says. "It feels like the home I've never had. There's this nostalgia about it, like I'm imagining memories that don't exist. Strange, huh?" Her eyes glimmer in the pink twinkle lights. "I want to kayak in the summer and build snowmen in the winter. Live off the land. Ride horses and catch rainbow trout. And on the night of my twenty-first birthday, I want to go to Porcupine Mountains Wilderness State Park and try to see the northern lights. It's a big dream of mine, and that park is supposed to be one of the best places to view them in the whole United States."

I wonder if she realizes she's smiling, a purely authentic tip to her lips as dreams and wishes unfurl behind her eyes. "When's your birthday?" I ask.

"November twentieth." Ella leans back, surveying her handiwork with an air of triumph. "There. All set."

My fingers rise to skim along the bandaged wound. I feel my own smile lifting as that pocket of peace swells and simmers, creating something almost palpable between us. A friendship in motion.

A dance.

Rhythm.

Our gazes tangle as I touch along the edges of the gauze. "Thanks."

"Of course." She clears her throat and stands, swiping her hands along her cotton shorts. "You can take my bed. I'll sleep on the floor."

"No way."

"Don't go all lionhearted on me. You have a hole in your head. Take the comfy mattress." As she moves toward her queen-sized bed and throws back the covers, she falters. Then she spins around to face me. "Wait. You shouldn't go to sleep if you have a concussion."

Damn.

Exhaustion bubbles to the surface as I stare at her fluffy blankets and collection of ten thousand pillows. "I'll be fine."

"No. I'll keep you awake." Her cheeks puff as she blows out a breath. "Let me find a shirt for you to wear. I still have a box of Jonah's clothes in my closet… I couldn't bear to part with some of his favorite T-shirts and hoodies." She turns to the closet. "They probably smell like a moldy attic, so that should keep you from getting too comfortable. Unless..." Faltering, she swivels back around. "Is it weird wearing his stuff?"

"No. It's fine."

This seems to appease her, and she steps into the closet.

While Ella rummages through boxes, I pull myself up from the chair and assess my equilibrium. I don't feel quite as woozy and I don't stagger sideways, so I take a few cautious steps over to the bed. Ella is bent over in the closet, her sleep shorts riding up her thighs.

It's then I stagger a little.

I tear my eyes away. "How do you plan on keeping me awake?" When I take a seat on the edge of her mattress, I wonder if that came across too suggestively. I'm sitting on her bed, half-naked, trying not to ogle her curves like a pervert.

Luckily, she's not privy to my intrusive thoughts, so she doesn't read into any innuendo as she lifts up and approaches me with a white T-shirt bunched in her hands. "You underestimate how annoying I can be."

A smile pulls. I take the shirt and glance down at the design across the front. "Winnie the Pooh?"

"Yeah," is all she says.

Ella looks away, pivoting to fiddle with her loose hair while I pull the shirt over my head. The shirt is a little tight around my biceps, but it'll do. The smell of musty cardboard box and a hint of sage fills my nose as I scoot across the mattress to the headboard, the box spring creaking.

Tentatively, Ella crawls in beside me.

My mind goes blank.

Cotton balls fill my mouth as I stretch out my legs and our hips bump together.

I'm eighteen, so it's not hard to fixate on the fact that I'm lying in a pretty girl's bed, even though it's not like that with Ella.

I feel like this is the part where awkward silence is about to fester between us. We're side by side, backs to the headboard, shoulders smashed together.

But I should know her better than that by now.

She immediately starts to sing. Off-key and extra terrible.

It's her own rendition of Fleetwood Mac's "Rhiannon," and I think she's really trying to be annoying. Voice cracking, lyrics jumbled, Ella leans over, crooning right into my ear, giving me the performance of a lifetime. Goose bumps pucker my skin as her breath tickles my earlobe with every bum note.

She snorts a laugh. "Is it working?"

My head tilts, our faces inches apart. I memorize her smile because it's such a rare, fleeting thing. All I say is, "I'm definitely awake."

"Good. I'm just getting started." When she forgets the rest of the lyrics, she moves on. "Did you know there's a species of fungus known as *Ophiocordyceps unilateralis* that infects ants, takes over their bodies, and turns them into zombie ants? You should Google it."

I shudder. "No, thanks."

"Google it, Max. The ant clamps onto plant foliage using its mandibles and then it dies. The fungus erupts from the back of its head, growing into a stalk that releases spores to infect the other ants below."

"Jesus. I'm never Googling that." She does it for me, tapping away at her cell phone and shoving horrifying pictures in my face. "What the hell, Ella?"

"I'm trying to keep you awake. You'll never want to go to sleep again."

"Correct. You've made sure of that," I grumble, swatting at the phone still waving in front of my eyes. "The irony is I'll be up every night with nothing to do, so I'll be forced to climb through your window. And, in turn, I'll be keeping *you* awake."

"You know what else is ironic?" she chirps. "Hippopotomonstroses-quippedaliophobia means the fear of long words."

I pinch the bridge of my nose and sigh, soaking up that revelation. Then a burst of laughter falls out of me and my head falls back to the headboard. I wince. "Where do you learn these things?"

She shrugs. "Never minimize the power of being a loner and a nerd."

"Well, no need to be a loner anymore. You have me."

"True. Oh, we could arm wrestle. I've been practicing with my left arm."

I chuckle. "Nah. I'm not bored."

"That's valid. You're far too annoyed to be bored right now." She does a little hand maneuver like a makeshift bow. "I'll be here all night."

My chest fills with gentle warmth as I inhale a deep breath, almost like I'm drinking in the air of a sun-kissed morning. I send her a sideways glance, my tone softening. "I'm really grateful for that."

I don't fall asleep that night but Ella does.

She drifts away, her head lolling onto my shoulder as the night presses on and the hours tick by. The only thing that moves is my heart. My muscles are stiff and tight, but my heartstrings are pliable, the beats skipping and alive. The sensation is as rare as her smile.

When the sun crests, I slip away from her, carefully inching myself off the mattress. She doesn't rouse. Doesn't wake. She looks like an angel as she sleeps, haloed by the rising sun. I climb back out the window the moment first blush spills into her bedroom, coloring her orange walls with splashes of gold.

Before I turn to leave, I peer through the glass, glancing at her dream-stolen face as she lies propped up against the headboard, her head tilted slightly to one side where my shoulder once was. The smallest smile paints her lips and I wonder where she is.

Fishing on the Great Lakes and cooking pink salmon over a firepit.

Watching a sunrise from the open fields of her very own horse farm.

Lying underneath the stars as the northern lights dance across the sky.

Riding her favorite horse.

She's galloping free with the wind in her hair and the sun on her skin, that smile beaming, burdenless, and bright.

One day, maybe…we can ride together.

Warmed by the thought, I traipse back home and sneak in through the patio door, feeling utterly restored.

Chapter 15

ELLA

*Y*OU CAN TRY ALL YOU WANT, BUT I ASSURE YOU, I'M NOT GOING TO THE FALL FLING."
That was me, yesterday, walking down the school hallway with Brynn!
as she tried desperately to convince me that the Fall Fling was a necessary part
of the high school experience and a rite of passage that would forever remain as
an incomplete stain on my memory without my partaking.

Famous last words, I suppose.

Turns out, I'm going to the Fall Fling.

But let it be known that I am going stag. There is no date. There is no
romantic companionship of any kind. There's literally no one because I turned
down the only person who asked me.

I have Max to thank for giving me a change of heart—even though I'm not
going with him. And that's fine. He'll have fun with Libby and her pickled pigs'
feet. After all, pickling is an art. I bet Libby is full of fun facts about brine ratios
and fermentation times. It will be a night to remember.

Anyway…

The reason I'm going now is because Max left another Post-it note in one
of my books when he came by yesterday after school. It's become something
of a tradition. A week has passed since he showed up at my window that
night, bloodied and broken-down, needing an escape. I still don't know why
he came to me, but maybe he felt the same thing I felt that day at the lake.

The day we skipped stones and the foreign sound of my own laughter fused with the breeze.

That afternoon sure felt like an escape.

So, maybe I get it.

The book he left open for me was a poetry compilation by T. S. Eliot called *Four Quartets*. The poem was titled "Little Gidding" and the following passage was underlined:

> **"What we call the beginning is often the end. And to make an end is to make a beginning. The end is where we start from."**

The quote has little to do with senior-year Fall Fling festivities, but something about it had me reconsidering.

I even bought a dress.

After classes let out today, I rode my bike into town. I strolled over to a nearby consignment shop and browsed the dress selections, armed with a devil-may-care attitude and my fifty dollars from Grandma Shirley. I spotted it instantly, sandwiched between two black dresses on a cluttered clothes rack. A beacon of vivid orange. A fireball of adolescent dreams.

A tangerine tube dress glowing bright amid a sea of drab neutrals.

My fate was sealed.

I was going to the dumb dance.

I sprawl the new dress out across my bedspread, smoothing the wrinkles and grazing my fingertips down the bright-orange front. It's a simple dress, sleeveless, with a straight-cut neckline. It cinches slightly at the waist while the hem kisses just above my knees.

As I hold it up in front of me and turn to face the mirror, my mother knocks on the door. "Ella?"

"Present."

She enters, poking her head inside. When she spots me doing something other than sulking, she gasps and the door swings open wider. "Honey, that's beautiful. You look terrific."

I make a sour face. *Terrific* is such a weird word. "It's okay," I reply with a shrug, even though a smile teases my lips.

"Is that for Fall Fling?"

"No, it's for a funeral. I seem to have died and been reborn as a teenager who attends school dances." I tilt my head and pop a hip, assessing the dress from all angles. "Dead Me deserves a punchy send-off."

Mom never appreciates my humor. She folds her arms and leans against the doorjamb, her chestnut hair freshly colored as it waterfalls over her shoulders. Silver flecks were beginning to spawn, which almost sent her into a midlife crisis at forty-five years old. I guess she's about due. Luckily, she works at a hair salon, so now all is right with the world. The crisis has been postponed.

"Are you going with Max?" Mom wonders.

Instinct has me glancing at my bed—the bed where I fell asleep against his shoulder last week like it was just a normal, everyday thing to do. Heat blossoms on my cheeks, so I swivel away from my mother's probing eyes to discard the dress. "No, I'm going alone. Can you give me a ride tomorrow night?"

"Of course. Why are you going alone?"

"Because Max asked me and I said no. Now he's going with Libby." There's no bite to my tone. There isn't.

"Hmm," she hums in that *Mom* way. "He's handsome."

My heart jumps a little. "He's all right. What are your thoughts on molecular genetics? We're learning about that in biology."

She sighs. "My thoughts are that you picked up the gene of swift subject changes just like your father used to—" Mom cuts herself short when my head whips toward her and tries to blink away the words. "Sorry."

I'd be a hypocrite if I gave her crap for the Dad slip, considering the number of times Jonah's name has tumbled from my lips. It's funny how the two most important people in our lives have been reduced to instant conversation killers. "It's fine."

"I, um, I actually have something for you. These came in the mail." Straightening from the doorframe, Mom pulls an item from the pocket of her black dress pants. Envelopes, folded in half. "Here."

At first I think they're checks from Grandma Shirley, since she's the only person who sends me mail and Lord knows she wouldn't miss another fifty dollars. But when I step closer and scan the letters scribbled on the front of one of them, the handwriting doesn't match. It doesn't match at all.

My stomach lurches.

RIVERBEND MAXIMUM SECURITY INSTITUTION
NASHVILLE, TENNESSEE

Our eyes meet. Mine widening, Mom's misting with a gloss of tears. My hand trembles as it reaches for the envelopes and I try to find my voice. "Thanks."

"I didn't read them. I've hung on to them for a while… I was worried about how you'd react."

All I do is nod.

"Ella…I've seen progress over the last couple of weeks." Swallowing, she lifts an arm and gives my shoulder a firm squeeze. "You're smiling again. You seem like you're in a better place."

I keep nodding, mindlessly. I'm nodding because if I don't do something to distract myself, I'll burst into tears and collapse at her feet. I don't want to burst into tears. I don't want to collapse. Crying is exhausting and collapsing will skin my knees and make me bleed. I'm just so sick of hurting. I've been collecting fresh wounds as often as I collect new books.

Mom swipes at her eyes and retreats slowly, monitoring my condition. My excessive nodding condition. "I'm here if you need me," she says. "I'll be in the kitchen."

The moment the bedroom door closes, I race over to my bed and tear open one of the envelopes, revealing a hand-scrawled note inside.

Jonah.

Jonah, Jonah, Jonah.

I cup a hand around my mouth and begin to read.

Piglet,

I had a dream about the Hundred Acre Wood last night. I go there a lot when the days are long and the nights are longer, and that's where I find you. You're always waiting for me like a home on two legs. Only, last night was different…you weren't there. I stood on our favorite bridge with a stick in my hand and watched through the trees, waiting for you to come and join me. But the woods remained silent and my stick slipped from my fingers into the river below, carried away by water.

I haven't heard from you and I understand why. You think I killed them. I saw it in your eyes that last day in court. You think I deserve to be sentenced to death for a crime constructed by thirsty prosecutors and media mongrels.

You think I belong here.

But in my dreams I belong at home. With you and Mom. I should be watching over my little sister, protecting her like I swore I always would.

I go by a lot of names these days: Monster. Murderer. Psychopath. Sicko. Inmate #829. But I hope that when you think of me…

I'll forever be your Pooh Bear.

Love always,
Jonah

The letter flutters to my bedcovers as a painful gasp is wrenched from my throat.

I burst into tears and collapse.

Jonah's letters are tucked inside my hobo bag like some kind of security blanket as we roll up to the dance at seven thirty the following evening. I don't know why I brought them. The words and sentiments sweep through my mind as I stare at the strobe-strewn glass of the gymnasium with my ass glued to the passenger seat.

Piglet,

Can I still call you that? I hope so.

A lot of things have changed, but I pray that'll never be one of them.

I got into a fight with one of the guards, Olsen. He's a no-good prick in a lot of ways, but want to know why I snapped?

He disrespected my baby sister.

He saw a picture of you that Mom sent me before telling me in detail what he wanted to do to you. So I showed him where that train of thought will take him.

My cuffed hands were around his neck before he could take another useless breath. I kind of blacked out, but I guess I managed to get a good hit in before another guard tore me off him.

They placed me in an isolation unit for a while, and I'm sure there will be more bullshit consequences. They say Olsen will recover just fine, but I'm betting his shattered nose will be a reminder for him to watch his fucking tongue.

Anyway, I'm still protecting you.

Even from hundreds of miles away.

Even on death row.

Jonah

Mom glances at me as I try to shake off the gloom, the image of Jonah beating up a prison guard playing out in my mind over and over. When I was younger, I felt like Jonah's violent outbursts in my honor were respectable and brave. Now, it's just a chilling reminder of why he's sitting in a jail cell on death row.

"Are you okay?" she asks.

"Fine." I'm lost in his letters, wondering how he held up in isolation, wondering if there were consequences, and wondering why I should even care.

Stop caring, Ella.

Life will be so much easier if you stop caring.

There's a little white stone tucked inside my hand, growing sweatier by the second. I've stopped pondering why I carry it with me these days; I just do. For whatever reason, it brings me comfort. It centers me, acting as a calming tether to the girl I once was. The girl who curled her hair and who laughed more than she cried.

I thought about curling my hair tonight but didn't. It looks the same as it always does, blow-dried and loose, hanging over my shoulders in red-brown waves. I tried to cover up the evidence of my sleepless night with concealer and a few strokes of shimmery champagne eye shadow. My lips are glossy. My dress fits nicely. Overall, I don't look nearly as terrible as I feel.

My mother stares at me. I see her studying me in my periphery as the headlights across from us shine light on my nervous jitters. I squeeze the stone tighter.

"You'll have fun tonight," she tells me, putting the car into park when I don't move. "And you look so pretty."

Pretty.

Max told me I was pretty while we stared out at the lake together and a bonfire roared with laughter behind us. It was the nicest thing anyone had said to me in years. I ran from the compliment, just like I ran from his proposal to go to the dance together. He said we'd make it fun and I believed him. It's the only reason I'm here right now, looking pretty. "Thanks," I mutter, throwing Mom a weak smile. "I'll find a ride home later."

"I'll stay up. I have a lot of work to do, anyway. Text me if you need me to come get you."

I have no idea what work she has to do, but I force a nod.

She gives my bare knee a squeeze, her irises glimmering grayish-green. Mom looks happier than she used to. There's a flicker of real joy shining back at me.

"Have a good time," she says before I hop out.

I scoot from the seat and push open the passenger door, plopping the stone into my ratty old hobo bag. Not exactly a fancy dance accessory, but fancy doesn't suit me anymore. "See you later," I say. Then I shut the door and dally on the curb, awkward and alone, while the car pulls away and disappears into the night.

I glance at the front of the building, picking at my thumbnail. A blur of colorful dresses and swinging hair moves in time to overproduced music while seizure-inducing lights filter through the double-glass doors.

With a deep breath, I step forward in my worn-out high heels and enter the building. The DJ blasts me with a poppy rendition of "Take Me Home Tonight" by Eddie Money as I clutch the strap of my hobo bag and try not to trip and face-plant into a sea of glitter-filled balloons. Mercifully, a punch stand is set up in the corner of the gymnasium, so I beeline toward it as a source of distraction.

I'm gulping down my second helping when someone from my art class slides up beside me. I think his name is Brandon.

"Ella, right?" he says, reaching for a plastic cup of punch. "I'm Landon. We have art together."

"Cool." I don't think it's very cool.

He nods, his gaze assessing me in a lazy pull, from my apricot scuffed heels to the hint of cleavage peeking out from my neckline. "You look terrific," he says.

I blink.

Terrific.

"Terrific" is one of those words that becomes less of a word the more you say it. I don't know why. It makes my nose scrunch up and my eyebrows crinkle every time I hear it, and then I proceed to repeat it over and over inside my head until it becomes an un-word.

I realize my face is doing the opposite of what it should be doing in the wake of a compliment, so I overcompensate with crazed eyes, a full-toothed grin, and a sluggish nod, making me look like that GIF of Jack Nicholson nodding creepily from *Anger Management.*

Landon backs away slowly.

One down.

I steal another cup of punch in hopes that my bladder will save me from this nightmare and I can hide out in the bathroom for a while. Shuffling over to the far wall that looks to be void of human contact, I lean back and twirl the cup between my fingers. The gym is alive with strobes and noise as my gaze floats from one gyrating body to the next in search of someone familiar I can latch onto.

Brynn!.

Kai.

Even McKay.

Mostly, I'm searching for…

Max.

I straighten against the wall, my grip on the cup tightening when I spot him by one of the round tables. Brynn! is a vision in flamingo pink as she whispers something in McKay's ear and they both grin, while Libby stands beside Max in a silver-sequin dress and a short blond bob that's been partially pulled up with glitz-studded pins.

Her manicured hand is clamped around his bicep. She's leaning in toward him while he looks around the room, notably fidgety. Possibly bored. Dressed in a modest white button-down tucked into dark slacks, he still manages to look striking. Hair lightly tossed with gel and sleeves rolled up past his elbows, Max scrubs a hand over his face and scratches at the shadow of stubble along his jaw.

He keeps looking around.

Scanning. Searching, just like I was.

My instincts scream at me to bolt, to run, to flee the scene before he sees me. I shouldn't have come. Libby is clearly his date and I'm the weird chick ogling him from across the room after turning down his multiple invitations. It's kind of pathetic if I'm being honest with myself, and I don't want to add that to my laundry list of glaring flaws.

But my feet remain firmly planted on the linoleum floor.

My body doesn't move.

Pathetic wins.

I freeze further when I notice Max falter, then blink. He pivots toward me, almost like he felt me somehow. His attention is on the floor first, gaze aimed at my heels, before it travels up my legs in a languid slide until, finally, he lands on my face.

Our eyes snag.

We hold tight across the strobe-lit dance floor as my pulse revs and my heart skips.

I watch a look cross over his face. Something I can't describe. It's almost like a time-stopped beat of pure awe.

Swallowing, I glance around me, thinking perhaps he's staring at one of the sexy cheerleaders in a slip dress shaking her ass to my left. But when my gaze pans back to him, I know that he's not. He's looking directly at me. And his expression hasn't wavered, hasn't dimmed or grayed. He sees me and he's seeing something that brings him awe.

Me with tired eyes and everyday hair that isn't curled.

Me in a neon-orange dress plucked from a thrift shop rack.

Me...

Staring back at him with the exact same look in my eyes.

Chapter 16

MAX

THERE'S A FEELING THAT COMES OVER A PERSON WHEN THEY'RE WAITING for someone to walk through a door and they finally do. At a party or a date. It's a moment of unrestrained elation, something almost indescribable, and yet we've all had that moment—waiting impatiently, anxious with nerves, wondering if maybe they might not walk through the door at all. Maybe they won't come. Maybe they changed their mind.

And then the door cracks open.

You look up.

Your eyes fixate on their feet first, eager to get a glimpse of that well-worn sneaker you bought for them or their favorite jeweled high heel. Your gaze trails upward, your stomach pitching with triumph, with awe, with *thank-fucking-hell* when you finally settle on the face you were waiting for.

Ella stares back at me with a similar expression, then pops her shoulders a little. A self-deprecating shrug, as if to say, "Here I am."

She came.

She's actually here and I can't bite back the slow-stretching smile as our eyes continue to tangle from twenty feet away.

"Do you want to dance?"

I flinch, forgetting there's a hand pinching my arm. A high-pitched voice floats to my ear and severs the connection, and it's not the voice I'm longing to hear. The girl beside me smells like pickling jars and floral perfume, but I miss the scent of citrus and honeysuckles.

"Not really." I shrug her hand off my arm. I hadn't even noticed it was there because I was too busy looking for someone I was never expecting to find.

I'm about to step forward when McKay tugs me back, his opposite arm slung around Brynn's shoulders. "Check it out, man," he says, scrolling through his text messages. "Party at Morrison's after the dance. He's got a keg."

"It's going to be a blast!" Brynn chimes in. "Morrison's parents live right on the lake. They're setting off fireworks later." She clasps both hands over her heart and glances up at my brother with a dreamy expression. "Think of how pretty the water will look painted in all those colors. How romantic!"

There aren't many things I'd rather do less. "Great. Drop me off at home on your way over so I can avoid that." When my focus pulls back to Ella, she's already been cornered by one of McKay's basketball buddies, Jon. He's leaning forward, whispering something in her ear. One meaty hand lifts to her waistline as her knuckles go white around the punch cup in her fist.

I'm on the move.

"Max!" Libby calls after me. "Where are you going?"

I ignore her. She's not my date so I don't feel bad about it. In three seconds, I'm worming my way between Ella and the basketball douche. "Hey, Jon. I heard they're giving away free beer at the punch stand. All ages. Tonight only."

Jon's eyes widen. "Sweet." He steps away, giving Ella a wink before he vanishes into the crowd.

I remove the punch from Ella's hand, set it down, then take the opportunity to circle my arms around her waist and tug her flush against me.

"Max." Ella's palms plant on my chest, though she doesn't push me away. "What are you doing? They never give out beer to minors. And he was just telling me about alley-oops." She feigns interest.

"I'm being a good friend and saving you."

"Saving me from an innocent conversation?" She glances up at me with only her eyes, long lashes fluttering thoughtfully. "You know me so well."

A grin spreads as my hands dip to her hips, holding loosely while our feet begin to move. Ella blinks away from my gaze but doesn't pull free. Her fingers splay against the front of my chest before she slowly glides them to my biceps and lets them rest there.

I swallow. Her touch is soft and hesitant, like she knows exactly where to put her hands but doesn't know if she should. "I didn't think you were coming tonight," I tell her, my voice hitching slightly. "I'm impressed."

We keep moving, keep swaying. The song changes to something slower, a sleepy country song. She glances across the dance floor toward my table. "I didn't mean to steal you from your date."

"She's not my date."

"I don't think she got that memo."

"I think she's got it now."

Ella's eyes lift to mine again. Tentative, unsure. Her hands are on my arms and my hands are on her hips, and she smells like citrus trees in the springtime. There's a feeling in my chest. It's the same feeling I had when I was in her bedroom that night, when she knelt between my legs and brushed careful fingers across my face, patching more than just a head wound.

On cue, her attention flicks to the butterfly bandage still taped to my temple. "How's your head?"

"Healing." My heart feels like it's healing, too, but I don't say that.

"I'm wearing a dress." Ella scrunches up her nose like the notion is detestable, then chuckles under her breath. "I haven't worn a dress in years."

"I like it." Smiling, I take a step back, pluck one of her hands from my arm, and motion to spin her. She's caught off guard at first, stumbling in her peach heels, but she follows my lead and does a clunky pirouette before tumbling against my torso.

When she pushes herself up, her cheeks are flushed and a sheepish smile pulls. "Sorry. I told you I can't dance."

"It's all about the rhythm and the glide," I remind her.

"Right. Because that worked like a charm when it came to stone skipping."

I twirl her again and it's marginally more graceful. "You'll get the hang of it."

"Dancing or stone skipping?"

"Both."

A slackening steals her shoulders and a lightness overrides the uncertainty in her eyes. She relaxes with a weighty exhale as my right hand laces with her left hand and we find a mutual rhythm. Ella glances down at our feet before peering back up at me, still clinging to that smile. "I look like a giant carrot," she says.

"I like carrots." I spin her and this time it's effortless. "How's the crayon doing?"

"Healthy and thriving."

Spin.

"Have you been watering it?" I ask.

Twirl.

"Yes. I even moved it to my desk for prime sunlight."

The song changes again. The music picks up with a livelier beat as "Gold" by The Ivy spills from two giant speakers propped on the stage. Our feet move faster. I spin her a few more times and watch as a sheen of sweat glistens on her hairline and multicolored strobes sprinkle gemstones in her eyes. Her hands are curled around my biceps again, this time with conviction. She's looser, more comfortable. Our chests press together, and when our eyes meet through the flashing lights, I decide to dip her.

My hand snakes around her back as I latch onto her hand to hold her upright.

And when I dip her backward...she squeals.

It's an organic burst of joy, her leg lifting, her hair coasting behind her in a mass of red ribbons. She squeezes my hand in a deathlike grip before I swing her back up and she spills forward, collapsing against me in a heap of laughter.

I'm grinning like I'm drunk on something. My lips are stretched wide, teeth flashing, cheeks aching. Both of my arms wrap around her and I hold her to me as we continue to dance.

"I can't believe you didn't drop me," she says, hips swaying, legs in motion.

"Really? I thought you had more faith in my arms. You're always looking at them."

"Ugh." She gouges her fingernails into said arms. "You're imagining things. Your arms are uninspiring at best."

"We'll see about that whenever we finally decide to arm wrestle."

"We can right now. Let's settle this once and for all."

I shake my head. "I'm not bored."

After twirling her in another successful spin, I take my chances and dip her again. This time her ankle gives out, not expecting the maneuver, and she clings to my biceps with a white-knuckled grip, her leg flying out to wrap around my thigh for steadiness. I'm too busy catching her to fixate on our precariously tangled limbs. My heart stutters for a moment before I pull her into an upright position, ensuring her balance is restored.

We both pause, breathless, faces mere inches apart.

And then she smacks me on the chest.

"What the hell, Max?" A big smile spreads, overriding the outrage in her voice. "You almost dropped me."

"I would never drop you." Her leg slides down mine until her heel is planted back on the dance floor and our pace slows to a steadier rhythm. "I'm good at catching things, too."

It's not long before Brynn rushes toward us, pulling McKay with her as he continues to text on his phone one-handed.

"Ella!" she shrills over the thundering music. "Oh, my God, I'm so glad you're here."

Reluctantly, I release Ella as Brynn slithers between us, a beam of hot pink. Ella's eyes flick to mine, her smile still gloriously intact, before her gaze pans to Brynn.

"I'm here," she says, her hair knotted and dance-mussed.

Brynn shoots me a sideways glance. "Do you mind if I steal your girl?" She follows it up with a wink.

My hands slide in my pockets. "She's not my girl, Brynn. We were just dancing."

"Guess you don't mind, then." She grabs Ella by both hands and flails their arms around. "Woo!"

I can't help but laugh and Ella can't, either. I watch the girls bop and sway, hair flying, sequins glittering with grins to match.

McKay sidles up beside me and bumps my shoulder with his. "You looked like you were having fun."

"I was."

We both glance over at Libby at the same time. She's dancing with Jon and another group of girls. I wait for McKay to say something scathing. To bust my balls or give me shit.

But he surprises me.

"Glad to see it."

We share a soft look and I bump his shoulder right back.

Another hour rolls by, filled with dancing, laughter, and tropical punch. McKay brought a flask to strengthen his drink, which worries me because of our father's history with substance abuse. I hate that he needs alcohol to have fun.

I sure as hell don't need it. I'm already soaring, high on a natural buzz, watching Ella let go and set herself free in the school gymnasium, her hair damp with sweat, mascara running, and eyes more vibrant than I've ever seen them.

As she gifts me with another smile, I zone in on a smattering of freckles along the bridge of her nose. I've never really noticed them before. They resemble a faint constellation, little stars that only come alive when you take the time to truly look.

I frown.

It's then I realize I might be in trouble, because I shouldn't be noticing things like that.

Legs? Sure. Tits? Of course.

Nose freckles?

Doomed.

It's a short ride back to the house where we make a pit stop to drop me and Ella off before the kegger. I'm smooshed in the back seat of the truck between Libby and Ella, while Brynn sits up front with McKay and details every second of the last few hours. She's driving, since McKay was drinking and also because it's been her "biggest dream in life" to finally drive our junky truck.

The enthusiastic pitch of her voice fades out because I'm too aware of my body pressed to Ella's on my left. Arms flushed, thighs smashed together, her bare knee knocking with mine every time the tires skim over a pothole. Long hair tickling my shoulder, the scent of it overpowering the smell of stale cigarette smoke and old leather interior.

Her hands are fisted tightly in her lap as her giant purse rests between her feet, and I catch the way she glances up at me every now and then in my periphery. The evening's adrenaline has dampened, turning her quiet, and it's been a valiant effort to keep my palms clasped around my kneecaps. All I want to do is reach for her hand and lace our fingers together, which is borderline concerning. I don't know why I want to do that.

When we pull into the driveway, Ella shuffles out of the truck first, her heels crunching atop gravel. "Thanks for the ride," she says, already motioning to take off across the street. "See you guys on Monday."

I slide out behind her, offering the group a hurried goodbye, then slam the door shut and chase after Ella, who is halfway to her house. "Hey, wait up." The truck pulls out of the driveway and guns it down the quiet street until all I hear are high heels clapping along the pavement and singing cicadas. "Ella."

She falters, glancing over her shoulder at me. "What's up?"

"You're running away."

"I'm not running. I just thought…" She slows her feet, glancing at my house across the road, then back at me. "I thought the night was over."

My eyes pan skyward. The moon hangs high, a silver glow in a stretch of black, and the stars are twinkling and bright. The dance might be over, but the night isn't. "Let's go to the bluffs."

This brings her to a full stop. Ella pivots to fully face me, the breeze stealing a few pieces of her hair and tossing them across her face. "The bluffs?"

"Yeah. I promised you stargazing and it's the perfect night for it."

She blinks. "Stargazing."

"Why not?"

"I'm…" Squeezing the strap of her purse, she peers down at her dress and high heels. "Well, look at me. I'd love nothing more than for this dress to be stripped off of me and discarded on my bedroom floor."

Her eyes pop.

My throat works as a flickering of heat zips across my chest.

"Yikes." She forces out a laugh and looks away. "That came out remarkably suggestive. And now I'm mortified."

I school my brain to conjure up less indecent thoughts because friends don't picture friends naked. That would be rude and inappropriate.

When I don't respond because my brain is being rude and inappropriate despite my redirection attempts, Ella clears her throat and steps toward me. "You know what? It's fine. We can be fancy for the stars tonight. This will be the only time I wear this dress, so I might as well make it last."

Elation trickles through me. "Yeah?"

"Sure. Let's do it."

A smile tugs at my lips when I think about spending more time with her. Just us, one on one. I can't even remember when I preferred the company of another person over my own solitude, but it's been years. McKay used to be that person. "Great," I say, trying not to sound too eager. "I'm going to check on my dad real quick and grab a blanket. Do you mind waiting out here?"

Her gaze drifts to my house across the street, settling on the side window where a yellowy light glows from behind the makeshift curtains. She looks at me, blinks. "No problem. I'll change my shoes."

I can tell she wants to join me, but that's out of the question. We're finally making progress in the friendship department, and the last thing I want to do is scare her away when she fully comprehends the disaster that lies on the other side of that piss-poor siding.

Sending her a quick nod, I jog toward my house and slip in through the front door. My father took sleeping pills before the dance, so he's probably passed out cold. I grab an old quilt off the back of the sofa before calling out to him. "Dad?"

To my surprise, he answers. "In here, son."

When I reach his bedroom, I spot him sitting up in bed with a book in his lap. "Hey," I say. "Thought you were sleeping."

"I was." He stares off into nothing before glancing my way. His cloudy eyes defog as he gives me a brief once-over. "You look handsome, Maxwell."

"Thanks. The Fall Fling dance was tonight."

"Did you take a pretty girl?"

I think of Ella dancing in my arms, looking stunning in her sunny-orange dress, her eyes and smile just as bright. "Yeah, I did."

"That makes your old man proud. I should get some pictures for the wall."

Once upon a time, we had walls brimming with photographs, canvases, and mismatched frames. Memories lined the plaster. Fishing trips, camping adventures, and family barbecues were displayed in every hallway and love-filled room.

Now the hallways are empty, the rooms barren and cold.

Even saying we have walls is a stretch.

Before I can respond, my father sits up straighter and his attention snags on my butterfly bandage. "What happened to your head?" he asks, tone laced with alarm.

Swallowing, I lift my hand to the covered wound. He doesn't remember that night. He has no recollection of smashing a lamp to the side of my head and tackling me to the floor in the exact spot I'm standing in. "I fell down by the lake," I lie. "I was running and tripped over some hedges."

His face screws up with distress. "I worry about you, Max. You're always running off alone and I fear one day you'll never come back."

A dark sadness rolls through me as I step backward out of the room. "I'll always come back, Dad. Don't worry." What I want to add is: *I have nowhere else to go.*

But I don't.

"You should give her flowers."

I hesitate, stopping in place before making my exit. "Flowers?"

"For the girl you brought to the dance," he says. "Girls like flowers. Your mother enjoyed white roses because they symbolized eternal loyalty." His silvery-blue eyes glass over for a beat before he picks up the book in his lap and settles against the shoddy headboard with a sigh. "I preferred to get her red roses. Maybe that's why she left me."

I stare at him for a few breaths before scratching at my hair and retreating from the room. "Good night, Dad."

"Good night."

Moments later, I'm in the middle of the street with an ivory quilt bunched underneath my arm. Ella fidgets near the side of the road, toeing at a patch of grass, adorned in a fresh pair of sneakers. She's still wearing her dress. "Sorry for the wait," I tell her. "Ready?"

I watch her eyes pan to my house before she nods. "Ready."

We make it to the bluffs after walking in comfortable silence, and I lead Ella to a small clearing atop a grassy hill underneath a sky of stars. My heart fumbles at how romantic the scene feels, despite my original intent. Something has shifted between us, and I'm not sure how I feel about it. It's alarming, exciting... unanticipated. It's the last thing I ever wanted, and yet I seem to be chasing the feeling head-on, caught in a whirlwind of new emotions.

I glance around at the little oasis as grass smashes beneath my feet, still damp from recent rainfall. The horizon blends dark earth with a deeper blue sky, and everything looks so...*magical*. I've been here a hundred times and it never felt like anything more than nature splashed with starlight.

The difference is I've never been here with her.

My throat feels tight as I inch forward and mutter, "Come on. I'll lay the blanket out over here."

"Wait." Ella snatches my wrist, stopping me, her eyes filled with the ancient glow of the moon. Letting out a sigh, she straightens and lifts her chin. "I will stargaze with you in my orange dress, Max Manning, but only under one condition."

"Okay. Anything."

She lets go of my wrist, glances up at the sky, then turns back to face me. "Promise me that this is not a date."

A smile blooms. I untuck the quilt from under my arm, drape it out across the grass, and gesture for her to have a seat. "I promise you, Ella Sunbury," I lie through my teeth. "This is not a date."

Chapter 17

ELLA

THIS FEELS LIKE A DATE." I LIE SPRAWLED OUT ON THE QUILT BESIDE MAX, my eyes turned up to the Tennessee sky. The scent of dewy grass and damp earth hangs in the air as the dull hoot from a faraway owl serenades the darkness.

Wrinkling my nose, I turn to Max to gauge his reaction.

He doesn't seem to react. "Maybe it is a date."

"What? No. You promised." I glare at him and his web of lies. "I don't date. I don't do romance or kissing or any of that stuff. I'm going to die a virgin and possibly a nun. I haven't decided yet. Churches smell weird, but nuns are really nice and *Sister Act* made it look appealing. Pros and cons, I guess."

He stretches out his legs and his dark slacks brush against my partially exposed thigh. "What does virginity have to do with this?"

My cheeks grow warm. "I don't know."

"It doesn't have to be a romantic date," he says, still staring skyward. "We're just friends. Friends go out on platonic dates all the time."

"We danced together and now we're stargazing."

"And losing your virginity is next on the list? Sounds logical."

"If this was a real list, then yeah, it would probably be fourth or fifth. Kissing is third. Or maybe hand-holding." I consider the imaginary list and nod as the bullet points come together. "Dancing, stargazing, hand-holding, then kissing. Virginity-losing is definitely fifth."

"If this was Andy Sandwell's list, maybe you'd be right."

"No. Andy would never be caught stargazing."

This gets a grin out of him. Max tilts his head toward me, his eyes flickering with twinkle lights. "Well, my list is different. No kissing, no virginity-losing. You're safe with me."

There's a chilly bite to the air but I don't feel cold. And I know our conversation is all in good fun, but the statement rumbles through me like he just wrapped me up in the warm quilt we're lying on. Tipping my head back to stare up at the star patterns, I release a small sigh. "I do feel safe with you," I admit. "You make me feel like…"

He's silent for a beat. "Like what?"

There's a knot in my throat. A burning lump of feeling that I don't know whether to swallow down or purge. "You make me feel like a regular girl."

"You are," he says softly.

"I'm not. But it's nice to feel like I am sometimes." When he doesn't respond right way, I fidget beside him as our shoulders graze and blades of grass tickle the back of my neck through a worn hole in the blanket. My thoughts take on a somber edge and I blurt out, "Jonah sent me letters from prison."

Max glances at me. "Do you usually send letters back and forth?"

"No. I've considered contacting him…but I haven't yet. The last time we had any correspondence, I was watching the guards lead him out of the courtroom in handcuffs and that was nearly two years ago."

That moment is seared in my brain like a nasty burn.

The verdict was read:

Guilty on all counts.

I remember every word, every whisper, every tense beat of silence as Judge McClarren drank in the verdict and gathered his thoughts.

And then he read off Jonah's sentence to the packed courtroom. "In all my years on the bench, rarely have I encountered a case that has affected me so deeply, both as a judge and as a fellow human being. The senseless loss of Erin Kingston and Tyler Mack is a stark reminder of the fragility of life and the darkness that can reside in humanity. This verdict, though aligned with the law, will never truly compensate for the void left in the wake of such a gruesome tragedy."

My heart was in my throat. Between my teeth. It felt like I was chewing on it as blood sluiced across my tongue, but it was only the shredded inner lining of my cheeks that I'd been biting raw.

My fingernails gouged into the heels of my palms.

I was sweating, hardly able to breathe.

Adjusting his silver spectacles, the judge took a deep breath and continued, tone stern and grave. "Given the severity of the crime, the pain caused to the victims' families, and after considering all presented evidence and testimonies, it is the judgment of this court that the defendant shall be sentenced to death as prescribed by the laws of this state."

I screamed.

My mother howled beside me as she collapsed.

We were the only two people in that courtroom mourning while everyone else stood, cheered, and cried completely different tears.

Mom and I were also sentenced to death that day.

Jonah stared over at us when he was hauled from the courtroom, his face a mask of pure pain. Our gazes caught from a few feet away and he said loudly, tortured, with tears streaming down his cheeks from red-rimmed eyes, "I didn't do it. Please, believe me."

I hate that I don't believe him.

I hate that I still love him, miss him, need him here beside me, giving me warmth on my darkest days. I think that's why I'm so broken-down and damaged.

Forgiveness without love is one thing.

But love without forgiveness? That's like a tree without roots; it can't stand for long. It can never truly live.

That's why I'm so resistant to the idea of falling in love. I can't go through it again.

Brynn! told me I have "anti-love" eyes, and I think it's because of all the horrible things they've seen in the name of it.

I turn to Max and can hardly make out his expression through the blur of tears. All I know is that he's staring at me. He doesn't pull his eyes away, even though a sky full of stars hangs over us. "Sorry," I murmur. "I'm getting all emotional."

"Don't be sorry. I know it's not the same but, in a way…I can relate."

"You can?"

He nods, maintaining eye contact. "My mother walked out on us and never came back," he tells me. "She's not dead but she's not here. I can't put my arms around her or eat her blueberry waffles, but I also can't bring flowers to a gravestone or whisper words to the clouds and pretend she can hear me."

Max's knuckles graze against my own. I'm not sure if it's intentional or not, but I don't move away. I do the opposite by inching my hand closer to his until his featherlight touch evolves into willful brushstrokes. Rhythm. The sensation prompts my belly to clench and my skin to sizzle.

"There's no closure in something like that," he continues, the words breathy. "That kind of grieving is an entirely different beast. Grieving someone still alive becomes choice, instead of chance, and I've had a whole lot of experience with that." He swallows, dusting his thumb across the back of my hand. "Sometimes I think it's the only thing in this world worse than death."

I hear him but his touch is louder. It feels like a song, an orchestra trumpeting through my bloodstream. My heart is a bass drum, and when his fingers slowly, delicately, begin to lace with mine, the drumbeats crescendo.

For as good as I am at catching things, I can hardly catch my breath. It slips away from me, as does time. We stare at each other, our fingers gently tangling, our hands locking to parallel our gazes. Max's breathing is shaky, my limbs are quivering, and I've never been this close to anyone before. Not like this. The stars are overhead, but some may have fallen and crash-landed in my chest. At least a few. At least one.

Max's eyes close for a beat with a slow, lazy blink. And then he whispers, "Look at the sky, Sunny."

His words register like thick molasses and I can't seem to tear my eyes away from his. I think I'm in a trance. A spell-glazed stupor.

He smiles at me, gives my hand a tender squeeze. "Look up."

Finally, I catch that breath. It filters through me, unlocking me, and as the strange haze dissipates, I blink myself back to the bluffs and let his words sink in.

I look up.

Above me, stars begin to emerge, one by one, as if someone is gradually lighting up a giant cosmic pinboard. My eyes adjust to the night as the darkness opens up, unveiling an extravagant show of constellations. Then, out of nowhere, a bright streak flashes across the sky.

I turn to look at Max again. "What was that?" I choke out, the words all gasp and wonder.

"The Taurid meteor shower."

My gaze pans back up and my heart jumps. The Taurid meteor shower. The meteor is cutting across the night like a sharp, swift brush streak on an inky canvas. Then comes another and another, each one more enchanting than the last.

I can feel my pulse racing, matching the rhythm of each fleeting meteor. Every fiery trail feels like a hello, a postcard from the farthest reaches of space. Being under the open sky makes me feel tiny, insignificant. But there is also a strange sense of belonging as light beams slash through a backdrop of deep, deep blue.

"Ella?" Max whispers.

Tears gather in my eyes as my chest fills with a smothering feeling. "Yeah?"

"I lied about something."

I frown, tipping my head toward him. "You did?"

"Yeah. I said you were a regular girl…but you're not." His tongue pokes out to wet his lips and he turns to meet my eyes. "You're more."

He doesn't elaborate. And within everything unsaid, that heavy feeling in my chest ruptures and those tears begin to leak from my eyes. I don't apologize this time. I don't tell him I'm sorry for letting my emotions spill out, for allowing this moment to make me feel something other than the comfortable wash of nothingness. I'm not sorry.

I'm grateful.

When teardrops gather at the corner of my lips, I lick away the salt and inhale a wobbly breath. "We're hand-holding," I say. "What comes next on your list?"

It can't be kissing. He said there would be no kissing.

I don't want to know how soft his lips are, or how rough his stubble would feel against the skin of my jaw. I have no desire to feel his tongue against mine. I don't wish for any of that.

I don't.

Max's gaze slips to my mouth and holds. "Nothing," he answers, a slow smile stretching before his eyes pan back up. "This is where the list ends."

When the words register, my own smile spreads and I give his palm a gentle squeeze. The quote from "Little Gidding" flashes through my mind as I stare at Max, his hand filled with mine and his eyes filled with stars.

> **"What we call the beginning is often the end. And to make an end is to make a beginning. The end is where we start from."**

I like this ending.

"HOW TO CATCH THE SUN"
STEP TWO:

Embrace the Golden Hour

Seize the warmth before it fades.

Chapter 18
ELLA

M Y EIGHTEENTH BIRTHDAY ARRIVES TWO WEEKS LATER, AND I WAKE UP TO a bouquet of orange roses on my front porch. The late-November sun sets them ablaze like the embers of an autumn campfire, and I glance around the yard as if a secret admirer might be lurking in my hydrangea bushes. Mom already left for work, leaving my favorite breakfast spread out on the kitchen table with a bundle of balloons, their ribbons tied to chairbacks.

I gulped down orange juice, then feasted on the meal of citrus cakes and scrambled eggs with candied bacon. A few months ago, I was dreading my birthday. I had no plans, no friends, nothing to celebrate but another year lost to sadness. But I woke up today feeling oddly renewed. My belly is full, it's a bright and shimmery Saturday morning, and there are orange roses on my doorstep.

Bending over, I pluck them up by the stems and read over the attached note. My heart skips.

Ella,

Happy birthday. I Googled the meaning of orange roses and I guess they symbolize energy, new beginnings, and good fortune. I also found this: "Orange flowers

are a symbol of the sun and all things positive." I
thought they were perfect because the sun suits you.
Flowers do, too.

—Max

PS: Get your dancing shoes on—we're going to
Knoxville.

I smile.

Guess I'm going to Knoxville.

Following an overly ecstatic text message from Brynn! an hour later, I'm now standing in the middle of her kitschy living room after snagging a ride over from Max and McKay. The walls are plum purple. The carpet is bright green. Neon-red furniture is littered throughout the space, eclectic art pieces stare back at me from all angles, and Cher's "If I Could Turn Back Time" serenades us from a record player in the corner of the room.

"Ella!" A man in a Halloween sweater crocheted with black bats and jack-o'-lanterns appears from the kitchen, his hair a shock of white-blond.

Oh, my God. It's another Brynn!.

A second man appears, his hair darker, his sweater brighter, and he pretends to sing into a spatula as he leans back and lets loose. Then he turns to me and grins wide. "Ella!"

Oh, my god. It's *another* Brynn!.

I can't help but return the smile because it's impossible not to. "Hey." I give them a little wave that feels lame and listless compared to the greeting I've received. Then I frown with confusion. "Uh, Halloween was last month. It's almost Thanksgiving."

"Halloween lasts until Christmas Eve around here," one man says.

"*Hocus Pocus* is always in season," adds the other.

I blink slowly. "Oh."

Brynn! skips between the two men and waves madly at me. "Ella!" she calls out, her enthusiasm on another level. "You finally get to meet my dads. This is

Daddy Matty," she says, pointing to the blond man. "And this is Papa Pete. I call them Daddio and Pops."

Max and McKay are seated side by side on the red floral sofa. Max shoots me a small smile, his eyes sparkling.

I blink back to Matty and Pete. "It's so nice to finally meet you. Thank you for the fruit tray when I was sick."

"Sugar is the only thing that works for me when I have a lung infection," Pete says, sliding the spatula into his waistband. "Feeling better?"

"I am."

"It was the sugar."

I grin. "Antibiotics are overrated."

Brynn! trots forward in her knee-high cowboy boots and denim skirt, plopping down beside McKay on the couch. As soon as she sits, the doorbell rings and she jumps back to her feet.

"Oh, it's Kai! We've been bonding in art class, so I invited him. I hope that's okay?" She glances at me before moving to the front door. "I know it's your birthday. I hope I didn't infringe."

"Of course not. Kai is awesome."

Kai trudges through the threshold, looking timid and supremely out of place. He glances between the five of us, brushing jet-black bangs out of his eyes and slamming his hands in his pockets. "Hi."

"Kai!" both fathers and Brynn! announce at the same time while Kai stands there like a cat at a dog show.

Five minutes later, our group shuffles out the door in preparation for our hour-plus drive to Knoxville.

Matty hollers from the porch step as we make our way to the slew of vehicles packed in the driveway. "There will be treats aplenty when you get back! Spiderweb taco dip, hot dog mummies, graveyard cake, and my ultra-famous bat wings. Mwahaha!"

Pete quickly snags the spatula from his waistband and shoves it in Matty's face. "Redo that."

"Mwahaha!" Matty repeats into the spatula.

A giggle falls out of me as we all wave goodbye and I beeline to the back seat of Max's truck.

"You're riding shotgun with me," Max says.

McKay grumbles. "Hell, no. I always ride shotgun. Ladies can do their girlie gossip in the back." When Kai clears his throat, McKay adds, "And Kai."

"Actually, let's take two cars," Max suggests. "Brynn, are you cool driving?"

"Sure!" she chirps.

"Then we need two DDs," McKay snaps.

"A non-issue. You're the only one with whiskey in your Coke."

"We don't need two rides, Max. Waste of gas. We can all fit."

"I want some alone time with Ella."

Everyone goes silent. My ears burn underneath my beanie as my gaze ping-pongs from face to face. The memory of holding Max's hand beneath the Taurid meteor shower flashes through my mind like a falling star zipping across the sky, and the heat from my ears travels to my cheeks.

McKay sets his jaw and tosses Max the keys with more force than necessary. "Fine. See you there."

Brynn! does a funny, hurried skip over to me while everyone else tromps to their respective vehicles. She snatches both of my wrists and shakes them up and down with a little squeal, her pigtails bobbing over her shoulders. "Ella!" She manages to both shout and whisper my name, which is impressive. "There is an *actual* chance we could be sisters."

The moment has escalated. "Sisters?"

"If you marry Max and I marry McKay, we'll be sisters-in-law. That would be amazing!"

My cheeks never had a chance to cool before another wave of warmth permeates them. "Um, it's not that serious. We're just friends."

"The way he looks at you, though! And he wants to spend 'alone time' with you." Her grip on my wrists strengthens. "I saw the way you danced together at the Fall Fling. Max has never taken much interest in girls before. I thought he was gay."

"He could be. We're just friends so I wouldn't know." Something tells me he's not.

Max rolls down the passenger's side window and leans over the console. "Ready, Sunny?"

Brynn! grins wider, her eyes bugging out. "*Sunny*. Oh, my gosh—text me updates during the car ride!" Another squeal, and then an extra smooshy hug until we almost tip over. "See you there!"

My beanie is lopsided and my hair is full of static when she finally releases me. I can't help but chuckle as I watch her flounce over to the black sedan beside the truck and hop inside.

I fling open the door and nearly topple again from the weight of it. "Ready," I mutter, steadying my balance before tugging off my beanie and tossing it to the floor of the truck.

"That was quite the hug. It's almost like she never planned to see you again."

"The opposite, actually." I slam the door shut and yank the seat buckle across my chest. "She wants to be sisters-in-law. Bound together by our respective matrimony to the Manning twins."

Max hesitates before sticking the key in the ignition. "Interesting."

"Mm-hmm."

"The pressure is on for a proposal now," he says. "At least I set the scene with the roses. Did you like them?"

When he twists around to glance out the back window while he reverses out of the driveway, I watch his biceps bulge and flex for a beat before slinking further in my seat and staring straight ahead. Then I study my fingernails as we pull out onto the road. "Sure. They were beautiful."

"I thought so. What kind of rings do you like?"

I chuckle and bite my lip. "The candy ones. Orange, specifically."

"Low maintenance. I can appreciate that."

"Thank you, by the way. For the flowers." Still gnawing on my lip, I peer over at him and catch the smile he's wearing. "The last time someone gave me a flower, I was seven," I say pointedly, playground magic sprinkling across my memory. "Then my dad came along and ruined everything."

"I still remember picking that flower for you. It was bright like the sun, and the sun was bright like you." Smiling softly, Max reaches for a pack of cigarettes on the dashboard, then falters. He leaves them there, untouched, and turns the dial up on the radio instead as a crisp wind shimmies through the open window. "Tell me about him."

"My dad? He left us all for good a few months after that. Drove me back to Nashville to live with my mom because my teacher's tits were more appealing than taking care of his daughter. They'd agreed to split up the siblings for whatever stupid reason, and Dad didn't want to deal with Jonah's anger issues, so he chose me. Mom and Jonah became close during that year we were all apart." My teeth grind together as I stare out the window. Grudges are a burden on the heart, so I turned my heart into stone. Too bad there are cracks. It would be a lot easier to hate him if there wasn't. It would be easier to hate Jonah, too. "Anyway…he's a bastard."

"Tell me about the before," Max prompts after a moment of silence. "Before he left."

I clasp my hands together in my lap and glance down. Memories, like water, always seem to find their way through even the smallest of fissures. I think about the times when love was effortless and trust wasn't so hard-fought. I wish I could seal the cracks and remain watertight, but hearts—even stone ones—have a way of remembering what they once held dear. "My father took me to a Stevie Nicks concert a week before he ditched me for my teacher," I tell Max, ignoring the stinging in my throat. "He propped me up on his shoulders so I could see better. I was so young at the time, but I still felt the magic of that moment."

Max sets his elbow on the console between us, his bare arm grazing the sleeve of my sweater. There's a heavy charge in the air, so he tamps it down by singing. "'This magic moment…'"

A smile breaks through my sorrow and I throw him a look of gratitude for redirecting the mood. Then I purposely avoid thinking about the lyrics that come next. The part about lips. "I'm excited to see the bands tonight. You should play some of their songs for me."

"Open up my Spotify," he says, gesturing at his phone. "I made you a playlist."

"Ooh, another list. But in song form."

"Yep. Sorry this old truck doesn't have Bluetooth, but you can play it off my phone."

Nodding, I reach for the cell phone and browse through his library that features a single playlist.

It has a title.

Sunny Songs.

I blink over to him.

He answers before I have time to question the discovery. "Those are some of my favorite bands and a lot of the songs have lyrics about the sun. They make me think of you." He sweeps a hand through his tousle of hair and clears his throat. "Two of those bands are playing tonight at the concert. Wilderado and Bear's Den. They're kind of—"

"You have songs that make you think of me?" I interrupt, because that's all that registered.

He hesitates, swallows. "Yeah." When we stop at a red light, Max plucks the phone out of my hands and scrolls through the list, landing on a song. He presses Play. "Especially this one. It's called 'Surefire' by Wilderado."

Melodies burst to life as he turns the volume up. The song is upbeat. Happy. I wonder why it makes him think of me. I'm constantly a dark cloud raining on him, and this song is so pure. It feels like living. Real, authentic living.

And suddenly...

I'm angry.

It happens so fast.

My hands clench in my lap as the lyrics ring loud and hot pressure burns behind my eyes. I see Max turn to glance at me in my peripheral vision.

"What's wrong?" he wonders, pulling off onto an open road as sunlight pours down on the infinite stretch before us. Rocks and pebbles light up, a tapestry of gold. Tree branches sway and shake.

"Nothing," I croak out while my fingernails dig into the heels of my palms.

He presses down on the accelerator and the landscape becomes a blur of motion. "If you're mad, let it out. You're safe with me."

I shake my head. "No."

"Let it out, Sunny." He rolls both windows down all the way. "Let it go. You'll feel better."

"I can't."

"Yes, you can."

Anger blooms in my chest, searching for a way out. I try to keep it contained like I always do, but it teases me, pokes me, and then it starts to claw. Right between my ribs. A sharp talon, jagged and mean. My breathing escalates, morphing into steady pants. "Fuck Jonah," I hiss through my teeth, emotion balling in my throat. "Fuck him for being on death row, for abandoning me. Fuck my father for leaving us behind without a backward glance, and fuck my first-grade teacher and her stupid tits. They deserved each other."

"Fuck them," Max agrees, his fingers bleaching white around the steering wheel. "Fuck them all."

"Fuck them all," I repeat. "And fuck the kids at school who look at me like I'm some kind of monster. The teachers, too. Mrs. Caulfield, especially. Fuck her and her pointy head and cruel words. She's supposed to be a teacher, but all she's taught me is that people can be so horrible to one another."

"Fuck her."

"And fuck Andy Sandwell and Heath and all of their asshole friends. Fuck my mother who worked so hard for her money and then worked so hard to lose it, hiring the best lawyers, thinking she could set Jonah free," I confess, feeling positively rageful. "He wanted to take the plea deal, you know. A guilty plea for life without parole. Mom begged him to go to trial. She was certain he'd get off, because she's convinced he didn't do it. Turns out, she was wrong. She sentenced him to death."

Max remains silent, glancing at me every few seconds as we gun it down the vacant dirt road.

I keep going.

"Fuck everyone who crucified me for that interview, who punished me for my sad, bleeding heart. It's not fair. It sucks. I hate being so mad." I'm near hysterics, so I turn to Max and ambush him with what's left of my pain. "And fuck you, Max Manning. Fuck you for being kind to me. For making me feel safe and vulnerable when I know it's a mistake. For dancing with me, for holding my hand beneath the stars, and for making me laugh like there are still things worth laughing about. Fuck you for giving me flowers, then and now, as if I really matter to you, and for making my birthday special. And for playing me this stupid song that I absolutely love because it makes me feel the same way *you* make me feel." I catch my breath and swallow hard, my voice softening to a hoarse whisper. "Like…I have no reason to be mad anymore."

A few tense beats roll by.

He says nothing, his hands still curled around the wheel, his jaw tense. He's looking straight ahead, processing my tirade, probably thinking I've lost my mind.

I have. I really have.

My face burns with shame. My palms are close to bleeding from my angry nails and my stomach coils into anxious knots.

I'm about to apologize. Maybe tuck and roll from the car while we're going seventy—broken neck be damned. I'm going to. I am.

But then…

"Fuck you, Dr Pepper," Max finally says.

I suck in a sharp breath. A laugh almost falls out, but I'm too stunned to laugh right now. He heard me that day at the vending machine. He heard me and he remembered.

I stare at him and nod slowly, my heartbeats ricocheting. "Fuck you, Dr Pepper," I murmur.

"Say it louder."

I straighten in my seat and tip my face to the truck's ceiling. "Fuck you, Dr Pepper!"

"Again."

I'm breathing like I just ran a marathon. High jumps, long jumps, pole vaults. Lifting up, I lean out the open window as my loose hair obscures my vision and the wind tries to choke me. And then I shout at the top of my lungs, "*Fuck you, Dr Pepper!*"

No one is around us, not a single car on the road. Only Max can hear me. Only the wind feels my grief as I release it with wild abandon, my hands clinging to the passenger side door, my heart in my throat. I scream it again. And again. I purge and shriek and bend and break.

I laugh.

I laugh with mania, with defiance, with soul-churning awareness. The song plays loud, volume up all the way, a forever soundtrack to this moment.

This magic moment.

When I flop back into the passenger seat, I'm breathless, boneless, and more alive than I've ever been before. It takes a second for me to notice the wetness trickling down my cheekbones, creating little pools along my lips and jaw. I stick out my tongue and taste the salt.

Tears. I'm crying.

I'm crying.

I swipe at the teardrops with the sleeve of my sweater, another sob-drenched laugh spilling from my lips. I'm crying, but not because I'm sad. It's because I finally found what I've been searching for. What I've been desperately craving for years.

Peace.

Just one peaceful moment.

I'm not broken. I'm not beyond hope. I'm worthy; I'm *so worthy* of this moment. Of this precious pocket of peace.

It's here.

It's mine.

I found it.

I found it in this rusty old truck on an open road, the music loud, the sun blood orange. I found it with dust in my eyes and wind in my hair as Max reaches for my hand and links our fingers together with a tender squeeze.

And I realize it's not the first time I've found it. It's merely the first time I've let myself acknowledge it.

I'm a mess of tears and joy when I look over at Max, our hands tightly locked together. He holds on to me. He's with me. He feels it, too.

The truth is I've had many peaceful moments.

And every single one of them has been with him.

Chapter 19

ELLA

Brynn! prances beside me as we wind through college kids and hand-in-hand lovers, music filling the air and spilling out from the crowded venue. I'm slurping down a blue-raspberry slushie when she links our arms together.

"What do you think of Kai?" she asks me.

It's an odd question. Her perma-smile wavers when I glance at her. "He's really sweet. Shy, introverted. Surprisingly funny when he's comfortable with you. Why?"

"No reason."

There's always a reason. "Elaborate."

"Well, McKay insists he has a crush on me and he's pissed that I invited him today. He's wrong, right? Kai just needs some friends. And I love making friends."

"I agree with McKay." When Brynn! whips her head toward me, she blanches a little. Honesty has never been difficult for me. "Sorry, but Kai definitely has a crush on you. I don't blame McKay for mentioning it, but I don't blame you for making Kai feel included. Just tread carefully."

She sighs, blowing out a long breath through pink, glossy lips. "It's my Christopher Robin eyes."

It takes a minute for the statement to process, and when it does, a burst of laughter falls out of me. "Well, that's not a bad thing. I wish everyone had Christopher Robin eyes."

"No. It's a curse. And now McKay is mad, thinking I might cheat on him."

"He doesn't think that."

"He cornered me outside the car and said those exact words. He's been acting really jealous and angry lately and it's stressing me out."

My nose crinkles, and I can't help but think of Jonah.

No.

McKay isn't Jonah; he's just a high school kid.

I banish the thought and try to ease her worries. "He's intoxicated and being insecure. Christopher Robin is loyal."

"Which character are you?" she asks.

I pause. I'm about to say Piglet, but then I wonder…*who is Piglet without Pooh Bear?* Swallowing the quickly forming knot in my throat, I shrug. "I don't know anymore."

Brynn! sips her apple cider and smiles softly, still holding on to my arm as we weave through the masses. It's a chilly fifty-degree evening, and everyone is bundled up and huddled together with friends and loved ones while dallying outside the venue. Considering we're heading into December, a lot of people are dressed up in holiday sweaters. I'm still stuck in Halloween with my all-black attire, blueish lips, and pale skin, so I probably look like Wednesday Addams.

I bet Matty and Pete were proud.

The guys are dressed comfortably. Max snagged a hoodie from the back of his truck after we parked, and when I sneak a peek at him sauntering a few feet to my right, he pulls his hood up over his head to counter the chill in the air.

Our eyes meet.

Hopefully mine aren't rimmed red from the embarrassing waterworks show on the drive over. His are as soft and blue as they've ever been.

McKay is on the other side of Max as Kai trails behind the group with his gaze on the ground. Brynn! unlinks our arms and peers over at a line of food trucks boasting the best barbecue in Tennessee. "Ooh! They have vegan kabobs. Pit stop?" She eyes the group.

I shake my head. "I'm good."

Kai immediately tags along, prompting a glare from McKay, while Max follows with a comment about smoky-garlic pulled pork. That leaves me and McKay standing off to the side, dodging a group of drunken twentysomethings.

He uncaps his Coke and takes a big swig, eyes narrowed at Brynn!'s billowing pigtails. "He digs her," he mutters, swishing the soda concoction around in aimless circles. "I mean, she's perfect. I don't blame the guy. But she acts flirty with him."

McKay and I hardly speak, let alone about anything serious. In fact, I would have put money on him not liking me all that much. Clearing my throat, I toe a groove in the pavement and try to act cool. "She acts the same way with me. She's a friendly person."

"It's different. She kept glancing at him in the rearview mirror on the drive over."

"That doesn't mean anything. I'm sure she was just making sure he was comfortable."

"Yeah. I guess."

"Are you guys going to the same college?" I pivot.

He sniffs. "No. I have no grand plans after high school. Might see the world, might not."

That's strangely relatable. I toss him a glance and a smile. "The world is vast and intimidating. Maybe it's more about finding our place in it, rather than seeing all of it."

His mouth twitches when he looks at me. Nodding, McKay slips one hand in the pocket of his baggy jeans. His shoulder-length hair flies behind him when a breeze whips through, and for a moment, he bears a striking resemblance to Max. The tiny smile, the stance, the eyes a similar shade of blue in the low-hanging sun. But there is no trace of dimples.

I'm about to say something else when Max returns, tugging the hoodie over his head and handing it to me. "Here, take this. You look freezing."

"But then you'll be freezing," I reply, frowning at the gesture while regarding his bare arms. "I'm the idiot drinking a slushie on a cold day."

"I'll be fine. Take it, Ella."

Reluctantly, I accept the offering with a look of gratitude. "Thanks." The hoodie is warm, scented with earthy cologne and the faint aroma of cigarette smoke. The sleeves hang past my palms as I wrap myself in a one-person hug and inhale deeply.

Max steps toward me, his gaze trailing me as his throat rolls. "Looks good on you."

"It's comfy," I say with a smile.

"Ready for music?" He doesn't wait for me to reply as he closes the gap between us and reaches for one of my concealed hands.

I shake it through the sleeve hole and our fingers interlock. It feels effortless, like our hands were made for holding, and warmth spreads to every limb. I lift my eyes to his as he towers a foot above me. "Ready," I say.

I'd be ready for anything with his hand in mine.

We commandeer a high-top table that overlooks a giant stage. Dazzling strobes splash an array of colors across the band as attendees wave their hands on the dance floor and music pulls everyone to their feet.

Bear's Den is playing—one of Max's favorite bands. I recognize a few songs that played on the drive over. Kai sways back and forth to my right, so I nudge him with my elbow. "Having fun?"

He glances beside him at Brynn! before clearing his throat. "Sure. The music is good."

"And the company is exceptional."

"The company is mostly exceptional."

We share a glance, and I know McKay's passive-aggressive comments are what have tainted the exceptional company.

When the band announces their next song called "Red Earth & Pouring Rain," Max leans in to me on my left. His rich voice tickles my ear and sends a shiver up my spine. "This one is my favorite."

"Oh, yeah?" I twist to look at him, and he's closer than I expect. I suck in a quick breath as our noses almost kiss. "I can't wait to hear it."

The crowd goes wild when the first chord rings out. The lights dim and a lone spotlight shines on the lead singer, casting him in a white glow. As his voice croons into the microphone, harmonizing in perfect sync with the instruments, energy surges through the audience and causes bodies to undulate and arms to swing back and forth. There's a huge smile on my face as I watch, transfixed, my shoulder glued to Max's arm. When I pull my chin up to catch his expression, I drink in his closed eyes and soft smile. There's a dreamy, soulful wrinkle to his brow and I find myself staring at him instead of at the band. He must feel my attention on him, because a moment later, his arm is around me, tugging me closer.

I melt into him.

The song picks up, the crowd whistling and bopping. Couples sway and slow dance as magic creeps beneath my skin and zaps my heart. I lean in to Max with my whole weight, nestling in the crook of his arm, flush against his torso as he holds onto me like a treasure. Just as the singer belts out lyrics about pouring rain, a sprinkler system activates, dousing the crowd in a cool shower. I gasp. A laugh follows, and my head tilts back while a gentle stream of water mists my face.

Max blinks down at me, a smile pulling at his lips, the moisture from over-head dampening his bangs until they're stuck to his forehead.

Nothing else exists. Just this song, this boy, and this look between us.

And then he's bending over, ushering me behind him. "Climb on," he tells me, voice pitching loud over the guitar riff.

I can't help but laugh. "What?"

"Climb on my shoulders. I'll lift you up so you can see better."

He's dead serious.

I falter for a beat, but then my legs are moving, guiding me behind his back. Max hooks both arms underneath my knees and hauls me up like there's no weight at all. I'm soaring skyward until I'm propped up on his shoulders, my legs crisscrossing at his chest, and my hands flying to his hair for balance. A squeal shreds my throat. I teeter sideways and Max locks his forearms at my thighs to keep me steady.

If my life were a book, this would be that moment where everything shifts.

A scene readers would tab, highlight, and revisit. Where the protagonist isn't just observing the story but is truly alive in it. Up here, the world feels different. I'm both a part of the crowd and above it, with Max as my anchor, grounding me through the lyrics, melodies, and makeshift rain. If this is what living in the moment feels like, I want every chapter to be just like this one.

I fist his hair with one hand and throw my other toward the ceiling with a whoop of joy. Water droplets sparkle under the stage lights as the singer bends over and sings like the lyrics are so much more than words. In turn, I hold on to Max like he is so much more than a pair of sturdy shoulders. He feels like a tether, a lifeline. An escape. We are two sticks tossed over a bridge, swimming side by side, floating away from it all.

When the song ends, Max slides me down his back and my boots hit the floor. My hands don't leave him right away. I want to press my cheek into the arc of his spine, but instead, I slowly trail my hands down his hips until my arms are dangling at my sides. A slower song begins to play next and I settle beside Max again while Brynn! plops down in McKay's lap in one of the tall chairs, and Kai stands off to the side sipping a soda. I steal a glance at Brynn!, and the smile we share says a thousand words.

These are my people. I finally feel like I belong.

"Come here."

Max's voice startles me from the moment, and I glance at his arm extended out to me. "What?" I ask.

"Come here, Sunny."

My gaze travels down his lean body, then back up to his face. A small smile gleams back at me as his wet hair curls along his temples and forehead. My heartbeats tangle at the notion of being fully wrapped in his embrace, my back pressed to his chest as a slow, dreamy song serenades us from the stage and those strong arms hold me tight.

Butterflies swarm low in my belly with dizzied wings when I inch over to him, allowing both of his arms to curl around my middle. "Okay," I murmur, avoiding eye contact. I lean back, hesitant and careful. Nervous and scared shitless. I'm not sure what I'm scared about, but my heart is accelerating at a lethal speed and oxygen feels like a tangible knot in the back of my throat.

Max leans forward a little. I feel his own heartbeat pulsing through the back of the hoodie, and it's gunning it at a similar pace. He squeezes me, taking a step forward so his legs are caging me in and his pelvis is flush with my lower back. Warm breath beats against the crown of my head in quick, steady puffs. His scent wafts around me, pine-steeped soap and woodsy cologne, fusing with the aroma in the air of fog machines and fried food.

The song plays, echoing through the crowd. It's called "Shadows." It's slower and kind of sad, and a few girls in front of us are crying, but miraculously, I can't relate. I'm not sad right now.

I lean back further against Max's chest, prompting his head to drop forward until his lips are whispering along my ear. I can tell by his breathing that he isn't sad, either. Melancholy dangles in the air, but we're in our own bubble and all I feel is his body heat warming me, his shaky breaths kissing my ear, and his hand as it slides from my hip to my thigh and begins to graze up and down the damp denim. Tendrils of silken heat slither through me as my eyelids flutter closed.

"Is this okay?" he asks softly.

My hair flutters from his breath and my heart flutters from his words. I have no idea if this is okay, but the reply spills out anyway. "Yes." Something inside me thinks it's okay.

Sighing, Max presses into me, and then his other arm wraps around my middle and pulls me even closer.

I make a sound.

I don't mean to; it just falls out like air.

His hand is on my thigh, and his arm is wrapped around me, and I've never felt anything like this before. I've never made that sound.

He hears it and makes a similar sound in return, right next to my ear. A breathy groan that feels like a fireball to my heart, a blaze of detonation traveling south and causing a throbbing heat to unfurl between my legs.

Oh God.

What is this?

What is happening?

My limbs are paralyzed but my insides are in motion. Spinning and free-falling. I'm frozen yet melting. Nothing makes sense.

Everything makes sense.

Max's hand trails up and down my thigh while the other splays across my abdomen, drifting and searching. His fingertips inch underneath the hem of the hoodie, just barely. A weightless touch. One finger skims the waistband of my jeans, and his thumb brushes the skin of my stomach. It feels like dozens of flickering fireflies have breached me. Starlight infiltrates. Sunshine leaks into my soul and thaws every patch of frost.

And when he whispers my name against the curve of my neck, everything is golden. "Ella."

My skin comes alive with goose bumps. My heart is pounding, my core achy.

A little voice inside my head yearns for him to dip his hand lower, to the space between my legs.

No, no, no. Stop it, Ella.

Terrified by the strange new thoughts, I tilt my head to the side and look at him. I'm not sure why I do that, but part of me needs to know what he's thinking and feeling. I need to see his eyes. Maybe to him this is harmless, friendly, playful. Maybe my body is responding in all the wrong ways and I can laugh it off, and we can be normal again.

But looking at him is a mistake.

When his head tips up, his eyes are glinting with crystalline intensity, far from mirroring laughter or playfulness. His gaze is unwavering, heated, steadfast—and in that split second, I realize we're on the same page, consumed with the same tension, the same pull. Normalcy feels miles away.

He leans in closer.

His lashes flutter, lips part.

Our mouths are a centimeter from locking together.

My instincts fire and panic overthrows me.

The light snuffs out as I scramble away from him. "I–I think I need to go."

Max inhales a breath and releases me like my leaking light just burned him. "Go?"

"I need some air." I move away on teetering legs, unable to look at him. He calls out to me again, but I'm already fleeing. Running away like a coward.

I shove my way through a mass of bodies, tripping over chair legs, earning glares and annoyed remarks from the crowd.

Brynn! shouts my name.

I keep running.

"Ella!" It's Max this time, chasing after me.

Tears cloud my vision. Tears of terror and confusion. I didn't want this… I didn't want *that*. There's a burning ball of need in my belly and I want to claw it out of me. It's a wretched invader. A trespasser. When I make through the double doors and into the cool air, I slow my pace, bend over, and clasp my hands around my knees as I try to catch my breath.

Max jogs up beside me, his sneakers coming into view on the sidewalk. "Ella."

"Don't… I can't."

"Can't what?"

Still winded, I lift back up and swat sections of damp hair out of my eyes. His brows are bent with concern, but a small smile still bleeds into the look he sends me. It's soft, gentle. Kind. His gaze scans my face, my pink cheeks, my wild eyes and tangled hair. I don't know why he's smiling. I hate that he's smiling. "Don't, Max," I repeat. "Don't smile at me like that." There's a hiss to my words. Each syllable is infused with lethal snakebite venom.

His smile withers, poisoned to death. "Why not?"

"Because you smile at me like I *matter*," I snap. "Like I mean something to you."

"You do matter. You do mean something to me." His throat works through a swallow and he shakes his head at my words as if he can shake them out of the stratosphere. "You matter a lot. You're my friend, Sunny Girl."

"Am I?"

"Yes."

"Then what was that?"

Max doesn't miss a beat, tilting his head as he asks, "What did you want it to be?"

He's not afraid of the answer because the answer is clear as day, despite what my audible response might be. It's written into my glassy gaze and the flush of

desire on my cheeks. It's in my shaky limbs and quivering lips. He knows exactly what I wanted it to be and that's why I'm running.

He also knows I'll never admit it.

I cross my arms over my chest and look down at the concrete before glancing back up. "I think...I think I want you to take me home."

Max blinks once, then nods. "Okay. I'll text McKay that we're leaving."

"Okay. Thank you."

I send a text to Brynn! at the same time and she responds instantly.

Me: I have a stomachache. Too many slushies. Max and I are taking off if that's okay. Tell your dads I appreciate the invitation for snacks later tonight, but I'm going to head home.

Brynn!: No problem! Is this code for sexy, naked shenanigans? *shifty eyes*

Me: Negative.

Brynn!: Only a matter of time according to EVERYONE in the crowd tonight ;) Text me later!!

Now I have an actual stomachache.

I slip my phone in my pocket and follow Max out to the parking lot a few seconds later. We don't say much during the hour-plus drive home. He doesn't hold my hand. Only the playlist he made for me serenades my tumultuous inner thoughts as I stare out the window and watch the sun sink behind the horizon for good.

When I fall asleep that night, Max is there.

Haunting my dreams. Altering my dreams.

We're riding horses, side by side, galloping down a trail beneath a sky of clouds and blue. He turns to me, the brim of his hat shadowing two crystal-like eyes. "The sun is extra bright today, Sunny. We should try to catch it."

I glance at the yellow-orange ball of fire in the sky and shake my head. "I don't know how."

"Easy," he says. "Prepare your net and begin at dawn."

That doesn't make any sense.

I don't answer him and look off to the horizon as horse hooves clap against the dusty terrain. There's where I see Jonah, standing at the edge of a ravine, his mouth moving with words I can't make out. His copper hair catches the light and a smile shines back at me.

I want to hug him. I want to race toward him, hold him in my arms, and never let him go. But he's too far away, too out of reach. I'll never make it before the sun sets and darkness paints the world black. Fighting back tears, I squint my eyes and stare into the sun before glancing back to where Jonah once stood.

He's gone.

Some things are too hard to catch, even for me.

Chapter 20

MAX

I've lost my mind.

Madness has taken over, infecting me with the absurd idea of bringing this shitty house back to life. I'm not entirely sure what came over me in the days since the concert, but I woke up one morning with the burning desire to finish what Dad and I had started years ago. Maybe it's Ella. She's allowed me to believe that broken things don't always need to stay in ruins.

My heart, for one.

And now...this house.

In a passing conversation with my neighbor, Chevy, I mentioned the blossoming idea, thinking he'd look at me like I'd grown a second head. But he didn't. All he said was, "When do we start?"

I've quickly realized that restoration is no joke. It's hard, grueling, and time-consuming. It's easier to let something rot away than to restore it.

But as I glance across the street at Ella pedaling down her driveway on her red bike with the sun in her hair and a smile on her lips, I know that it's not impossible.

She skids to a stop in front of my yard, planting both feet on the ground. "Hey," she greets me. The smile sticks, despite the fact that I was a heartbeat away from kissing her last week at the music festival. Luckily, I refused to let us simmer in awkwardness, so I taped a list to her bedroom window on Monday morning before school:

Reasons Why You Shouldn't Avoid Me Forever

1. You'd miss my amazing lists too much.
2. Who will you play Pooh sticks with? Yourself?
Lame and you know it.
3. We still haven't arm wrestled yet. A life filled
with regret is a life wasted.

—Max

It was dumb but seemed to do the trick. Ella ate lunch with me by the willow tree at school that afternoon and every day since. I haven't tried to kiss her again, even though it's all I've thought about. While I've made peace with my shifting and growing feelings for Ella, I realize her walls are more shatterproof than mine. Just like this old house, it's going to take time and patience to mend what's broken and build something new.

"What are you up to?" she asks, glancing at the tools strewn across my front lawn.

"Fixing up the house."

Her eyebrows swing up to her hairline. "Really?"

"Chevy offered to help me. He's already renovating this huge property a mile from here, so he knows his stuff and has a ton of leftover materials. McKay offered, too, but I'm not holding my breath with him." I pop a hammer in the air, giving it a twirl, then catch it by the handle. "I figure it might take months, maybe even a year, but it'll get there eventually. Progress is inevitable when you put in the work."

Chevy jogs over to us from the adjacent yard, wearing a backward ball cap and a grease-stained tank. He's covered in tattoos, putting my singular tattoo to shame. Chevy is a midthirties bachelor who lives by himself and always has a thousand projects going on at one time. Auto repairs, house flips, landscaping, you name it.

"Hey, darling." He nods at Ella as he approaches, a few pieces of a honey-blond hair sprouting from underneath the cap. "Is Max putting you to work?"

She wrinkles her nose, shifting her weight on the bike. "No, I'm heading into town to grab coffee with Brynn. I've given up on the job hunt at this point, so I'll settle for drowning my sorrows in a lethal amount of espresso."

"That'll do the trick," he says.

"Thank you for the bike, by the way. Sorry I haven't said that yet."

I blink. *Whoops.*

"Uh, sure." Chevy glances at me and flips his hat around. "I fixed it up and gave it to Max years ago when he was still a kid. I'm glad someone is getting use out of it again."

I don't say anything as I stare at Ella and rub the back of my neck.

Realization dawns, filling her eyes. Her lips thin and she nods slowly, gaze fixed on me. "Yeah," she murmurs. "I'm glad, too."

The sound of the screen door creaking open behind us has me whirling around, my attention locking on my father, who hobbles onto the porch step.

He leans forward on his cane, his pants two sizes too big and drooping off his hips. "Is this the pretty girl you brought to the dance?" he wonders, motioning at Ella.

All of my worlds are colliding. I stumble for a response, my throat thick. "Yeah, Dad. This is Ella. She lives across the street."

Ella tosses her bike down and moves across the yard. "Nice to finally meet you, Mr. Manning."

"Call me Chuck." His face lights up. "Did my son get you flowers?"

Sighing, I rub the space between my eyes and wish for a swift death. "Dad, c'mon. She has somewhere to be."

"He did, actually," she replies. "Orange roses."

"Orange?" He frowns. "Interesting. Never gotten those before."

"Orange is my favorite color."

"Suits you. Hey, why don't you come by for dinner this weekend? I'm making brisket."

My eyes pop and I rush forward, stepping between my father and Ella. There's no way she's coming over for dinner. I will take out a credit card and fly her first class to Italy for the most authentic, expensive Italian cuisine I can find before I subject her to the inside of that embarrassing house and Dad's drunken outbursts. *No way.* "Ella doesn't eat brisket."

She huffs. "I love brisket. Thank you for the invitation. I'm free tomorrow."

"No, you're not." I turn to fully face her, my eyes pleading. "We have that thing."

"What thing?"

"The thing with the…*thing*. I can't believe you forgot about the thing."

Chevy tries to come to my rescue. "I remember the thing. It's a stellar thing. You can't miss it."

Ella glances between the three of us, chewing on her thumbnail. Her shoulders slacken for a breath and I think she's about to concede. But then she straightens, stretches a full-toothed grin, and bobs her head at my father. "I'll be over at six." She waves and retreats.

Shit.

Dad looks positively slap-happy. The newfound twinkle in his eyes should have me beaming with relief if I didn't have a heap of damage control dropped into my lap. Chevy sends me an apologetic look before I bolt and chase Ella over to her bike. "Ella, hold up."

She ignores me and begins to pedal, her pace slow and sluggish as she rides up an incline.

"Ella." I jog beside her, watching her auburn hair fan out behind her. "You can't come over for dinner. Dad hasn't cooked in a decade. We don't even have a real oven." Shame heats my cheeks, but I keep jogging beside her, my gait quickening to a run when she picks up speed.

"You think I'm one to judge?" she scoffs, already out of breath. "I'm still living out of boxes because I can't bear to go through some of my old things."

"We barely have walls."

"That's fine. I'll be too busy eating brisket to notice the walls."

"I'm serious. I'll take you out to dinner if you really want to have a date with me." She side-eyes me with a squinty glare. "There's a place off Braxton. They have great risotto."

"I prefer brisket."

"Dammit, Sunny. Slow down so we can talk about this."

"Can't be late for coffee." Ella glances at me, then at my swiftly moving feet like she can't believe I'm keeping up with her. She pedals faster. "See you tomorrow at six." Lifting up, she uses all her strength to ride ahead of me until I give up and slow to a defeated stop in the middle of the road.

I scrub both hands over my face, wondering if I can make history by renovating a house in twenty-four hours.

Fuck my life.

———

I have to put a stop to this.

The moment I see Ella arrive home at dusk and park her bicycle along the side of her house, I slip on my shoes. I wait a few minutes for her to settle inside while I pace the living room and peer out the unglazed window, tug down the cheap roller blinds, then storm out the front door. Dad is sleeping. He'll probably be sleeping tomorrow, too, when Ella comes over for make-believe brisket. And that's if he's not passed-out drunk on whiskey.

The horror of that probable scenario has me racing across the street in record time.

When I make it to her front porch, I knock softly. Footsteps approach and the door widens, revealing a middle-aged woman wearing a blush loungewear set. Two green eyes, a shade darker than Ella's, flare when she spots me hovering in the doorway with my hands buried in my pockets. "Oh, hello there."

"Hi." I locate my manners and step forward, extending a hand. "Max Manning."

She greets me with a surprised smile. "Candice. Are you looking for Ella?"

"Yeah, is she home?" I know she's home, but I don't want my first real impression with Ella's mother to give off stalker vibes, so I attempt to look oblivious.

"She just got home. She's in her room."

"Thank you."

"Max," Candice adds before I make my way down the hall. "It's a pleasure to finally meet you more than just in passing. I never did thank you for saving my daughter's life that day at the lake."

"Oh, uh…" I pause to scratch the back of my neck. "I'm glad I was there. Right place, right time."

"You two have become close, yes?"

"Pretty close. We're friends."

"Did you get her those roses?" Her eyes drift to the kitchen table in the adjoining room where a cerulean-blue vase holds the slightly drooping bouquet.

Those flowers are haunting me.

I fold in my lips and nod.

"Well, they're lovely." She grins brightly. "Let me know if I can make some food for you two."

"I appreciate that. I won't stay long… We're just working on a project together. For school." When she sees me off with another warm smile, I traipse down the short hallway until I land at a closed door. There are three closed doors, but this one has a custom wooden hanger dangling from a nail in the frame in the shape of a horse, personalized with Ella's name in block letters.

Bingo.

I forget to knock and whip open the bedroom door.

Then I freeze.

Ella whirls around to face me, wearing only a lacy black bra and matching panties. She gapes at me, mouth hitching with surprise.

As for me, I just stand there staring at her, not moving, my own lips parted with shock. With more than shock. My gaze rolls over her curves and alabaster skin in slow motion before drawing back up to her face and mess of static-infused hair.

I'm still not moving.

Not. Moving.

"Max, get out! Jeez!" she shrieks, her cheeks flaming. Instinct has her grabbing a bed quilt off the mattress and wrapping herself up like a mortified burrito.

"Right. Shit. Sorry." Still not moving.

She throws a slipper at me.

"Christ…I'm going," I fluster before swiftly exiting the bedroom and closing the door behind me. I lean against the wood and take a deep breath, begging my nether regions to calm the hell down. As I drop my head back, the horse nameplate falls on me and everything is chaos.

I'm putting it back into place when the door pulls open again and Ella stands before me, newly clothed in pajama pants and a tank top that's flipped backward, the tag poking out through the top of her chest.

I blink at her.

"Did my mother let you in?"

"Yes." Blowing out a breath, I do everything in my power to cleanse my mind of the last thirty seconds but fail tremendously. "Sorry. I should have knocked first."

"You think?" Blotches of bright pink dapple her cheeks and neck as she avoids eye contact.

"Can I come in now?"

"No." She swallows, crosses her arms. "Fine."

I sweep past her into the bedroom and try not to trip over the wadded-up blanket on the floor. When I collapse on the edge of the mattress, I brave a glance at her. "I'm used to climbing through your window. I thought the door was a step up."

"Knocking is standard etiquette in both scenarios."

"Noted." I twist my lips and track her as she flits around the room, tossing laundry into bins and stacking textbooks into piles. "How was coffee?"

"It was great. The barista there is super cool. Her hair is blue."

"Impossible to be below average with blue hair."

She throws me a small grin but then it dissolves. "Andy and some guys from school came by for coffee and entertained me with their lack of intelligence, so that was fun."

My hackles rise. "Did you punch them in the face? Please say yes."

"No. I enjoy having a clean record, thank you."

"Self-defense, obviously. Their existence is offensive."

A chuckle slips out. "In Andy's mind, he was on good behavior, I'm sure. All he did was order a coffee with cherry syrup and make a comment about popping *my* cherry."

"He made a comment about wanting to take your virginity?" I stand from the bed, every muscle going rigid as I stalk across the room to where she's

standing by her desk. The top is littered with bookbinding accessories, ivory-and-cream paper stacks, and an assortment of multicolored crafts. It's a little literary oasis of fairy tales and imagination.

I cross my arms and stare at her, awaiting her response.

Ella appears nonplussed. "Yep. I suppose when it comes to goals, you should always set the bar high. After the girl he's dating scribbled the word 'whore' on my locker last week, I snapped and told them all I was a virgin. Now that's the new angle—getting in my pants."

"You're, uh…not interested, of course." I'm clearly fishing. I hover beside her as she aimlessly organizes her desk and then skips over to do the same with her bookcase. It's like she's trying to physically run away from the topic.

"Am I interested in losing my virginity to one of those creeps?" Disgust has her nose scrunching up. "Eww. No. God."

Relief swims through me. I reach for her and curl my fingers loosely around her wrist, pulling her attention away from the scattered books. Her eyes flick to my hand, then up to my face. I have no idea what prompts the next statement, but it probably has something to do with the fact that I just saw her half-naked and now we're discussing sex. "So…you are a virgin."

She frowns. "Don't act so surprised. I told you I was."

"I didn't know if the status had changed since you last told me."

"That was only a couple of weeks ago, Max. And if it *does* happen to change…you'd be the first to know."

"I would?"

"Sure. Cross my heart. If I ever uncross my legs, there's no way you wouldn't know. Immediately. Firsthand."

I sense some kind of hidden meaning, so I squint at her. "Why is that?"

"Because…" She sighs before looking away and then back to me. Nerves skate across her face as her cheekbones tinge a rosy shade of pink. "If I had any desire to lose my virginity, it would probably be with you."

I stop breathing.

I think I make a choking sound.

Fainting and subsequent humiliation are bound to follow, so I swallow hard and inhale a shuddery breath. "Me?"

Blinking repeatedly, she pulls away and stalks to the other side of the room, now interested in a cobweb in the corner. Pulling a duster from a drawer, she swats the webs away. "That part is irrelevant."

Excuse me? I chase her down. "It's not irrelevant to me, Ella." Her face is beet red but she emits cool composure as she returns the duster to the drawer and turns her back to me. This girl just confessed in a roundabout way that she wants to sleep with me. There are a thousand questions teasing my tongue, but all I can muster is, "Why me?"

Ella clears her throat and offers a small shrug. "I mean…you're basically my best friend. And I trust you."

My heart beats like a caged bird longing for the sky. Her words are a shot of sunlight to my veins. Still, I try to act unruffled as I tilt my head and study her through narrowed eyes. I search her profile when she twists around, then fold my arms, trying to keep the smugness out of my tone. "Generally, sex involves some level of attraction. Are you attracted to me, Sunny?"

Her cheeks pinken further. "No, eww, never," she rushes out. "Maybe it's just something to do eventually and I might as well do it with someone I don't find repulsive."

"That's so bleak."

"If I've given you any reason to believe my thoughts veer in a more frolicsome direction, I truly apologize. I'm ashamed."

Sighing, I run my tongue along my top teeth. "Presumptuous of you to assume I'd be interested."

"You would be."

"What makes you so sure?"

She faces me and arcs a brow. "You're an eighteen-year-old straight male. And despite my laundry list of personality flaws, I'm not a monstrous ogre. Physically, I'm at least a six-point-five. Maybe a seven." She shrugs again. "Also, you're staring at my boobs right now."

My gaze shoots back up. "You have a little mole on your chest. I've always thought it was cute. It's shaped like a *T. rex.*"

Ella fidgets, bouncing from foot to foot. "Fine." She clears her throat, glances up at the ceiling. "Seven-point-five. For the intriguing dinosaur mole. But that's where I tap out."

A grin spreads and I catch the way her gaze falls back down and settles on my mouth for a beat. She swallows, flicks her eyes up to mine, then swivels around and runs away from me.

Again.

"Ella. Come on." Begrudgingly, I chase her down for the third time as she glides across the room to make her bed. I watch her gather the giant blanket on the floor and drape it over the mattress. "You can't just drop that bomb on me and pretend nothing has changed."

"Nothing has to change. I was just being honest."

"I like your honesty. But honesty usually comes with a follow-up conversation. You just said you wanted to have sex with me."

She fluffs her pillows, smacking them multiple times until they're the opposite of fluffed. They are now flattened, cotton pancakes at the head of her bed. "I didn't say that. I said *if* I wanted to sleep with someone, it would *probably* be with you. But I also told you I was dying a virgin, so do the math."

I stare at her for a few beats, processing the situation. Doing the math.

The math is in the way she leaned out my truck window and bared her soul to me, crying while our hands locked together, her heart bleeding out of her as I picked up the pieces and kept some for my own safekeeping.

The science is in the way she melted against me at the concert with my favorite songs alive in the air, filling me with hope and promise.

The chemistry is in the way she lights up, brighter than any Taurid meteor shower, every time our eyes meet.

I'm good at math.

The math only adds up to one thing.

I come up behind her until my torso is nearly flush with her spine. Startled, she whirls around, her palms flying up and gently splaying across my chest. She doesn't back away. She gazes up at me with wide, curious eyes, waiting for me to speak.

I school my expression to stay passive. I keep my racing heart in check and do everything I can to keep the quiver out of my voice. "Well...you were right about one thing," I tell her, bending slightly until my lips brush the shell of her ear. "I would be interested."

Fuck it—I might as well be honest, too.

She trembles, inhaling a sharp breath, fingers curling and pressing into the hard planks of my chest.

Ella loves to pretend she's unaffected by me, despite the hand-holding, the heated looks, the compliments and flirting. Her aloof disposition serves as a coping mechanism, gives her power, and it keeps her in survival mode. Because of that, I've respected her brush-offs and stone walls. I let her pretend because that's what she needs to get by.

But she can't pretend right now.

I feel her skin heat. I see her eyes hood. Her breaths are coming quicker and her chest is heaving up and down with anticipation. She's responsive.

She feels me. Everywhere.

Leaning in closer, I murmur, "You were right about that, but you were wrong about something."

Her eyes flutter closed. "What's that?" she asks breathlessly.

I place a soft, featherlight kiss on her temple, drag my lips down her cheek, then whisper in her ear. "You're a fucking ten."

And then I step away.

Her eyes open slowly, like my words were a drug to her veins. She doesn't say anything and just watches me retreat as her arms make a languid descent back to her sides, swaying on shaky legs.

"I'll be over at five thirty tomorrow night," I say, my voice gravelly as I saunter over to her bedroom door. "You're not coming over for dinner. I'm taking you out."

"Max—"

I don't let her argue and walk out of the room, all while pretending like that tiny kiss to the side of her head wasn't the greatest moment of my life.

Chapter 21

MAX

I TOWEL OFF MY SHOWER-DAMP HAIR AS I MAKE MY WAY OUT OF THE DINGY bathroom off the hallway. Tools are scattered at my feet. Tarps are laid out, as if the dirty subfloor needs protection. The house smells like the meshing of sawdust and despair, but there's a flickering of renewed optimism hovering between these barren walls that feels like a subtle but striking parallel to my relationship with Ella. Chevy helped me work late into the night and I have no clue how I'll ever manage to repay him. On the flip side, the only trace of McKay I've witnessed over the past few days has been around school, which is no surprise. I had a feeling he'd make himself unavailable to help with the reno despite his half-hearted agreement over leftovers last week.

After throwing on a clean button-down and my only pair of dress pants, which I wore to the Fall Fling, I tousle my hair in the mirror with some gel and dab a bit of hand-me-down cologne on my neck and wrists.

There's a fresh box of condoms sitting on my nightstand.

It's not like I'm jumping to conclusions or anything, but based on my conversation with Ella yesterday and the electricity that swam between us at school earlier, it's better to be prepared.

Just in case.

At five thirty, I snatch up my wallet and prepare to head over to Ella's house to pick her up for our dinner date. I made a reservation at an Italian restaurant downtown. One of my aunts who lives a few towns over gave me a gift card to Roma for my birthday this past September, so it's the perfect time to use it.

I call out to my father before traipsing down the hall. "I'm going out, Dad. I might be home late."

Rustling sounds ensue. "Wait, wait…hold up, Maxwell."

Sighing, I pause in front of his bedroom door. A few seconds pass and the door swings open, revealing a sight I never expected to see.

My heart flounders. My eyes flare with surprise.

My father stands before me in a dark-gray suit with freshly styled hair.

He clears his throat and straightens out his emerald tie, a timid smile tipping his mouth. "Well?" he prompts, holding his arms out at his sides. "How do I look?"

I scratch my head then rub a hand down my face. "Um…you look great, Dad. Why are you dressed up?"

"For dinner tonight, of course. Your girlfriend is coming over for brisket."

"I…" I don't even know what to say. Not only had I assumed he instantly forgot about the dinner invitation, but I also figured he'd be passed out on sleeping pills or booze. And never in a million years did I expect to see him in a dress suit. My father hasn't worn anything other than ill-fitted jeans and grimy T-shirts in years. "Dad, I–I canceled the dinner. We don't have any brisket."

"Hmm." His eyes narrow. "I was wondering where you were running off to. Well, no matter. We can make something else. The pantry is stocked with pasta and jarred sauces. I'll whip it up."

"We don't have a pantry. We have a shelf of expired canned food and I haven't restocked the fridge yet. There's nothing." My shock is trumped by terror because he's serious. But he can't be serious. I'll die of embarrassment if Ella comes over here and eats our "limited edition" cans of mystery meat. "We can reschedule. I'll pick up some fresh groceries tomorrow."

"Nonsense." He swoops past me, smelling like McKay's cologne. "We'll figure it out. She'll be here at six o'clock, yes?"

"No, I—"

There's a knock at the front door.

Kill me now.

I blanch, my skin starting to sweat.

"Oh, she's early. That's a shining characteristic, Max. Everyone is late these days with no consideration for others." Smiling, he hobbles to the front of the house, his aluminum cane clapping along the subfloor.

I hop over power tools and buzz saws, racing ahead of him to get rid of Ella. It must be Ella. Clearly, she misheard me and thought we were meeting here.

When I reach the small foyer, I yank open the door and come face-to-face with pure beauty.

Words jumble in my throat, catching on my stalled breaths. "Hey."

Ella is a stunner in a little black dress, her hair styled in ribbons of dark-red curls that flow over both shoulders. And in her hands is a foil-wrapped dish. She holds it up high. "I brought the brisket."

She brought the brisket.

She brought the brisket.

I'm not sure whether to yell at her or vomit out a love confession. I settle for a few slow blinks, my eyes panning from the dish in her hands to her face. She's wearing a touch of makeup, her lips ruby red and her eyelids painted with silvery shadow. Long, inky lashes flutter back at me as her smile lifts, looking brighter. "You…brought brisket," I repeat dazedly.

She nods. "I did. You said you didn't have an oven."

"We hardly have a suitable table to eat at. It's a folding table with garage-sale chairs."

"I'm adaptable."

You're perfect.

That's what I want to say, but my father makes his way over to the open door and pokes his head around me.

"Aren't you lovely?" he says with an air of magic in his tone. "Max, look at her. She's beautiful."

Dad latches onto my shoulder with a proud squeeze. I finally make a coughing sound and take a step back, knowing I have no choice but to let her inside. "Yeah, she is."

Ella spears me with a smile and passes through the threshold, her gaze dancing around the messy living area. Normally, I try my best to keep things clean and uncluttered in my limited free time, but we just started this reno, so the space is worse than it's ever been. There's dust and Sheetrock everywhere. There's a blue tarp over the couch because it's the one piece of decent furniture we own and I didn't want it to get ruined by paint and falling debris.

Only one word can sum up how I'm feeling right now as this gorgeous girl I'm quickly falling for assesses my current living conditions.

Mortified.

But her smile doesn't waver as she glances around and then peers back over at me. "Thanks for having me over."

I sigh through a weak glare. "Totally."

Dad nods at the adjoining kitchen. "Let's get the table set up. I'm starved. I can't remember the last time I had a nice hot helping of brisket. Did you make this yourself?" he asks Ella.

"Yes," she says. "Let's just say my mother won't be auditioning for *MasterChef* anytime soon."

"Impressive."

It is impressive. I'm not sure what's more impressive—Ella cooking us brisket, or the fact that my father is coherent, sober, and wearing a full-on suit. My emotions are all over the place. Embarrassment warms my skin, but seeing my father like this warms my heart. And seeing Ella in a pretty dress with curls in her hair and a smile on her face warms my whole damn soul.

She trots over to the folding table in clunky heels and sets down the foiled dish. "Do we need plates or silverware? I'm happy to run back home for anything."

"We're good." I make my way to a hall closet to grab an old tablecloth before pulling Mom's vintage dishware out of a cupboard. There's leftover spaghetti we can warm up for a side. We also have one of those premade salad kits and a jar of French dressing. And a half-full jug of orange juice.

It'll have to do.

Chair legs squeak against the raw underfloor when my father pulls a chair out for Ella. I monitor them carefully as I move from counter to fridge to cupboard.

"You and my son are high school sweethearts, yes?" Dad probes, making a slow descent down to his own chair across the table from her. He leans his cane against the plastic, floral-patterned tablecloth. "Met my wife back in sophomore year of high school. Got her roses every single day until graduation. I know you'll make my son very happy."

Ella flusters, toying with a long curl. "Oh, I don't..." She seems to catch herself, clear her throat, and flicks her eyes to me. "Thank you. You've raised a great son, Mr. Manning."

I've raised myself for the last six years, but I don't say that. Plopping a lump of spaghetti into a cast-iron pan, I crank on the wood-burning stove.

"Call me Chuck," Dad reminds her. "Hey, do you play Scrabble?"

"Oh, um, not really. I played a few times with my brother years back," Ella responds.

"Yeah? I haven't seen him around."

"He...relocated. He's four years older than me."

"Off seeing the world, I bet. That's great. Smart." He nods. "Is he a romantic like you?"

Groaning, I pace over to the table and set down three plates, then unwrap the brisket from the tinfoil. "Dad," I warn. His weird subject changes and personal questions are almost as off-putting as this day-old spaghetti I'm reheating.

Ella shakes her head, sending me a tiny smile. "It's fine. And I'm not really a romantic, if I'm being honest. I'm kind of the opposite."

"Nonsense." Dad swipes a hand through the air like he's slicing her words to smithereens. "You've got a lot of love in your eyes. A lot of it, indeed. You just need to pull it out of you and share it with the world. It's trapped right now. Romanticize your own life."

I'm about to interject again, but Ella holds her hand up, sensing my interference. She stares at my father with a glassy look in her eyes. "What do you mean?"

"I mean what I said, honey. Romanticize your life. Don't live every day like it's your last. Live every day like it's your first. Lasts are tragic. Firsts are exciting and full of celebration. Look at every sunrise like it's the first time you've ever seen colors like that before. Listen to your favorite song like you've never heard such a precious melody. If you make every day a celebration, you'll never get bored in your own story."

I pause on my trek back to the stove. My father's words sweep through me like a tidal wave of warmth. I haven't heard him make so much goddamn sense in years, and the notion nearly brings me to my knees. When I glance at Ella, she's gazing at him with an expression that reflects my own. Her irises glitter with tears; her lips tip up with soft wonder.

What's gotten into him?

Ella inhales a breath. "That's...very wise. Thank you."

"I have my moments." Dad reaches for a serving fork and digs into the brisket. "Let's eat."

We eat.

We laugh.

We play Scrabble until the sun sets and Ella's chair scoots closer to mine, her bare leg flush against my pant leg. When I reach down to grasp her hand, she interlocks our fingers and we stay like that until the fire from the stove flickers to embers and starlight seeps through the window. It's not the first time we've held hands, but I pretend that it is.

It feels like it is.

As the night presses on, I reach over to a dusty shelf and snag the book lying there, the one I planned to give to Ella at dinner. "Hey. I have something for you," I say, tossing it to her. She catches it. "Have you read this one?"

To Kill a Mockingbird.

"Of course," she replies.

Grinning, I watch her glance down at her lap and flip through the old copy of the book, searching for something she knows is hidden inside. When she finds it, she pauses with her head bowed, her orange-tipped fingers curling around the edges.

Ella looks up at me, her smile turning radiant as it catches the light.

"You rarely win, but sometimes you do."

We play one more game of Scrabble.

We're all seated together, having a normal conversation, making jokes and playing board games after devouring the best brisket ever made, as the book sits beside us like a quiet reminder.

And somehow, even with the broken-down walls, plastic tarps, and unpainted plaster…

Ella makes this house finally feel like a home.

Chapter 22

ELLA

IT MAKES SENSE THAT WE'D END THE NIGHT TOSSING STICKS OVER A BRIDGE with moonlight glinting off the water. Silver ripples stare up at us as we lean over, side by side, then race to the opposite railing.

Laughing, I point down at the stream. "I win again. You suck at this."

"I didn't realize there was any strategy involved."

"There must be. I've never seen anyone lose every single time."

Max sighs, shaking his head as he bends over the rail. "The water is cursed."

"Not from my perspective." I match his stance against the railing and our elbows bump together. Even the slightest brush has a shot of heat zipping through me. Glancing at him, I trail my eyes over his profile peeking out from his black hoodie. "Your father was...unexpected," I murmur. "He's not who I thought he'd be."

His jaw tics as he stares down at the glimmering stream. "Yeah. I haven't seen him so clearheaded in years." Max pulls his chin up and stares skyward. "I haven't noticed him drinking lately. He must be past the detox stage."

I twist around, my back to the rail. "He seems like a good man who just lost his way."

"That's what I've been saying," Max agrees. "McKay thinks he's a lost cause."

"Your brother was notably absent at dinner tonight," I note, fiddling with my long, baggy sleeve. I'm wearing Max's hoodie over my black cocktail dress—the one he let me borrow at the festival. It still smells like him. "I'm sorry he's not more supportive."

My knees knock together when a bitter wind whips us in the face and the chill travels down my bare legs.

Pivoting to the same position beside me, Max folds his arms and glances down at the bridge. "Yeah. I keep trying to pull him back and he keeps running farther away. But he's my family, so I won't give up. Blood is thicker than water, you know?"

I gnaw on my lip as his statement slithers through me like tar. "Funny enough, that phrase was intended to mean the opposite of how we say it these days."

Max frowns, looking over at me. "How do you figure?"

"The original passage is actually, 'The blood of the covenant is thicker than the water of the womb,'" I tell him, meeting his eyes. "Contrary to popular belief, it emphasizes that the relationships we choose can be stronger than our family ties. It highlights the value of bonds formed by choice over those we were born into."

"That's interesting."

"Yep. Whenever I want to hate Jonah a little extra, I try to remind myself of that. He's blood but he's no longer my family. He lost the title when he pulled that trigger." I shrug, inspecting my fingernails. "It doesn't really work. I still love him, so it only makes me hate myself."

The human mind is a reckless beast. It clings to memories and bonds, no matter how much logic tells us otherwise. Trying to separate love from resentment, especially for family, is like attempting to untangle intertwined threads. One always follows the other.

"You're freezing."

My legs are bobbing up and down and my teeth are chattering. "It's cold out."

"Michigan is colder," he says.

I can't help but smile as I glance up at him. Max Manning's memory is a steel trap. "I'd rather be cold there."

"Why's that?" His face falls as he moves to fully look at me, his brows creasing.

"It's far away from here."

That's what I keep telling myself, anyway. Miles away from these soul-sucking memories, this judgmental town, and the high-security prison that's a mere three hours away—a place I'm inexplicably drawn to. Far from my mother who poured every ounce of love and savings into her murderous son and left her daughter to deteriorate in the aftermath.

But as I swivel back around to stare out at the open sky, I feel a hand curl around my bicep to pull me back.

Max whispers softly, "It's far away from me."

My heart skips as a shot of sadness rolls through me and our gazes tangle beneath the moonlight. "Max…"

He drops his hand and pulls his cell phone out of his pocket, then begins to scroll. Moments later, a song starts to play.

I grind my teeth together to keep the emotions at bay. "What's this one called?"

"'Atoms to Atoms' by Eyes on the Shore," he tells me, setting the phone atop the bridge rail. "Do you want to dance?"

"Yes."

The answer falls out so easily.

I plan to leave Tennessee behind for good next summer and begin my horse-farm dream. I'll save up for a cut-rate car, or maybe Chevy will hook me up with something cheap yet reliable. Hell, I'll hitchhike if I have to.

But if Max asked me to stay…

I can't help but wonder if that same answer would fall out just as easily.

Hey, Sunny.

Stay.

That's what he said when he pulled me from the lake, and those words still skate across my mind. But I'm in his arms before I can think about them too long. He pulls me close, snuffing out the chill in my bones. He wraps two strong arms around me and props his chin to the top of my head. My face is smashed against the front of his chest as we begin to sway to the music, and visions of a snow-dusted Michigan backdrop melt into images of a future just like this. Dancing on bridges until the end of time. I wonder if he sees that. I wonder if he wants that.

I wonder if I want that.

I lift my head to gaze up at him, my hands dipping lower and clinging to his hips. "If money, time, and distance were off the table and you could do anything…what would you be doing right now?" I ask. I want to know his dreams. Would he be here with me? Would he be somewhere far away from here, chasing a different life? Would he be scaling a mountain, diving deep beneath the wave-spun sea, or writing stories in a secluded cabin in the woods?

Maybe he wants to see the world. Maybe he wants to change the world.

"Anything?" he whispers back.

"Yes. Anything at all."

"I'd be kissing you, Ella."

My heart slams to a full stop inside my chest. It's like a stoplight switched from green to red and forgot about the yellow. I inch backward, hardly able to catch my breath. "What?"

"I'd be kissing you."

"I heard you."

He smiles and ducks his head, lifting only his eyes to my face as his arms drop to his sides. "Want me to clarify better?"

I take another step back, then another. Terror grips me, even though I knew this was coming. That's how these things start. That's how it started with Jonah and Erin.

Friendship.

Hand-holding.

A kiss.

Love.

Everyone dies bloody.

The end.

Panic and terror fuse as one as I swing my head back and forth and swallow hard. "I—I already told you… I'm not looking for romance. I don't want that."

"But you want to lose your virginity to me."

I swallow again. Harder. I try to swallow down that confession in my bedroom yesterday and rip it from his mind. From the universe. It was a stupid thing to say, honest or not, and now Max will never let me live it down. "I didn't mean it like that. It wouldn't be about intimacy or, God forbid, *love*. It would just be about—"

"Getting laid?" He frowns. "That doesn't sound like you."

"An experience. An experience with someone I trust."

"Kissing is an experience, too. Have you ever been kissed before?"

I close my eyes and keep shaking my head, ignoring the burning ball of heat blooming in my lower belly as I envision Max's lips on mine. "Kissing is different. It's more."

He takes a step closer to me. "Your logic is flawed, Sunny. If you think you can only have meaningless, experience-driven sex with me and not feel *more*, I'd be willing to call your bluff."

The feeling blossoms into fireworks and I squeeze my thighs together. "Are you implying you want more?"

"What I want is beside the point. It would be more. That's just a fact."

"Because you're so masterful in the bedroom," I say, forcing out a chuckle. "I'd have no choice but to fall madly in love with you?"

My attempt at levity falls flat. The look in Max's eyes is light years away from anything resembling humor.

He takes a slow step forward, his gaze boring into me. And when we're toe-to-toe and face-to-face on this old bridge beneath the stars, he lifts a hand and grazes his knuckles along my jaw. "I wouldn't know."

His words are overridden by the feel of his skin against my jaw. A rough thumb brushes over my bottom lip and I choke on a small gasp, my eyes fluttering closed. His scent invades me, pure and clean. His touch unravels me. My legs quiver and my heart thumps, and after a few dazzled beats, his statement finally registers. "You wouldn't know what?" I murmur.

"If I'm a master in the bedroom or not."

My eyes slowly open. "I'm sure you're well aware."

All he offers is a stiff headshake.

A frown forms between my brows as implication unfurls inside my chest and I murmur, "What are you saying?"

Max lets out a tapered breath and leans in close, his lips dusting my ear and sending shivers up my spine. Then he confesses gently, "I'm a virgin, too, Ella."

The world stops.

My world stops.

Never once did I ever consider the notion that Max Manning was a virgin at eighteen years old, with a face like his, with a heart like his, with the silent power to take my bleak, loathsome stance on romance, shred it into tiny bits, and toss those pieces to the wind.

Max is a virgin.

When he pulls back, he's staring at my stunned, parted lips. His palm cups my jaw, fingers sliding into my loosening curls. "I didn't want this either," he admits, his throat working, eyes still fixed on my mouth. "There's been no place for girls or relationships in my life. I have too much baggage, too many responsibilities, too much of nothing good." His other hand reaches for my shaking palm and presses it against his chest. He holds it there, his dizzied heartbeats vibrating into my fingertips. "But there's a place for you, Ella," he says. "I have all the room for you if this is where you want to be."

Tears rush to my eyes.

It's too much. This moment, his words, my fingers splayed over his beautiful heart.

I wrench my hand from his grip and run.

"Ella."

He calls after me as my sneakers smack the bridge planks in time with my heartbeats. Crisp air bites at my skin. Want nibbles away at my resolve. Indecision chews me up and spits me out until I don't want to run anymore.

I slow to a stop, out of breath.

When I spin around to face him, I see that he's still standing in the same place. Not running after me. He hasn't moved, but his face is equal parts torture and hope. His hood is pulled back and his hands are balled at his sides like it's taking all of his self-control to keep his feet glued to that spot on the bridge.

"Stay," he says, so softly I almost don't hear him over the howl of the wind.

But I do.

I hear him.

I start running again.

This time I run toward him. I run *to* him. The jaded part of me sprints alongside me with heaving lungs and an achy chest, and I try to beat her in this heartrending race I've never been able to outrun before.

She's a worthy competitor, but I leave her in the dust.

I run until I catch him.

I run until I throw my arms around his neck, lift up on my toes, and pull his face to mine as the song reaches its climax and my heart bottoms out of me.

I win.

My trophy is in the way his hands fly out and cup my face. The gold medal lies within the first brush of his lips against mine.

Max's breath hitches and his mouth instinctively parts to let me in. Our tongues touch, gentle at first. The first note of a song or a single raindrop escaping the clouds. I make a whimpering sound to match the hitch of his breath, not expecting the heat that funnels through me from a single swoop of his tongue.

His tongue flicks mine one more time, then pulls away, and we both go still, waiting, breathless. He inches back slightly, his eyes closed, grazing only our lips together. "This is my first kiss," he murmurs against my mouth as one hand curls around the back of my head and he draws our foreheads together.

"Mine, too," I whisper back, the words shaky, my legs shakier.

My first kiss.

Our first kiss.

His eyes open briefly before he moves back in and presses our lips together. My hands dive into his hair, and I fist the night-dark strands while he parts my lips with his tongue. I open for him. I let him in entirely, and it's no longer a first note or a wayward raindrop. It's a crescendo. A storm. Lightning, thunder, a heart-stopping orchestra.

I moan when our tongues tangle hotly.

All hesitation is snuffed out.

Everything feels perfectly, magically *right*.

I've never felt anything like it before.

Max spins me around and braces me against the guardrail, one hand on my jaw, the other sliding into my mess of loose curls as he squeezes his fist and holds me to him. His tongue strokes against mine, hungry as it explores my mouth. The taste of peppermint gum sets my senses ablaze, fusing with the smell of his earthy cologne and a trace of pine in the air. Our faces angle, tasting deeper, and my leg draws up to link around his upper thigh. A groan rumbles in his throat as we lick and seek and savor. I pull at his hair and he pulls at mine. I grind against him, feeling his erection dig into the juncture between my legs. My head falls back with a gasp, and he trails open-mouthed kisses down the side of my throat. I press further into him, chasing the feeling. Tingles bloom and climb, lighting me up. Wetness slicks my underwear as my dress rides up my thighs.

I'm weightless and floating. Nothing else exists. My whole body trembles as his tongue slides up my neck and he nicks my jaw with his teeth on a ragged exhale.

I want to keep kissing him. I never want to stop.

"Max," I rasp, my grip loosening on his hair as my fingers sift and touch.

His lips are pink and swollen, glistening under the starlight from our kisses. Drowsy, half-lidded eyes stare back at me as he trails his hands down to my hips and tugs me closer. "You taste so good."

"I like kissing you."

"We don't have to stop."

My mind is dizzy, my eyelids fluttering closed as I drag my hands to his shoulders and hang on to him. "I don't want to."

He kisses my forehead. "Come here."

Max lowers himself to sit on the bridge and pulls me into his lap, his back against the railing and my chest flush with his. I cradle his stubbled cheeks in my palms as I straddle him, the hardness between his legs setting me on fire.

We kiss again. We kiss until time freezes, the earth stops spinning, and his tongue in my mouth is all that exists.

I'm breathless when I pull back, buzzing all over. Achy for more. I graze my fingertips down his cheek, the bristles tickling my skin. When his light-blue eyes lift, a vision flashes through my mind. I see a glimpse of a future so different from the one I always imagined. Stargazing in open fields, dancing under the moon, and magical kisses above a slow-gliding stream as music fills the air. "Your eyes," I murmur, cupping his cheek with one hand. "They make me feel seen."

He smiles, blinking slowly like he's drunk on my words, my touch.

Sighing, I press my lips to his hairline and banish the strange new thoughts away. All I want to think about is this moment. "Your smile makes me feel cherished." Then I snuggle closer to him and finish, "And your arms make me feel safe."

Max leans in to press a soft kiss to the side of my head, and I feel his lips bloom with a grin as he whispers back, "I always knew you had a thing for my arms."

Chapter 23

MAX

THE FOLLOWING EVENING, I DREAM OF A SUNLIT HORSE FARM.
Ribbons of gold glimmer off alfalfa fields and chocolate-brown manes as I cast my gaze around the setting. The sweet scent of leather and hay mingles with manure, and I step toward a red barn towering in the distance. Three horses graze behind a locked fence where a girl stands in a bright-orange sundress and straw hat. She's petting one of the horses, humming a lullaby. The melody floats to my ears, sounding haunting.

I keep moving forward, curious about the girl.

Wanting to see her face.

Her hair is tucked into the hat, hiding the color. I call out to her but no sound leaves my mouth. It's a silent plea. Only her eerie ballad echoes in my ears as my feet pick up their pace and I break into a run.

She hears me approaching.

She senses me, even though I can't speak. I can't sing with her. I can't do anything but run, my heart boomeranging in my chest and my boots burrowing in mud.

The moment she spins to face me with the brim of the hat shielding her eyes, the image dissipates. I'm pulled away by something.

Startled, I open my eyes as reality sinks into me and I'm lying in my bed, the room dark, my mind muddy. I blink myself awake as a cool wind whips through the open window and chills my bare skin. My vision is blurry as it adjusts to the haze of black.

And then the scent of citrus wafts around me. Orange honeysuckle and clean shampoo.

The mattress shifts with an added weight.

I lurch to a sitting position and twist my head left, my eyes meeting with Ella's through the dark. "Ella? What…" My voice trails off.

She's crying.

"I'm sorry," she whispers, the words raspy. "I had…a nightmare."

"Shit. Come here." I don't hesitate in wrapping my arm around her shoulders and pulling her against my chest. She collapses onto me, warm tears slicking my skin. "It's okay, Sunny. It's okay."

Sniffling, she reaches for one of my hands and holds on tight. "I had a dream that…h-he killed you."

"Who?"

"Jonah."

Closing my eyes through the pang in my chest, I squeeze her hard. "I'm here. It was just a bad dream."

"It felt so real." She shakes her head, her sweet-smelling hair tickling my chin. "I thought it was real."

"It wasn't real. He's in jail and he's never getting out."

She cries harder, jabbing her nose against the crook of my neck. "He stabbed you," she whispers, splaying her fingers over my heart. "Right here. And then you were bleeding. Dropping to your knees in front of me. I tried to run to you but my legs were frozen. My shoes were stuck like glue to the floor. All I could do was watch."

"Shh." I kiss the top of her head. "It was just a dream."

"I woke up terrified," she says. "I had to see you. Touch you. Know for certain you were still here."

"I'm here."

When her tears subside to addled breaths, she lifts up and sweeps her fingers through my hair. "I'm sorry I woke you."

"Don't be. You can always climb through my window."

A sad smile crests as a quiet beat passes. Then she whispers, "The bicycle was from you."

Swallowing, I nod, holding her tighter. I was wondering when she'd bring that up. "Yes."

"Why? We weren't even friends then."

"Weren't we? I seem to recall you asking for my hand in friendship at the clearing the day of the bonfire." Hesitating, I retract that. "No…we were friends long before that. I saw you in the schoolyard reading a book when I was seven years old. You smiled at me. And that was all it took."

Her irises glitter in the soft glow of moonlight, lashes fluttering thoughtfully. "Thank you for the bike, Max."

"You're welcome."

Ella props her chin on my shoulder and lifts her puffy eyes to me. "Do you really sleep naked?" Her gaze dips to the white sheet pulled up over my hips, then flicks back up.

"Boxers only."

She swallows, glancing away. "I should probably go."

I don't want her to go. She smells like citrus and feels like sunshine. Her palm still rests atop my chest, grazing lightly over my ribs. Her breath warms the side of my neck. One of her legs is twined with mine beneath the covers and there's nowhere else I'd rather be.

When her breathing placates and her hand stops moving, I tilt my head until my temple kisses the top of hers. "Stay," I whisper.

But she's already asleep.

It's still dark and quiet when my eyelids peel open and I stir from a dreamless sleep. There's an added weight draped over me. A drowsy smile tips my lips as I stretch, my limbs stiff but my heart an elastic band of contentment.

Ella rouses beside me, the arm across my chest sliding up until her hand is in my hair and her body is spooning my side. The repositioning has her leg lifting higher until it grazes against the steel rod in my boxers. *Shit*. Maybe I was dreaming, after all.

Must've been a good dream.

She freezes when she notices, because it's impossible not to notice.

I hear her breath hitch, feel the shaky little gasp against my neck as she stills beside me. The moment is charged, heavy. I'm wide awake now, staring up at the stretch of black ceiling. I don't move. I'm afraid to touch her, considering I'm half-naked and rock-hard in my bed with the girl of my dreams fused against me.

She's breathing heavily, husky and ragged. When she presses a tiny kiss to the skin below my ear, I nearly convulse. My fists clench tightly as one knee draws up beneath the covers. Swallowing hard, I inhale a flimsy breath and close my eyes, waiting to see what she does next.

She kisses me again, lingering longer. Then again. Tugging on my hair with her right hand, she lifts up higher to kiss the side of my jaw. She peppers kisses down the bristled edge and makes an achy little sighing sound.

And when her tongue pokes out, I lose it.

I turn my head, bury my fist in her hair, and crush my mouth to hers.

Ella melts into the kiss with a groan, her leg coiling around me in a needy clutch, her boy shorts riding up her legs. She whimpers, moans. She grinds herself into me as I groan right back, our parted mouths pressed together for a moment of stopped time. When her hand releases a fistful of my hair, she drags it down my torso and brushes it over my hardness. I almost die. I'd put money on the fact that my soul leaves my body for one weightless, divine second and levitates through the paneled ceiling.

"Ella," I rasp, pulling back and squeezing my eyes shut as she strokes me through my boxers. I'm scared as shit that I'm going to come. No one's ever touched me there before, save for my own hand. I turn on the pillow until we're face-to-face, her wide, glassy eyes meeting with mine. Moonlight pours in from the open window, highlighting her flushed cheeks and static-mussed hair.

I glance down at her heaving chest cased in a peachy tank top. Pebbled nipples poke through the thin layer of fabric and the animal inside of me reacts. A growl rumbles in my throat as I reach for the hem of her top and start dragging it up her body. Ella gasps again, removing her hand to help me discard it. Seconds fly by as the shirt is tossed to the floor and her milky-white breasts are at eye level. Inching down the mattress, I palm both breasts with my hands and lurch forward, taking her nipple in my mouth.

"Max…oh my God…" she moans, arching her back, pressing into me as she latches onto my biceps.

I nip and suck, then move to the other breast. She is all soft skin and sun-kissed daydreams. Ropes of long hair cascade over her breasts, and when I'm out of breath I grab a handful and pull myself back up, inhaling deep and diving back at her mouth. Both of her arms wrap around my shoulders and yank me as close as I can get. Her leg curls around me until I'm pressed between her thighs and her chest is smashed to mine.

Her head falls back at the contact. "Max," she moans. "Touch me."

I don't hesitate.

We're both inexperienced, but inexperience means nothing when you're fueled by need. Guided by raw feeling. Everything feels right. Every touch, every new discovery, makes sense. Hands simply know where to go and limbs tangle accordingly, while lips and tongues dance in an age-old rhythm.

I slide my hand inside the waistband of her shorts and stroke the damp piece of fabric between her legs.

She cries out.

My other hand whips out to cover her mouth, to hold back the shriek that will have my brother or father barreling into the room, destroying the moment. And that will destroy *me*. I will absolutely drop dead if Ella is forced from my bed before I can make her come.

Her eyes pop over my hand when I slip my fingers into her underwear. She moans helplessly against my hand before I slowly pull my palm back and drop my forehead to hers.

I close my eyes through a low groan as my finger dips inside of her and starts to pump, in and out. Silken warmth tears through me. Velvet fire. Our faces are centimeters apart on my pillow and her warm breaths beat against my lips as little whimpers catch in her throat. My finger is slick, and I insert one more as the curl of her leg tightens around my waist.

When the heel of my palm grinds against her, she bucks against me. "Oh God…" she husks, her fingernails digging into my bare arms. "Max."

"I've got you. I'm here." I open my eyes to watch her unravel. "Hold on to me. Let it go."

She squeezes me tighter. "I… That feels…"

"It feels good, doesn't it?" I swallow, my boxers tight and smothering. "You like it?"

"Yes."

"Do you want to come?"

"Yes…Max…" Her lips are parted, cheeks flushed pink. "It feels so good."

I lean in to kiss her, mouth open and tongue hungry. She kisses me back with the same urgency, both of us moaning and grinding and feeling fucking *everything*. "I have condoms in my nightstand," I murmur, pressing our foreheads back together.

She manages to shake her head. "This…this is good."

My hand picks up speed, two fingers filling her deep, curling into her, angling higher. I thrust hard.

That's when she freezes on a small yelp.

I pull my face away from hers, my eyes flaring. "Did I hurt you?"

Her jaw clenches but she shakes her head. "I'm okay… Keep going."

"Ella." My fingers begin to retreat, but she snatches my wrist to keep me there. To keep me inside of her.

"Please don't stop."

Indecision grips me…until *she* grips me.

Ella slides her hand beneath the covers and inches her fingers inside the waistband of my boxers.

"*Fuck*," I curse, my head rearing back through the wave of pleasure snaking up my spine.

She strokes me. Up and down, her fingers firm.

I keep fingering her, keep grinding my hand against her.

Furious, desperate, both of us on the edge.

I yank my boxers down my hips, sliding them midthigh until I'm freed from the constraints, giving her better access. I'm shameless as I ride her hand and she rides mine. Heat unfurls. Tingles bloom and climb. The mattress creaks as the headboard lightly taps the wall. Ella grinds against me, the slippery sound of my fingers pumping in and out of her echoing through the still room.

My tongue is in her mouth again, messy, clumsy, spurred by rampant need.

She tenses when my hand finds the perfect rhythm, her mewls and whimpers pouring into my open mouth. Her eyes slam shut. Her hand jerks around me as she comes undone.

I force my eyes open to watch as her face twists with pleasure and she lets out a silent, raspy cry, vibrating in my arms.

She strokes me faster, even through it.

And that's all it takes.

My body tightens, ignites, and releases.

A hoarse moan falls out of me as I spill onto her pale stomach before we both collapse with a simultaneous burst of breath.

Ella's eyes flutter open across from me on the pillow, her hand slick and sticky as she loosens her hold. Sweat glimmers on her brow while she stares dazedly at me. I pull my fingers out of her and she winces, a slight hiss slipping through her teeth.

My breath stops. "I hurt you."

"You didn't. I'm fine."

Blinking at her, I yank my hand from her underwear, twist around, and turn on my bedside lamp. When I glance down at my hand, both fingers are tinged with blood.

I whip my head toward her. "Ella…"

"I'm fine, Max. It just felt like a little pop of pressure. It's not a big deal." She leans over the side of the bed and searches for something to clean up with.

I readjust my boxers into place as I inch off the mattress, then pull a fresh T-shirt from my dresser and bring it to her. I turn away while she tends to the cleanup. "I'm sorry," I murmur. "I was caught up in the moment. I should have been more careful." Sparing her a quick glance over my shoulder, I watch as she pulls her tank top back over her head. "I wasn't gentle."

Ella flattens her mess of hair, dragging her fingers through the tangled strands. She looks at me, her cheeks bright pink and eyes still glazed. "I'm okay."

"It shouldn't have happened like that. It should've been when we…" Swallowing, I let my voice trail off, my insides pitching with guilt. I snapped her precious barrier with my fingers like a total idiot. Blowing out a strained breath, I run a hand through my hair and lower my gaze. "I'll be right back."

I pad out of the bedroom and make a quiet retreat to the bathroom across the hall. My reflection stares back at me, revealing flushed skin, disheveled hair, and nail marks on my upper arms. Nail marks from Ella. Because my fingers were inside her and I made her come.

Holy shit.

The gravity of what just happened slams into me as I flip on the faucet and exhale a shuddery breath. As I rinse off in the sink, I watch the water run red with her blood.

The image stabs at my chest.

When I return to the room with a warm, damp towel, Ella is burrowed underneath the blankets with only her head peeking out. I hand her the towel and climb in beside her, flipping off the light. We're silent for a few beats, lying side by side on my bed, before I turn to her. "Are you okay?"

"Yes," she whispers back.

"Are you sure?"

"I'm sure."

"Are you okay…emotionally?"

"Max."

"Yesterday you were loath to even kiss me. Twenty-four hours later, you're in my bed with your hand wrapped around my—"

She slaps three fingertips to my mouth, shushing me. "*Max,*" she repeats.

I open my mouth and bite her fingers, making her squeal with laughter as she scoots closer to me on the bed. We're face-to-face again. As my eyes adjust to the light, her porcelain features slowly come into focus and she lowers her fingers, dusting them against my chin before letting them fall away. Ella inhales, swallowing a frayed breath. "I don't want to run anymore," she confesses.

My gaze skims her face through the darkness. She looks lighter somehow. Softer. "I'm on board with that."

"I'm sorry it took so long for me to say that," she says. "I'm not trying to give you whiplash or make you doubt what's happening between us, because that's not fair. I just... I made a promise to myself that I would never do this. I'd never open my heart to anyone because that would leave me exposed and vulnerable to real pain. And so I've been running for years. No rest breaks. No water. Strained muscles, sore joints, bruised feet."

"Sounds exhausting," I murmur.

"It has been." Pausing, she adds, "But all that running was worth it."

"Yeah?" I press a kiss to her forehead, my hand sliding up and down her arm as I wait for her to continue.

Ella's eyes close through a sigh as she cradles her palm to my cheek. "Eventually, I ran into you."

My heart pounds, bursting with a sense of completion. Because I've been running, too. Running through a dense forest on loop, calling for help, begging for someone to find me before the sun sets and darkness swallows me whole. And then there was Ella. Adorned in an orange dress with red hair and a golden smile, glowing prettier than any molten sunset.

My way out.

I raise my hand and tuck an errant strand of hair behind her ear. "A favorable collision," I whisper, leaning in to kiss the peak of her nose.

A drowsy smile tips her lips as she curls into me with a yawn, her palms clasped around my neck. A few blissful minutes tick by before she murmurs, "Max?"

"Ella," I respond, sleep pulling me under.

"I think I'm Eeyore."

I blink myself from the edge of slumber, an amused frown twisting my brow. "What?"

"I'm Eeyore. From Winnie the Pooh," she says. "I don't want to be, but I am. His friends would try to cheer him up, try to pull him out of his dark hole, and it would work for a while...but then he'd always crawl back inside." She sighs, her eyes fluttering closed. "Eeyore never had a happy ending."

Melancholy trickles through me. I pull her closer, lowering her face to the space between my jaw and my chest, my chin resting atop her mound of hair as I graze my hand through the tresses. "We'll just have to rewrite it then," I tell her softly.

Ella makes a sighing sound, her body going lax against me. "You rarely win…but sometimes you do, right?" she mumbles, her voice fading, her breath shallowing as sleep steals her away.

"Yeah, Sunny. Sometimes you do."

I fall asleep moments later with a smile, knowing that this moment is a beginning.

But as everyone knows…

A beginning is often an end.

Chapter 24

ELLA

Johnny Mathis is music to my ears.

But the only thing echoing louder is my own moaning as Max brings me to ecstasy against my bedroom door with his fingers between my thighs. The mellow vocals are drowned out, overridden by the feel of Max's tongue in my mouth, his opposite hand sliding up my dress and cupping my breast. I arch into him with a whimper. "Oh God…"

"Mmm." His fingers pump in and out, pace quickening. "Kissing you feels like catching the sun," he rasps, his lips dipping to my neck and trailing wet kisses down to my collarbone.

Not that I've had a ton of experience with romance, but that is, by far, the most romantic shit I've ever heard.

It'll be impossible to top.

I smile through the spasms buzzing down below that are funneling into a spine-tingling release. Max presses his face to the curve of my neck as his speed kicks up and he hits just the right spot, causing another loud moan to fly past my lips.

His free hand whips out to clamp around my mouth when I gracelessly unravel and jerk forward. I pull at his hair, my emerald party dress bunched at the waist. "Mmmphxx," is my muffled version of *Max* that doesn't quite articulate right with his hand over my mouth.

I get it, though.

His dad is right down the hallway in the living room. And his brother.

My mom, too.

Actually, everyone is here, and they all probably heard me, including Johnny Mathis.

Yep. He knows.

I come down from the euphoric high and collapse into a sated heap against the door. Slowly, Max drags his hand away from my mouth, his fingertips catching on my bee-stung bottom lip. Turns out, I didn't even need to bother with makeup. My lips are kissed raw, mascara smudged beyond repair, and my cheeks are stained with the natural blush only an orgasm can provide.

I stretch a drowsy, idiotic grin and drape the back of my arm across my eyes as I catch my breath.

Max drops his hand from between my legs, looking smug. "I think you're getting louder."

"You're getting really good at that," I mumble, floating somewhere far, far away. Removing my arm, I blink up at him, my punch-drunk smile still in place and matching his. "Your turn?"

His eyebrows arc. "Sure."

As Max reaches to unhook his belt buckle, a knock sounds on the bedroom door behind me.

Crap!

"Max. Get out here and help us with this stupid lasagna," McKay blares from the other side. "It looks like it had a midlife crisis. You can fuck later."

My cheeks burn to heat-stroke level as I rearrange my dress, searching the floor for my underwear. "Coming!" I call back.

"Yeah. We heard." McKay's footsteps stomp away.

Eyes bulging with horror, I step into my underwear and nearly topple over as I do a one-footed hop. "Shit. Mortifying."

Max follows suit, glancing in the mirror to fix the buttons of his dress shirt, smooth down his hair, and relatch his belt. "I told them we had to finish up a project real quick."

"Mm-hmm. Project: 'Bring Ella to Soul-Fleeing Ecstasy with Nothing But Your Hand' has been well-documented across Juniper Falls. Thanks."

"I tried to shush you."

"We should have waited. There's a dozen people in my house right now."

"You gave me a look, Sunny. And your hair was all pretty against the Christmas tree lights. And that dress…" He pivots toward me, giving me an appreciative sweep with his eyes. "I was toast."

"And then you turned me into melted butter." Grinning, I fluff my hair in the mirror and scrub at the black streaks under my eyes before unlocking the door and hauling it open, while also praying the musk of sex and teenage hormones doesn't seep out.

Max exits beside me, readjusting himself in his pants.

I grin wider.

I'll repay him later.

Music pours from the record player that Brynn! and her dads brought over and "Winter Wonderland" fills the air with snow-sprinkled magic, even though my internal temperature is hovering around the dead of summer in South Florida. Clearing my throat, I tromp across the living room and give a little wave to the party guests scattered across the space.

Everyone stares.

Brynn! pretends to be oblivious as she pops up from the couch in a cherry-red dress patterned with snowflakes. "Merry Christmas!" she beams brightly. She says it like she's bursting through a giant gift-wrapped box, her arms raised high, tinsel raining down on all.

Max gives my hip bone a squeeze before joining McKay in the kitchen to assist with the lasagna, while I mutter a "Merry Christmas" to Brynn! and hope that my dress isn't caught in my underwear. It might be.

Our house is brimful of twinkle lights, savory casseroles, and all my favorite people. A fresh pine tree stands slightly slanted in the main room, taking up half the space. Max helped my mother and I chop it down; then we spent an enchanted Sunday afternoon decorating it with vintage-colored bulbs, silvery tinsel, and nostalgic ornaments we plucked from dusty boxes in the shed.

Almost a month has passed since my first kiss on the bridge with Max, and now it's Christmas Eve. We decided to host a "Friendsmas" to celebrate what feels like a well-earned new beginning for all of us. Honestly, there's a lot to celebrate this year. My relationship status is evolving from "lame and alone, forever and ever" to "tentative girlfriend, even though I loathe titles." I haven't had any notable mental breakdowns recently, Mom and I are on better terms because she's been in a strangely good mood lately, and Max's dad has seemingly crossed over the line into consistent sobriety.

December has been a good month.

Brynn! wraps a shimmer-lotion arm around me and guides me over to the couch, discreetly untucking my dress from my underwear in the back.

Ahh! I knew it.

My cheeks heat, paralleling the warmth in the room from the nearby oven. We both plop down on the giant sofa with Matty and Pete on our right and Mom and Kai's father, Ricardo, on our left. Kai sits across from us on the ottoman, sipping from a tumbler of holiday punch, while the Manning men graciously tend to the potluck feast in the kitchen.

I catch my mom stealing glances at Max, her unspoken approval echoing louder than the clinking of utensils and the subtle hum of conversation in the room. Her gaze trails him as he organizes salad bowls and casserole dishes before she gifts me with a warm, genuine smile. She doesn't say anything. Words unsaid spill between us, and her eyes tell me that she's proud. Relieved. Grateful for Max and our budding relationship that has pulled me from rock bottom, giving me a lifeline.

"My son and I very much appreciate the invitation," Ricardo says, breaking through the quiet moment and leaning back with a cocktail in hand. "It's hard acclimating to a new town."

Mom nods. "We know the feeling all too well. It's nice knowing we're not alone."

"I admire your gumption and strength, Candice. Getting to know you this evening has been eye-opening in the most positive way." When Mom blushes and bites her lip, Ricardo pivots with a timid smile. "Kai told me how kind your daughter has been to him."

"I'm right here, Dad," Kai mumbles through a slurp, his bronzed cheeks pinkening.

Brynn! lifts her foot and gives his ankle a little knock. They share a smile.

"I don't know if I'd say *kind*," I add with a shrug. "I more or less aggressively pursued his friendship. Force was involved. He had no other choice but to submit."

Brynn! giggles. "That's what I did with you, Ella. And now look at all of us!" She sighs dreamily. "One big happy family."

I lean over to whisper in her ear with a grin, "Sisters one day, perhaps?"

Her face falls.

She recovers quickly, bobbing her head up and down and plastering on a smile. "Yep."

Hmm.

Matty pipes up beside us, hoarding an entire tray of Christmas cookies in his lap. He says through a crumbly bite, "Whoever made these cookies is my new best friend. We'll be inseparable."

"We have a spare room at the house," Pete chimes in.

"The offer is on the table."

"As long as cookies are on the table."

Kai lifts a hand then brushes his bangs aside. "Um, thanks. I'll pass on the room and board, but I'm happy to make you cookies whenever."

The cookies actually *do* look fantastic. Every one of them is intricately designed with a different holiday theme, from snowmen to reindeer, looking like they came straight from a prestigious bakery. The guy has talent.

I reach across two laps to snag a candy cane cookie, my eyes popping when I take a bite. "Holy shit. These are crazy good."

"Language, Ella," Mom scolds.

"Holy barnacles. These are crazy good."

"Barnacles are horrific," Matty says, visibly shuddering.

"He has trypophobia," Pete says.

I blink. "Holy frijoles. These are crazy good."

Everyone seems satisfied. Mom and Ricardo continue conversing, inching closer together on the couch with every giant sip of rum-infused punch as their hands wave with extra gusto and the laughter loudens. Matty and Pete are still on the topic of trypophobia, so I decide to leave the adults, grabbing Brynn!

and Kai by the wrists and dragging them away from the new debate about why lotus pods are more distressing to look at than clusters of insect eggs.

Kai looks oddly tipsy as we sneak out the front door to mingle on the porch. I narrow my eyes at him, the crisp December air tamed only by the bright sun. "What are you drinking?"

"Punch," he says.

"More specific."

"Punchy punch."

Brynn! gasps. "You rascal! Can I have some?" He hands her the tumbler with a cooky grin and she chugs it down.

I watch them for a few seconds, taking in their dynamic. They look comfortable with each other. Maybe a little *too* comfortable, considering McKay is on the other side of the white siding. Brynn!'s reaction to my "sisters" comment earlier swirls through my mind and I wonder if there's trouble in paradise.

I blurt out my suspicions, never needing alcohol to loosen my tongue. "How are things with McKay?"

A swallow gets caught in Brynn!'s throat and she forces it down. "What? Why?"

"Just curious. You two have seemed distant lately."

"Oh. Well…things have been a little tense. We've been arguing a lot more, and he seems angry all the time. Besides, I'll be heading to college soon, so I'm not sure where that's going to leave us." Nibbling her ruby-red lip, she averts her gaze and stares down at the porch. "I'm moving to Florida in June. I'll be staying with my aunt while I get acclimated."

"Oh, wow. You were accepted?"

She nods, unable to hold back a smile. "Florida State."

"That's amazing. Congratulations," I tell her, giving her a celebratory nudge with my elbow. "McKay doesn't want to go with you and try to make it work?"

She shrugs. "I don't think so. He wants to stay here with Max."

"Really?"

"I guess. He said they made a pact when they were kids. They're going to travel together. See the world."

This is news to me. Max doesn't really talk about the future, and I suppose

that warrants our *own* discussion. I have no desire to stay in Tennessee, but leaving Max behind sounds terrible. Maybe he'll come with me. McKay can look after their father while he figures out his own path in life.

Kai leans back against the porch rail beside Brynn! and takes back the tumbler, swallowing down the last few sips. "My father wants me to pursue medicine. He's a dermatologist."

"Is that what you want to do?" I ask.

"Nope. I want to be an artist," he says. "Dad says the term 'artist' doesn't exist unless it's paired with 'struggling,' so he's trying to pivot me in a more favorable direction. Favorable for him, anyway." His nose wrinkles with disappointment. "What about you, Ella?"

"I don't really know anymore," I admit, my chest feeling heavier. "My dream was always to move to Michigan and work on a horse farm one day. Maybe even buy it…if I could ever afford to. Lots of acreage, horses that become family, and the prettiest sunrises and sunsets lighting up the stables."

They both smile at me, but I can't manage a smile back.

The vision feels shaky, filling me with confusion. It's strange to think that a lifelong dream, carefully stitched together piece by piece with heart-laced strings and soulful knots, could untangle so easily. Unraveled by a boy and his magical kisses and strong arms. A bridge, a playlist, and a forever dance.

The Michigan dream is hard to catch when my arms are so full of something else.

And it feels too soon to be thinking like that, but I can't escape the overwhelming feeling that Max is becoming a *new* dream—one I never expected but can't seem to ignore.

The door creaks open a minute later, revealing McKay. A scowl paints his face when he glances at Brynn! and Kai standing so close together against the rail, their hips touching. Kai pulls up and sweeps a hand through his hair.

"Food is ready," McKay mumbles before glancing at me. "Max was looking for you."

I clear my throat. "Great. I'll be there in a minute."

He sends us a terse nod, shoots a glare in Brynn!'s direction, then disappears back inside the house. Brynn! doesn't say anything as she moves

past me, her heels clacking against the porch and her bubble-gum smile all chewed up.

I watch her shuffle into the house, her dream of settling down with McKay now morphing into Florida coastlines and a promising new career…while my own dreams hang in the balance.

———————

After dinner, we open grab-bag gifts by the light of the Christmas tree and an assortment of red-and-green candlesticks. Our bellies are full of cookies and lasagna and the room is laughter-lit and song-filled. I'm sitting cross-legged near the tree, fiddling with the fringe on the new jade scarf I received in the exchange.

Max is beside me, his legs sprawled out as he leans back on his palms. "I got you something," he says softly so only I can hear him.

"You did?"

"Yep. I want to give it to you in private."

My eyes flare and my cheeks heat. "Is it another finger trick?"

He snorts a laugh. "I'm saving that for later."

Grinning, I gather my hair and drape it over one shoulder. We haven't had sex yet. I'm still acclimating to the idea of being someone's girlfriend after years of building anti-romance walls made of stone, steel, and bitter bricks. Every time we approach that heart-stopping line, I pump the brakes, overthinking everything. It's ridiculous because we're both eighteen and I know he's ready. I think I'm ready, too, but my bone-deep fears always sneak inside me the moment I'm about to give in. I guess that's what happens when you spend years conditioning yourself to run away from emotional connection and intimacy. You find it's not a switch you can just flip back on when the longing hits.

Luckily, Max is patient.

I pull myself up from the floor and make a clean break from the living room while everyone else is absorbed in conversation and buzzed on punch. Max follows, his hand gently pressed to the small of my back, and we swerve

into my bedroom. I watch as he bends down and draws something out from underneath the bed.

"What's that?" I wonder, eyeing the neatly packaged gift. Silvery paper twinkles under the ceiling light, topped with a big red bow.

"Your present."

"I only got you a gift card to Spoon," I say miserably, which is a local coffee shop in town. It was for fifty dollars, at least. Coffee and scones to last an entire month if used wisely.

He smiles, handing me the gift. "I love the gift card. It's an excuse to take you out for coffee."

"You caught on to my ulterior motives, huh?" Sighing, I reach for the gift and lightly tinker with the bow. "This is too much, Max."

"You don't even know what it is yet."

"I can tell it's too much. And you wrap better than me."

"Yes."

Chuckling, I take a seat on the edge of my bed and begin to peel back the wrapping paper. Max sits beside me and my eyes water. It's true that I don't know what it is yet, but something tells me it's going to cause my heart to dribble out of me and leave a gooey puddle at my feet.

It's probably going to make me fall head over heels in love with him.

Max wrings his hands together as he watches my fingers work. I unwrap slowly because his wrapping job is too precious to ruin. When the tape is undone, I take a deep breath, pause, and then pull open all four sides.

A leather-bound book stares back at me.

I blink a few times.

Stare at it.

Hold my breath.

My fingertips glide along the smooth, coffee-brown texture as my heart does exactly what I expected it to do—it melts.

"Open it," he says softly, our shoulders pressed together.

I spare him a quick glance through dampening lashes, then open the book. The title page shines back at me and my tears fall like rain.

Eeyore's Happy Ending.

I cup a hand over my mouth to hold in the sob.

Max's arm encircles me as he inches closer. "I'm not an expert bookbinder like you, Sunny. But I tried."

"Oh, my God." My hands are violently shaking as I peel back pages and pages of cream and ink. "Max…"

"Kai helped me with the drawings," he says, showcasing the intricate sketches designed with colored pencils. "It's our story."

As I thumb through pages etched with deep woods and vibrant colors, the story comes to life, taking me through a journey of an often-overlooked donkey finding happiness with a fellow reclusive donkey in the Hundred Acre Wood. Their favorite spot is a little clearing where they watch orange sunsets and enchanted meteor showers together. Images detail them skipping stones across the lake while they dance to sun-charged playlists and toss sticks over their favorite bridge, triggering a quick-blooming friendship. As days turn into months, their bond deepens and they find solace in each other's company, their tails securely fastened and swishing happily. Our defining moments are sprinkled throughout the ivory pages, sending my heartbeats into a tailspin.

A childhood park date with an orange flower caught between the donkey's teeth.

Sitting side by side at a bonfire years later.

Dancing together at the Fall Fling.

Watching the Taurid meteor shower in a secluded field.

Playing Pooh sticks on the bridge until the night is sealed with a sweet kiss.

And when I turn to the final page, a new picture stares back at me. A moment yet to come.

A future.

We're sitting beside a beautiful white horse, watching the sky above us sparkle with pretty green lights. "The End" is scribbled in loopy letters underneath the picture.

I break down and cry, covering my face with both hands as my entire body shakes with soul-shattering tremors.

"Don't cry, Sunny," Max whispers, pulling me closer. "Please don't cry."

I feel his lips graze my temple, my hair, my tearstained cheek. Words are elusive. Words are utterly pointless in a moment like this because there are no words that can describe how I'm feeling.

I wrap both arms around him and tackle him to the bed, crying against the crook of his neck as he holds me to his chest and strokes my hair. I can hardly catch my breath as I murmur, "Thank you. That was so beautiful."

"It wasn't lame and cheesy?"

I shake my head. "It was perfect. You're perfect. I don't deserve you."

He kisses the top of my head, still smoothing back my hair. "You deserve so much more than you know."

Sniffling, I scoot off him and curl up against his side, my finger drawing lazy designs across his chest, when a light tapping at the door startles us from the moment. I shoot up in bed and scrub the tears off my face while swatting down my mess of hair.

Mr. Manning pokes his head inside. "You kids all right?"

"We're fine, Dad," Max says, clearing his throat. "Be out in a minute."

"Okay. Well, the camping gear is in the truck. We should try to get there before dark," he tells us, leaning on his cane as his eyes stare off over our heads. "You know your mother hates putting the tents up in the dark."

I stiffen beside Max, my hands squeezing together as my heart thumps.

Mr. Manning must have gotten into the spiked punch.

Max stands, glancing at me before looking back at his father. "Dad?"

He doesn't respond right away, gazing out through the far window with a pinched brow. Finally, he blinks a few times and returns his attention to Max. "Dessert is ready. Blueberry pie." Sending us both a quick nod and a smile, he slowly pivots around and disappears from the doorway.

I watch Max's fists ball at his sides, the planks of his back rippling with tension. I wait for him to acknowledge the odd interaction, but he doesn't. He just swallows and glances my way. "Pie?"

Nodding slowly, I force a smile. "Pie sounds great."

Letting out a long breath, Max ducks his chin to his chest and walks out of the room.

My eyes close as a sad feeling floats across my heart like a rain cloud. But I don't have time to wallow in it because I'm jolting in place when Brynn!'s voice startles me.

"Dessert time," she says, peeking around the door. "Are you okay?"

Her tone is lacking its usual enthusiasm, the words void of exclamation points. "I'm okay. Are you?" As I glance at her from the bed, I swear there are tears in her eyes. Rims of red and smudged mascara.

She bobs her head with extra force. "Sure! Of course. I'm excited for dessert." The smile is also strained as she folds her hands together. "Oh, hey…you should come to Morrison's New Year's Eve party with us," she says. "It's going to be a lot of fun. Live music, fireworks, catered food."

"Oh, hmm. Max and I haven't discussed plans yet." I absently pick at the stitching on the bedcover. "I'll let you know."

"I'm sure Max will go. We can dress up and ring in the new year in style!" She infuses animation into her voice, though it still falls flat. "I have the perfect outfit. We can get ready together. I–I think I need a distraction from all these big decisions."

"College, you mean?"

She bites her lip. "Something like that."

I stand from the bed with a nod, knowing what it's like to need a distraction. A friend. An escape from life's bitter throwdowns. Smoothing down my dress and hair, I lift my chin and send her an agreeable smile. "Okay, sure. It sounds like fun," I concede. "Count us in."

"Really?" she beams.

A subtle unease settles in, a voice inside my head whispering to take it back and choose a quiet night at home with Max.

But I don't listen.

I push aside the feeling and widen my smile. "Yeah," I tell her. "We'll be there."

Her face lights up when I join her in the hallway and we link arms, sharing a tender look before heading to the kitchen for blueberry pie.

I say yes.

I agree to go to the party.

And for the strangest reason, I can't help but feel like I just agreed to a goodbye.

Chapter 25

MAX

D ^AD!"
  Glass shatters. Curse words bounce off the half-painted walls. My heart recoils in my chest as my stomach drops out of me.

This cannot be happening.

No, no, no.

I call over my shoulder for my brother. "McKay, I need a hand!"

The small Christmas tree McKay helped me cut down lays tipped over at my feet, shards of multicolored ornaments scattered across the still-in-progress floors. Dad is on a rampage and it came out of nowhere—first he was helping me with my tie for the New Year's Eve party tonight, his hands shaky as he worked through the stubborn knot. I wanted to look nice for Ella, so Dad offered to let me borrow his dress suit. Money is tight and it didn't make sense to buy something new.

"You look so handsome, Maxwell," my father said, his eyes prideful, smile warm.

"Thanks, Dad."

Trembly fingers fiddled with the teal-blue fabric, sliding down the length of the tie. Everything was fine. Everything was perfect. An enchanted evening of music, fireworks, and midnight kisses that just might lead to more commandeered my mind as the clock ticked down to 8:00 p.m.

Then he paused. My father swayed on the chair across from me, his glimmering eyes turning dull and dazed. He stared straight ahead, attention locked on my chest, before his chin slowly tipped back up and our gazes tangled.

I frowned.

I blinked at him.

"What's wr—"

He erupted.

With one staggering lurch, he reached for Mom's old dishware set on a nearby shelf and started heaving dishes at the far wall, one after the other.

I was frozen with shock.

"You son of a bitch," he snarled through yellowing teeth. "You have no right to be in my goddamn house after what you did."

I grabbed his wrists in an attempt to stop him. "Dad, don't!" I begged, confusion strangling me. "Nobody's there. It's just you and me."

His eyes were feral as saliva dribbled down his chin and he struggled out of my grip. "You're a bastard, Rick. A no-good parasite who stole everything from me."

I reached for him again before another plate left his hand and shattered near the front door. "I'm taking you to the hospital."

"The hell you are!" Dad sliced an arm through the air and everything on the kitchen table went flying: a vase of poinsettias gifted by Ella's mother, two half-filled mugs of cocoa, and a candle that caught on the lacy tablecloth and quickly bloomed into a deadly spark. I raced to put out the traveling flame before it burned the entire house down and looked up at my father as he headed to his bedroom, knocking the tree down along the way.

Smoke billows now as my heart dismantles, one horrified piece at a time. "McKay! *Fuck*," I seethe, knowing my brother is in his room, right down the hallway. I yank the cloth from the table and wad it into an angry ball, the acrid odor of burning fabric making my stomach roll.

McKay slogs down the hall looking like shit. Dark, glossy eyes meet with mine as my chest heaves. I toss the tablecloth aside and fist my hair. "Something is going on with Dad," I tell him, kicking at the mess all over the floor.

My brother sniffs, glancing around at the destruction. "You sound surprised."

"He's sober. He's been *sober*," I insist. "Something is wrong. I don't care what he says, I'm taking him to the hospital."

"Good luck with that." More crashing sounds blast from the other side of Dad's bedroom door.

Frowning, I narrow my eyes at McKay. "Are *you* sober?"

"Nope."

"Awesome. Fucking brilliant." I scrub a hand up and down my face. "I need you, man. I can't keep doing this alone."

He lets out a humorless chuckle. "Alone?" he parrots mockingly. "You're not alone. You have a pretty redhead on your arm who thinks you're the center of her universe. You have Dad's undying love and always have. You have a shining future ahead of you."

I gape at him, still frowning.

"You have everything and I have jackshit." His jaw tenses as he folds his arms. "Brynn dumped me."

I can't help the stab of sympathy that hits me, despite it all. Swallowing, I look away, down at the scattered glass. "I'm sorry."

"I'm sure you're devastated."

"I am. I was hoping it would work out between you two."

"Mmm." McKay steps forward, his balance wobbly. "You knew it wouldn't. When does anything ever work out for me?"

Anger overrides the sympathy. "Knock it off with the self-loathing bullshit. You're better than that."

"But not better than you."

"It's not a competition!" I shout, throwing my hands up. "What happened to you? What happened to us?"

"*You* happened." He shoves a finger in my face. "You and your good luck, your moral high horse, your inability to ever see me as your equal…and *her*." His finger shoots to the front window, aimed at Ella's house. "Your happy ending is written in the stars, isn't it? You get the girl. You get the fairy tale. And I get nothing. The-fucking-end." He punctuates each word, his fury climbing.

Mine does the same.

His words aren't fair.

"Guess so," I mutter. "I'm leaving after graduation." My heart palpitates at the admission because it's not something Ella and I have discussed yet. But I know it's what she wants…and I think it's what I need. Stepping closer, I cross my arms and stare him down. "I've held down the fort for years, ever since Mom left. I've sacrificed everything for you, for Dad, for this house and this family. Now it's your turn. You can take on some fucking responsibility for once. You can take care of Dad while I try to live a semblance of a life."

McKay's teeth clack together as he processes my tirade. "You're leaving with her?"

"Yeah, I am."

"You're an asshole."

"*I'm* the asshole?" I counter. "Christ, McKay. I've done *everything* for you. Cooking, laundry, taking on the role as Dad's caregiver while you drink with your buddies, play basketball, date, live, and enjoy your youth. I finally have something worth living for now and I…" I let my voice trail off, regretting the words instantly.

His eyebrows rise with distinct hurt. Silence festers between us, only compromised by the echo of my careless words. McKay looks down at his feet, his expression wilting. Muscles locking. "Something worth living for, huh?"

I blink, shaking my head. "I didn't mean it like that."

"You did."

"No…no, I just meant that I finally have something for *me*." I slam a palm to my chest. "I deserve that. I've earned that."

"Right." The fight leaves him as he takes a step back and glances down the hallway to where the noise has since quieted. "I need to clear my head."

"McKay—"

"Don't follow me," he says, spinning on his heel. "You're right, Max—you deserve a life free of your useless tagalong brother. Doesn't matter the pact we made when we were kids. It doesn't matter that I've spent years distracting myself with pointless bullshit, begging for time to speed up so we could finally get out of this town together and chase the dream you promised me."

My lips part but no words fall out.

Tears blur my vision.

I think back to summers at the lake when we'd dunk underneath the water and stare at each other through the wall of murk and gray. A future unfolded there, a future for both of us. Somewhere far away from here, the two of us traveling the world, sightseeing and leaving it all behind for good.

I promised him that.

"You and me, McKay," I said to him as we dried out by the embankment's edge, staring up at the clouds. "One day, it'll just be you and me."

Guilt gnaws at me, mingling with bitterness and bone-splintering sadness. We were just kids then. I didn't think he'd be hanging on to those innocent words through adulthood, waiting for me to pack my bags and haul him away from here.

I don't know what to say. I realize now that words have weight. Words have consequences, a power to root themselves deep within a person, shaping futures, and disassembling even the most resilient bonds. Words are never innocent. They're either weapons or remedies. Like seeds, they grow and expand, becoming skyscraping trees or invasive weeds.

McKay stumbles into his shoes and searches for the keys to the truck. "Happy New Year," he mumbles, headed for the front door.

"McKay, wait. You can't drive."

"Try and stop me."

"I'm sorry. Please, let's talk about this and—"

The door slams shut and everything goes silent. I glance around the chaotic house, my emotions in my throat, my heart still pounding. I think about Ella getting ready with Brynn, excited to ring in the new year with me, eager for an easy, romantic night watching fireworks paint the lake in every color.

I rub my face with both hands, then loosen my tie. Stomping toward the bathroom, I pull a pill bottle out of the medicine cabinet, sprinkle two tablets in my palm, and fill a paper cup with water.

Dad is belly-flopped on the mattress when I enter his bedroom. "Dad," I call out. "Take these to help you sleep."

"Mmmph," he says.

"Please."

I wonder if he hears how much pain laces that single syllable. He lifts up slightly, twisting his head toward me on the pillow. "Maxwell," is his groggy greeting.

"I'm taking you to the doctor tomorrow, first thing in the morning. You're not well."

He slow-blinks in my direction as I set the pills and water on his bedside table. My father reaches for the items with a quivering hand and swallows down the sleeping pills. "I'm fine, Son. I just need to rest." He chugs the water and collapses back to the mattress with a tired sigh. "Thank you for taking care of me."

"Yeah." My jaw is tight, my fight weak. "Happy New Year."

"Hmm," he mumbles, his eyes closing. "Give your girl a kiss at midnight."

I try not to let his words coil like a snake around my heart. "Good night," I whisper, leaving the light on as I move out of the room.

There's no way I can get Dad to the hospital on my own right now. I need McKay's help and he left me here alone...*again*. I have no wheels, no hope, and no girl to kiss at midnight. All I have is this mess to clean up and a daunting new year ahead that looks a lot less clear.

After standing the tree back up, I call Ella, one hand fisted in my hair as I pace back and forth in my suit, the teal tie hanging loose.

She picks up on the second ring, her voice chipper. "Hey. Brynn and I are almost ready to head over to the party. Just give us five more min—"

"I can't go." I squeeze my eyes shut, heavy disappointment stinging the back of my throat.

A long pause. "What?"

"I can't go to the party, Sunny. It's Dad. I don't know what the hell is going on...one minute he was helping me with my tie, the next he was chucking dishes at the wall." I swallow hard, forcing back tears. "He was hallucinating. Seeing things that weren't there."

"Oh, my God. I'm on my way. Brynn can drive me—"

"No," I say quickly. "You can't come over. It's not safe here."

"Max—"

"I'm serious. Something's wrong. It's like he was having one of his drunken outbursts, but I don't smell any alcohol on him. I gave him some sleeping pills to get him through the night. I'm going to take him to the hospital tomorrow..."

My voice trails off as I scrub my jaw. "I thought it was the booze before, but he's been sober, Ella. I'm scared that it's something else. Something worse."

"Max," she whispers. "I'll go with you tomorrow. I want to be there."

I nod, grinding my teeth together. "Yeah. Okay. Tomorrow."

Her raspy sigh filters through the phone. "I'm so sorry, Max. Where's McKay? Is he with you?"

"No. We had a fight and he stormed out a few minutes ago." I pinch the bridge of my nose, shaking my head. "Brynn dumped him today, so he's drunk and miserable."

"Yeah," she murmurs. "She told me."

"He said he needed to clear his head. If he comes back, maybe I can meet you out for a little while. McKay can watch over Dad. Otherwise…have fun. Have the best time, okay?"

She sounds like she might cry. "I want to be with you."

"I know," I tell her, wanting that more than anything. "But you deserve this. Dance the night away with Brynn, eat a shit-ton of carbs, watch the fireworks over the water. And then tell me all about it. Please don't worry about me."

"Max…I don't know. I feel like I should come over," she insists. "It won't be the same without you."

A sad smile crests as I squeeze the cell phone in my hand and inhale a hard breath through my teeth. "Call me later, all right? I'll be here."

"Are you okay?" she asks softly. "Did…he hurt you?"

Yeah.

He hurt me.

But I don't say that. "He didn't hurt me. He's sleeping now. I'm fine."

"You're sure?"

"Yeah, I'm sure. I…" *I love you. I want to climb through your window later and make love to you until the sun rises and a new year dawns. I want to ride horses in fields of gold and catch sunsets and marry you on our favorite bridge.* Reining in my emotions, I whisper a final send-off before disconnecting the call. "Happy New Year, Sunny Girl."

I toss my phone on the couch, pull off my tie, and collapse on the floor strewn with glass.

Chapter 26
ELLA

PARTY NOISE BLASTS MY EARDRUMS AS BRYNN! GUIDES ME THROUGH A SEA of people in her Barbie-pink cocktail dress. She did an impeccable job of covering up her swollen eyes after crying on my shoulder for an hour while we got ready in her bedroom.

I don't exactly want to be here without Max, but my friend needs me, too. She's grieving.

Flamingo-tipped fingers curl around my wrist as Brynn! pulls me between a cluster of fellow seniors. "This house is amazing!" she declares, chugging down a tumbler of punch.

I don't like alcohol, so I'm sipping a watered-down Coke, wishing it was Dr Pepper. "I guess."

Pursing my lips, I follow her into the dining area, where four football players are tossing ping-pong balls into cups of warm beer. I cringe. One of the guys happens to be Andy's minion, and it would be a disservice to his character if he didn't take the opportunity to torment me.

"Sunbury!" He sends a catcall my way. "I called dibs on one of the bedrooms for us. Nice king bed and silky-ass sheets. There's one of those vanilla-scented candle thingies in there. Heard it's an aphrodisiac."

If my eyes rolled any harder, they would land in last week. "You couldn't arouse me if you came with a user manual and a troubleshooting hotline."

"We'll see."

His eyes track down my body, from my cleavage to my bare legs that Brynn! insisted on spritzing with shimmer-dusted body mist. They are still as pale as the Michigan snow, but now they glitter. My black party dress is the same one I wore to dinner the night Max and I had our first kiss and is one of three that I currently own.

Three dresses, glitter, and an end-of-the-year kegger.

I don't even recognize myself.

The party presses on amid flip cup tournaments, loud music, and drunken laughter as I lean back against a wall and wave hello to Kai when he appears, looking dressed to impress.

"Kai!" Brynn! singsongs, leaping into his arms for a bone-crushing hug. "You made it!"

Kai grunts softly at the impact, then blushes, his cheeks tingeing pink as he wraps one careful arm around her waist. "I had to sneak out. Dad says parties are for troublemakers and social butterflies. We'll see which way I'm leaning by the end of the night."

"You'd make a lovely butterfly," Brynn! says, inching back to fix his collar. "You already have the grace for it. All you're missing are the colorful wings and a penchant for flowers." She bops him on the nose, her laughter infectious, all remnants of McKay tucked away for the time being.

A sad smile hints when I think about Max. I imagine him here in his dressy clothes, hair gelled up, dimples gleaming. Sighing, the vision only amplifies when I watch Kai and Brynn! start slow dancing to a moody ballad, drifting toward the kitchen, lost in the moment. Something is clearly brewing between them, and I can't help but wonder if it triggered the breakup.

As I lean against the wall, spinning my empty cup between my hands, something catches my attention on the other side of the patio doors.

My heart stutters.

Max?

I blink, frowning.

No…the hair is too long, the sweep of his shoulders notably different. My eyes narrow, making sure I'm seeing things correctly. With no alcohol in my system, I can only determine that I'm indeed staring at McKay stumbling through the backyard.

That's weird.

I have no idea why he'd show up tonight, knowing Brynn! would be here.

Swallowing, I pull up from the wall and weave through the crowded room. McKay looks awful. His shirt is wrinkled, his hair a disheveled mess as it teases his crooked collar. My pulse trips with empathy. He's my boyfriend's twin brother and he's grieving, too.

Brynn! said he took the breakup hard.

I watch as he slumps down in the grass near the edge of the lake and dangles a beer bottle between his knees. Nibbling my lip, I look over my shoulder at Brynn!, finding her deep in conversation with Kai in the corner of the room, both of them in their own little world as they sway to the music, a small-sized gap between them.

I shouldn't tell her he's here—it'll only put a damper on her night.

Though my loyalties feel divided, I decide to see if McKay is okay and slip out through the patio door, quietly closing it behind me.

It's barely forty degrees outside and the late-December air nips at my skin. I pull the sleeves of my black cardigan down over my palms and cross my arms across my chest for warmth. McKay doesn't notice me as he faces the opposite direction, slinging back a few clumsy swallows of beer. I clear my throat as I approach. "McKay?"

He pauses mid-sip and slowly lowers the bottle, his head tilting slightly until I appear in his periphery.

"I didn't think I'd see you here."

"Mmm. Can't find any place I belong these days."

My ballet flats smash along the chill-laden grass. I've never been great at comforting people and that's probably because I've never been a notable source of comfort. It's hard to be sunshine in someone's cloudy sky when *you're* a dreary gray cloud.

I glance out at the lake, the water calm and free of ripples. When I'm standing right beside him, I hug myself tighter to counter the biting temperature and let out a sigh, my breath falling out in a plume of white. "Not belonging anywhere is relatable," I tell him. "If you need someone to talk to, I'm willing to offer up my dubious services. No guarantees, no refunds."

He looks up at me, his eyes glazed and intoxicated. "Why would I want to talk to you?"

"Valid point."

"No offense," he adds, taking another swig of beer.

"None taken. Which, might I add, could be a reason in itself. I'm impossible to offend. If I'm part of your problem, you can ambush me with your anger and misery and I'll take it like a champ." I flash him a smile of forced enthusiasm. "Give it a shot. Do your worst."

His eyes narrow through the lowlight as he stares up at me. "You're kind of weird."

"Love that. Keep going."

"Off-putting, too."

"Part of my charm, if I have any at all."

"I'm not entirely sure what my brother sees in you."

"Right there with you."

A partial smile slips as McKay looks up at me, his beer bottle half-tipped over in the grass. When he peers back down at the ground, the smile fades. "He wants to leave town with you after graduation and I don't understand it. He promised that he'd leave with me. *Me*," he says, agony lacing his words. "He barely knows you and I'm his twin brother. It's bullshit. It's not fair. He says I've abandoned him, but he's never once tried to chase me down or win me back. He's never fought, never made me believe we're a team…so why bother? Why fight for a father who doesn't even know I exist? Why rebuild a house that has never felt like a home?" He closes his eyes and lets out a rattled breath. "I thought I was the endgame, the grand plan…but I guess I've always been the *backup* plan. I was there until something better came along." When he glances up, his dark-blue eyes look black. "You came along, Ella. *You're* the endgame."

My heart stutters.

It gallops with surprise, because I didn't know Max wanted to leave town with me.

It teeters with guilt, because now McKay is an innocent casualty in our escape.

And I know what that's like. I understand what it feels like to be abandoned and overlooked by the people you love. The people you trust. The ones who always said they'd be there.

I blink back the mist glazing my eyes and duck my chin.

I'm not offended… I'm just sad.

I'm sad for McKay.

Shaking his head, he pulls himself up from the grass on wobbly legs, leaving the near-empty beer bottle behind. He sweeps past me, smelling like booze and cheap cologne. "Let's go for a walk."

My head pops up, a baffled frown furling. "What?"

"Come on."

He's already trudging ahead of me, toward the tree line that borders the lake. Hesitating, I glance over my shoulder at the brightly lit house swarming with life and music. Silhouettes dance and sway behind curtained windows and teenagers fill a bubbling hot tub, squealing and splashing with cocktails in hand.

When I look back at McKay, he's yards ahead of me, dissolving into the stretch of darkness.

Worried about him going into the woods alone and intoxicated, I follow.

I jog forward, catching up to him before he reaches the trees. "Did I infect you with my invaluable advice and positive spirit?" I ask, my feet moving at double the speed to maintain his pace. "Maybe I'm cooler than I thought."

"You're not," he mutters. "But you're not a terrible listener."

"I'll take it."

We walk in tandem for a few minutes, sticks and leaves crunching under the soles of our shoes. McKay's balance is unsteady as he swats bare branches out of his way and staggers left and right. He doesn't say anything, so my lone skill as a semi-decent listener feels wasted.

The path through the woods is inclined, causing my calves to ache and the bottoms of my feet to throb through the thin shoes. I'm in no position to be hiking right now. I glance at McKay, still trying to keep up with his longer strides. "We should probably head back. How drunk are you, anyway?"

"Not enough." He ducks underneath a leafless branch. "What has she said about me?"

"Brynn?" I wonder.

"Obviously."

We make our way through the thick trees until we come out near a sloped bluff overlooking Tellico Lake. Moonlight serves as an eerie flashlight, casting a glow on the still water. "She's really upset. She was crying all night before we got to the party."

His breath is a tangible cloud when he exhales. "Not what I asked."

My throat tightens through a swallow. Our feet come to a stop and McKay falls to a sitting position just before we meet the edge of the promontory, collapsing with a graceless plop. I follow suit, taking a seat beside him and crossing my legs. "She just said that it wasn't going to work out. She said you were acting jealous over Kai and things were tense. She's leaving for Florida in a few months, and you're staying behind, so breaking up felt like the right thing to do."

"Jealous," he mutters with contempt. "You think? They've been all over each other since he moved here. It's impossible not to feel pissed off and hurt when I'm constantly catching them together, flirting and making moon eyes at each other."

I pick at the blades of grass. It's not my place to speak on my friend's behalf, so all I say is, "I'm sorry you're hurting. I know it sucks."

Grumbling, he pulls something out of his front pocket. It's a miniature liquor bottle that he quickly pops open, then tips back, drinking it all in one swallow. "It won't last between you and my brother, you know."

I frown. "Why not?"

"He's never had a girlfriend before. He's completely clueless."

"I don't think that matters. I've never been in a relationship, either."

"You guys fuck yet?"

I blink over at him, my cheeks warming despite the chill in the air. "That's none of your business."

He shrugs, spinning the empty bottle between his fingers. "Just a question. You don't strike me as a prude."

I tinker with the hems of my sleeves and fold my arms, looking back down at the grass. "No. We haven't."

"How come?"

"I haven't felt ready yet. Romance was never a part of my plan, so I'm taking it slow." I feel him staring at me, waiting for more. "Sex complicates things. It makes it harder to let go, and I wasn't sure what direction we were going in after graduation."

He makes a humming sound. "Well, congratulations, he's whipped." McKay flicks the bottle aside, then kicks it over the ledge of the bluff with his shoe. It makes a tinkling sound as it plummets down below, reminding us of how high up we are. "Tell me, Sunbury…what makes him better than me?"

My arms cross tighter across my chest. "Nothing. You're just different."

"We're nearly identical."

"Your personalities are different. You're not the same person."

"So, what makes him better than me?" McKay takes out a second bottle of liquor and downs it, tossing the empty glass beside him.

Then he slowly cants his head in my direction, his eyes looking cloudy and glazed against the moonlight. I'm not sure how to respond to the question without upsetting him further. I can't put a definition on a feeling. Max speaks to my soul. He complements me in all the best ways.

Inhaling a breath, I look over at him and our eyes meet. "He saw me when no one else did," I murmur. "He heard my truth when everybody around me whispered gossip and lies. He wanted to know *me*…not the rumors. Not my past. Just…Ella." I watch his brows dip with a thoughtful expression. "Max found me when I was lost," I tell him gently. "And I think that's the only way to recognize your real home. You need to be lost first. You need to be wandering, forgotten, misplaced. Only then will you truly know where you belong."

My heart twists with epiphany. With realization. My pulse speeds up and my breaths falter as the weight of my words trickle through me like a warm waterfall.

McKay seems to sense the gravity of my admission and his eyes soften. Nodding, he stretches out his legs and stares out at the dark water bleeding with darker sky. "I envy you both. Must feel nice to finally belong somewhere."

A small smile lifts and I extend my hand, placing it atop his knuckles in the patch of grass between us. "You'll find your place. I know you will. My brother used to tell me…" Emotion causes my voice to hitch, so I pause to regroup. "My brother would tell me that when things don't work out, it's because something better is waiting for you."

"Sounds cliché. Bullshit to help us cope when we can't do it ourselves." McKay's words start to slur as he sways side to side. He glances down at my hand on his, his Adam's apple bobbing in his throat. "Not to mention, he's a murderer."

I ignore that last part. "There's nothing wrong with needing help."

"You offering to help me, Sunbury?" His dark eyes lift, half-lidded. "Maybe you're not so bad."

Part of me wants to say: *The notion that you thought I was "bad" in the first place is one big difference between you and Max.*

But I don't want to make things worse.

I pull my hand away and offer him a shrug. "Sure. I can try."

"Yeah?" He scoots closer to me on the grass until our hips bump together. The alcohol has him nearly toppling into me as his face tilts and his nose skims my hair.

I stiffen.

"Mmm," he says. "You smell nice."

My stomach pitches, his proximity causing me to inch away. "Um, thanks," I mutter. "We should probably get out of here. It's almost midnight and the fireworks are going to start soon."

When I move to stand, his hand whips out and curls around my wrist, pulling me back. Frowning, I glance at the contact.

"Don't leave," he mumbles.

"McKay," I state, slithering free from his grip. "We should go."

"Don't want to. I jus' need a friend. You said you'd try to help me."

"I don't know how to help you right now. You're drunk. We can grab coffee tomorrow if you want."

"No." He snags my wrist again. "Stay."

Stay.

Somehow, the word sounds far less reassuring coming from him.

I shake my head and try to move away. "I don't want to. I'm cold."

"I can keep you warm." His eyes dip to my mouth.

A tense beat passes between us and I freeze in place. I can't move, can't form a cohesive thought. His eyes hood as he stares at my parted lips, still swaying, drunk on booze and bitterness.

And then he leans in.

He leans in to kiss me.

Oh my God.

All my senses whoosh back like a sharp wind and I pull back quickly, horrified, shoving at his chest. "What the hell are you doing?"

My heart pounds.

Anxiety prickles the back of my neck and dances down my spine.

He's still leaning in, far too close, a smirk lifting half his mouth. "Think I was gonna kiss you."

"That's not okay. I want to leave now." Glancing around the empty bluffs, I become fully aware of the fact that we're all alone up here. I can barely make out the lights from the house across the lake. The cold breeze picks up, sprinkling more goose bumps up and down my arms and legs. "I'm going back to the party."

As I move to pull myself up, McKay snaps his hand out and latches onto my cardigan. "Why would I wanna go back there? My ex-girlfriend is there, probably getting naked with that Kai kid. Fuck that. I like it better here." He yanks me down with surprising force and I tumble into his lap. "I like you more. I want to know what my brother sees in you."

Fear grips me like a barbed noose. I scramble to get free as both of his arms wrap around my middle to keep me in his lap. He moans when my ass grinds against his groin in my attempt to escape. "McKay...let me go," I say, my voice shaky, tone pitching. "I'm serious."

Logic tells me this is McKay. This is Max's twin brother and he would never hurt me. He's drunk and not thinking clearly, and any minute now, he'll apologize and let me go.

This is a misunderstanding.

An awkward, uncomfortable misstep.

But my instincts are flaring, telling me otherwise. They sense danger, regardless of who he is.

"That feels good," he whispers in my ear, grazing the tip of his nose through my hair. "Feels good when you wiggle like that."

Then his hand crawls up my torso to cup my breast and he buries his face in my neck, inhaling deeply.

No, no, no.

This is wrong.

This is so wrong.

"McKay, stop it. Don't touch me." I peel his hand off my chest and rocket forward, my heart in my throat.

He pulls me back.

I scream.

"What the hell," he growls, his head popping up while one hand slaps across my mouth to keep me quiet. "Jesus. Someone'll hear you."

I keep screaming, the sound muffled by his palm.

"Knock it off, Ella. Fuck…just hold still!" He grips me tighter, squeezing me, until I can hardly catch my breath.

Kicking my legs, I try to find stability to haul myself up. I scratch at his arms, writhing, desperate to flee. Terror sinks into me as my adrenaline spikes and my survival instincts fire tenfold. When one of his hands trails down my body and slips between my legs, prying them apart, I swing my head backward until my skull connects with his forehead.

He gasps out a pained groan and releases me. A bone-rattling scream lets loose as I struggle to find my footing, and then I jump to my feet and run.

I hardly make it a few steps when a hand flies out and grips my ankle.

I shoot forward, landing facedown in the grass, my chin connecting with hard earth. My teeth slam into my tongue and blood fills my mouth.

Tears blur my vision as pain renders me paralyzed long enough for McKay to flip me over and snatch both of my wrists, pinning them above my head.

He straddles me.

I stare up at him, blood coating my mouth and jaw, my chest heaving with panic. Dark, shaggy hair drapes over his face and his eyes glint with black ice. "Please, please, get off me," I beg, squirming beneath his heavy weight, trying to rip my hands free. "Get *off* me!"

"I don't wanna hurt you," he slurs. "Jus' hold fucking still."

"McKay, stop! You *are* hurting me!" I shout. Tears slide down my cheeks, mingling with blood. "*Somebody help me!*"

He clocks me across the face.

"Shut. *Up*," he hisses, eyes wild.

More pain zips through me, head to toe. I watch as something takes him over like a sinister possession. He looks crazed, out of his head.

I fight.

I'm screaming and pleading, kicking my legs and struggling to free my arms. The moment he uses one hand to tug my dress up my thighs and yanks down his zipper, I pull free, lifting enough so I'm able to draw my knees up and fling my legs forward, kicking him in the chest.

I jump to my feet, my tongue swollen, blood spilling down my chin and neck. My cheekbone is bruised, my body racked with tremors and mind-numbing shock.

McKay is on me before I can gain any speed. He flings me around, grabbing me by the upper arms and yanking me against him.

We stumble.

"Christ, hold still!" he says through his teeth, spit misting my face. "Stop running!"

Sobs tear through my chest. I've never been more petrified. He grapples with me, his panicked hands in my hair, around my neck, trying to contain me. "Stop it, stop it! Help me!" I shriek, fighting back, slamming my knee between his legs and connecting with his crotch.

He howls with pain and lets me go. I cry out as loud as my lungs will allow and spin around to escape, but he grabs my elbow and swings me back toward him. He yanks me hard, with more force than my body can process.

I slip.

My shoes have no traction as they struggle for support.

My arms wave desperately, trying to latch onto the cold wind to keep me upright.

The moment moves in slow-motion. McKay lunges forward to grab me, to reach for me, to keep me from falling.

But then he hesitates.

He stops dead in his tracks, his eyes widening as I tumble backward, rocks and rubble kicking up beneath me.

He doesn't reach. He doesn't move.

He just…watches.

And I realize in that split second what's behind me.

I know exactly what's there to catch me.

Nothing.

A scream explodes from my throat as the nothingness snatches me up, jerks me in reverse, and I tip backward over the drop-off.

The last thing I see is McKay fisting his hair with both hands, his eyes rounding with horror as orange fireworks flash across the sky.

The last thing I feel is my stomach lurching into my throat and icy wind and tree branches slicing my skin as I fall, fall, fall.

The last thing I think about before my body hits the ground…is him.

Max.

And I wonder if he'll ever find out that his brother killed me.

Chapter 27

MAX

S HE DOESN'T CALL ME AT MIDNIGHT.

I pace my bedroom, the cell phone sweaty in my hand as I stare at it.

12:04.

12:05.

I call her for the third time and no answer.

She's probably having fun with Brynn, watching the fireworks, laughing, and enjoying herself. It's okay. She didn't forget about me; she's just enjoying her night.

Blowing out a breath, I run a hand through my hair and drop my arm, tapping the phone against my thigh as I glance out my bedroom window. I see her mother in the living room across the street, the lights yellow and warm. She's on the phone, pacing around in aimless circles, just like me. The difference is she's smiling. She looks happy.

I tell myself it's Ella on the phone. She wanted to call her mother first.

Waiting a few more minutes, I traipse down the hallway and pace some more. The living room, the kitchen.

12:11.

I call her again.

No answer.

I decide to dial Brynn instead, knowing they're likely together. It rings three times before she picks up.

"Max, hey!" she chirps, her voice high-pitched and full of its usual enthusiasm. Noise and static filter through the speaker. "Haaaappy New Year!"

I start pacing again. "Is Ella with you?"

Giggles fuse with raucous cheers. Fireworks boom in the distance.

"Brynn?"

"Sorry, sorry! Fireworks are still going off. Super loud. One sec." A few seconds pass until the voices and external noises quiet and a patio door sounds like it slides shut. "Hey! What's up?"

"I'm looking for Ella. She didn't call me."

"Oh…um, she's…" Another long pause. "I don't see her anywhere."

"What do you mean? I thought you were ringing in the new year together."

"We were. I–I didn't even realize she wasn't here. God, I'm sorry. I've been drinking, and Kai and I were catching up, and…" The line goes quiet, save for various rustling noises. "Shoot. I can't find her. She must be in the bathroom."

I pinch the bridge of my nose, my chest prickling with anxiety. It seems silly to stress. Knowing Ella, she probably ditched the party to watch the fireworks by herself near the lake. "When's the last time you saw her?"

"Um, I'm not sure. Maybe an hour ago? No…probably less. It hasn't been that long."

"Okay. Well, can you have her call me?"

"Of course! I'm sorry. I should have been paying more attention. I feel like an awful friend."

I swallow. "It's fine. I should have been there, too. Just…have her call me right away. I want to say good night."

"I will. Promise."

I hang up, scrubbing a hand across my mouth and jaw as I glance out the main window at the empty driveway. If I had the truck, I'd already be on my way.

I call McKay next, hoping he'll have an ounce of sympathy for me and bring the truck home.

I tap his number.

Straight to voicemail.

I try one more time with the same result.

"Dammit," I mutter under my breath, a sheen of sweat dotting my hairline. He was intoxicated when he stormed out, and the thought only heightens my nerves.

He's fine.

Ella is fine.

It's ridiculous to be worrying this much. It's only a quarter past midnight and it's a sprawling lake house. Ella could have fallen asleep in a spare room for all I know, and McKay is probably at a friend's house.

But…

But.

That's the issue. There's a nagging "but" hovering over me like a storm cloud, howling in my chest and pinwheeling in my stomach. I can't explain it. I could never begin to explain the strange, instinctual feeling zipping through me, telling me that something is wrong.

My Sunny Girl needs me.

I wait fifteen more minutes before checking on Dad and tugging on my shoes. He's sound asleep, his face buried in the pillow, arms at his sides. Snores echo through the bedroom, giving me a shred of relief. Ten seconds later, I'm marching through the front lawn, across the street, and landing on the Sunburys' doorstep. I knock three times and wait for the footsteps to approach.

Candice cracks open the front door and peers out at me. When recognition fills her eyes, she widens the door, a cell phone pressed to one ear and her hair in curlers.

"Max," she says, a frown of confusion competing with a hesitant smile. Holding up her index finger, she tells the person on the other line that she'll have to call them back. Then she clicks off the call, lowers the phone, and gives me her full attention. "I thought you were with Ella?"

I'm fidgety, restless, my feet shuffling back and forth as I shove my hands in both pockets. I don't want to worry her, because my fears are unfounded, so I force myself to remain neutral. Still and calm. "Something came up, so I couldn't go to the party," I explain, glancing over her shoulder. A slew of open folders and papers is strewn across her work desk in the corner of the living room. The laptop is on, surrounded by multicolored coffee mugs. "I, uh, wanted to ask you a favor. My brother took the truck and I'm trying to meet up with Ella. Her phone must have died."

Concern flickers in her eyes. She fiddles with a pink curler that matches the sweatsuit she's wearing. "Is everything okay?"

"Sure." I clear my throat. "Of course. It's not an emergency or anything, so I feel weird asking…but can I borrow your car?"

Her chestnut eyebrows arch with surprise. "Do you need a ride?"

I quickly shake my head. "No, no, it's not that serious. You look busy," I note, my eyes panning to her workstation. "The party is only a few miles from here. I can walk if you're not comfortable."

"You're sure everything is okay? Is Ella in trouble?"

"She's fine. I just talked to Brynn." I'm hopeful the vagueness of my statement gives her a semblance of solace. "I wanted to meet up with her. I'll drive her back home in a bit."

She chews on her thumbnail, weighing my words and taking note of my movements, my expressions. I must fake it well because she nods slowly, moves away from the door, and fetches a ring of keys from her purse. When she returns, she holds them out to me. "You haven't been drinking?"

"Not at all. I've never touched alcohol in my life." It's the truth, thanks to my firsthand experience with watching both my father and my brother succumb to the destructive allure of the bottle.

Candice nods again and folds in her lips. Then she plops the keys in my hand. "All right. Please have Ella call me as soon as you get there. I'll wait up."

"I will. Thank you." I force a smile, fist the key ring, then spin around on the front stoop. My gait is laced with panic as I fumble for the right key, launch myself into the front seat, and jam it in the ignition. The red Nissan Sentra revs to life and I waste no time in careening out of the driveway, uncaring that Ella's mother is watching from the front porch with a hand fisting the collar of her pale-pink sweatsuit.

She's fine, she's fine, she's fine.

I drive on autopilot down familiar back roads with the window down to keep me from suffocating on my own fear. When I swerve into Morrison's packed driveway, I park sideways, blocking in multiple vehicles, and kill the engine. I don't care. All I care about is finding Ella. Instinct has my eyes assessing the dimly lit street for our truck, wondering if McKay made it to the party. I don't see it, so I keep moving.

The door is unlocked. I barge through in my baseball cap, ratty jeans, and white tee, shoving my way through dancing and sweaty bodies, and ignoring the cherry punch that splashes on my shoes when I collide with an aggravated brunette.

Someone calls out for me. I ignore them.

My gaze scans the crowded living room and adjoining kitchen, taking quick note of every face that doesn't belong to my girl. Two blonds are perched on the white quartz island top, their arms swaying to "Something in the Orange" by Zach Bryan. The melody haunts me as I barrel down hallways, burst through closed doors, and disregard the blow job taking place in one of the bedrooms.

"Don't you knock?" someone blares.

I slam the door and keep moving. Five minutes pass and I can't find Ella. My heart is beating like a snare drum as I march out onto the patio, glancing at the hot tub to my left, then panning right to survey the veranda strung with bulb lights and tiki torches. Nothing. Only a bunch of teenagers partying and laughing without a care in the world.

As I glance out toward the lake, I spot a silhouette just before a familiar voice reaches my ears.

"Ella!" the voice calls out, another body trailing beside her as the two figures stare out at the slow-rippling water.

Brynn and Kai.

I race forward, cupping my hands around my mouth. "Brynn!"

Her high ponytail whips her in the face when she spins around. "Max…I'm still looking for Ella. I–I can't find her anywhere."

It's after 1:00 a.m. now. Fear grinds into me like a dull knife. My gait slows when I reach them, sweeping shaky fingers through my hair. "Do you think she left with somebody?"

Brynn's face is pink and panicked. Her eyes bulge to saucers and glimmer against the moon as she shakes her head, arms crossed over her chest. "She wouldn't leave without telling me, right? That's not like her. I looked in all the bedrooms, the bathrooms, the garage…"

"Me too," I whisper. "Fuck. Do you think she went for a walk? Got lost? Fell?"

It's fucking cold outside. My mind races with images of Ella with a broken ankle, dragging herself through sticks and branches in the deep, dark woods. Both hands link behind my head as my thoughts spiral. "We need to look for her. She's not answering her phone."

"I know. I keep calling her," Brynn says.

Kai points over to the shadowy tree line a few yards away. "Over there is a hiking path. Maybe she wanted a better view of the fireworks."

I'm running before he finishes talking. "Why isn't she answering her god-damn phone?" I wonder aloud, listening to their footfalls jogging behind me.

"No service?" Kai calls out. "I never get service in the woods."

A few cracks of lagging fireworks paint the sky in splashes of violet and blue as we make our way through the opening, trudging up the inclined path. I pluck my phone from my pocket and switch on the flashlight, trailing the light over the rugged terrain in hopes of spotting something of relevance. Gnarled roots, moss, underbrush. Nothing of value.

"Ella!" Brynn calls out, Kai's voice following.

I shout her name into the midnight sky and dancing tree branches. "Sunny!"

"Ella!"

Our voices pitch and bleed together as we tromp up the craggy hill, pelts of icy wind stinging my skin. Brynn bolts ahead of me, her ankles twisting in her glittery high heels. "Ella!" she yells, veering toward a small clearing overlooking the lake.

My chest aches from breathing so hard, more panic than exertion. The only thing I see littered along the bluff is a miniature bottle of Jim Beam.

Ella doesn't drink. She's not here.

I move to the left, while Brynn and Kai swing right. I'm slicing my way through tall brush when I hear it.

The scream. The ear-splitting, hair-raising scream.

My blood chills. My muscles lock up as the universe shrinks to a pinpoint. And I know.

I fucking know my world is about to be rocked, shaken, and split in two.

Brynn's scream morphs into an ugly, wretched sob, and I turn, turn, turn, the moment a slow-motion swirl of horror. She collapses to her knees, her gaze pinned on whatever nightmare lies below. Kai's face twists with agony. They both stare over the edge of the bluff until I find myself beside them. I don't remember moving. I don't remember the howl that wrenches from my throat, even though I hear it echoing back at me and shredding my eardrums.

But I'll forever remember that image of Ella.

Lying in a heap, thirty feet below us.

Motionless and bloody.

My Sunny Girl.

My mind is a cloud, a lethal blur. I squeeze my hair in both fists as I stare down over the ledge of the cliff to where Ella is sprawled out in a bed of grass and weeds, having missed the lake by a few feet. Dark water laps at her hair like it's trying to draw her in.

A sob sticks in the back of my throat.

Bile crawls up my esophagus.

I move.

I swing my legs over the ledge of the bluff and climb down, my feet catching on jagged earth, my hands cutting on rock. "Ella!" I cry out, repeating her name over and over. Kai tells Brynn to stay put while he follows me down. I'm only halfway along the embankment when I launch myself forward and jump the rest of the way, landing on my hip with a bruising thunk. I drag myself over to her, ignoring the pain that shoots through me.

"Ella, Ella...*fuck*," I cry, crawling on my hands and knees. Blood oozes from her mouth, already dried and crusty, as locks of dark hair fall over her eyes. When I reach her, I push her hair back and search her face. A blink, a breath, anything. I check her pulse, my own on overdrive. One arm is draped above her head, her fingertips submerged in the shallow water, while the other extends out at her side. "Sunny, baby, please," I choke out, pressing my ear to her chest and pleading for a sign of life. I don't hear anything. I'm going to puke.

Kai dashes beside me, his sneakers kicking up a cloud of dust, and drops to his knees on the other side of Ella. He's calmer than me. Coolheaded as he takes the lead. "Pulse?" he asks, snatching up her wrist.

I hardly register his words. All I hear is my own misery and Brynn's terrified wails from above us as I bury my face in Ella's neck.

"She's alive," Kai says.

I take her battered face between my hands and sprinkle tear-salted kisses along her cheeks and forehead. "Sunny, Sunny…Ella, please. Fuck…*please*."

"Max!" he shouts again. "She's alive."

My head jerks up, finally processing his words. A cell phone is pressed to his ear as he gives a location.

Girl. Fell. Bluffs. Near Plankton Street. Breathing.

Breathing.

Alive.

Tipping his head skyward, Kai calls up to Brynn. "She's alive!" he repeats.

"Oh my God. Oh my *God*," she sobs.

I pull Ella's hand out of the water and press the pad of my thumb to her wrist, forcing my breathing to placate so I can concentrate on her pulse.

But I can't feel anything.

Dread whispers along the back of my neck as I place my ear to her chest again, then try for a pulse, then repeat. Kai notices my unraveling and balances the phone between his ear and shoulder as he leans over Ella to help me.

"I'm still here," he says into the receiver before lowering the speaker and addressing me. "Right here, Max. Press two fingers right here. It's weak but it's there. She's alive."

I inhale a deep breath and close my eyes, holding my index and middle fingers to her pulse point.

There's a flicker.

A soft, beautiful beat. The faintest trace of life.

I lock eyes with Kai and he nods at me. "They said not to move her unless she stops breathing and then we need to administer CPR. Ambulance is on the way. I'm going to stay on the line."

Falling back on my haunches, I slam both hands to my face and let out a tortured moan. Relief and terror. *Thank fuck* melded with sickening disbelief. I look up at Brynn, who's halfway dangling over the ledge, a hand cupping her mouth as her body shakes with tears.

I glance at Ella.

I stare at her shipwrecked body, her porcelain skin marred with scrapes and scratches, her face bruised and bloodstained.

Leaning forward, I press my lips to her forehead and stroke her hair as I squeeze my eyes shut. "Stay, Sunny Girl," I whisper, choking back my pain. "Please stay."

My girl fell off a fucking cliff.

She fell.

And I wasn't there to catch her.

"HOW TO CATCH THE SUN"
STEP THREE:

Weather the Eclipse

Even the sun navigates through shadows.

Chapter 28

E L L A

JONAH BRINGS ME LEMONADE.

I tip my chin, my eyes squinting underneath a wide-brimmed hat as sunlight pours down from the clear-blue sky. My denim romper is stained with mud. Worse, my fingernails look almost black from working with the horses all day as my hand curls around the sweating glass. "Thanks," I tell him, my lips searching for the straw. "Mom makes the best lemonade."

"It's the honey syrup," Jonah says, his thumbs hooked in his belt loops. Shaggy copper hair curls at his ears and his bangs are damp from hard labor under the sun. "Erin is coming by for dinner tonight. I can't wait to finally introduce her as my girlfriend."

"No, shit!" I say, grinning wide. "It's official?"

"Official as a judge's gavel."

"She's really sweet, Jonah. And pretty, too." I think of Erin and her long blond hair and perfect bangs. I tried to give myself bangs once and I looked like a bewildered sheepdog who'd had an unfortunate altercation with a hacksaw. "Is Mom losing her mind?"

"She's made three casseroles, seven pies, and enough lemonade to hydrate the entire state of Tennessee for years to come."

"Sounds legit." I giggle. "I'm happy for you."

"Thanks, Piglet." He leans in to ruffle my hair like I'm a toddler. "No clue what she sees in me, but no complaints."

"She sees what I see, of course."

"Hope not. That would be creepy."

My arm shoots out to swat him on the shoulder. "She sees your heart, Jonah. You know…that big, beautiful thing inside your chest."

"You think so?"

"I know so." Sighing dreamily, I sip my lemonade and imagine what it would be like to fall in love one day. I picture a rugged cowboy with dark hair and broad arms. He's fit and strong because he works on a ranch all day, tending to horses and baling hay. Sunrises are filled with songful birds and floral breezes, and sunsets are the prettiest color orange I've ever seen.

"Where'd you just go?" Jonah wonders, his head tilting to the side.

I blink back to the stables, the fantasy dissolving. "I was just thinking about my future love story."

"Oh, yeah? You're only fourteen. You've still got a ways to go."

"I know. But it's fun to think about," I muse. "Besides, you always wanted me to find love one day."

Jonah glances off over my shoulder and his sage-green eyes brighten. "Well, he's here right now. You should introduce yourself."

I cough when lemonade catches in my throat. "What do you mean? Who's here?"

"Your future love story."

My future love story? Did Mom accidentally spike the lemonade?

"What the heck are you talking about?" My nose wrinkles with confusion. He points off into the distance. "Look."

Hesitation grips me for a beat before I whirl around, my attention landing on a man with the lightest blue eyes and the nicest arms in the whole wide world. I may only be a freshman in high school, but I know nice arms when I see them. When the man smiles at me, dimples pop on both cheeks, making me swoon. He stares at me like he knows me.

I think he does.

I close my eyes and memories churn and spin. Stones skip across water and the sky lights up with dazzling star patterns. Music fills my ears as a crisp wind rushes in through an open window, tires flying down a deserted road. He takes my hand. Our fingers interlock and everything is golden.

"Max," I whisper.

I swivel back around toward Jonah, excited to tell him everything.

Max.

It's Max.

"Jonah, you're right. That's—"

A scream rips from my throat. Erin stands beside Jonah, spattered in stains of crimson. Blood oozes from holes in her chest as she sends me a wave and a smile.

Jonah wraps his arm around her waist, tugging her closer. "Erin is here," he says, looking proud and in love. "Isn't she beautiful?"

Her face is a mess of gore.

Her body is riddled in bullet holes.

Terror sinks me as I look down at the lemonade in my hand, watching as the pale-yellow liquid swirls with red. This isn't right. This isn't real.

No, no, no.

There's a beeping noise filtering into my psyche. Persistent and shrieky. I slam both hands over my ears and shake my head. "What's that noise?"

Jonah smiles. "It's time to go."

"Go where?" Anxiety cinches my chest. "There's nowhere left to go."

"There's always somewhere. No one stays lost forever."

"But…I didn't finish writing you that letter," I tell him. Suddenly, that's the only thing that matters. I need to finish my letter. Jonah has been gone for years and I never wrote to him. I never told him that I still care, that I still love him and miss him terribly.

I was never able to piece together my fairy-tale letter, the one where I fell in love with a boy in the forest who swung from vines and feasted on berries and rainwater. Somehow, it feels important. He has to know that I'm okay. My love story prevailed.

Jonah nods agreeably, still holding on to a bloodied Erin. "So write the letter, Piglet. There's still time."

"I can't."

"Sure you can."

"But—"

He snaps his fingers.

And I'm in the clearing.

Birds chirp from tree canopies as sunlight seeps in through leafy branches, casting ribbons of gold at my feet. Max is seated across from me, his knees drawn to his chest, both hands dangling between them as he leans back against a giant trunk. There's a notebook in my lap, a pink pen fisted in my hand. I blink up at Max, studying him. Taking in his mop of hair and crystalline eyes.

But before I can process anything, there's a small stone barreling toward me at the speed of light. I don't think as my hand flies out and catches it with eerie precision.

"Nice reflexes," Max says, his dark eyebrows pinched together.

"I'm…good at catching things."

"Yeah. You mentioned that."

I unclench my fingers and glance down at the stone. It's smooth and white. Comforting in some strange way. It feels like a tether to solid ground, to a world I used to know.

Swallowing, I look over at Max.

"Are you going to that bonfire tonight?" he wonders, plucking tall weeds from the space between his parted legs.

"No."

He nods. "Me neither."

The notebook sits heavily in my lap and my hand sweats around the gel pen. I peer down at the unfinished words, wondering why I never gave them life. I should write the letter and mail it to Jonah. I should let him know that I'm okay.

Am I okay?

Even if I'm not, I can lie. I'll lie to him.

"You should finish that," Max tells me.

His voice fades out, sounding miles away. It's replaced by a whooshing in my ears like a white-hot whip lashing at my brain. I'm freefalling. Cold wind bites at my skin as tree branches gouge and scrape, a faraway scream trickling into my mind.

The beeping noise returns and I can't block it out.

Beep, beep, beep.

"Go ahead, Sunny," Max urges, just a whisper. An echo.

Beep, beep, beep.
I drink in a deep breath.
And I lift the pen.

Dear Jonah,

Today I fell in love with a boy who

———

My eyes fly open.

Oxygen fills my lungs with a razor-sharp inhale as my body stiffens and arches up off a springy surface. The beeping sound picks up speed and my gaze flits around the unfamiliar space. Bright, fluorescent lights streak across my vision. I hear a muddle of voices over the beeps, a flurry of words I can't comprehend. I can hardly make them out.

Awake.

Awake.

She's awake.

Panic sets in. My fingers latch onto a starchy fabric and a biting sting in my hand makes me aware of something sharp. *A needle?* My throat feels parched, my lips dry and cracked. An attempt to call out results in a raspy whisper, my vocal cords protesting after what feels like an eternity of silence. More panic rushes through me. I'm scared, lost, alone.

I'm not alone.

Faces blur above me, faces I don't immediately recognize.

Where am I?

I want to cry but I can't remember how.

A shadow moves closer as someone tinkers with something attached to me that burns the back of my hand. Movement is fast-paced. A confusing mess of motion.

I'm scared.

So scared.

I blink the haze from my eyes. I keep blinking, a million times over, until one of the faces morphs into something familiar. Dark hair spills over blue eyes and chiseled cheekbones. A man. A man I know. His eyes are wild and filled with concern. His lips are moving but I can't hear his words.

I freeze.

Flashes of memory skate across my mind.

That face looming over me.

That same dark hair swinging over two eyes glinting with malice.

Hands grip me, holding me down.

Rocks dig into my back and blood fills my mouth with warm copper.

Screams.

I'm screaming then, and I'm screaming now. My body thrashes and fights. Someone holds me down again. Maybe two people. So many hands, so many voices.

But I'm acutely aware of something else. Something tucked inside my own hand. It's smooth and small, held tightly in my sweat-slicked palm. I squeeze and squeeze as a sense of calm washes over me. Peace. A peaceful moment.

I drift away to the clearing again.

Sun beats down on my face as Max sits across from me, smiling from his perch against the tree.

I look down at my outstretched fingers.

And there is the little white stone, resting in the palm of my hand.

Chapter 29

ELLA

WHEN I WAKE AGAIN, IT'S NOT AS LOUD. NOT AS VIOLENT. MY MIND IS groggy, my eyelids heavy, as I allow my surroundings to take physical form. It feels like there are lemon peels over my eyes as I pry them open, one at a time.

I hear the beeping noise again.

Sunlight from my dreams mutates into brassy, artificial light and a white sheet stares down on me. As my eyes slowly crack open, I blink away the thick film, ceiling panels taking shape from above. I'm in a room, lying on my back. I move my fingers. Wiggle my toes. Noise sounds muffled as it seeps in from behind a…curtain.

I stare at it. It's cornflower blue, fluttering gently when shapes sweep past it on the other side.

I'm in a hospital bed.

There's a powder-white blanket pulled up to my chest and an assortment of IVs and needles attached to my body. When I splay my fingers on my right hand, a piece of tape stretches my skin. My mouth is dry, my muscles stiff, and the back of my head itches.

I've hardly registered my surroundings when a head of raven hair pokes through the curtain. "Miss Ella," says a soft voice. "I'm Naomi, one of your nurses."

I blink at her, taking in her big, braided bun and rose-stained lips. Purple eyeglasses rest on the bridge of her ebony nose as she steps farther into the room.

She smiles warmly. "It's so good to see those eyes of yours open. How are you feeling? Can you understand me?" Naomi glides over to me, adjusting the bed to make me more comfortable.

"I understand you," I reply, my voice raspy, barely audible. "What happened?"

"You're in the hospital. What do you remember?"

I close my eyes. My mind is a blank canvas, my urge to recall is the brushes and paint. Images drag across my memory as I lift my paintbrush and watch colors brim to life in careful strokes.

Orange.

Spatters of orange flicker across a night sky.

I'm staring up at shimmery streaks of light as loud booms echo through the darkness and mingle with far-off cheers.

"Fireworks," I murmur, my eyes still closed. "I remember fireworks."

"That's good, Miss Ella," Naomi responds, pulling a chair closer and sitting beside the bed. "You've been here for a while. Do you remember what happened before you got here?"

I pull from the deepest parts of my brain, but everything is a blurry cloud. Orange fireworks…and then darkness. "It all goes blank after that," I whisper.

"That's okay. Memories can take hours or days to return. Sometimes longer," she explains. "Do you remember anything before the fireworks?"

My breath hitches.

A kiss.

I remember kissing a beautiful boy. My back against a door, my hands in his hair. Pale blue eyes look hungry and adoring as he pulls back and smiles at me like I'm his truest treasure.

"Kissing you feels like catching the sun."

I exhale slowly. "A kiss," I tell her. "I think I'm in my room. I hear… Christmas music."

Naomi nods, assessing my vitals. "You were found at the bottom of a steep bluff. You took a hard fall," she says. "Some tree branches slowed you down and lessened the impact, making you a very lucky girl. That type of fall could have been a lot worse."

"How long have I been here?"

Her eyes soften with sympathy. "Four weeks."

A stab of panic slices through my chest.

Four weeks.

Four. Weeks.

Naomi presses a hand to my shoulder and squeezes gently. "I'll send the doctor in shortly. There's a lot to go over. We're going to prohibit visitors for a while as we monitor your condition. The first time you woke up, you were highly agitated, so we had to sedate you."

Four weeks.

It's all I can hear.

All I can process.

Tears burn my eyes as my body starts to tremble. "M-my mom…is she here?" I ask, voice quivering.

"She is. She's in the waiting room with your boyfriend. They've been here every day."

My boyfriend.

"Kissing you feels like catching the sun."

The tears fall as I shake my head back and forth and lift both hands to my hair. Cords tangle as the beeps on my machine quicken with urgency. When I sweep my hair back, I notice that it's not all there. Anxiety pokes me as I touch along the back of my head and hardly feel anything.

Half an inch of hair at most.

"My hair…" I croak, more panic taking over. "Where's my hair?"

Naomi stands to tinker with the machine. "Yes, honey. They had to shave the back of your head to perform surgery. It will grow back. You look beautiful."

I start to sob. "No…no."

"It's all right. You rest now. When you wake up, the doctor will be here to talk to you."

"No, please. I want… I need to…"

"It's okay. Just rest."

Her voice sounds far away as I tilt my head and stare out the window, everything fogging. A peaceful feeling reaches for me, eager to steal me away.

Before I black out, my eyes settle on the bedside table.

Orange roses. Red roses. Pink roses.

And beside them sits a tiny terra-cotta pot with an orange crayon sticking out of the dirt.

Memories trickle into my mind of a boy climbing through my window. Carrying me from the lake. Dancing with me, holding me, kissing me on an old bridge.

"*Stay*," he says.

I reach for him.

I can't let him go.

"Max," I whisper as the world fades out.

There's a man in my room. The sunlight that was streaming in through the window has now been replaced with a pane of black. Even the fluorescent lights overhead have dimmed, telling me it's nighttime.

I pick at the scratchy bedcovers and lift my eyes to the figure standing over me.

"Hello, Ella. I'm Dr. Garcia, the neurologist overseeing your care." The doctor hovers near my bedside with a clipboard in his hand, donning a crisp-white set of scrubs. Bushy eyebrows pinch together as he studies me. "I'm sure you have many questions, so I'll start with your injuries and the treatment you've received over the past four weeks."

Four weeks.

I still can't believe it.

I've been in and out of consciousness for two days now.

Processing. Remembering.

Simmering in those memories.

Pieces have settled into place, one by one, hour by hour.

For a while, I was caught between dreams and reality. Fiction and truth. At one point, I swore I saw Jonah sitting at my bedside telling me I was going to be okay. But then I drifted again, and when I awoke, I was alone. It had only been a dream.

I squeeze the little white stone in my hand, the one that was placed next to the terra-cotta pot. "Okay," I respond in a rasp-laced voice. "Go ahead."

The doctor with tan skin and inky hair pauses as he stares at me, assessing my reaction. "You've been through a lot, young lady. When you were brought in, it was clear you had sustained a traumatic injury that caused significant swelling in your brain after a hard fall," he explains, monitoring my micro-expressions for any sign of stress. "We had to perform an occipital craniotomy. This surgery involves temporarily removing a part of your skull to allow the brain to swell without causing further damage. The piece was replaced once the swelling subsided."

What?

My eyes ping wider and I can't breathe.

The thought of my skull being removed and my brain being jabbed and prodded has nausea swirling in my gut. I try to keep my face impassive but my bottom lip quivers as I cling to the stone.

Dr. Garcia offers a reassuring smile, leaning over and pressing his hand to my bicep. "Your skull has been fully repaired now and you responded well to the surgery. You've also had multiple CT scans to monitor your brain's condition. As for your other injuries," he continues, "you suffered a fractured pelvis and a dislocated hip. You also broke a couple of ribs. You're very lucky you didn't puncture a lung." He takes a deep breath, his brown eyes warm as they skim my face. "The coma was induced initially due to the swelling in your brain. Your body then took over, keeping you in a natural coma for the remainder of the time, allowing it to heal. The good news is your other injuries have been recovering nicely. In a few more weeks, we'll transfer you to a rehabilitation facility."

I inhale a frayed breath. "I'm not...paralyzed?" I choke. It's clear that I'm not by the way my legs wriggle underneath the covers, but the notion still fills me with panic and dread.

"No, not at all," he says. "Your spine was remarkably unimpaired, save for bumps and bruises that have since healed. You can thank some tree branches and a patch of heavily weeded undergrowth for cushioning your fall."

He pauses, blinking down at me. "In terms of prognosis, every brain injury is unique. While we are hopeful given your current progress, there might be challenges ahead. You'll require physical therapy for your hip and pelvis, and possibly some occupational and speech therapy. As for cognitive or emotional changes, they can vary. Memory issues, mood fluctuations, and trouble with concentration are not uncommon. How are you feeling right now?"

Physically, it feels like I took a frying pan to the back of my head and I'm chewing on a wad of cotton balls. And mentally…

"Confused," I murmur. "Scared. Tired."

"That's perfectly normal," he says. "You've been through a lot. I'd like to ask you a few questions to understand your cognitive state. Would that be all right?"

Anxiety seeps inside me, but I swallow through a slow nod.

"Can you tell me your full name?"

"Ella Rose Sunbury."

"And your mother's name?"

"Candice. Candice Sunbury."

"Good. What's the last date you remember?"

Fireworks and sparklers flicker through my mind.

A pink party dress. Music, laughter, noise.

"December thirty-first. New Year's Eve."

He jots down some notes. "It's currently February first. Do you recall any of the events leading up to your fall?"

I hesitate, drinking in a shaky breath. "I remember…going for a walk. I wanted a better view of the fireworks and…the party was loud. Crowded. I don't like parties, but I wanted to spend the night with my friend. She was going through a hard time." I swallow down more grit. "I wandered up to the bluffs a little before midnight. And…I tripped. That's the last thing I remember."

"Your blood results showed no alcohol in your system. No drugs. You were clean."

I nod. "I don't drink or do drugs."

"Was there anybody with you?"

My eyes slam shut as I pretend to recall the moment.

But I don't need to pretend.

The final pieces rushed back to me as I drifted awake an hour ago, my chest on fire, my stomach in knots, and my heart in pulpy fragments.

"Christ, hold still! Stop running!"

"Stop it, stop it! Help me!"

"No. I was alone," I lie.

"That's okay. Don't push yourself too hard," he assures me. "We can circle back when your mind is clearer."

"We don't have to. That's all I remember. I was alone when I fell."

Dr. Garcia studies me, folding one arm across his white scrubs while the clipboard dangles in his opposite hand. "There was a bruise on your cheek that wasn't consistent with the fall. It looked like a fresh impact, possibly from a hand or an object. Do you remember how you got that?"

Instinct has my fingertips lifting and coasting across my left cheekbone.

"Shut. Up!" he hisses.

My heart rate spikes as cold sweat forms on my brow. Memories flood me, but I push them down, trying to keep my face neutral. "I–I don't know. I can't remember. Maybe I bumped into someone at the party? Everything is a little hazy."

The doctor raises an eyebrow, not entirely convinced but not pressing further. "All right. Well, it's important for us to understand the events leading up to the fall, not just for medical reasons but for your safety as well. A detective will be stopping by with further questions as soon as you're ready."

"There's nothing else," I insist weakly. "I fell."

His smile is tight. "Do you feel ready for visitors? Your mother and your boyfriend are in the waiting room. If you prefer to rest, I'll let them know."

I think about my mother trudging through the past four weeks, sitting in a waiting room chair, uncertain of my prognosis. Unsure if I would ever wake up. Not knowing whether or not she would be living the rest of her life alone, with both of her children cruelly taken from her.

I roll the stone between my thumb and fingers and nod. "Can you bring them in one at a time? I'd like to see my mother first," I tell him.

"Of course. I'll send her in."

He walks out through the blue curtain and my mother rushes into the room two minutes later.

"Oh, Ella." She stops in place, her hand shooting to her mouth to hold in the cry. "My God…"

"Mom," I murmur.

For as distant as we've been over the past few years, somehow it feels like there is no distance at all. Only the few feet between us that she quickly erases when she dashes to my bedside and falls to her knees, taking my stone-clasped hand in both of hers. She kisses my knuckles, her tears falling freely. "My baby girl," she croaks out, forehead resting on our joined palms.

I haven't heard her call me that since I was fourteen. The nickname has my own tears escaping in warm rivulets down my cheeks.

We spend the next few minutes crying quietly, taking in the moment. Taking in all the moments missed over the last month. When my mother finally stands and drags over a chair, she gazes upon me like I've been brought back from the dead. Almost like I'm lying in a gold-encrusted coffin, sprinkled with floral arrangements, and then my eyes snap open.

I'm still alive. Please don't bury me.

Mom fills me in on the prior four weeks of lost time, informing me of my grandmother's ailing health, her own leave of absence from work, and the investigation into my mysterious fall.

She asks me what I remember.

I lie to her.

I don't know why I'm holding on to my memories. I've always prided myself on being honest and forthcoming. My rational voice says I should be shouting it from the rooftops.

It was McKay. McKay Manning attacked me in a drunken rage and let me fall to a presumed death. He could have caught me, grabbed me, pulled me back. But all he did was watch. He knew that a dead person was a silent person, and his secret would be safe.

His inaction was a silent assassination.

Just as my silence now betrays the truth.

But that truth catches in the back of my throat like an acidic knot. Pieces claw their way up, then die out on my tongue. I curse my own cowardice and squeeze the stone clutched in my hand, only half listening to my mother's voice as she drones on.

As time ticks by, Mom leans back in the chair and sweeps trembling fingers through her hair. She fidgets, her eyes panning around the room before settling back on me. Her usual bouncy curls hang flat and listless as they tease her shoulders, while her gaze gleams with trapped words.

"Ella...sweetheart," she says, her face a mess of tears and hesitation.

I blink at her, my chest tightening.

Squeezing my wrist, Mom presses her lips together and exhales through her nose. "There's something else. There's something you should know."

"What?" I whisper, anxiety prickling the back of my neck.

"I..." Her lips part but no more words leak out. Seconds sweep by. Wobbly, unsettled heartbeats.

Then she shakes her head, her throat bobbing as she swallows hard. "Nothing, honey. I'll send Max in. He's dying to see you."

"No, wait. What were you going to say?"

She strains a smile, still shaking her head. "We'll talk when you're feeling better."

"I'm fine. I'm feeling fine." I reach for her hand as she scoots the chair back, preparing to leave. "Mom, please."

"It's okay, Ella. We'll talk later." Pulling free of my grip, she stands from her seat.

My throat burns as I watch her walk out of the room. She sends me a quick, nervous smile over her shoulder before the curtains flutter closed behind her.

It's the fall.

Everyone thinks I was pushed off that cliff...and *God,* how I wish it was some random bully from school who had been there. I wish Andy or Heath had been the one to have pried my legs apart, held me down, beaten and bruised me, then left me for dead at the bottom of the bluffs.

It would be so much easier.

I'm still swallowing down the true events when the curtain swings open again and my heart stutters, the beats tangling. I hear him before I see him. I hear the sound he makes.

A groan.

A tortured, audible groan of pain and relief.

My eyes close briefly as I suck in a breath, and then I open them, trailing my gaze up his denim-clad legs to his forest-green T-shirt before landing on his face. Weeks' worth of scruff lines his jaw. His eyes are rimmed with dark circles and his hair has grown out, making him look even more like McKay.

Our eyes lock. Our breaths hold.

Max stands at the foot of my bed, his expression painted in pure torment as he holds my orange backpack in one of his hands. He sets it down, his fists balling to stones. His balance teeters as he fights back tears. "Ella," he says softly.

I stare at him, not knowing what to say. I should tell him that he never left my mind for four weeks. He was there in every dream, in every haze-drenched reverie, refusing to let me forget. Refusing to let me go. Calling me back home.

My dry lips part to utter a single word. "Hi."

If he was searching for more, he doesn't say it. The lone syllable is enough to carry him toward me, his dark brows pinched together and his jaw tight with emotion. Max inches himself beside me on the bed with equal parts gentleness and urgency. He's careful of my cords and needles, yet desperate for my touch. I stiffen at first, the guilt of my secret keeping me guarded and sealed up tight. But when his hand lifts up to cup my cheek and his fingers tilt my face toward his, my tension deflates like a popped balloon.

Icy-blue eyes gaze back at me. And not icy like the cold dread trickling through me, but crystalline and clear. A peaceful lake on a winter morning. "Sunny," he says, dragging two fingers down my cheek with a featherlight touch that makes me tremble. "You remember me, right?"

I dip my chin, finding it hard to look at him. "Of course I do."

"Every time you woke up, you were afraid of me. You'd look right at me, but it was like you were looking at someone else," he says. "They kept having to sedate you."

"I want to know what my brother sees in you."

"Knock it off, Ella. Fuck…just hold still!"

Hot pressure burns behind my eyes. "I'm sorry. I don't remember that."

Max tips my chin up with his finger but my eyes remain squeezed shut.

"The doctors were worried about amnesia." When my eyes still don't open, he drags his thumb along my damp cheekbone. "Hey…look at me, Ella. It's okay."

Goose bumps pimple along my skin at his touch. My body wants me to curl into him, inhale his scent, and kiss him until I can't breathe, but my muddled mind has me slamming on the brakes.

I shake my head a little.

"You're safe with me." His voice sounds pleading.

"I know, I just… It's a lot." Sniffling, I allow my eyes to slide open, revealing a fresh coat of tears. "A month of my life is gone. Half my hair is gone. I don't even know if I can walk."

"You'll walk."

"You can't know that."

He leans in until our noses touch. "Then I'll carry you if I have to."

My lips wobble with grief, fear, and trapped guilt. "Max…"

"I found you, you know," he says, curling his palm behind my neck and pulling our foreheads together. "I found you at the bottom of that cliff. Me, Brynn, and Kai. We thought you were dead. I thought I'd never see these eyes again. Never get to touch you, hold you… It *killed* me."

My whole body shakes as I cry. "I'm sorry."

"*I'm* sorry. I'm so fucking sorry I wasn't there with you."

"You couldn't have known. Nobody could have known."

Inhaling a hard breath through his nose, Max's grip loosens on my neck as his head moves side to side. "Fuck, Sunny. I can't believe you're here."

Am I?

I feel half here, half gone. Half the girl I was and half this scared, empty shell. I must look terrible. Chalky and ghostlike, feeble and bruised.

I pull away from Max and roll onto my back, glancing at the bedside table. The potted crayon stares back at me. "I thought it would be a carrot by now," I whisper hoarsely. He doesn't respond and I wonder if he feels rejected. Shunned by my pullback. I keep my eyes pinned on the orange crayon and try to ignore the ache in my chest as I murmur, "You brought me my stone."

"Yeah," he says. "I thought it might help."

"It did." I curl my fingers around the little stone, letting it anchor me.

Letting it soothe my anxious heart like it always has for some strange reason. "Where's McKay?" I inquire. The question falls out stupidly and out of place, so I quickly try to cover it up. "And Brynn? And Kai?"

He pauses before answering. "They've been here. They're worried about you."

I swallow. "All of them?"

"Of course. McKay asks about you every day. If you're awake, if you're making progress. And Brynn has been a mess. Every time I see her, she's crying."

My lips purse into a flat line as my eyes shift to the darkened window. I can see a sliver of moon peeking out through the treetops. I should reply but my lips feel numb. My tongue frozen.

McKay isn't worried about me, Max. He's worried about himself.

Another silent beat goes by and then Max asks, "Do you want me to go?"

His tone sounds wounded, and heartache grips me like a noose. He's waited a month for me to come back and I can hardly look at him. I can't look at him without seeing his brother, without feeling the heat of my secret burning into me like a red-hot poker.

And this is exactly why I never wanted any of this. I never wanted these feelings because I *knew*. I knew that falling leaves you with broken bones and shattered pieces. I knew that falling leaves you in ruins and sometimes dead.

I never wanted to be conquered, overthrown, another victim of *love*.

But I fell anyway, despite everything I knew. I fell for him.

I fell head over heels for Max Manning, and now I have to live with the knowledge that his twin brother tried to kill me.

My tongue darts out to catch a tear dangling on my upper lip. I refuse to look at him as I mutter, "I'm a little tired. I should probably rest."

Silence permeates the space between us. The kind that chafes and scratches like a mosquito bite that can't be soothed.

"All right," he finally says, inching his way off the mattress. "I'll let you sleep."

The bed shifts and his body heat dissolves, leaving me colder than ever. It takes all my effort not to look at him, not to pull him back to the bed and let him hold me until dawn.

A zipper whirrs and rustling ensues, but my eyes stay locked on the window. A solid minute ticks by before I feel something placed beside me on the bed.

"I brought this for you," Max tells me before his footfalls retract from the hospital cot. "I'll come see you tomorrow. If you want me to."

"Bye," I say quickly, snapping my mouth shut before a sob cuts loose.

I hear him sigh, a sigh of pure anguish. Just like the groan he made when he first walked into the room and saw me. My stomach swirls with nausea as I listen to him walk away. The curtain draws back with a swish and a metallic clink, and then he's gone.

I look to my right and discover what he left behind for me—it's a copy of *The House at Pooh Corner*.

Max brought me one of my favorite books.

Tears slide down my sallow cheeks as I open the book and flip through the pages, knowing a message is waiting for me. Knowing there's something he wants me to see.

I flip and skim and search, until my eyes land on a string of words about rivers and streams, highlighted in orange.

I read them.

I read them over and over again before I cry myself to sleep.

"There is no hurry. We shall get there someday."

Chapter 30

MAX

AFTER SIGNING IN TO THE REHABILITATION CENTER AND STICKING THE name badge to the front of my shirt, I make my way down the winding hallway. Ella is in the open therapy area today. The receptionist guides me to the observation seats where I can watch her finish up her session before visiting with her when she's done.

Two months have flown by in a blur of tedious schoolwork, house renovations to keep my mind busy, and visiting Ella while she finishes up physical therapy in preparation for returning home. She's getting stronger every day. Stronger, brighter, braver.

And yet…it still feels like she's slipping.

Slipping away from me.

McKay insisted on driving me over, just like he always does. He never wants to see Ella. Says it hits too close to home with Dad's rehabilitation after the job accident that rendered him temporarily paralyzed. I get it. And I appreciate that he wants to be here for support, even though he waits in the lobby.

As I take a seat in one of the stiff burgundy chairs, I spot Ella on a padded therapy table, a therapist by her side, guiding her through delicate leg movements to mobilize her hip joint and strengthen her weakened muscles. Ella grimaces slightly with each stretch, a testament to the effort each motion requires. But with every repetition there's a sense of triumph, another step closer to a full recovery. Sweat slicks her brow line as her arms quiver through pulls and stretches. Her cheeks are flushed, filling with deep breaths before she blows them back out.

Ella's therapist, a tall woman with silver hair, talks her through the movements, offering words of encouragement and technical instructions. She occasionally adjusts Ella's posture or applies resistance to specific maneuvers. In another section, a parallel bar is set up, the next stage for Ella to practice standing and walking with support.

I watch her for the next twenty minutes before she's led out of the therapy room with the assistance of her walker. When she spots me waiting, she pauses, her knuckles bleaching white as she squeezes the padded grips.

I stand from the chair, a bouquet of orange roses tucked inside my hand.

Ella glances at them, lingering on the brightly colored blooms. Then her gaze pans up to my face. "Hey," she greets, her voice stronger despite the notable crack.

She looks at me differently.

It's like she remembers me…but she doesn't remember me the same.

"Hey," I reply. Hope laces the word, then dies out when she pulls her eyes away.

"Come on," she murmurs. "We can go to the visitation room."

I follow alongside her as we make our way to a consultation space with pale-blue walls and soft, ambient lighting. Spring sunlight pours in from multiple windows, causing her shorter hair to glitter its usual shades of red and brown. It's been newly cut into a reverse bob, cropped in the back due to her surgery and longer in the front. She fiddles with the longer pieces as she takes a seat in one of the cushy chairs.

I pull another chair over to her and hand her the roses. "You look good."

Ella doesn't maintain eye contact as she holds the flowers in her lap and tinkers with one of the petals. "I still look like death. But thanks." Her eyes flutter closed through a long exhale. "You don't need to keep bringing me flowers, Max."

"I know. But I want to."

"You don't need to visit me every day, either. I'm sure you're busy."

"I'm never too busy for you, Sunny."

She swallows hard. "They said I'm almost ready to go home."

Home.

There was a time when I imagined that I was becoming her home. Somehow, I don't think that's the case anymore. "That's great news."

"Yeah."

The chitchat eats at me. My skin itches from head to toe and all I want to do is fall to my knees in front of her, bury my face in her lap, and feel her fingers sink into my hair like they used to. I want to breathe in her scent. Oranges and sunshine. I want to gather her in my arms and carry her home…to a home that includes me.

Leaning forward on my elbows, I scrub my hands over my face and leave them there as I try not to have an emotional breakdown across from her. "Ella. Talk to me."

"I am talking to you," she whispers.

"This isn't talking. This isn't us. Something broke between us and I don't know how to fix it." I lift my chin and steeple my fingers. "Did I do something wrong?"

Her eyes are wide and wild as she shakes her head. "No, you didn't do anything wrong. I'm just…not myself. I'm trying to reacclimate and that takes time."

The words don't ring true. "I see the way you are with your mother. With Brynn and Kai. It's like nothing changed with them, but with me…" Emotion catches in my throat. "It feels like everything changed."

"That's not true."

"Are your memories misfiring somehow? Are there gaps, missing pieces? I've been racking my brain, trying to figure out why there's this wall between us. If you need a reminder, I can do that."

"Max…" She shakes her head, flattening her lips.

"I'll tell you about the way we played Pooh sticks on the bridge, and how I taught you how to skip stones across the lake. You couldn't skip them, but my heart nearly exploded just watching you try, watching you laugh and smile like nothing else mattered. Only that moment mattered…that moment with me."

I pause to catch my breath. "I'll tell you about the concert and how you laughed through your tears on the ride over, looking so goddamn free, so perfectly at peace as our hands locked together and music sang through the speaker. And how I held you against my chest as the band played, my arms around you, my lips grazing your ear. I wanted to kiss you so fucking badly it physically hurt. And I'll tell you about that night on the bridge when I did kiss you. Time stopped, Ella. The world stopped. Everything stopped," I confess. "And *dammit*…sometimes I wish it really did. I wish it stopped right then and there, freezing the moment, so I could hold on to you forever, just as you were. Just as *we* were."

I don't even realize tears are sliding down my cheeks until they pool at the corner of my lips. I lick them away, heaving in a shuddering breath as I choke on the final words. "We were happy."

Ella stares at me with glassy eyes, the bouquet of roses shaking in her lap. Her lips part with quick, uneven breaths as tears pool, her cheeks glowing light pink.

My heart drags over broken glass when she doesn't respond. She doesn't say anything and just gapes at me like I spouted off the Declaration of Independence in French. "Fuck," I curse under my breath, swiping both hands over my face, erasing the evidence of my pain. "Sorry. I'll go."

"Max…"

I stand from the chair and pivot to leave.

"Max, don't go," she cries out. "I do remember. I remember everything."

I pause, facing away from her. I rub the back of my neck and dip my chin, unsure what to do. Two months have whirled by in this painful purgatory and I have no idea how to fix it.

Swallowing, I slowly spin to face her. "If you need space…time…" I begin, watching her lips quiver with emotion. "I can do that. I'll wait. But if it's over… just tell me. Say it. Make it quick."

Tears trickle down her cheeks as she clutches the bouquet to her chest. Then she lifts a hand to me, beckoning me forward.

Biting down on my lip, I release a strained sigh as my legs carry me toward her. I sink down in the chair across from her and pull it forward until we're inches apart. Our knees kiss. My hands reach out to take hers and I bring them to my lips, peppering kisses along her dry knuckles.

Ella pulls free and wraps her arms around my neck, tugging me close.

I practically moan at the contact. At the feel of her face burrowing in the crook of my neck. I hold her. I hug her. I squeeze her tight, feeling her slight frame mold against me. Warm and alive. Small but strong.

She never does answer me.

She doesn't tell me if it's over, or if she just needs space.

But I don't press the matter. I don't beg for more than what she's giving me. I just hold her.

And I pretend we're on the bridge again, dancing and kissing underneath the stars, forever caught in that moment of stopped time.

McKay stands from his seat the moment he spots me rounding the corner. "Hey," he mutters, tousling his shaggy hair, looking just as fidgety as me.

I don't say anything as I zip past him and barrel through the double doors into the warm sunshine. His footsteps catch up to me. He calls my name as I dig through my pockets for a pack of cigarettes.

I went months without smoking. I always knew it was a bad habit, but it lessened my burdens and eased my stress. Then Ella came along, and *she* became my reprieve. Instead of reaching for a cigarette, I reached for her.

But nothing good ever seems to last.

"Max," he says again, latching onto my elbow to halt my quickening gait through the parking lot. "How is she? What did she say?"

"You can go ask her yourself," I reply, my answer muffled around the paper and nicotine. Smoke fills my lungs with sweet relief and I blow it back out through my nostrils. "You'll probably make more progress than me at this point. Let me know how it goes." I try to keep walking, but he pulls me back.

"She didn't say anything?"

I sigh, finally turning to look at him. My brother looks pale, the sun brightening the sheen of sweat casing his brow. "Not really. She hardly says anything to me."

He releases a slow exhale, his shoulders slackening. "That's…so weird," he says. "Do you think she has amnesia? Lost memories?" McKay stares off over my shoulder, shuffling on both feet.

"According to the doctors, she remembers everything."

Which is why none of this makes any sense.

Nodding slowly, he rubs a hand across his jaw. "Fuck, man. That's gotta suck. I can't imagine having to live with those memories…" He swallows, ducks his head. "Falling off a cliff like that. Waiting for someone to find you. Not knowing if you were going to make it or not."

My heart aches, my stomach coiling with fresh knots.

I can't think about that. The images haunt me enough in my dreams.

"Let's go," I mumble, tucking my misery away. I take a few more hard drags off my cigarette before stomping it beneath my shoe. "We should check on Dad, then try to figure out that electrical issue with the wiring."

McKay has been surprisingly helpful over the last couple of months with the home improvements and helping me take Dad to a slew of doctor appointments as we try to get to the bottom of his strange behavior. His initial hospital visit was put off by a few weeks due to Ella's fall. But then, after a trip to the emergency room that came on the heels of another bizarre night terror—one that earned McKay a bruising slug to the jaw—the tests came back inconclusive. We were referred to a specialist and still have another appointment on the horizon.

We don't have answers, but they've ruled out a lot. Vitamin deficiencies, thyroid problems, a brain tumor, various neurological conditions. The relief I feel when nothing serious is revealed always shrivels up and dies the moment Dad has another episode. Last night he was convinced Rick was outside, lurking in the bushes. He made us turn off all the lights and lock the doors as he hid underneath the kitchen table, armed with a baseball bat.

The stress is eating me alive.

Ella. Dad. Knowing high school will be over soon and I have no fucking clue what I'm doing with my life. No college aspirations, no grand plans, and no Ella to guide me through the terrifying unknowns. I've never felt more beaten down and defeated.

McKay follows me to the truck as we hop inside and I rev the engine.

"It'll be okay," he says to me, leaning back in the seat and staring out the window, his expression tight. His knees bounce up and down as he repeats, "It'll be okay."

I don't reply as I reverse out of the parking space and speed off into the deceptive sunlight.

In another life, I might believe him.

Chapter 31

ELLA

HOME SWEET HOME.

My bedroom looks the same, not a thing out of place. Bookbinding items lay strewn across my desk and my bedsheets are rumpled from the last time I slept in them. Even my lava lamp burns bright, splashing a magenta glow across my cantaloupe walls.

I lean into the walker, my fingers curling around the grips.

"I'll give you some privacy," Mom says from behind me, her hand extending to squeeze my shoulder. "Take your time and relax. I'm going to make us a hot meal."

I stare blankly at a horse poster taped to my wall and imagine myself riding under a Michigan sky. "I'm not hungry."

"You should eat. You'll need your strength while you heal."

"I'm healing fine. Moving around, getting stronger every day." True enough. My muscle atrophy has dwindled, thanks to weeks of physical therapy. I even took a few steps without the walker this morning. "I'll eat when I'm hungry."

"Ella."

"What was it you were going to tell me at the hospital that first day when I woke up?" My teeth clench as I keep my gaze pinned across the room. I hear my mother's sharp intake of breath behind me before it ghosts along the back of my neck. "You haven't brought it up again. Sounded important."

A few quiet beats tick by. "Your grandmother is in hospice care. I didn't want to worry you."

"You already told me she was sick."

"Yes, but it's worse than I led you to believe. She doesn't have a lot of time left."

My heart twists. Grandma Shirley and I have never been all that close, but she's my family. And aside from me, she's all my mother has left. "I'm sorry. I wish I could visit her."

"I know, sweetheart," Mom says. "I'm going to make us some din—"

"But that's not it," I interrupt.

She pauses, sucking in that breath again. "What?"

My chest thrums with a tug of intuition. Mom is keeping something from me. I know it. She's upset about Grandma Shirley, sure, but that's not what she was going to tell me at the hospital that night. I turn around slowly, holding on to my walker for support. My mother stands there, one hand pressed to her collarbone as her eyes shimmer with unspoken words. "Tell me," I urge her.

Her eyes dip to the carpet.

"Mom…please."

"Fine," she relents, her throat bobbing through a swallow. "It's…about Kai's father. Ricardo."

I blink.

It takes a moment for the words to process because I wasn't expecting them. "What about him?"

"Well, we became closer over the past few months while you were in the hospital. We started dating," she confesses. "I didn't want to shake you up. I know it's strange. I haven't dated anyone since your father left and that was over a decade ago, so I hope you don't think any less of—"

"Mom," I cut her off. "I think it's awesome. Why would you be afraid to tell me that?"

Her lips thin as her head swings back and forth and her shoulders lift with a shrug. "I…don't really know. I'm sorry. I thought you'd be rattled and take it the wrong way."

Frowning, I shake my head back at her. "No way. I'm happy for you. Of course I am."

"Really?"

"Really." My eyes narrow as I simmer in the bombshell. "Brynn didn't tell me."

"I asked her not to. I thought it would be too much for you to process. You were so fragile, Ella. I wanted to be careful."

"Well, it's fine. It's more than fine," I say, feeling a prickle of joy for the first time in a while. Mom has been lonely. She deserves to settle down and enjoy romance again. "I'm happy for you."

Her smile tightens as she bobs her head quickly. "Thank you. I'll go whip up a casserole. You should eat something."

I go to protest, but she's already marching down the hallway toward the kitchen. Sighing, I close the door behind her and drink in the quiet. I stand in the center of the room, taking it all in, my eyes panning around the small space and its piles of organized clutter.

As my gaze catches with sullen green in the mirror across the way, I pause to look at my reflection. Truly look at her. She's an accurate representation of my insides, I decide. Sickly and sapped. Anemic. My pale skin is almost translucent with gray circles underlining my eyes. Once-shiny hair hangs in drab and stringy sections as it frames my face, thanks to the cheap toiletries provided by the hospital and rehabilitation center. Mom brought over my favorite conditioner, but it never left my backpack. Healthy hair didn't seem important at the time when every other part of me was running on empty. An ailing soul and bedridden heart.

The doctor told me that depression and mood swings were likely. A therapist came in to talk to me a few times, but what could I say? Last December I was on the precipice of falling in love with a boy, and that boy shares an eerily similar face with the person who attacked me and left me for dead.

No.

There is no healing there. There is only a gaping wound bleeding with irony.

While Brynn has been a notable source of warmth and solace, I've noticed that, somewhere along the way…I stopped adding the exclamation point to the end of her name. I slowly make my way over to bed and wrench a quilt from the mattress, carrying it to my mirror and draping it over the glass. I don't want to see the physical evidence of my decline.

There is no healing there, either.

Before I shuffle back to bed, I falter near the window. I glance outside at the dusky sky that's painted with the final remnants of a setting sun. Blood orange and dark pink. The colors spill over the roof of the Manning residence, making it look like it's aflame with otherworldly fire. It's haunting and beautiful at the same time. I savor the view for a few minutes before I tug the window up a crack, grateful it isn't sticking, and crawl into bed.

Mom knocks on my door an hour later, telling me dinner is ready, but I ignore her and feign sleep. Her footsteps retreat and everything is quiet again. Dusk transitions to nightfall but sleep never comes. The hours tick by in slow motion as I toss and turn, kicking off my bedsheets then drawing them back up. I roll onto my back, my side, trying to get comfortable. But comfort can't find me.

I wonder all night if he'll climb through my window.

He never does.

Day two brings another round of detectives to my doorstep. They'd filtered in and out of the hospital with notepads and stoic faces in the days following my revival from the coma, asking questions and interrogating me about the fall.

Names were thrown around.

I denied everything.

With no evidence aside from the mysterious bruise on my cheek, their hands are tied. They saunter out of my house thirty minutes later, no closer to the truth. I make my way out to the front porch, my walker leading the way, and watch the patrol cars zoom out of the gravel driveway.

As tires shoot up a cloud of rocks and grit, I squint into the sunlight. A lawn mower throttles from across the street as the dust settles. Max stands in the center of his lawn, yanking the rope-start multiple times to no avail. Sunshine washes down on him from above, making his skin glisten against a dark-navy tank. His biceps bulge with every rough tug on the rope-start.

He gives up after five tries, blowing out a breath and taking a step back from the mower. I watch as sweat trickles down the side of his neck and dampens the roots of his hair.

He stalks toward me a moment later.

I straighten on the porch, my grip on the walker tightening, but less for physical support. I watch Max cross the street that separates our properties, his eyes on the ground.

"Hi," I call out when he marches through the spring-green lawn.

I can't believe it's already spring.

It still feels like winter, in more ways than one.

"Hey." He stops in front of me, still nearly a foot taller than me despite my elevation on the porch step. "How are you?"

"Doing better. I feel a lot stronger." I lift my arm and flex my bicep, infusing lightness into my tone. "But you'd definitely win at arm wrestling right now."

Finally, his chin rises and our eyes catch, causing electricity to crackle. Eye contact alone has neon heat fizzing between us. "That's great, Ella."

I bite my lip and drop my arm. "Lawn-mower complications?"

"Apparently," he says, hands sliding into the pockets of his running shorts. "What did the cops say?"

I shrug, feigning nonchalance. "They're still investigating my fall. I'm not sure why."

"Some guys at school have been under the microscope. Word got out that you were tossed in the lake last year." Max's eyes thin, reading me for a reaction. "You'd tell me if someone hurt you, right?"

"Of course."

Of course I'd tell you if some bully pushed me off a cliff. Unfortunately for both of us, the truth is far more devastating.

Forcing a flat smile, I glance over his shoulder. "What's McKay up to these days? I haven't seen him around." My tone is remarkably even. I don't even blink.

"He's been staying with one of his basketball buddies for the last few days. Said he needed to hunker down on a project they're working on for biology."

Convenient. "Gotcha."

"He sends his regards."

My chest strains as I hold in the laugh of contempt. My eyes burn, a prickle of angry-hot tears threatening. "That's nice of him."

"Yeah." He nods. "I wanted to give you space while you settled in," he continues, ruffling his slick hair. "I didn't want to smother you. I'm sure it feels like I have been."

"You don't smother me, Max. You…"

My words trail off.

I want to say that he grounds me, heals me, makes me feel like surviving that fall wasn't just a lucky blip. But I can't, because those feelings are at war with the paralyzing image of his twin brother's face. Every time I look at Max, I see the haunting resemblance, and it taints the warmth he once provided. My silence hangs there, heavy, pregnant with the unspoken truth. The conflict in me rages on, torn between the solace he offers and the echoes of the past.

"You mean a lot to me," I mutter, looking away. "I appreciate you visiting me every day. And for giving me all those flowers."

I notice his hands are void of orange roses today. I understand. He can only afford so many flowers. He can only afford so many heartbreaks when those flowers wither away on my bedside table and we're no closer to what we were.

"Ella…" he murmurs, stepping closer until the toes of his shoes are flush with the wooden porch step. One hand reaches out to cover mine as it curls tightly around the walker. "If I did something wrong…if I upset you somehow…you'd let me know?"

I watch his throat bob with turmoil as I unclench my fist. I twine my fingers with his, my balance teetering from his touch. Our hands lock together.

A perfect fit.

"You haven't done anything wrong," I whisper. "Not a single thing. Not ever."

Pain skates across his face, burrowing in every crease. His grip tightens on my hand as he nods, blinks, and lets go. "Text me any time, Sunny. I'll be here." He doesn't wait for me to respond before spinning around and walking away.

I stare at his retreating back and then watch as he fights with the lawnmower again. He yanks, jerks, snaps at the rope-start. Once, twice, twelve times, pulling harder with each attempt. He curses and growls as sweat pours down his face.

Then it starts.

A guttural purr slams into my ears.

Max glances over at me as the tension drains from him and he pushes it forward along the grass.

A tear slips out and I head back inside.

By nightfall I'm restless and antsy, the anxiety I've been harboring spilling into my dreamworld as I doze in and out of sleep. I dream about Phoenix, my childhood horse. My beloved, long-lost friend. We're riding through pastures of gold and green, the sun beating down on us as we gallop for miles. The air is warm. The clouds are marshmallow white. Everything is perfect as birds sing and a balmy wind has my hair taking flight.

And then McKay appears out of nowhere, blocking our path.

It all happens so fast.

With a flick of his wrist, he slashes my horse's throat with a knife, grinning evilly as blood splatters across his face. He kills Phoenix right in front of me. I scream, tipping over as the stallion bleeds out with a terrified neigh and topples sideways.

McKay's voice haunts me as I rocket toward the ground. "Stop running, Ella."

I shoot up in bed, drenched in cold sweat.

My heart is in my throat.

My pulse jackknifes.

Text me any time. I'll be here, Sunny.

My face crumples in a mess of tears as I scramble for my cell phone, nearly knocking it off my nightstand. I don't think as I pull up his name and type out a quick, frantic text message.

Me: Come over. Please.

There's no way he's awake. It's after 2:00 a.m.

I drag my fingers through my hair and slump forward, trying to steady my breathing. And to my surprise, my phone dings a few seconds later.

Max: Two minutes

I left my window open again, which isn't smart. McKay still lives across the street from me, despite the fact I haven't laid eyes on him since I've been back. I'm making it so easy for him to slip inside my bedroom and take care of his unfinished business. To bury his secret for good.

All I have is a baseball bat hiding underneath the bed, even though it won't do much if I'm ambushed in my sleep.

But it's not McKay who widens the window two minutes later. It's Max. He's wearing gray sweatpants and a fitted white tee as one leg slides into the room, followed by the other.

My back is to the bed frame, my knees drawn to my chest. I'm still shaky and out of sorts, the dream fresh in my mind. "Max," I say, voice torn.

He stands there for a few beats, staring at me through the wall of darkness, his arms hanging at his sides. His fingers clench and splay like he doesn't know if he should reach for me or not.

I make it easy for him. I lift my hand and hold it out, a silent plea for comfort.

Max crawls in my bed, those strong, safe arms wrapping around me and pulling me close.

Relief. Reprieve. Completion.

A ragged sigh spills out of both of us when I bury my face against his chest and breathe him in. Clean, earthy familiarity. A trace of smoke. Woods and pine. Max nuzzles his nose in my hair, his hand curling behind my head, gentle against my incision scar—a purplish zigzag across the back of my skull. A few inches of new hair growth sprout around it that he lightly skims with his fingers. He goes to speak, but I don't want to talk. There's nothing to say.

I lean up and find his mouth instead, severing his words.

Max goes still, freezing against me as our lips fuse together. I'm not hesitant or soft. My tongue thrusts into his open mouth and his breath hitches at the contact, startled. Uncertain.

Pulling back on a sharp exhale, he cradles my face between his hands and frowns. "Ella…"

No talking.

No words.

My eyes are wild as they skim over his beautiful, staggered face.

I kiss him again.

I lift my leg and curl it around his waist, yanking him fully against me as my tongue plunders his mouth and we both groan. His tongue slides against mine, hesitation dissolving, the kiss turning feral and all-consuming. His hands glide to my neck, thumbs pressed to my jaw as he tugs it down and opens me wider. Our tongues become a desperate tangle. A hungry, wet dance. Moans bleed together as our faces slant, searching for more places we can reach and taste. It's been too long. Months without his kisses have left me starved.

I reach down and tug my shorts off my hips, my underwear following. Without breaking the kiss, I snatch one of his hands and drag it lower until his palm is pressed between my thighs. His tongue stops moving as he shudders on a groan, paralyzed.

I'm soaking wet.

His fingers disappear inside me, plunging deep and fast, the sound of my need a slippery echo in the quiet room.

But it's not enough. I need more.

"Condom," I whisper breathlessly, pulling away from his thoroughly kissed lips.

Max drags his fingers out of me, rubbing me until I jerk forward. "I didn't bring any," he says.

My eyes close and my mouth hangs open on a silent moan as I thrust against his hand. "Doesn't matter. I just need you."

So reckless. So heedlessly reckless.

"Ella." His fingers keep moving, working me into a frenzy as his forehead dips to mine. "Are you sure?"

"I…" My body is sure. It's so damn sure. But my falter hangs heavily between us and his fingers stop moving.

"Ella," he repeats, going still, cupping me gently down below. "I need you to be sure."

"Don't stop," I mutter, my hands sinking in his hair.

"Look at me."

My eyes remain closed. I can't. I can't seem to open them.

His hand disappears from between my legs and I hear him sigh as he pulls back. Blindly, I reach for him, tugging him back to me and burying my face against his collar. "You won't hurt me."

"That's not the only thing I'm worried about," he replies, pressing a kiss to my temple.

Tears bloom behind my closed eyelids as I hold on to him as tightly as my weakened muscles will allow. "Please," I whisper. "I need you."

His heart pounds against mine. His hands snake around me, cupping my bare bottom, then trailing underneath the hem of my tank top.

Warm, steady breaths beat against my hair.

"Fuck." And then he's sliding down my body, gently moving me onto my back as he settles between my legs and parts my knees. Heartbeats leap up my throat. My hands grip handfuls of his hair as he slings his arms underneath my thighs to hold me steady before he lowers his head.

I cry out when his tongue thrusts inside me.

"Oh God...*Max*." My whole body trembles, my back arching off the mattress on instinct. Any pain or resistance I might feel peters out, overridden by his mouth devouring me. His fingertips gouge my thighs. My hands fist his hair with a violent squeeze. If I'm hurting him, he doesn't notice. Doesn't care.

I'm already close. Achy, needy, full of pent-up feelings.

My thighs clamp the sides of his face, tremors rippling through me, overtaking me one tongue flick at a time. His mouth latches onto me and he sucks hard as two fingers slide inside me.

He pumps in and out. Over and over.

Rhythm.

The perfect rhythm, a recipe for detonation.

His mouth was made for me. It knows what I need. He knows what I crave and he's relentless in bringing me over the edge.

It's heartbreaking how this boy is everything I could ever want and more, and yet...I can hardly look at him.

I glance down, my shorts and underwear dangling off one ankle. I wrap my legs around his upper back and burrow my nails in his scalp, hanging on for dear life. Hanging on to the moment, the feeling, the stopped measure of time when nothing else matters. Everything falls away but him. It's just us… only Max and me.

I buck up against his face as tingles bloom and climb. A raspy cry tears through me. He quickly lifts his hand to cover my mouth, to silence my scream that could wake the dead, and I bite down when two fingers slip inside my mouth.

The orgasm slams into me, a lightning bolt shooting across a black sky. I want to wail, shriek, sob, and laugh. The feeling is electrifying, freeing, soul-shattering. I'm flying…

I'm falling.

Tree branches tear at my skin. Cold wind snaps into my lungs. Fireworks burst from above as McKay stares down at me, watching, waiting, begging for me to die.

The bliss ebbs and terror sneaks in. I deflate on the mattress, becoming a sagging, wretched heap of defeat.

Max doesn't notice at first as he slowly works his way up my body, pausing to graze his fingertips along the scar on my lower abdomen, left behind from my pelvis fracture surgery. It's long, curved, and pink as it dips toward my bikini line.

Bending, he presses a soft kiss to the marred skin, only pausing when he feels me shaking. His lips fall away from me as he lifts his head and stares up at the expanse of my shivering body while my silent sobs mangle the intimate moment.

The pleasure is gone, replaced by grief-soaked memories.

"Sunny Girl," he murmurs on a tortured breath, army crawling the rest of the way up until we're face-to-face. "Ella…God. Please don't cry. You're safe. I'm here."

I wrap my arms around his neck and haul him to me, shoving his face to the curve of my neck and twining my legs around his waist. Minutes tick by in silence and my tears dry out, my pain retreating into its dark, bleak hole, having sapped me of strength like a parasite draining its host.

The moment is over. Time presses on and a single word hovers on the tip of my tongue.

Stay.

I want to say it, scream it, brand it on his heart.

Stay, stay, stay.

But all I muster is the gravest lie. "Go."

Max freezes on top of me, a breath catching in his throat. It whispers like a ghostly chill along my neck when he lets it back out.

He pulls up, stares down at me.

My lip wobbles as I tell him, "You should go." I can see a baffled frown twist, illuminated by the soft moonlight seeping into the room.

He swallows. "You don't want me to stay?"

"Mom will be checking on me. It's not smart."

"Ella, I don't care—"

"Thank you," I blurt out. The words sound awful and grating. Selfish. Like he provided me with a service and now I'm sending him on his way. "I'm sorry. I just…I think I should try to sleep now. I'll text you tomorrow."

Head falling, chin lowering to his chest, he blows out another hard breath, stewing in my dismissal. Then he nods and pulls away from me. "Yeah," he mutters. "Sure."

Nothing else is said as he moves off the mattress and pads across the floor to my window. He hesitates briefly, just for a second, swiping a hand through his hair before he climbs out the window and fades into the darkness.

The routine continues on for the next two nights.

Max slips into my bedroom through the open window after midnight and takes me apart with his tongue and his fingers. Then I vibrate with tears in the breadth of his arms as he strokes my hair, shushes my demons, and tells me it will be okay. I let him hold me for a few minutes, savoring his touch. His warmth. His love. Reveling in the few precious seconds I allow us.

But the seconds pass and I send him away under the guise that my mother will discover him in my bed come sunrise. He knows that's not the reason. He doesn't know what the real reason is, but he knows it's not that.

Max can't stay because I'm afraid of the words that will tumble from my lips.

I'm terrified of the truth that will escape my mouth when I fall into grisly nightmares. I fear that when I startle awake in the night, I'll think he's someone else.

And I'll be scared of him.
I never want to be scared of him.
So I don't let him stay.
I make him leave. I push him away, even though it breaks us both.
And I count down the painful minutes until he returns.

Chapter 32

ELLA

On my fifth day home from the rehabilitation center, I'm reclining on my bed, immersing myself in the final chapters of the book *Monster*. Despite being well aware that the assignments are overdue and that I'll be pursuing my GED once I've fully recovered, I felt compelled to finish it. I've never stopped reading a book before, even when I didn't enjoy it. Nothing feels worse than an incomplete story, the characters dangling in limbo, the plot points collapsing into unknowns. The notion has always brought me anxiety, so I trudge through pages and pages until I reach the end. No matter what.

Luckily, this book is great.

No regrets.

My mother approaches and lingers in the doorway as I lie curled up under an old quilt Grandma Shirley stitched for me years ago—it's my way of feeling closer to her since I'm unable to visit. It was buried in a box in my closet, but after a quick wash, it now feels as good as new. I idly wish I could apply the same simple steps to my own well-being.

"Ella, honey," Mom says, her hand curled around the edge of the door. "Can you meet me in the living room?"

I toss the book beside me on the bed, next to my notebook of unfinished words. I've been working on a letter to Jonah, but my thoughts are jumbled and nothing feels right. Nothing feels good enough to send him. After starting over dozens of times, all I'm left with are wads of crumpled lined paper strewn across the bedsheets and my own disappointment.

When I glance up, my eyes fixate on my mother. She looks blanched, her complexion paler than mine. "What's wrong?" I ask.

"Nothing." Her voice shrinks on the word.

Unlike me, she's a terrible liar.

She sweeps her hair back, her fingers quivering. "You're feeling better, yes?"

"Yes. I was moving around without the walker this morning."

Her sigh sounds like relief, which is a valid response, yet it hollows out my chest. Suspicion blossoms between my ribs. "Is this about Kai's father? Are you going to officially introduce him to me as your new boyfriend? Because it's not a big deal. I already told you that."

Darting her eyes away and fidgeting with her hair, Mom clears her throat, neither confirming nor denying. "I'll meet you in the living room in a minute," she says. Then she dashes from the threshold so fast I swear she leaves a cloud of smoke behind.

I rub the heel of my palm to my chest.

My cell phone sits on my nightstand beside the potted crayon and the white stone. I reach for the phone before climbing out of bed, desperately needing a shower but needing to know what my mother is up to more.

Dangling my legs over the side, I smile at the string of messages and GIF wars with Brynn that have brightened my spirits over the last few days, then pull up my recent text to Max.

Me: I miss your lists.

My smile buckles.

I sent it at 4:00 a.m., hours after he left me sated and spent, his tongue working me as long as he could. He brought me to the edge multiple times, then tore me away, reveling in my squirms and protests, knowing he needed to savor the small amount of time I offered. When I broke, I broke hard. After, I wrapped my hand around him as he kneeled over me, caging me in and exploding onto my stomach, his fist in my hair, the other gripping the bed frame as he came apart with a tapered groan.

I let him hold me through the tears.

And then he left.

My heart wilts when I discover that he hasn't responded to my text. It shows Read a minute after I sent it. I can't blame him for it, just like I can't blame my poor heart for caving in on itself at the radio silence that I set in motion.

I plop the phone back down and rise slowly from the mattress. It takes a minute for me to gather my bearings, my balance, and then I move forward on weakened legs. They don't feel like jelly anymore, at least. More like overcooked spaghetti. I refuse to reach for my walker as I pad across the carpet toward my bedroom door. Mom's voice carries down the hall from the living room, inciting a new wave of curiosity.

I'm confident I'll see Ricardo and Kai sitting in my living room, their nerves high as they inform me of the new relationship status.

A sigh leaves me as I press forward.

I'm careful down the short hallway, my hand grazing along the cream-painted wall to keep me steady and upright. I'm smiling again when I reach the end, alight with accomplishment. So far, that was the farthest walk I've taken unassisted.

Mom stands from the love seat across from me, her eyes flaring wide, hands wringing together at her abdomen as she blinks repetitively. "Ella."

"I walked the whole way," I tell her. "I did it."

Tears sluice her eyes. She's happy for me.

But before I can say anything else, a shadow steals my attention, pulling me from the proud moment. My brows draw together and my gaze holds tight with my mother's as she swallows hard and her tears fall freely down chalky cheeks.

A feeling sinks into me.

A jab of awareness. An elbow to my gut.

I turn around slowly when a flash of copper hair catches in my peripheral vision.

And I freeze.

A cloud of disbelief swirls around me as my eyes meet with familiar dark green.

I gasp. Choke. Teeter, sway, and shake.

He stares at me from the edge of the kitchen, heavy emotion glowing in his gaze. His voice hitches as he says with a smile I haven't seen since I was fifteen years old, "Hey, Piglet."

The last thing I hear is my own wailing cry.

Then my mother's arms are around me, catching me as I go down.

Chapter 33

E L L A

J ONAH SITS BESIDE ME ON THE COUCH.

Jonah.

Sits.

Beside me.

On.

The.

Couch.

Mom holds a tissue over her mouth and nose, seated on my opposite side, stroking my hair back as my body shivers violently through the earthquake.

"I told you to wait in the kitchen," Mom scolds, her voice a distorted garble. "I wanted to ease her into it. She's still fragile, Jonah."

"I've waited years. I couldn't wait any longer."

This is a trick.

This isn't real.

I'm still in a coma.

Holy shit—*I'm still in a coma.*

I pinch my skin, pull at my hair, stomp my feet.

Wake up, Ella.

Wake. Up!

The scenery doesn't change.

I tilt my head left and Jonah is still next to me, his arm draped over the back of the couch, his expression creased with affection and concern as he rubs my back and tells me it's okay.

"No," I croak out. "No, no, no. You're not real. I–I'm not—"

"I'm real." Jonah takes me by the shoulders, holding me still while I mentally and physically unravel. Finding my eyes, he forces me to look at him. "Take a deep breath. Breathe, Ella. I'm real. I'm right here. I missed you so fucking much."

My face crumples. "No."

Mom squeezes my forearm, sniffling on the other side of me. "Honey, I'm so sorry I didn't tell you sooner," she chokes out. "I didn't want to get your hopes up if it didn't work out… You'd come such a long way. And then the accident happened, and I was terrified. It's so much to process, and you were barely hanging on. I thought I was getting my baby boy back, only to lose my little girl. It felt like the universe was forcing me to trade."

Her words bleed into fog. "How…how long?"

A pause.

"January," Mom whispers.

January.

It's now April. It's April and my brother has been out of prison—off *death row*—for three months, and I am just now finding out.

I feel like I might puke. From astoundment, from despair, from heart-sinking disbelief.

"He's been staying with a friend in Charlotte," she continues, voice brittle. "I thought it was for the best, until you were fully healed. We didn't know what the long-term effects of your brain injury would be, or how you would process such a massive shock. I wanted to—"

"How." The world falls out as a demand, not a question. I'm staring at Jonah in a daze. I've dreamt of him so many times, in so many different ways. Brutal and terrifying. Sweet and tender. Fear mulled with memories, pain sweetened by warm nostalgia.

But never like this.

Never real, in the flesh, close enough to touch.

At twenty-two, he looks older. Weathered by time, by barren cell walls, and by God knows what else. A scar ropes along his right cheekbone and dark shadows gray the space beneath his eyes.

I stand.

I find some source of strength and jolt upright on wobbly, stringy legs, my mother's hand shooting out to hold me steady. "*How*," I repeat, emotion climbing, brewing, swelling to a peak. "Tell me how. Tell me how this is real. I can't believe it. I don't, I refuse. This can't possibly be happening." Tears fall rapidly, violently.

Jonah's jaw flickers as he stares up at me. A big hand lifts to sweep through thick, coppery hair. Light brown with reddish tints. Full on top, shaved to the skin on the sides and in the back. His nails are rimmed with dirt, and another scar drags across his knuckles, a puckering of pale, raised flesh. "It's a long story," he says.

"I'm sure it is. Tell me everything. Right now." I can't stop crying. My voice sounds ten octaves above normal, squeaking with desperation. "I was there, in that courtroom, when they sentenced you to *death*," I screech. "Death, Jonah! People don't just walk off death row."

"Sometimes they do," he murmurs.

"Did you escape?" I tug my hair back with both hands, grateful my mother is still holding on to me. I'm mentally free-falling and can hardly stay standing. "Oh, my God…you broke out."

"What? No. Jesus, Ella."

"Then tell me how it's possible. I can't even begin to comprehend this," I cry, shaking my head, my fingernails burrowing in my scalp.

Mom answers first. "I was working on overturning his sentence for a long time, Ella," she tells me. "This didn't happen overnight. I've been at it from the moment they read off that verdict. All those late nights at the computer, on the phone…that was me, fighting for your brother's freedom."

"You didn't tell me," I breathe out.

Heartbreak shimmers in her eyes. "I couldn't, baby girl. I saw the toll it took on you, both emotionally and mentally. You were angry, confused, lost. I chose to keep this hidden from you because I didn't want you to bear the weight of new disappointment if it didn't work out. It was my way of shielding you from the unpredictable roller coaster that comes with fighting for justice."

I lower myself to the living room floor, collapsing and shaking. "But people aren't just sentenced to *death row*," I grit out. "The…the evidence. I even thought you were guilty. *I* did!" I slam a palm to my chest as my gaze pans to Jonah, the guilt suffocating me. My lungs are waterlogged with it, shrinking with it. "Jonah…you were there, at the scene. You were covered in their blood."

His face is unreadable, eyes skimming across my face. "The DNA evidence was compromised. Mom worked her ass off to prove that," he says. "And there was jury tampering. Erin's fuckhead father had a friend on that jury, put there to skew the verdict. The juror admitted it. He confessed." He swallows, pauses. "The whole trial was a farce, a sham orchestrated to get me convicted. They needed someone to blame, to slap with a guilty verdict, because the entire goddamn world was watching."

My throat constricts. "But the blood…why were you covered in their blood?"

He inhales, looking away briefly before meeting my gaze and steepling his fingers. "Like I've been telling you all along, I tried to *help* them. Tried to resuscitate them. It wasn't my crime, but I was there after the fact, attempting to save them. I knew it looked incriminating, so I left the scene. I fucked up, yeah, but I didn't deserve a goddamn death sentence for it."

The weight of my doubt crushes me. All these years I had allowed the visuals of that night, the evidence presented, the media frenzy, to direct the narrative. I let suspicion cloud love. All of it overshadowed the boy I grew up with, the man I knew, deep down in my soul.

Our mother chimes in, dabbing a tissue to her eyes. "The lab that was processing the evidence had a contamination incident," she explains. "Some of the samples got mixed up, including Jonah's. Your grandmother helped pay for Dr. Jensen's services—the forensic expert I've been in contact with for the past two years. He was the one who brought it to light. He discovered that the DNA results from the bloody clothes didn't just have anomalies; they were fundamentally flawed."

My heart races, trying to grapple with the enormity of such an oversight. "How was this not caught during the trial?"

Jonah shrugs, his frustration evident. "Inefficient cross-checking, maybe. The prosecution built a strong story and everyone got swept up in it. Erin was my girlfriend, and I was the jealous lover who caught her cheating. No one thought to question the authenticity of the evidence. They trusted the lab results and followed the seeds planted by thirsty prosecutors. But this wasn't just a simple error. Dr. Jensen revealed that the lab had faced similar issues before, but they were brushed under the rug. This time it cost me years of my life."

I'm still shaking my head, still buzzing with incredulity. "And then you had a second trial? How did I not hear about it?"

"I didn't go to trial again. With no witness testimony to put me directly at the scene, the verdict was entirely based around that DNA evidence. The rest was circumstantial and hardly enough for a credible case. The odds of a guilty verdict were fifty-fifty."

I stare at him for a heavy beat. "But…you *were* there," I breathe out. "Who else was there? Did you see the real killer?"

Jonah doesn't blink, doesn't break eye contact. Harrowing seconds pass before he replies. "No. And it doesn't matter. There's no concrete physical evidence now, no witnesses to corroborate anything. It's not my job to figure out who really did it."

I wasn't there…but I saw him.

He came home, covered head to toe in blood.

They never found the murder weapon, but Mom always kept a gun in the house and still does. The ballistics matched one of them.

Still, it was circumstantial. It was a common pistol—a 9mm firearm. A Glock 19.

His bloody clothes were the smoking gun. If the DNA evidence was no longer credible, they had nothing to go on but assumptions: Jonah's lack of an alibi, his relationship with Erin, and Mom's weapon that she told the packed courtroom was stolen years prior; she'd just never reported it.

Jonah pulls his bottom lip between his teeth. "The prosecutor chose not to retry the case due to the publicity and notoriety it gained," he continues.

"Given the errors in the initial trial, they felt that a new trial could further erode the public's trust, especially if there was a chance they might lose. Which there was." Jonah stands from the couch, hovering over me as I sit slumped on the floor, still trembling, still reeling. "Piglet…it's over. I'm a free man," he says softly, crouching down in front of me and pushing a piece of hair off my eyes. "And I'm so fucking glad you woke up. That you're okay. I thought about you and Mom every damn day. I worried, I stressed, I wrote you letters. I missed you both so much."

Tears glimmer in his eyes. Raw pain reflects back at me, filling me with the same sentiment.

He sinks down lower until we're face-to-face.

I'm looking directly into the eyes of my brother. The man I thought was lost forever. The man I slapped with my own guilty verdict.

Jonah.

He's no longer sitting on death row, awaiting a needle to the arm. He's here and he's free.

He came back to me.

I break into pieces, throwing myself at him with the remaining fragments of my strength. He holds me tight, pulling me to his chest as we stumble back against the front of the couch. Strong arms wrap around me, and his face drops to the crook of my neck, his tears falling and dampening my blouse. He smells like cedar and cigars and the stale musk of lost time.

We break together.

Mom slides down from the sofa to join us, slinging her arms around us both. We sit like that for close to an hour, huddled up on the living room floor.

Sobbing, releasing, healing…*together*.

Mom.

Jonah.

And me.

We're a family again.

We sit together by the sun-kissed lake, set only a few feet from the road. My walker rests beside me for support after Jonah drove me over, eager to spend alone time together.

The afternoon was filled with reminiscing and swapping stories over the years: Jonah's tales more harrowing, and mine a mix of sweet and sour. The sweeter moments took over as we ate chicken casserole at the kitchen table—my brother's favorite meal. We made it together and I savored every bite.

It was the best casserole I've ever had.

My orange backpack is settled in my lap as we stare out at the glimmery lake and I fiddle with the key chains.

"I can't believe you still have that thing," Jonah says, flicking stones at the water.

They skim across the surface and my memories bleed together.

Flashes of Jonah trying to teach me to skip stones when I was just a little girl fuse with images of Max's chest flush against my back, his careful arms instructing me as he whispered in my ear.

It's all about the rhythm.

I glance at the backpack decorated in black Sharpie, then up at Jonah. "It's the most precious thing I own," I tell him. "It was the only tangible piece of you I had left."

He nods. "I wrote to you. Did you get my letters?"

Guilt nibbles at my insides, leaving tiny holes. "Yes," I croak out. "I read them thousands of times."

"You never wrote me back." His features crease with disappointment. "I thought you hated me."

"Part of me did," I admit. "But part of me loved you, too. And that's the part of me that hated myself."

"You really thought I did it?" he wonders, voice cracking on the last word.

"Yes." My eyes close tightly, pain skittering through my veins. "I don't know," I mutter. "Some days I couldn't believe you would do that. I couldn't fathom such a thing. You were Jonah. My devoted, heroic big brother who always kept me safe." I drag my finger down the front of my backpack, tracing the Winnie the Pooh design. "But those were the days that hurt too much…to the point where I could hardly function, could barely breathe without choking on the lump of grief. It was easier to imagine that you were where you belonged, instead of a reality in which you were going to be executed in cold blood for a crime you didn't commit."

Jonah leans back on both palms, his hair tangling with the warm breeze as he soaks up my words. It's a perfect sixty-five-degree day, the sun a brilliant yellow, the treetops undulating against a blue sky. He tips his head up and squints at the clouds. "Remember that day we were playing Pooh sticks on the bridge and our sticks kept getting stuck in the weeds?"

Golden memories flicker through my mind as sunlight slants across the lake. "Of course I do. I remember everything from our childhood."

"You were only five or six. I think it was the summer before Dad separated us and took you away from me," he recalls, bitterness seeping into his tone. "Anyway, you started crying. Said it was unfair and the river was cheating."

I snort a laugh through my heartbreak and shake my head. "So dramatic."

"You were." He smiles. "Then you made us walk down to the water's edge and pluck all the sticks out of the brush. You wanted to give them a second chance."

Sighing, I tuck my chin to my chest. "I never thought I'd get a second chance with you," I tell him sadly. "So I started playing Pooh sticks by myself." I look over my shoulder at the bridge standing tall above us, a few yards away. "I'd play them on that bridge over there and I'd pretend you were with me." I consider telling him about Max and about how he gave *me* a second chance—a second chance at living. A second chance at peace. My eyes water but the words dry out. "I guess I don't need to pretend anymore."

"When you're stronger, we should play," he muses, pulling at some blades of grass and letting them flutter from his fingers. Then he sits up straighter and looks at me, a question in his eyes. The mood shifts, a cold front rushing in. "Tell me more about that night. About the fall."

My heart thunders. "What? Why?"

"I want to know the truth."

"You do know the truth. I tripped and fell. It was stupid."

He studies me, rubbing his fingers over his short goatee. Dubiety shimmers back at me, lingering deep within the green. "Sorry, but I have a hard time believing that. You're savvy when it comes to the outdoors. I taught you everything you need to know. There's no way you'd stumble off a cliff all alone at night."

"Well, I did. It was dark and I was trying to see something over the ledge."

"What were you trying to see?"

My mind races with fictional scenarios, twisting up my tongue. "I–I don't know. A snake or something."

"A snake in December?"

"I don't remember, Jonah. My memories are still hazy." My pulse thrums faster as sweat slicks my brow, trying to give me away.

He frowns. "You said you remembered everything about our childhood, but you can't remember what was so appealing that it made you topple over a thirty-foot cliff?"

Heat blooms on my cheeks. "You think I'm lying?"

"Are you?" Jonah stares at me for a few seconds, then turns to look at the water as a family of ducks coasts by. "I promised you I'd always keep you safe," he tells me, his timbre sounding tortured. "Kills me that I wasn't there. It absolutely slaughters me that you've been by yourself for all these years, and I was one month too late to prevent you from a traumatic fucking brain injury."

I close my eyes, shoving aside the memories. "I haven't been alone. I've had Mom." It's a partial truth—Mom was there, even though she was always so wrapped up in her "work." Work that I now realize was her mission to set Jonah free. Part of me is angry that she kept it from me, but the bigger part of me understands her reasoning. I hadn't made it easy for her to open up—especially about Jonah. I carried my own burdens and, in doing so, unintentionally contributed to the isolation she must have felt in her mission. "Anyway," I continue with a sigh. "I fell. And I'm okay now. Everything is okay."

My brother sighs, swallowing down his fight. It's not the time for it. Maybe it never will be. "I really wish you wrote to me," he says, eyes dipped to the grass. "Would've felt like the sun on my skin, just reading your words, hearing your voice in my mind."

"I'm sorry," I rasp. "I'm sorry I abandoned you. I'm sorry I doubted you, even if it was for my own protection."

He nods slowly, simmering in my answer. "I suppose if that was how you stayed safe and protected, despite it being at my own expense…I'll take it."

My mind swirls with sweet-spun memories of Jonah defending my honor when we were kids, of telling off bullies, of sticking up for me, even to our parents.

Even if it cost him. Groundings, punishments, spankings. He would willingly accept the consequences, no matter what.

As long as I was okay.

"I can't believe you beat up a prison guard," I say, recalling one of his letters.

Jonah shrugs like it was nothing. "The fucker deserved it for running his mouth about you. I'd do it all over again if I had to."

"What was it like?" I probe. "Being on death row?"

His eyes glaze over and a hardness creeps into his expression, jaw clenching, hands fisting the grass between his legs. Then he glances over at me and his features soften, almost like he's staring at a shimmering rising sun. "Painfully lonely." He flicks his eyes to the ground and exhales a long breath. "You know, we have a lot of time to make up for. I want to know everything about you… school, future plans, boys." A smile quirks. "Any love stories in the making?"

I blush when Max's face skips across my mind. "There was a boy," I admit, nibbling my lip. "I'm not sure where we stand right now, but if I introduce you, you can't go all crazy protector on me and beat him up if he tries to hold my hand or something. I'm eighteen now."

Levity bounces between us as Jonah chuckles, looking back over at me. "No promises."

I smile, a peaceful feeling washing over me.

Like I'm home again.

Like things are finally looking up.

Like…maybe everything *will* be okay.

And when I catch Jonah's eyes once more, I say something I haven't been able to say for years as my favorite storybook tale flashes through my mind. "Pooh Bear?" I murmur.

His gaze lights up. He already knows what comes next.

A smile tips his lips as he holds out his hand for me. "Yeah, Piglet?"

We're in the Hundred Acre Woods again.

Magic kisses the air, innocence fills my heart, and my own bright smile stretches back at him.

I take his hand and everything is right with the world. "Nothing. I just wanted to be sure of you."

Chapter 34

MAX

SHE BUCKLES BENEATH ME, HER CRIES RAGGED AND MUFFLED BY HER OWN hand as she peaks. The sound of my name escaping her well-kissed lips when she bottoms out on a wave of pleasure is pure music to my ears. Better than my favorite song. Better than all the songs in the whole damn world.

I withdraw my fingers from her and press a kiss to both inner thighs, her taste coating my tongue and driving me wild. More kisses make their way across her half-naked body as I crawl up to find her lips. She's breathing heavily, eyes closed. Her arms fling around my neck as she pulls me down on top of her and sifts her fingers through my sweat-damp hair.

My T-shirt is tossed beside the bed, my sweatpants tented. I settle between her legs and grind against her, only a thin layer of clothing between us. We both moan.

"Max," she whimpers, gently grazing her nails up and down the planes of my bare back. "We could go further…"

My throat rolls with trapped desire. Fuck, I want that more than anything.

No…that's not true.

More than anything, I want us to go back to what we used to be. Before the accident. Before she started looking at me like I was a stranger.

Like someone she fears.

Those are the most debilitating moments. The times when I catch her off guard or accidentally startle her. She'll flinch, her gaze locking right on mine as genuine terror sparks in her eyes. It's fleeting, just a flash. But it's *instinct* and that's what murders my fucking heart and has it drying out like concrete inside my chest.

And then there are these moments.

The too-short nights in her bed, a cool midnight breeze sweeping in through the window, moonlight setting her aglow while she unravels beneath me. I banish her fear with my tongue and execute her demons with my soul-deep kisses. She's mine again. She's mine until the sun crests and dawn shines new light on her darkness.

I frame her face with both hands and sprinkle more kisses across her face. "I can't move forward, Sunny. Not until we go back."

Her eyes fall closed. "We can't go back."

"Then this is where we'll stay."

"I want more," she murmurs, lips quivering.

"So do I."

Every night, I stay a little longer. A half an hour, an hour, two hours. Daybreak lingers on the horizon and I wonder if tonight will be the night I fall asleep in her arms and wake up beside her, her hair haloed across the pillow, our limbs perfectly entangled.

"Hold me, Max," she says, pulling me close.

I inch up and settle beside her, tugging her to my chest. My heart pounds with hope. With desperate, foolish hope that this is that night.

"I need to tell you something," she whispers, dragging her index finger down my chest.

Tension infects the small gap between us, but I focus on her finger making lazy designs near my heart. "You can tell me anything."

Anything except that it's over.

Anything but that.

She inhales deeply and it falls out with a noticeable shake. "God…I don't even know how to say this. I still haven't processed it."

My muscles lock up as I find her eyes, nerves racing all the way down to my toes. I wonder if she's going to tell me about the fall. Tell me that some motherfucker pushed her, that someone tried to kill the girl I love. I swallow. "Tell me."

"It's…about my brother."

A frown bends my brows. "Shit," I murmur. "Did they schedule his execution already?" That can't be right. It's hardly been three years—even I know it can take decades.

She shakes her head. "No."

"Then what?"

"He…" Ella moves away and rolls onto her back, rubbing both hands over her face and through her hair. "He's free, Max. Jonah's sentence was overturned. The charges were thrown out and he was released."

What?

Her words freeze me.

Choke me.

I pull up on my elbow, leaning over her, thunderstruck. "How?"

"Contamination of DNA evidence. Jury tampering. That's the short version."

"Are you safe?" It's the first thing on my mind. The only thing on my mind.

She turns, her own frown staring back at me. Hesitating, she nods slowly, carefully. "Of course I am. Why would you think otherwise?"

"Because he murdered two people, Ella."

"No, he didn't. I just told you that the charges were thrown out. He's innocent."

"They proved that?"

Her breathing is unsteady as she sits up straight, putting more space between us on the bed. "They couldn't prove anything either way."

"So, he's not necessarily innocent. He's just free."

"He's not guilty."

My heartbeats are in a tizzy, the cold prickle of fear seeping into my bones. "Ella…you thought he was guilty. You told me yourself. What changed? Was there new evidence discovered? Was the real killer captured?"

Tears light up her eyes as she scrambles to put her clothes back on. "I was wrong, okay? Jonah would never hurt me. You don't even know him," she says.

"It's hard enough living with the notion that I ever doubted him in the first place. I don't need you adding to it."

"You can't blame me for worrying. He was on death row for a brutal double homicide and now he's been released on a technicality. That fucking terrifies me." I try to reach for her but she swats me away, yanking her tank top over her head. "Sunny."

"You should go now. It's almost morning."

"Ella…please." My voice breaks on the word. "I love you."

I didn't mean to say that.

Fuck.

I've meant to say that all along.

Silence follows, my confession dangling between heartbreak and healing. It teeters on the edge of putting us back together and tearing us apart for good.

Ella stares straight ahead, her eyes wide and glazed. Breath caught, hands trembling as she fists the bedcovers. When she finally inhales, a small cry falls out. She dips her chin and shakes her head back and forth. "Don't," she says huskily.

Her response pulverizes me. Emotion snags in my throat as I move in, reaching for her. "I mean it. I should've said it months ago."

"Stop. Please."

"I won't stop. I won't stop loving you because you're scared. I'm scared, too." I take her hand but she rips it free. "I'm absolutely petrified that you're falling away from me, while I'm falling more and more in love with you. Every day. Every minute."

She covers her face with both hands, her shoulders shaking. "You don't love me," she says, the words muffled. "We're too young."

"You say that like it's insignificant," I shoot back, trying to hold it together. Trying to hold us together at the same time. "Jesus, Ella, young love is the purest fucking kind. I think I've loved you since the day I first saw you on that playground ten years ago."

"That's ridiculous. We were only kids."

"Doesn't matter. You smiled at me and I knew I was going to marry you one day."

"Stop!" she shouts, loud enough to startle me. We stare at each other, tears streaming down both of our faces. "Don't you get it, Max? *God…*" She forces out a laugh that sounds unhinged. "I may have been wrong about Jonah, but I was right about love. Love blinds you. That's its toxic trait. It blinds your soul."

I clench my jaw, hating her words. Hating her bleak, miserable stance on love. On *my* love. "Souls don't see, Sunny. Souls feel. They feel, and they yearn, and they *know*." Swallowing, I move in closer, refusing to give up on this. Refusing to give up on her. "I'd feel you in any lifetime, in any version of any reality. And I'd know, without a doubt, without a shred of hesitation…that your soul was meant for mine."

"No…" She breaks apart, draping both arms across her stomach like she's trying to keep all of her precious pieces from spilling out into the chasm between us. I reach for her again. She pushes me away. I do it again and again, until finally, she launches herself at me, wraps her legs around my waist, and sobs against me, every inch of us entwined.

Her hands grab my hair and pull my face down to hers.

Our tongues lash and tangle. Salt, grief, pain, love.

She kisses me desperately, taking everything I give her. And I give her my all. My whole heart. My life. I'm hers and she's mine, whether she lets herself believe it or not.

I know she knows.

Our souls know.

Tugging frantically at my sweatpants, she shoves her hand inside the waistband and curls her fingers around me. I jerk back with a hiss of pleasure as she moves down my body, shoving at my chest, pressing me flush against the headboard. I watch as she grips me and strokes hard, cheeks glinting with tearstains, moans falling out of both of us.

Ella takes me in her mouth and brings me to my knees in less than two minutes. I want to hold out as long as I can, but I'm lost to her, lost to the feel of her mouth on me, one of my hands in her hair and the other twined with hers beside us on the mattress.

It's over before it even began.

I release inside her mouth with a low groan, shuddering through the pinnacle, through that perfect moment of completion, while dreading the moment that comes next.

She sends me away again. Just like she always does.

I stalk back home, broken down and lost, sunk with the realization that I won't be drinking in the sunrise with her tucked inside my arms. Tonight wasn't that night.

Maybe tomorrow.

Chapter 35

ELLA

I FELT IT WHEN I WOKE UP THIS MORNING.

That weird intuition that sometimes pokes at you with no logic to back it up. A rock plopping into the pit of your stomach. A knobby finger jabbing at your chest.

Saying *yes* to an innocent New Year's Eve party invitation.

I brushed it off as residual stress and anxiety. After all, Max never climbed through my window the night before—likely due to the fact that I threw his love confession back in his face—so my dreams were filled with ghosts and black thoughts. Not to mention, it's also supposed to thunderstorm today. Storms always make me anxious.

Trying to counter the sinking feeling, I call Brynn over for some girl-bonding time. We sit cross-legged on my bed, facing each other, while I fill her in on Jonah's shocking return and watch tears stream down her pretty cheeks. We hug and cry as I binge a tray of brownies she brought over, courtesy of her fathers. I wish sugar had the healing powers her dads insist it has, but my heart still feels irrevocably wounded.

I devour five brownies, just in case.

After she leaves, the sky swirls with gray and silver as I step outside and look up. My itch to delve back into bookbinding has been clawing at me over the past few days, and I'm craving the therapeutic outlet. Our backyard is laden with colorful wildflowers—lavender, pink, and baby blue. I'm going to pluck a few handfuls, press them between the pages of an old book, then use them in my next project.

It's a slow, tedious walk to the backyard, my body sore from reacclimating. I've been doing exercises on the days I don't have physical therapy, and that paired with my late-night activities with Max, I'm feeling the burn.

I take a few moments to sit in the grass before the rain comes, stretching out my legs, the tendons straining. Then I gather up a collection of purple and light-blue flowers and tuck them in my palm. Satisfied with my haul, I pull myself up and head back toward the door, eager to start working.

I'm walking along the side of the house with a fistful of flowers when a figure catches my eye from across the street.

Everything blurs.

Icy fingers clamp around my heart.

A blizzard races down my spine.

McKay.

He's stalking toward me from his driveway, glancing once over his shoulder before beelining toward my house. Thanks to him, I'm not exactly limber these days, so my quick escape is more akin to a turtle trying to outrun a hare.

I've hardly had a chance to move when he calls out to me. "Ella, wait. I just want to talk to you."

I freeze in place.

Mom went back to work today after I promised her I'd be fine on my own. Jonah is on his way home from Charlotte, having left to grab the rest of his belongings so he can officially move back in. Max is still at school.

If McKay intends to hurt me, it wouldn't be hard, even if I do manage to lock myself inside the house. My heart beats swiftly, my stomach pitching with telltale fear. I knew this moment would come. He can't hide away forever.

I curl my fingers around the handful of green stems and try to center my breathing. "Leave me alone. I'll call the police." My cell phone is inside but he doesn't know that.

"Please, give me a chance to explain."

My eyes pop as he jogs the rest of the way over to me. "Explain?" I scoff with astoundment. He's too close. Only a few feet away from me now. Panic crawls through me, dozens of fire ants biting at my insides.

"I need to talk to you," he says, looking around, assessing the quiet street. It's midday on a Tuesday; most adults are at work, kids are in classes. He should be in class, too. "Please."

The flowers flutter from my clammy hand.

My whole body erupts with tremors.

"You need to leave," I demand. "Right now. Don't come near me again."

His shoulder-length hair catches on a storm-charged wind that whips through, sashaying among the treetops. He looks gaunter, sickly. The weight of his secret glows heavily in his eyes. Eyes that are rimmed with dark, hollow circles. Once-bronzed skin is now chalky and bloodless as he scratches at his cheek, fidgeting on both feet. "I was drunk. Out of my head. I hardly remember it happening."

My bottom lip wobbles. "I can jog your memory."

He presses his lips into a flat line.

"First, you tried to kiss me," I tell him. "When I resisted, completely disgusted, you grabbed me, hurt me, bruised me, then tried to rape me."

"That's an exaggeration."

"Don't gaslight me," I hiss back, anger and terror tunneling out my chest. "You pried my legs apart. Hiked up my dress and pulled your zipper down. Pinned me to the ground. And when I fought back, you fought harder. You yanked me toward the edge of the bluffs and then you let me fall. You almost killed me."

"It was an accident."

"You could have stopped it. You were right there, close enough to pull me back." Hot tears blanket my eyes, but I force them back. "You were jealous that your brother had something special. You were angry that you had no direction in life. You took it out on me."

"I didn't—"

"You left me for dead!" I screech.

McKay shoots forward, getting right in my face. "Be quiet," he grits through his teeth. "Someone will hear you."

Bitter memories flash across my mind—of his hand lashing out and covering my mouth, holding in my cries, my screams. Before I can shove him or slam my knuckles at his teeth, he jumps back, shaking his head.

"Sorry, sorry…" he tries, holding both hands up, palms forward. Sweat gleams on his forehead as raindrops sprinkle down from the clouds. "I'm just… I'm freaking the fuck out. I can't go to jail. I *can't*. It was a mistake, Ella…an awful, horrible mistake that I wish I could take back. I'd do it all differently, I swear."

I step away from him, almost stumbling when I trip over hedges. "I trusted you."

"I know… God, I know. I'm so damn sorry. You have to believe me, that's not who I am. I drank too much, got carried away, and then I panicked when I thought you were going to run off and tell somebody. I didn't push you. I just…"

"You just tried to rape me," I provide. "Then you watched as I plummeted to a likely death and forgot to call for help."

He grips his hair, swinging his head back and forth as his teeth gnash together. "I thought you were dead."

"You hoped I was."

"I was fucking wasted, Ella! I don't even remember how I got home. Think I slept it off in my truck in some parking lot, then I woke up the next morning hardly remembering what had happened."

"Well, I didn't wake up for four weeks. Four weeks!" I seethe, tears sneaking through and pouring down my cheeks. My face is hot, furious. "Nothing you say is going to fix this."

"I just…I need you to keep quiet. I'm begging you not to tell anyone." He steps closer, eyes glinting with ice and fire, arms shaking at his sides. "I'll do anything. Anything you want."

"I don't want anything from you."

"There has to be something." He reaches his hand out tentatively, but I slap it away like it's a deadly weapon. "You haven't gone to the police yet, and there's a reason for that. All I'm asking is that you hold on to that reason, whatever it is. I think you know, deep down, that I'm not a monster. I'm human.

I royally fucked up and I promise I'm suffering the consequences. The guilt is killing me."

"The *fear* is killing you," I correct, putting more space between us. "The fear of getting caught."

"No. It's more than that. I regret every second of that night." His throat works through a hard swallow as he glances down at his feet, then back up at me. "Please…keep this between us. If you wanted to rat me out, you would have already. You know I don't deserve to go to prison."

I stare at him, feeling numb. Feeling beaten down and torn. "Let me make something perfectly clear," I bite out, my balance unsteady as I try not to fall. "I'm not protecting you. I'm protecting Max. I'm protecting that amazing, beautiful, *incredible* man, who is more of a man than you will ever be." I jab a finger at him, my skin flushed hot, breathing erratic. "Shame on you for taking something precious away from him when all he ever did was love you. And you did, McKay. You stole from him. You succeeded tenfold because you ruined me. The girl he knew is long gone." I close my eyes through the pain, more tears leaking out. "And he doesn't even know why."

His blue eyes shimmer as the rainfall swells. Fat droplets tumble down, splashing across his hair and skin. Blinking the tears away, he swipes a hand down his face, forehead to chin, looking genuinely devastated. "I'm so sorry," he chokes out. "I am. Max has been my best friend from the moment my eyes opened, and the last thing I ever want to do is cause him pain. You two can fix this. You can—"

"Every time I look at him, I see *you*." My breath catches on a whimper as my teeth chatter hopelessly. "I've read hundreds and hundreds of books in my lifetime and nothing—*nothing*—could ever paint a tragedy like the one I'm living."

His face falls. His shoulders sag.

Rain drenches us in the sky's cold tears.

McKay closes his eyes and stares down at the damp grass, blowing out a long breath as he digests my words. A heavy moment trudges by before he whispers, "Okay." Another beat passes. "Turn me in."

"I—" My words fall off when the statement fully registers. I blink at him, my lips parting on a startled breath. "What?"

"Turn me in," he repeats, nodding slowly, coming to terms with his plea. "Do it. It's the right thing."

I'm stunned silent.

"Tell Max everything," he continues. "Talk to him first. He should hear it from you. And then go to the cops and turn me in. Or I'll do it. I will. Just… talk to Max first."

Thunder booms above us, crackling in the sky. My lips tremble from the chill, from indecision, from absolute misery. I don't know what to do.

I don't know what to do.

I tent my hands over my face, squeezing my eyes shut as mourning rakes through me.

"I'm sorry, Ella. For everything."

When I peel my eyes open, McKay is already moving away, stepping backward. His face crumbles before he swivels around and runs full speed in the other direction, heading toward his house. I watch him go, watch him cross the street, then disappear through his front door.

I tip my face to the sky and let the rain pelt me. I beg it for answers. I pray for direction.

McKay *should* pay for what he did to me.

But…

The one who will pay the ultimate price…is Max.

Some secrets are worth keeping. Some truths are better left buried.

And ultimately, some tragedies are worth living in order to protect the ones you love.

After only just getting Jonah back, I can't bear to lose someone else.

Minutes pass as I stand along the side of my house with rain-soaked hair and wildflowers sprinkled at my feet. I stand there long enough to see Max's truck pull in the driveway, tires splashing up rainwater puddles. There's a lump in my throat as I watch him hop out of the truck and stalk through the grass with his backpack slung over one shoulder before he enters the house.

I could tell him. I could go over there right now and confess everything.

But I don't.

I head inside my house instead.

Slamming the door behind me, I growl my pain into the quiet void as I tug at my hair and crouch down, my weight too heavy to bear. I take a few minutes to calm myself, collect my strength, and then I pull up to unsteady feet and make my way to my bedroom to decompress.

I stand in the center of the room and stare out the rain-glazed window, listening as the storm brews on the other side of the glass.

Seconds pass until I feel a presence behind me.

I jump in place, a yelp dislodging from my throat when my bedroom door slams shut.

McKay?

But when I whip around, my eyes land on Jonah leaning back against the doorframe, his every muscle taut and flexing. My chest fizzes, thrumming with relief when recognition settles in. I press a hand over my heart to calm the beats. "What are you doing here? I—I thought you wouldn't be home until dinnertime." I glance down at his hand clamped around a screwdriver.

I frown, confused.

His jaw is tight like a steel trap, green eyes wild and feral. "I got back early." Jonah traipses across the room, sits down on my bed, and sets the screwdriver beside him on my nightstand.

"What's that for?" I wonder, squeezing the front of my shirt, still trying to soothe my heartbeats.

"Fixing something for Mom," he says.

Darkness lurks within his tone. His eyes are pinned on me, burning hot. I feel the heat from a few feet away. Swallowing, I clench my jaw. "Did you need something?" I ask casually, despite the dread kissing the back of my neck.

"Tell me more about the fall." His words from the lake echo back at me, this time swirling with something sinister.

It doesn't take me long to figure it out.

My heart drops out of me. It plummets to the ugly beige carpeting.

I stare at him, unblinking, anxiety carving out my chest. "What…what did you hear?"

He heard us. He heard me talking to McKay outside the house.

He knows.

"I heard enough."

I crack on my inhale. "Jonah…"

"I need to hear it again," he says, tone steady but menacing. "Did he do all that to you?"

All I do is shake my head.

"Say it, Ella. Tell me."

My eyelids slam shut, my throat burning. "Jonah, please."

"Did he try to rape you? Attack you? Put you in a goddamn coma for a month?" Shadows curl around him. His eyes are like the devil's, his body flickering with suppressed fury. "Did he leave my little sister for dead at the bottom of a *fucking cliff*?"

I can't lie to him. I can't lie anymore.

He already knows.

I cover my face with both palms and nod, breaking apart as the truth finally spills free and slices every piece of me on the way out. "Yes."

Jonah jolts upright from the bed and stalks toward me, looking absolutely nothing like the brother I know. He looks like…

A monster.

I cry out when he grabs my cheeks between his hands and slams a hard kiss to my hairline.

When he pulls back, his voice is a terrifying kind of even as he says, "I swore I'd protect you, Piglet. And I'll be damned if I don't keep my word."

Then he whirls around and storms out of my bedroom, closing the door behind him. Shock renders me paralyzed for a beat before deadly realization sinks in, almost stopping my heart. "Jonah!" I screech, moving as fast as I can. I hear the front door bang shut. Fear grips me like a vise.

I twist the doorknob and yank.

My pulse stutters. It doesn't budge.

I pull and tug with all my strength, but I know it won't open.

It's locked.

My eyes quickly pan to the screwdriver, then back to the door as awareness sets in. He switched the doorknob around after he heard me talking to McKay. The lock is on the opposite side.

He trapped me in my bedroom so he could exact revenge.

"No!" I shriek, pounding my fists to the door, knowing it's fruitless. "*Jonah!*"

Hot tears stream down my face as I pivot back around toward the window and start banging on the pane when I see him marching across the street, his gait lethal. I try to pull the window open, but it's stuck. It won't budge, and my arms are too weak.

No.

I glance at the truck in the driveway, and I almost buckle.

Max.

They're twins. Jonah doesn't know they're twins.

He's going to attack the wrong man.

A sickly, beastly feeling washes over me. A feeling like…

Maybe Jonah is a killer, after all.

It's poison in my veins. Black tar oozing through my bloodstream. It's a thousand times more agonizing than the feeling that slithered through me when I plummeted thirty feet to the earth and landed hard, my bones breaking, heart shriveling, everything blurring to black.

I scream at the top of my lungs, slamming both palms to the window as I watch Jonah approach their doorstep.

Thinking fast, I scamper to the other side of the room, reach under my bed for the baseball bat, then race back to the window and smash it against the pane with all my might. Glass shatters. I move on instinct, uncaring of my injuries, indifferent to the way my still-weak legs resist the climb.

I haul myself out, shards of broken glass scraping my skin as I tumble out the window and collapse in the wet grass. Lightning flashes across a graphite sky. Thunder rolls but no louder than the soul-deep scream I release into the storm.

I glance up.

Jonah is already inside.

"Jonah! Jonah!" I shout, pulling myself up on shaky legs and racing forward. "No, no! They're twins! They're *twins!*"

I make it across the street. Rocks and rubble try to trip me. I see red, I see neon, I see stars across my eyes as my heart pounds in time with thunder.

I'm slipping across their front lawn, trying to keep from falling, when a shot rings out.

A gunshot.

I freeze in place, jerked back by an invisible force. My eyes widen into tearful, panicked saucers. I scream again as buckshot turns my insides to ashes.

I don't even remember heaving myself through their front door. I don't remember how I got there, shaking and screaming in their living room, staring down a blood-soaked body, unable to tell who is sprawled out at my feet.

Max, the love of my life.

Or McKay.

I can't remember what he was wearing. I can't remember anything.

I hardly notice Jonah standing there, his chest heaving, pistol aimed at the man writhing on the floor. The man with blood spurting from a gaping chest wound. Puddles of red pool beneath him. My screams are echoes, unable to penetrate the terror, the despair, the shock, as I drop to my knees beside him and press both palms over the hole in his chest.

I look up when another figure appears.

And that, I know, I will always remember.

I'll never forget the look on his face when he comes to a dead stop, letting out a howl of pain when he finds his brother bleeding out on the living room floor.

Chapter 36

MAX

FIFTEEN MINUTES EARLIER

I TOSS MY BACKPACK TO THE PARTIALLY TILED FLOOR AND KICK OFF MY WET shoes.

McKay is seated on the couch, slumped over, his face in his hands. "Hey," I greet, pausing to study him. "Everything okay?"

His head lifts slowly. Nodding, my brother rests his chin on his clasped hands, his eyes bloodshot. "Yeah. How's Dad?"

"Doing better. They're keeping him one more night for observation."

Dad had another night terror and fell and hit his head on the nightstand. Mild concussion. Four stitches. And a long, sleepless night in the ER before I dragged myself to school for a half day, hardly able to keep my eyes open.

I'm exhausted. Worn down and done.

I miss Ella.

Pulling my phone out of my pocket, I move into the kitchen to pour a glass of milk, then send her a quick text after chugging the whole thing.

Me: Sorry I didn't come over last night. I was at the hospital with Dad... long story. I have a new list for you. I know it's been a while. See you tonight. ♥

I backspace the heart emoji three times before saying, "Fuck it," keeping it, and tapping Send.

When I glance into the living room, McKay is slumped over again, rocking forward and back on the sofa cushion. I frown. "You sure you're okay?" I ask, setting down my empty glass of milk.

He looks sweaty, agitated, and paler than I've ever seen him.

"Stomach bug," he mumbles into his hands. "I'll be fine."

McKay offered to take Dad to the hospital last night, but I knew his big biology project was due today, so I volunteered to go solo. My brother was going to catch a ride to school with a buddy. "How did your project go?"

He blows out a breath and tents his hands over his face. "I called in because I feel like shit."

My arms cross. "You look like shit."

He makes a humming sound, then pauses. "You ever do something you regret?"

The subject change has me freezing, blinking slowly, and stepping forward. "What do you mean?"

"I said what I mean," he says, tapping both feet in opposite time as he stares out the front window. "Regret. It's the worst feeling in the world. It's like this knife in your gut that twists and twists, and you want someone to pull it out, but you don't know if that'll only make it worse. Either way, you bleed. Either way, you suffer. Either way…you've been stabbed. And you can't be unstabbed."

I stare at him, lips parted, eyes flaring. I'm not sure how to respond, so I move in closer until I'm standing over him, watching as he keeps looking out the window and tapping his feet. "McKay," I murmur. "Is this about Brynn?"

Jesus, he looks terrible. The sickest I've ever seen him.

"Yeah, sure," he forces out. "So, do you have any regrets?"

"Of course. Everyone does."

"What do you regret?" he wonders.

"I regret not being a better brother to you and for making promises I could never keep. I regret not being a better son to Mom and Dad. I've kept myself awake at night, wondering if I was the reason Mom walked out on us. The notion eats me alive."

"None of that's true," he says brokenly. "The knife hardly left a scratch on you. I'm talking about *real* regret, Max. The fatal kind."

I shake my head, confused. "What is this actually about?"

He finally stops rocking and fidgeting and tears his gaze away from the window, looking up at me. "Whatever happens…I hope you know how much I've appreciated everything you've done for me. I've seen it. I've seen *you*," he says. "And I'm sorry for not being there, for not being the brother you wanted me to be. I'm sorry for leaving you stranded with Dad, for abandoning you with a shit ton of responsibility when you deserved nothing more than to live an easy, carefree life. For making you feel like you've been all alone in this. I've always wanted the best for you, I swear. Even when I seemed ungrateful and self-absorbed. My coping mechanisms were fucked and I regret all of it. I regret so fucking much, Max."

His face falls back to his shaky hands as thunder booms outside the house, rattling the walls. I flinch, glancing out the window. Rain pours down in buckets, ricocheting off the glass as my brother's words ping-pong between my ribs.

"McKay—"

"You left the mower out in the backyard," he mutters.

I blink at him, my frown deepening. My eyes pan back to the window he keeps staring at.

"I can put it away," he says, standing. "We can't afford a new one."

As he sweeps past me, his collar drenched with sweat, I grab him by the arm and shake my head. "I got it. Sit. You look like you're going to keel over," I insist. "I'll be back in a minute."

He digs the heels of his palms into his eye sockets and nods. "Yeah, okay."

"Hold tight. We can talk more when I come back in." I spare him a final glance before heading out back and stomping toward the lawn mower, filled to the brim with uneasiness.

I've never seen McKay like this before. I know he took the breakup hard, but it's not like him to confide in me, especially with deep, uncomfortable topics. For years, he's kept me at arm's length.

Zoned out, I push the lawn mower into the shed, the rainfall a roaring soundtrack to my dark thoughts.

Hunched over to tighten the gas cap, I jerk upright when I think I hear Ella's voice.

Yelling, shouting, begging.

What the hell?

A popping noise follows. A thunderclap.

I freeze, pivot, race out of the shed.

Heart stuttering, I glance up, my face doused in cold rain. The sky continues to untether as lightning flashes across gray clouds in veins of pale yellow. I wonder if I imagined it. Maybe it's just the storm.

Maybe Ella is haunting me.

Anxiety prickles as I pull the door of the shed closed and swipe a hand through my sopping wet hair.

I'm jogging back toward the house when I hear something else. Something I know I don't imagine.

A scream.

A bloodcurdling, stricken, ice-fraught scream.

My ears ring, my pulse trips, my legs turn to jelly underneath me.

I run.

I run faster than I've ever run before, slipping in the wet grass, my heart shooting up my throat until I almost choke on it. The back door whips open and I barrel through, knocking over a small table, dishes clattering to the kitchen floor. Curving around the corner, I careen to a time-stopped halt at the edge of the living room.

And I see it.

I can't unsee it.

Ella, bent over my brother, her hands pressed to his torn-up chest.

McKay, lying in a pool of blood, his body twitching. Liquid crimson spurts out of his mouth and seeps through her hands as she screams and cries.

A man.

A man with a gun, standing over McKay, his shirt sprayed with red and fury in his eyes.

Gunpowder and copper fill my nose as Ella's ragged wails fill my ears. My own howl bleeds with hers. Horror, confusion, debilitating fucking *shock*.

I don't know how to move, how to breathe. My vision clouds, a haze of red, and a second later, I'm on the floor with Ella, covered in my brother's blood. I don't remember moving. I'm just there, shouting, crying, spitting, begging. "What the fuck, what the *fuck*," I cry out.

The man is looming over us, reaching for Ella. "Let's go. We have to go. Now." He grabs her bloody hands, but she swats him away, hysterical.

When I blink again, the man is gone, the front door swinging on its hinges.

"I'm sorry, I'm so sorry," Ella shrieks, hands newly clasped over McKay's chest. "I'm so sorry!"

I need to call 911. I think my phone is gone, but I don't remember looking for it because my eyes are pinned on McKay's blood-spattered face as he chokes and coughs up red fluid.

"No, no, no," I plead, snatching his face between my hands and forcing his eyes on me. "McKay, stay with me." His eyes flutter closed. I slap him. "Stay. The Fuck. With me."

I don't recognize my voice.

"I told him," Ella cries. "I told him, I told him. He knows... Oh God, Max..."

Her words seep through the madness. I lurch forward and snatch her by the upper arms, my bloody fingers smearing her skin. "Told him? Told him what, Ella?"

She's not looking at me. She's staring at McKay, in shock, shaking and screaming.

"What did you *tell* him?"

Another figure appears in my periphery, racing toward us, sliding to his knees. A phone. He has a phone pressed to his ear as he prattles off a location.

Chevy. It's Chevy.

"Jesus Christ, what happened?"

I hear him but I don't hear him.

"A man's been shot," says a faraway voice. "We need an ambulance, fast. I don't know what happened. Yes. No. You need to fuckin' hurry..."

Tears track through the warm blood on my cheeks. I grab McKay's face again, my thumbs bruising his cheekbones as I try to keep him with me. He wheezes, tries to say something. Nothing comes out but more blood.

"McKay, McKay…don't you fucking die on me. Stay with me. *Stay with me!*"

He sputters, still trying to speak.

His head tilts, eyes finding me through the black haze.

Lips parted and quivering, he hitches out a breath, and those eyes dim before me as a tear slips loose and trails down his temple.

A light flickers out.

His life is draining, expiring, and I'm helpless to stop it.

"No," I croak. "No…" I shake him hard, growling with horror. "Stay!"

McKay goes motionless on a final frayed breath, his eyes wide open and locked on mine.

He's still.

Completely still.

I don't remember what comes next. I'm hardly alive myself as noise trickles into my psyche, voices tangle, and strong arms haul me off my brother while I cling to him, sobbing, cursing, and shouting my grief and disbelief to his lifeless body.

Beeping noises. Defibrillator paddles. Men in uniform.

Ella.

Ella is in my arms weeping, and I hold her back because I don't know what else to hold on to. Her cracked words bleed into my ears as she apologizes, tries to explain.

"The bluffs…the fall… McKay…attacked me… I'm sorry… Jonah…"

I can't process it.

All I register are the external sounds. More beeping, a blur of uniforms, a slew of useless words, and a beat of harrowing silence.

And then…

A time of death.

For all of us.

Chapter 37

ELLA

ALL I SEE IS RED.

"What have you *done*?" our mother screams at the top of her lungs, collapsed on my bedroom floor as sirens screech in the distance.

I'm numb.

I'm split in half.

I'm crippled with shock.

Jonah stares at me, pleads with me, his eyes wild and his shirt sprayed with red mist.

McKay's blood.

No, no, no.

"I love you both so much," he tells me. "Believe that."

He kisses the top of my head as he holds me tighter than ever. Like it's the last time he'll ever hold me.

It is.

"Take care of Mom," he says brokenly.

Men in uniform storm into the room as I'm dry heaving on my bedroom floor.

Jonah goes with them without a fight.

He surrenders.

Wrists cuffed and eyes on me, my brother is guided out of the bedroom while Mom grabs helplessly at his ankle, and he tells her he loves her, that it will be okay.

I look over at her. Sprawled out on the beige carpet. She won't stop screaming.

We've been here before, but her screams don't sound the same.

The night Jonah came home covered in blood after Erin and Tyler were found murdered, she regrouped quickly, offering a trace of hope and composure.

"You didn't do this, Jonah," she said, repeating it over and over. "It's going to be okay. I'll get you out of this. It's a misunderstanding. A horrible tragedy, but I will fix it. I'll fix this, Jonah."

This scream is different. There is no hope seeping from the edges or bleeding within the ragged timbre. This time, there are witnesses to Jonah's crime.

This time, she can't fix it.

Somehow, I manage to drag my way up onto quivering legs that carry me over to the busted window. I glance down at my bloody clothes, the scratches on my skin from broken glass. My hands lift in front of my face, stained dark red. It's a horror movie.

My horror movie.

I raise my eyes slowly to the scene across the street. Police cars everywhere. Ambulances. Chevy stands at the side of the road, arms crossed, a few splotches of blood dappling his gunmetal-gray coveralls. He talks to a police officer as the man in uniform jots down notes.

And then there's Max.

Hunched over on his front stoop, face dropped to his red-slicked hands, his shoulders shaking. My heart crashes down to my feet, leaving more red stains behind.

I want to run to him. Be there for him. Hold him in my arms and rewind the last few months of this horror movie.

But I'm in the starring role—the villain.

And he's the helpless victim.

Max's head lifts as officers surround him and take his statement. I wonder if he felt me the moment before our eyes lock from a few yards away.

Miles away.

He's never been farther from me.

Tears slip down my cheeks as I mouth the words, "I'm sorry."

He shakes his head, his face stricken with more pain than I can process. Then he collapses forward while an officer takes a seat beside him on the stoop.

Just a few months after escaping death row, my brother is going back to prison.

I'll put him there myself if I have to.

The hours crawl by, until hours turn into days.

Trips to the police station, interrogations, debilitating grief competing with numbness.

Mom doesn't speak. All she does is cry and cook chicken casseroles. Burnt casseroles. Undercooked casseroles. She makes one every night in silence and I force-feed myself a few bites until my stomach churns with nausea and I drag myself to my room. I count the number of days that pass by the number of casseroles cooked.

Five days.

Five days since Jonah killed McKay.

Ricardo comes over to comfort my grieving mother, and Brynn stops by with sweets to comfort us both.

As for me, each day is a struggle to reconcile the conflicting emotions swirling within me. There's a profound sorrow for Max that cuts deep, leaving behind jagged edges of pain and confusion. Yet, beneath the grief, a simmering anger brews, fueled by the realization that Jonah truly *was* capable of such violence and darkness.

He always was.

Mixed with the anger is a battling of feelings toward my mother. I grapple with the frustration that she, in her unwavering belief in Jonah's innocence, inadvertently became an accomplice to the nightmare that unfolded. I can't help but feel a pang of resentment, wondering if her blind faith in him clouded her judgment and pulled all of us deeper into this web of heartbreak.

The failed casseroles serve as a reminder of this fractured reality we now inhabit. With each meal, I taste the bitterness as I navigate through the days like a ghost in my own home, all too aware of the daunting task of rebuilding my life once again.

On the fifth night, I startle in bed when I hear a tapping sound at my newly installed bedroom window that Chevy replaced for me.

My heart fumbles.

It can't be…

I slide off the bed and walk over to the window, my heartbeats tangling with raw hope.

But when I look outside, I don't see anything. There's no one there.

Only my hollow reflection stares back at me.

Chapter 38

ELLA

A MONTH ROLLS BY AND SPRING MELTS INTO HOT SUMMER.
I stay with Brynn most days, sleeping in her spare bedroom. Sometimes I find my way to her room at night and crawl in bed with her, loneliness clawing at me, nightmares soiling my dreams.

She never makes me leave. She just holds my hand and we cry together.

Ricardo moved in with my mother last week, so I don't feel too guilty for needing space. Living across the street from Max was too painful. Living a few yards away from a murder scene was too much for my heart to take when it hadn't fully healed in the first place.

I'm sitting at the Fishers' black eclectic dining room table on a balmy June evening, stabbing my fork into a heap of shepherd's pie. It resembles brown mush, but the few bites I've managed to swallow down taste great. Way better than Mom's casseroles.

Pete eyes me across the table. "We added extra carrots just for you," he says.

My stomach clenches.

My potted crayon is sitting on the nightstand in the guest room, a constant reminder of everything I've lost. "Thank you. I appreciate it."

"You should talk to him, Ella-Bella," Matty chimes in.

I inhale sharply, my fork clattering to my plate.

My jaw rolls, my hands shaking as they wring together in my lap.

"Daddio," Brynn interrupts, tenderly bumping her knee to mine. "It's complicated."

"True. It's more complicated than a Rubik's Cube in the dark." Matty pops a green bean in his mouth. "But it's not impossible. I've done it. Not this, of course—heavens above, not this. I meant the Rubik's Cube. The evidence is proudly displayed above our bed in a glass case."

A smile hints, despite myself. "I tried…but he said he needed space," I murmur. "And time."

Brynn rubs my back with affection. "I think we all need time," she says, voice cracking on the words. "I still can't believe he's gone. I can't believe he was here and now he's gone, and not only is he gone, but we're left with the horrible truth of what he did before he left." Her hand falls away from me. "I feel like I'm grieving the loss of him in multiple ways. McKay had his faults, but I never thought he'd… God, I never—"

"I know," I say.

"And Max…I can't even imagine how he's processing all this." Tears track down her cheeks as she stabs her mashed potatoes with a fork.

I saw Max at the funeral.

Well, it was more of a memorial, per se. McKay's body hasn't been released from evidence yet, so the actual funeral is to be determined. The thought alone has my insides curling and shriveling.

Max was emotionless.

Numb.

His father was a wreck, sobbing through the entire ceremony.

The sun felt extra warm and bright that day, which made everything so much worse. I ran over to Max before he left, winding my fingers around his elbow and stopping his retreat. Pain skated across his face when our eyes met. I wondered if he saw Jonah when he looked at me, just like I saw McKay when I looked at him. I couldn't fault him for that.

I still can't.

"Max…please," I pleaded in a raspy whisper, unable to let go of his elbow. "I'm so sorry. So unbelievably sorry."

He glanced at the contact, swallowed, then looked back at me. "Not your fault," he said, tone even. It was like the pain had rendered him passionless. "I'm sorry, too."

"Maybe we can spend some time together," I tried. "To talk."

"Yeah…one day," he replied. "Not today."

I nodded through the tears. "I understand."

Max didn't move away as we held eye contact, my grip on his arm tightening. He looked down at the grass for a beat before lifting only his eyes to me. "Ella…I know you're a victim, too. Brynn told me what happened at the bluffs. What my brother did to you." His eyes finally shimmered with crystalline sadness as his voice broke. "I'm trying…to process everything. I'm struggling…"

"I know," I choked out. "I know."

"I just need some space. Time. I want to talk to you, I do, but I don't even have the words…"

I let go of his elbow, inched up, and threw my arms around his neck. "I know, Max. I'm sorry for everything. I should have told you the truth."

"I get why you didn't," he breathed into my hair.

"Please don't hate me."

"I could never hate you."

We held each other until people trickled from the outdoor ceremony in black dresses, black suits, with handkerchiefs pressed to their noses.

Max pulled back first, unraveling my arms from around his neck, a choking sound escaping his throat. "I should go," he whispered. "But…I have something for you."

I blinked, sniffled, and swiped at my tears.

Then I watched as he stuffed his hand in his pocket and pulled out a crumpled note.

"I wrote this for you the morning of…" His voice trailed off, his tearstains glinting in the sun. "I wrote this for you."

I reached for the note, nodding as my heart pounded and my chest squeezed. "Thank you."

With one last tortured look, he glanced down at his feet, then stalked off, meeting his father in the parking lot.

I stared at their truck as it pulled away and disappeared down the street, the note shaking in my fist. Heaving in a breath, I opened it and skimmed over the familiar handwriting.

> How to Catch the Sun
>
> 1. Strategy? Still formulating, but persistence is key. I'll get back to you on that.
> 2. Once I figure it out, I'm never going to let it go. I'll bask in that glow, let it warm me, fill me up, and hell, I'll even let it burn me. A small price to pay for eternal sunshine.
> 3. You're my perpetual horizon, Sunny. I'll never stop chasing your light.
>
> This wasn't the structured list you anticipated. My muse feels distant. But then, so do you.
>
> Come back to me.
>
> —Max

I collapsed in the grass with the note pressed to my chest, my tears spilling out and dampening the paper.

Now it's folded up, resting underneath the white stone, right beside the potted crayon. It's all I have left of him right now: his beautiful words, a precious stone, and a little terra-cotta pot.

I glance up at the two Fisher men, the mood heavy and tense. The nice thing about the Fisher family is that tense moments never last long, always severed by a joke, a silly dance move, music, or words of love.

"Can I give you a bit of advice?" Matty asks, setting down his fork and folding his arms as he presses forward on the table.

"It'll be bog-standard at best," Pete adds with a smirk.

"You're a hog," Matty snaps.

"*Bog*, dear husband. I said *bog*."

"Nobody knows what that means. What does that even mean?" His eyes pan around the table, but we all shrug.

Screw the advice. I'm already smiling.

"*Anyway*," Matty continues, glaring kindly at his husband before swiveling back to me. "My bog-riddled advice is this: love comes first."

I blink at him, the words settling in my heart.

"Whenever this bonehead pisses me off, I repeat that, over and over."

"Thanks," Pete grumbles.

He grins. "But in all seriousness, Ella-Bella—remember that. *Love comes first*. You're grieving because love happened. You're bleeding because love sank its nasty, beautiful claws in you. You're crying because love filled you up and now it has nowhere to go." A solemn quiet washes over the table as he looks me in the eyes and his smile softens. "Love always hurts, honey. That's the price we pay to experience it. Sometimes that hurt is on a smaller scale, and sometimes it's big enough to move mountains. Either way, it hurts. You have to think of it as a cruel gift. Nothing good in life is ever free. There are always sacrifices and tough blows. And even if we never fully recover from those blows, we can appreciate the love while it was still sweet and untainted. After all, it was there first. It's the conduit for every raw, passionate, ugly heartache we experience in this life."

I don't even notice that Brynn's hand is linked with mine under the table, our fingers entwined, our palms gripping hard. I glance at her and see that she's crying. Silent tears stream down her face.

And I realize…I am, too.

I nod as I force a broken smile, sniffling, my lips trembling.

I think back to a summer afternoon on a swing set. The clouds looked like spools of cotton candy. A funny-looking caterpillar awaited transformation into a glorious butterfly. Sunshine beat down like a warm hug.

And at the center of it all, there was a boy.

A boy with dimples, with affection in his cloudless blue eyes and an orange flower tucked inside his hand.

"It's bright like the sun. And the sun is bright like you."

Yes.

Love came first.

Young, sweet, beautiful love.

Life goes on, life throws frost in your face, but it doesn't ever dull the warmth of that first spark.

Pete's eyes gleam with tears as he slings an arm around Matty's shoulders and tugs him close. "You can't go back, darling," he tells me. "You can't change anything. There's no changing the past. If you believe you can, you'll never move forward."

"So," Matty adds, "there's only one thing left to do."

"What's that?" I croak, swiping at my cheeks.

He reaches over the table, takes my hand in his, and squeezes. "Heal."

Chapter 39

MAX

LEWY BODY DEMENTIA.

My father's diagnosis rolls in on the heels of the worst month of my entire life.

"Your father has what's known as 'dementia with Lewy bodies,' or 'DLB' for short," a young doctor tells me, his light wisps of blond hair a contrast to his dark words.

My eyebrows knit together as anxiety washes over me. "What does that mean?"

Dr. Shay folds forward on the desk across from me, eyes empathetic. "It's a type of progressive dementia. The name comes from the presence of abnormal protein deposits in the brain known as 'Lewy bodies.' These affect chemicals in the brain, leading to problems with thinking, behavior, and mood." He pauses to allow the information to sink in. "It's different from Alzheimer's, though there can be overlap in symptoms. Your father might experience visual hallucinations, vivid nightmares, moments of alertness and drowsiness, and motor symptoms similar to Parkinson's."

Night terrors. Shaky hands. Hallucinations. Frequent naps. Memory loss.

Everything funnels through me like a cyclone.

Test after test had been coming up inconclusive, and I was beginning to think that my father was going to be okay. Maybe I'd exaggerated his symptoms.

Maybe he was getting older, and with age came memory loss. Maybe the trauma of losing his wife, paired with his injury, was simply catching up to him. Maybe he just had night terrors like some people do.

Scrubbing a hand down my face, I cup my jaw and close my eyes. "How do we fix it?" I wonder, wanting to check out. I want to disappear, fade away. I wish for the hard office chair to morph into quicksand. "What's the cure?"

Dr. Shay tilts his head with a solemn sigh. "Unfortunately, there is no cure, Mr. Manning. Current treatments can help manage some of the symptoms, but they can't stop the progression of the disease. Our main goal will be to ensure your father has the best quality of life possible, given the circumstances. We'll work together to develop a comprehensive care plan tailored to his needs."

He hands me a brochure.

I stare at it like it's a map of a foreign country I have no desire to visit.

No cure.

No money for treatment.

I'm lucky our state medical plan covered his hospital visits and testing thus far, but I know it won't cover long-term care.

There's only me.

No mother, no brother, no future.

I guide my father to his bedroom when I get home and help him on the bed. I give him the news, just like I had to give him the news about McKay four weeks ago.

Dad stares at me with glazed eyes, his hands shaking in his lap. "You're a good son, Maxwell," he tells me. "You've made me…very proud."

I'm not sure what he processed, but I guess it doesn't really matter.

And, in a way, I envy my father. I envy him because one day, I know…

He won't remember any of this.

I hug him, refusing to let myself cry. Refusing to break down because I'm the only stability he has left. I have to be strong…there's no other choice.

"I think I'll take a nap now," he says, nodding as he glances out the window. "Wake me up before your brother's game, will you? I want to be there."

My eyelids flutter closed as I stand. "Sure, Dad. I'll wake you in an hour."

"That's great, Son." He slips underneath the covers and curls his legs to his chest. "Thank you."

I stare at him for a beat before heading outside and collapsing on the front stoop.

School let out last week.

High school is over, and I graduated with solid grades and a glittering diploma.

And it means absolutely nothing because I've already lost everything.

Two black boots appear in my periphery and I glance up, my gaze landing on Chevy. He stands beside me, two beers in hand, his golden hair fluttering in the summer breeze.

"Hey," I manage.

He takes a seat beside me on the stoop and hands me a beer.

I shake my head.

When he offers me a cigarette instead, I falter briefly before snatching one from the box. "Thanks." I bring the rolled paper to my lips and watch as he lights the opposite end, cupping a hand around the flame. "I mean that, by the way," I add. "Thank you…for everything."

Chevy pockets the lighter with a nod. "No need to thank me. Neighbors help each other out."

"You're more than a neighbor. Always have been."

"Well, you're welcome, then." He sends me a partial smile before glancing out across the street. "Some of my fondest memories are of you two kids playing out in the front yard, tossing footballs, running through sprinklers. Reminded me of my own childhood back in Oregon. I have a brother, too. Not a twin—he's two years younger than me—but he's my better half. My best friend."

I can't imagine Chevy having a better half. He's already the best. "Are you still close?"

His eyes dim. "Not close enough," he says, cracking open the beer I rejected and taking a long pull. "He's in a cemetery near Cannon Beach."

"Fuck," I mutter, dropping my chin to my chest. "Sorry to hear."

"Leukemia. It was a late-stage diagnosis and he never stood a chance. He passed away three months after we got the news. Fourteen years old." Chevy sets his beer on his knee and looks back at me. "Anyway, if you ever need an outlet, let me know. I have a ton of shit lying around that you're welcome to break."

A smile slips as I blow a smoky breath out through my nose. "I might take you up on that."

Nodding, he studies me, the mood shifting again. "I don't know what it's like to lose someone in such a violent way…but loss is loss. Absence is absence. You can't fill it and you can't shake it. All you can do is accept that it's always going to follow you around like a shadow, and you do what you can to live with it," he tells me. "You fill your life with other things. Hobbies, people, dreams. I keep busy because I have to…house flipping, auto restoration, a bunch of random shit. I have a thousand projects going on at once because that's the only way the shadow takes a back seat and lets me appreciate what I still have. It becomes a silhouette." Chevy takes another swig of beer, then dangles the bottle between his knees. "I'll never lie and say it's easy. I'll never pretend like it doesn't suck your soul straight out of you sometimes…but I will tell you that it's still possible to find the light. The loss is permanent, but the darkness isn't."

My eyes fill with stinging tears as I stare across the street at Ella's house.

I think of her.

I think of McKay.

I think of myself submerged in Tellico Lake, staring at both of them as they floated across from me, our eyes locked together while sunlight poured down on the surface above.

Green eyes. Blue eyes.

Hopelessness and yearning.

Time stopped and sound faded as we held our breath and counted down the seconds.

Little did we know, the real drowning would come after we pulled ourselves out of the water.

Chevy presses his hand to my shoulder and gives it a squeeze, severing my bleak thoughts. "She's your light, Max. Trust me on that," he says with conviction, tipping his head toward Ella's property. "Don't let it get away."

With my throat in knots, I stare at him as he stands from the stoop and sends me a small nod.

"My real name's Eli, by the way." Walking backward, he raises his beer bottle with a wink. "Don't tell anybody."

I smile through the tears, a silent thank-you, and watch as he heads back to his house and gets to work on an old RV sitting idle in the front yard.

As I puff on my cigarette, Ella trickles through my mind like a sunbeam forcing its way through gray clouds.

I told her I needed space.

My brother is gone, but so is hers. My world is rocked, but she's in the same boat, getting tossed and thrown among tumultuous waves. We're both victims, both drowning in the shadows, both trying to find the light.

It's hard to think about what she went through that night with my brother. The secret she clung to. The pain she guarded and kept from me as a way of keeping *me* safe and protected from that same pain. Her spirit was so broken, and I had no idea why.

Never in a million years would I think it was my own flesh and blood who tore her down and rendered her paralyzed.

I'll never say McKay got what he deserved when Jonah put a bullet in his chest—*I can't*. Forgiveness is a complicated beast, but love has a way of lingering, despite it all. I can't think of the heinous acts he committed without thinking of the sweet, happier moments, too. I'm certain Ella feels the same way about her own brother.

Light and darkness. Yin and yang. Sun and moon.

They coexist.

But I do know what Ella deserves, and it's not this. It's not my radio silence or cold shoulder. She needs my light, my warmth, more than ever.

Chevy is right. She's my light and I'm hers.

My sweet Sunny Girl.

From that first glance in the schoolyard, her smile peeking out from behind a book in the golden afternoon light, I felt it deep inside my soul—she was, and always would be, my sun.

I pull the partially smoked cigarette from between my lips, frowning as I ponder why I ever craved the needless crutch in the first place.

With conviction, I stomp the cigarette beneath my foot, snuffing it out it without a second thought.

And I never look back.

Chapter 40
ELLA

I SIT ON THE HANDMADE BENCH AS THE SUN SINKS BEHIND THE CLOUDS, leaving splashes of fuchsia and burnt orange behind.

"We should find a clearing in the woods and make it our own special hide-away. Dad can help me build a bench for us to sit and read books together. We can talk about our day at school and watch the butterflies flutter by. It'll be our secret hiding spot."

My fingertips trail over the wood grains, lingering on the jagged carving: MANNING, 2013.

He did it.

He made the bench, just like he said he would all those years ago.

Tears rush to my eyes. I wonder how long he sat here, waiting for me to come back, to sit with him and read storybooks together and watch zebra butterflies flutter their wings. I told him I'd see him the next day, but my father turned that one day into ten years.

I inhale a shuddery breath as I glance at my phone.

Max: Meet me in the clearing at sunset.

I'm here.

I'm ready.

I don't know what comes next, but it has to be something. Healing only comes with a forward trajectory.

My head snaps up when I hear footsteps approaching. Branches cracking, leaves rustling. A moment later, Max appears, towering in the entryway of our secret hiding spot in navy running shorts and a light-gray tee, his eyes glittering in the fading daylight.

I'm already close to tears. I'm not sure how I'm going to get through this.
But I'm here.
I'm ready.

He steps inside, his throat rolling as he swallows. "Hey, Sunny."

The nickname almost breaks me in two. My bottom lip quivers so I stab it with my teeth. "Hey." I watch as he lingers for a moment, eyes on me, hair tinted with pink and orange. I scoot over on the bench, leaving space for a second person to sit beside me. If that person wants to. "I was surprised to hear from you," I confess.

He nods slowly, eyeing the vacant space on the bench as he takes another step forward, all the way into the clearing. "Sorry I've been distant. My dad's diagnosis came in right after everything happened with…" He swallows, stalls his feet. "It's called Lewy body dementia. There's no cure. I'm trying to figure out what to do, how to help him. There are treatment plans available, facilities that can care for him, but…I don't know. I'll need to figure out a way to collect an income. Chevy offered to bring me in on a house flip he's working on outside of town. Maybe I can do that."

I stare at him, dumbfounded. Heartbroken.

"God…Max," I murmur. "I'm so sorry."

"It is what it is. I'll figure it out." Shrugging, he gazes back at me, trying to hold it together. "I remember building that bench with Dad," he whispers, changing the subject. "We started it that same night. After you left the park."

I blink back tears. "Really?"

"Yeah. It was before Dad's accident. Before Mom left, before you left." He swallows, his jaw tight. "I think…I think that was my last really good day. Until you came back to Juniper Falls and stole my heart for a second time."

My brows wrinkle, a rock lodging my throat.

Max shakes his head. "No...that's not true. You never gave it back in the first place."

I dip my chin, the rock becoming a boulder. "We had one magical year together when we were kids. We were so young."

"It's really something, isn't it?"

"What?" I breathe out, lifting my head.

"Innocence." His gaze retreats from mine momentarily before floating back. "It's so fleeting, right? But, *God*—it's life-changing. Gone in a blink but powerful enough to shape every moment after. Every love story, every dream. We can't get it back once it's left, but we hold on to everything it gave us at the time," he says, emotion fusing each word. "I never let go of you, Ella. I thought I was an entirely different person when you returned, but I wasn't. Seeing you again felt like coming home." Max takes another step forward and drops to his knees in front of me, taking my hands in his. "Young love..."

I finish for him, tears traveling down my cheeks. "The purest fucking kind."

A smile stretches through the melancholy as he dusts his thumbs over my knuckles.

I glance over his head and out through the clearing opening. The sky grays before my eyes, the wind picking up like an omen. A sharp stab to innocence.

Color drains from the sky and thunder crackles in the distance.

Gunshots tears holes in sweet reveries.

Everything slams back into me, reminding me of all the things I long to forget. But there's no forgetting.

Letting go of Max's hands, I stand from the bench and move around him, staring out at the lake as the water ripples and churns. I fold my arms with a shiver. "I don't know how to move forward from this," I admit, my words aimed at the sky, at the lake, at him. "I don't know how to heal. Where does healing come from, anyway? Time? Therapy? Long walks and longer talks?" I shrug, feeling hopeless. "None of that feels like healing. It just feels like forcing happiness back into your life after it was ripped away from you."

"What other choice do we have?"

"I don't know. I don't think all the books or advice in the world can put our pieces back together." When he doesn't respond, I walk ahead, out into the woods. Warm wind sweeps my hair up as the treetops undulate overhead. "With every ounce of healing comes another hard blow. One step forward, two steps back. Maybe some people aren't meant to heal or overcome."

I feel him come up behind me as a few wayward raindrops slip from the clouds.

"Sunny," he whispers to my back.

I whirl around.

As we stare at each other, my bitterness heightens. Not at him but at life. At life's cruel *gift*. "How can you even look at me?" I wonder breathlessly. "How are we standing here talking about love and innocence and hope after everything that just happened?"

His expression falls as he repeats, more brokenly, "What other choice do we have?"

"There's always a choice, Max. Always."

He steps forward, body taut with tension. "You're right. McKay made a choice when he tried to force himself between your legs. He made a choice when he let you fall off a fucking cliff and when he walked away without calling for help, leaving you for dead." Anger and resentment flicker in his eyes. "Jonah made a choice when he stormed through my front door with a gun and shot my brother in the chest. He made a choice when he took justice into his own hands—justice for *you*. Every choice is a ripple. Every choice has a domino effect," he bites out. "And now, *we* have a choice. You and me. What's it going to be, Ella? How are you going to alter our next chapter? Where are you taking us?"

I gawk at him with wide, glazed eyes and swing my head back and forth. "I… It's not just up to me. What do *you* want?"

"I want to kiss you. That's what I want."

His words freeze me. My heart kicks up speed as the rain sprinkles down, dampening my hair. "That won't fix anything."

He shrugs. "Maybe not. But it's what I want."

"I don't think you know what you want. It's impossible to think clearly right now. I think…I think we need a break," I croak. "You were right when you said you needed space. Everything is too cloudy, murky. Messy."

"So, we clean up the mess."

"It's not that simple."

Letting out a hard breath, he glances down at the wet leaves and clenches his fists. "Fine."

"Fine?"

"Yeah. Fine. If that's what you want, we'll take a break."

"It's not about what I want. It's about what we need."

"Sounds like we need different things," he says. "I had space and I missed you like fucking crazy. No, scratch that—I had space for the last seven months when you left me stranded all alone in love with you and didn't tell me why. Fuck space. It's not what I want *or* need. All I need is you." He slams a flat palm over his heart. "You're the only thing that will repair this goddamn hole in my heart."

"I'm not the answer. I'm not—"

"You're *my* answer, Sunny."

"My brother killed your brother!" I shout, voice pitching over a roll of thunder.

He swallows hard, eyes flaring. "And we're not either of them. You're Ella and I'm Max. Why can't that be enough?"

"It's not. It can't be," I yell back. "McKay is dead because of Jonah."

"McKay did something unforgivable to you."

"He didn't deserve to die!"

"And neither do I!"

My face crumples as the rain splashes across my hair and cheeks. "Max…"

His chest heaves, body trembling, eyes darkening along with the sky. He scrubs both hands over his face and hair, shaking his head as he slams the heels of his palms to his eyes. "Fuck…sorry. You're right." Max stands there for a beat in the same position, only, his headshake morphing into a nod of acceptance. "You're right. Take all the time you need."

When he swivels away from me, I panic. My chest implodes with regret. I open my mouth to call him back, but nothing comes out.

So I race after him, grab him by the arm, and spin him around.

He stares down at me.

I whisper his name on the exhale, my heart bursting from the weight of it all. "Max."

He doesn't hesitate.

Our mouths crash together on our next breath.

Rain, tears, pain, love.

I fist his T-shirt with both hands as his arms wrap around me and yank me flush against his chest. His tongue pushes inside and I open willingly, longingly. We moan in tandem as I arch back, pulling him closer, his hands keeping me from tipping over.

No more words. No more talking, rehashing, or wallowing.

Only this.

Max and Ella.

Still holding me with one arm, he drags a hand to the side of my face and cups my cheek hard, his thumb tugging my jaw. I open wider. I kiss him harder. Everything blurs: the past, the present, the future. Rainwater sluices us as his tongue lashes mine and my hands lower to his hips.

He walks me backward. Our feet slide in wet leaves, puddles splashing with each clumsy step. We reach the clearing opening and he spins me around before collapsing down on the wooden bench and yanking me forward. Slick fingers dip underneath the hem of my halter top and drag it up my body, pulling it over my head. I gasp when the breeze kisses my skin. My wet hair slaps across my shoulders, my bare breasts spilling free and glimmering with rainfall. Max's breath hitches on a deep groan as he buries his face between them, his tongue flicking out, and then he moves to take a nipple in his mouth, sucking roughly.

My legs shake underneath me as I watch him move, an animalistic growl teasing his throat. I fist his hair and pull, desire pounding between my legs.

I climb onto his lap, my knees caging him in as he grabs my ass and thrusts his hips upward. His hard length stabs me through his running shorts and I don't think before sliding my shaky fingers under the waistband and tugging at his shorts.

Max lifts up briefly. The shorts slide down his thighs.

Frantic with bottled-up pain and lust, I wiggle my way out of my leggings, pulling one leg free. I mount him again, the leggings hanging off one calf as I reach down to fist his erection while my arm curls around his neck for balance and I grab a fistful of his hair.

Max cranes his neck back as my hand squeezes and strokes him. "Fuuuck," he grits out, face dropping to my breasts again, a nipple catching between his teeth.

I whimper, fiery tingles racing south. My knees shake as I try to stay steady, lifting up slightly and lining him up against me.

Tension races between us. An achy, breathless beat.

My eyes fall to his. They're hooded, half-lidded, as they lazily float up to meet mine.

I lower myself down onto him.

I feel him breach me, fill every inch of me, and when he's halfway inside, I wrap both arms around his shoulders and drop down all the way.

We both let out a loud, tapered moan, putting the sky's thunder to shame.

My hands clasp at the nape of his neck, nails gouging the skin. "Max," I mewl, a high-pitched, raspy slew of syllables. He's fully inside me, to the hilt. We are joined, connected, completely entwined. My barrier was broken, so there's no physical pain, yet tears rush to my eyes as the moment hugs me with desperate, shaky arms and squeezes tight.

I squeeze him in return, holding his face to my chest as I lift up then lower my hips.

I do it again and again.

He growls, groans, panting through the rhythm.

"Ella." He hisses my name, his arms twined around my body, one hand cupping the back of my head, fingers sifting through my hair. His other arm slides up and down my back, feeling my movements. Guiding them.

I need to feel more of him, so I grab at his T-shirt and try to yank it off him. Max holds me up with one arm while the other reaches behind his back, snatches the shirt by the collar, and hauls it over his head.

Skin to skin.

Chest to chest.

Heart to heart.

I press forward as I rock, my breasts smashing against his chiseled torso. I move faster, glancing down between us and watching as he slides in and out of me, up and down. When I lift up, almost all the way, the sight of him wet with my desire sends shivers down my spine. My pulse is on fire, my blood pumping hot.

I slam back down and he trembles in my arms, his breathing escalating.

As I rise again, our foreheads clank together and we both watch as my movements pick up speed and he thrusts up off the bench, chasing me.

My neck arches back and I ride him hard. Fast. Frenzied and reckless, so close I can feel the electric swell.

"Fuck, Ella...*fuck*, keep going," he pants, latching onto my hip bones, his fingers bruising as he rocks into me. "Feel how much I want you. Need you. God, you're perfect." His mouth hangs open, his eyebrows tightly knitted, as he stares down at our joining, our bodies slapping together while rain slaps at the earth all around us. "I'm gonna come in you," he groans. "Fuck, I'm close."

His words fuel me, set me aflame.

One of his hands falls between us and he rubs me with his thumb, taking me with him.

"Oh God," I whimper, head falling back, damp hair swinging. I feel it climbing, clawing, cresting. "Max..."

"Feel me, Ella," he rasps, forehead dropping to my chest. "Let it go. Let it all go."

I grind into him, and when he sucks my nipple into his mouth again, I break. I shatter into infinite pieces and land among the stars. Lightning streaks across my vision as white-hot ecstasy carries me away and then brings me right back home.

I collapse against him, boneless and thunderstruck, as Max grips my hips hard and rams into me two more times before tensing, shuddering, and letting out a feral groan with his face smashed between my breasts. I feel him empty inside me, releasing. Releasing everything.

Breathing heavily, he stays pressed against me as he comes back down. His hands slide up and down my back, one of them twirling my wet hair while we both process the last five minutes.

We lost our virginity.

He gave himself to me, and I gave myself to him, in the exact same spot we handed each other our hearts over a decade ago.

He's still inside of me as his head slowly lifts and his lips sprinkle kisses to the breadth of my chest, all the way up to my collarbone. I cradle his face between both hands, grazing his stubble, before angling his face up to mine.

We stare at each other for a few tangled heartbeats before I lean down to kiss him. Softly, gently. I don't think it's a goodbye, but as our tongues flick and our lips move, it almost feels like one. Emotion catches in my throat and I kiss him harder, hanging on to whatever we have left.

When I pull back, tears are in his eyes. Shining, gleaming, reflecting everything I'm feeling.

My lips quiver as I press a kiss to his forehead then rest my head on his shoulder. "Where do we go from here?" I whisper hoarsely. My lips brush the side of his neck as I wait.

And I wait.

Max squeezes me tighter, still sheathed inside me.

Then, on a frayed inhale, he croaks out three words that bring me to tears.

"I don't know."

An hour later, Brynn drives me over to the local pharmacy. I purchase the morning-after pill and chug it down with a bottle of Gatorade in one of the empty aisles with colorful boxes of cereal as my witnesses.

Brynn finds me a few minutes later, one palm clutching an eye-shadow palette. She approaches me with a smile and slides a loving hand up and down my arm. Sighing, she drops her temple to my shoulder. "Are you okay?" she asks.

I cap the Gatorade and try to catch my breath as I stare blankly at a box of Cap'n Crunch. Blinking slowly, I glance down at my muddy shoes and still-damp leggings, closing my eyes and holding in my grief. Then I whisper back, echoing Max's words, "I don't know."

Chapter 41
ELLA

A SCORCHING-HOT JUNE SHIFTS INTO AN EVEN HOTTER JULY, AND MY mother finally tells me that Grandma Shirley passed away in the weeks prior.

"You sure you don't want me to go with you?" Brynn asks, zooming by me in a streak of pink and baby blue as she hunts down her sandals. "I can reschedule with Kai. It's just a picnic."

A smile tips my mouth. "Nobody turns down a picnic, Brynn. Nobody."

She dismisses my claim with a beaming grin, slicing a hand through the air. "It's not a problem. The great thing about Kai is that he's extremely adaptable."

My lips purse.

You kind of have to be in this cursed town that's been privy to multiple tragedies in the span of a few months.

I should rephrase: You kind of have to be in this town that's been privy to multiple tragedies in the span of a few months, thanks to the cursed Ella Sunbury.

"He made a charcuterie board," I remind my friend as she gives her high ponytail a tug. "You don't turn your back on a complex array of fine cheese spreads on your first official date."

"I do like cheese."

"Cheese wins. Every time."

Brynn pauses, leveling me with a sympathetic stare. "I'll have my ringer on full blast. Please call or text if you need anything. I'm so sorry about your grams."

We hug each other as Kai pulls up in his dad's Volkswagen and races to the passenger side door to open it for Brynn. I smile and send her off, just as he's traipsing up the walkway. "Have fun," I tell her with a wave.

"I will!" she calls back. "Cheese!"

Fifteen minutes later, I'm pulling into our driveway.

Brynn let me borrow her car to make the few-mile drive over to the house. It was my first time behind the wheel in ages after my doctor finally gave me the green light, and it felt good to have a semblance of control over *something* in my life. All of my scans and tests have come back clear with no permanent brain damage, no vision impairments, and no issues with motor functions. Next, I'll be working toward my GED, courtesy of missing nearly six months of my senior year.

Gathering my courage, I climb out and meet Mom in the living room as she shares a mug of tea with Ricardo on the couch. His arm is draped around her shoulders and my mother is snuggled up against his chest, both hands cupping the mug.

I'm glad she has someone after I left her in the shadows with all these ghosts.

She glances up at me when I enter. "Ella."

"Hey." I set my purse down and slide out of my sneakers. "How are you?"

All she offers is a small shoulder shrug as her eyes glaze with sadness.

My poor mother.

Ricardo stands from the couch, sending me an empathetic nod. "I'm going to head out back to mow," he says, graciously leaving us alone.

"Thanks, hon," Mom replies, reaching for his hand and squeezing before he disappears through the patio door.

I stand in the entryway, lost.

Frozen.

Hopelessly unsure.

"Come here, sweetheart," Mom says, patting the space beside her on the sofa. "I miss you."

My eyes mist, her words triggering my legs into action. I collapse beside her as her arms envelop me, and I break down. "I'm so sorry, Mom. For everything."

"There's nothing to be sorry for."

"I abandoned you. I've been a really shitty daughter," I croak. "Selfish."

"Ella," she whispers, propping two fingers underneath my chin and lifting my head. "Every human being has a right to be selfish when it comes to grief. I abandoned you, too, in the wake of what happened with your brother." Her voice cracks on the last word. "I sacrificed precious time with you, so obsessed with overturning the case, when I still had a child here who needed me more than ever," she tells me brokenly. "I kept you in the dark. I was trying to protect you, trying to save you from another crushing disappointment if it didn't work out. So, no, Ella…you don't need to apologize for taking time to heal, no matter the cost. I'll always be your safe place to land when there's nowhere else to go." She strokes my hair back and shushes my tears. "I promise."

Her words make me cry harder as I bury my face against her shoulder.

In the midst of my tears, there's a solemn realization that bitterness—like a stubborn thorn—cannot be the sole foundation for our relationship. As my mom continues to comfort me, I sense a shared vulnerability bloom between us. Mom made a choice; her staunch belief in Jonah's innocence guided her judgment. Love always has a way of guiding the heart's will.

I can't fault her for love.

And I know that I'll need to make a choice, too.

"I love you," I whisper against her shoulder as she strokes my hair. "I don't want to stay angry, or to hold on to useless grudges. I just want to move forward. I want to live. And it's so hard to live when I feel trapped inside this bubble of tragedy and resentment." Inhaling a ragged breath, I finish with, "I just…I want to heal, Mom."

"Oh, sweetheart…I love you, too. So much." She sniffles, squeezing me tighter. "Do what you need to do to find your healing, okay? Whatever it might be. I will *always* be here. No matter what."

I nod, taking her words at face value.

Simmering in them. Spinning them over inside my head.

We stay like that for a few minutes, maybe ten, maybe twenty. It feels nice to be held, to still be loved after so much love has been sucked out of everything.

"I have something for you," Mom says, removing her glasses to swipe away her own tears. Smudges of mascara mingle with dark circles as she returns the wire-rimmed glasses to her nose. "It's from Grandma. She left you something in her will."

"She did?"

"Of course. I know she was stern and set in her ways, but she loved you very much." Mom stands and traipses across the small living room to snag her purse off a wall hook.

She hands me a manila envelope.

I lift up off the couch and pluck the envelope from her hands, grazing my fingertips over the starchy paper. A knot tightens in my throat.

"I'll give you a few minutes," she says softly. "Find me in the bedroom after you've read over everything."

Nodding distractedly, I feel her hand squeeze my upper arm, and then I listen to her footfalls move away as she heads down the hallway.

I peel open the envelope and reach inside.

I read.

My eyes bulge. My lungs squeeze.

Air leaves me in a staggered whoosh as I lean back against the wall for support, the world blurring.

Grandma Shirley left me $250,000 in her will.

She also left a note.

Warm tears stream down my cheeks as I skim over the shaky ink, drinking in her final words to me.

Dearest Ella,

Use this money wisely.
More importantly, live wisely and with love.
With all my heart,

Grams

I place a palm over my chest, rereading the simple words dozens of times.

Then I glance out the window, my gaze settling and lingering on the RV on Chevy's property across the street, before panning over to Max's house.

My chest contracts. My pulse stutters.

And it only takes two heartbeats for me to figure it out.

I make my choice.

I know exactly what I'm going to do.

Chapter 42

MAX

THUNK.

Footsteps clomp along my front porch.

My chin tips up from the book I'm reading, and I glance out the main window just as a shadow bolts by, disappearing before I can make out who it is.

I frown, wondering if it's Chevy bringing over a bag of groceries like he sometimes does.

Closing the book, I set it down beside me on the couch, slip my shoes on, and pull open the door. It takes a minute for me to notice it as my gaze dances around the yard, across the street, left to right. But when I peer down at the porch, a familiar item stares up at me.

An orange backpack.

I swallow, a sinking feeling swimming through my chest. An engine roars and sputters beside me, coming from Chevy's property, but I don't give it much thought.

I'm too focused on the backpack—Ella's most prized possession.

Crouching to my knees, I unzip the bag and peer inside. It hardly weighs anything at all.

And that's because it's only filled with one thing.

A note.

My hand trembles as I reach inside and pluck the folded paper from the bottom of the bag. When I peel it open, another rectangular piece of paper flutters out of it, landing at my feet.

I open the letter, my heart galloping, my breathing unsteady.

And I read.

> *Dear Max,*
>
> *You can't catch the sun, but there's no shame in chasing its light.*
> *I hope this brings you light.*
> *Thank you for being mine.*
> *Give your father the best care possible.*
> *I love you.*
>
> *—Sunny*

A choking sound falls out as I read over her note, two times, twelve times.

Then my attention falls to the other little piece of paper resting near my shoe. I pick it up and turn it over. And I almost fucking die when I see what it is.

A check.

A check for $200,000.

No.

No, no, no.

"Ella...*fuck*." I jump to my feet and rake a hand through my hair, just as the RV on Chevy's property revs to life and reverses full speed out of the yard.

I already know it's her. I already know she's leaving me.

My legs hardly feel attached as I stuff the check in my pocket and start to run. "Ella!"

My shoes kick up stones and rubble as the big rusted RV guns it down the neighborhood street. She sees me. She has to see me chasing after her, running toward her, desperate to catch her.

Chevy stands by his front door as I whip past his house. He shakes his head, tears in his eyes.

I keep running.

The RV is old, struggling as it climbs the steep hill. "Ella!" I shout cupping my hands around my mouth as the vehicle moves faster. "*Ella!*"

It keeps moving, the engine booming as she slams on the accelerator.

She's leaving.

She's leaving without a fucking goodbye.

My thighs burn and the soles of my feet ache as I run as fast as I can, catching up. Closing the gap, little by little.

I run like I've never run before. With Olympian speed. With the heart of a gutted, desperate man. Like it's my life's final marathon.

The RV keeps going and I keep running. I won't stop. I can't; I can't let her go. Not like this, not after everything we've been through.

I've hardly had her. I've hardly had a chance to love her.

That rainy night in the clearing will not be our swan song. I refuse to let her go without a real goodbye, without holding her one more time, without one last goddamn kiss.

No, no, no.

"Ella!" I call out, my heart pounding in time with my feet, my airways narrowing as oxygen fights to fill my lungs. As I fight to reach my fucking girl before she's lost forever. "*Sunny!*"

The RV zooms farther ahead, moving faster, leaving me behind.

My chest feels like it's going to erupt, my strength draining.

I can't catch her.

She's too far.

She's gone.

With a gasping howl from me, my feet finally slow to a painful stop, and I collapse to my knees in the gravel, inhaling, exhaling, every breath without her a breath with no purpose.

I stare out at the expanse of dusty, barren road as the RV becomes smaller and smaller.

I shout, I scream, I growl my agony into the sun, grief spilling from my eyes and tearing down my cheeks.

I stand upright, torn up and dying inside as I kick at a pile of rocks and fist my hair.

And then…

I freeze.

I blink, a sobbing breath catching in my throat.

Red brake lights flare. The RV jerks to a sudden stop up ahead.

I gasp again, this time with disbelief. My heart races and my legs start to move. A slow, cautious jog morphs into a full-out run when I see Ella spill out of the driver's side and land on her feet, staring at me from a few yards away.

The door hangs open.

She cries out.

And she runs.

She jogs toward me with a partial limp and I dash forward with renewed strength, my adrenaline spiking, hope firing in my chest. "Ella!"

"Max," she chokes, the space between us thinning. The distance dwindling.

"Ella."

We meet in the middle and she throws herself at me, her legs coiling around my waist as I drop to my knees, my arms holding her tight. "Max…Max," she weeps against my neck, gripping my hair with both hands. "I'm sorry."

I kiss every inch of her tearstained face, crying with her. "God, Sunny. I thought you were gone."

"I couldn't… I–I saw you running and I–I thought about that day my dad drove me away. I couldn't leave you without a goodbye. Not again." A ragged, mournful wail is muffled by my neck as she trembles in my arms.

"Ella…I can't accept this money," I grit out, squeezing her tight. "I can't. It's too much. Don't you dare leave me with this."

"Take it," she cries. "Please."

"No…the money is nothing without you. My life is nothing without you."

She shakes her head. "Your father needs you, Max. You need each other."

"I need *you*."

We rock together in the middle of the road, both of us in ruins.

With her lips pressed to my collar and her arms wrapped around me, she breathes out raggedly, "I need you, too. I'll always need you, b-but…I can't stay."

Pain.

Raw, violent pain crashes down on me.

Devastation competes with knowing, both funneling through me as I clutch her, feeling her soft hair sift through my fingers. "Sunny…"

"I can't, Max," she sobs. "I–I can't stay. I have to leave. Even though it hurts, it hurts so bad, I *need* to do this. I need to figure out who I am outside of this town. Outside of all this tragedy."

I think about everything she's been through. How broken she's been. How lost.

I think of her dreams, her precious, hard-fought dreams that she *deserves* to live out.

A horse farm in Michigan. A starlit sky beaming down on her. A quiet, simple life in her RV with books at her feet and wind in her hair as she gallops bareback and free on her favorite horse.

A peaceful life.

A life away from all this pain, all these sad reminders.

She can't stay.

And I can't go.

I let my tears fall down my cheeks and shower her hair. "I understand, Sunny Girl. I do." I choke out the words, pulling back and pressing my lips to her forehead as my heart shrivels up between my ribs. "I know this is what you need," I tell her with soul-crushing defeat. "I just needed to catch you one last time."

Her face crumbles, her cheeks flushed and soaking wet, her whole body shaking uncontrollably. "I'm sorry, Max. I'm so sorry. I just… It's too much. I need time…time t-to heal…"

I pull her back to me, stroking her hair. "Fuck," I murmur against her temple, squeezing her tighter. "I know."

I know. I fucking know.

It hurts so goddamn much, but I know it's right. I *know* it's what she needs, and I'll never stand in the way of her chasing her peace.

Her light.

Even if that light isn't me.

"Change your number," I force out, every word a dagger to my insides. "I'm begging you. Change your number and delete mine, because I swear I will reach out to you in my weak moments."

She nods, sobbing hopelessly against me.

"Don't let anyone tell me where you are. Make them promise you. I'll come for you, Ella. I swear to God I'll come for you and I'll never let you go."

"Okay," she cries. "Okay."

"I love you so much."

"I love you," she whispers raggedly. "I love you, Max."

It's the first time she's said the words aloud.

And she says them on a goodbye.

Every piece of me withers and decays like a dried-out rose under a hot sun. I deteriorate, petals falling as they're carried away with the wind. "Go," I manage, pulling back and gulping down a strained breath. "Go, Sunny."

"Max." She holds me tighter, kissing my throat, my cheek, my hair.

"Please," I beg. "Go live a good life, Ella. The best life. Meet new people, learn to skip stones, watch every sunrise and every sunset. Find a bridge and toss sticks into streams. Dance. Dance, no matter who's watching. Read as many books as you can, make lists, drink Dr Pepper, and ride horses until you can't catch your breath." I cup her face between my hands and place a final kiss on her lips. "And think of me. Bring me with you to all of those things," I plead, the pain eating me alive. "Don't let me go, Sunny. Don't ever let us go."

Nodding through her tears, she grips my shoulders, her emerald gaze shimmering with new adventures, new daydreams, a new chance at life. "I won't," she whispers back, giving me one last squeeze. "I'll never let you go. And maybe…" Ella swipes at her eyes, staring into mine. "Maybe I'll find you again one day. Maybe…we'll find each other."

Hope bleeds into her words.

Hope that someday, maybe, our timing will be right. Fate will bring her back to me, just like it did ten years after I first laid eyes on her smiling, beautiful face.

"Yeah," I murmur. "Maybe one day." I move away and take a step back, scrubbing my hands over my cheeks and jaw. Then I heave in a tattered breath and voice my final farewell. "Go live, Sunny Girl."

Hesitantly, slowly, she retreats, walking backward toward the RV, still nodding like she's reminding herself that this is right. And with one last poignant look, she spins around and dashes away, her red-brown hair swinging behind her.

Before she hops inside, I call out to her. "Ella."

She turns. Our eyes lock.

"Thank you."

I tap my front pocket, the check she left for me weighing heavily inside.

Her final gift.

A second chance for me, too. For me and my father.

She blinks away more tears and stretches a sad, knowing smile. "You're welcome."

Ella jumps inside the driver's seat with a closing glance, and I stare at the RV as it stutters to life, taking with it the girl I love. I watch it drive off, disappearing over the hill and leaving me behind.

I fall back down to my knees the moment it's out of sight.

Broken down and drained, I sit collapsed in the middle of the road as cars fly by, honking, zigzagging around me, shouting at me to get out of the street. I hardly hear them. It's all background noise. A distant hum.

I sit there until night takes over and minutes bleed into hours.

Daylight fades. The sky darkens to gray.

And I just sit there…

Watching as the sun sets.

"Goodbye…? Oh no, please. Can't we just go back to page one and start all over again?"
—THE MANY ADVENTURES OF WINNIE THE POOH, 1977 DISNEY MOVIE

"HOW TO CATCH THE SUN"

STEP FOUR:

Hold Out for Dawn

Just as the sun rises, so does the chance for a new beginning.

Chapter 43

ELLA

TWO YEARS LATER

Ella! I need you—*NOW!*"

Natine's voice spills in through the open door of my RV, yanking me into action. I jump from the bed, toss my book onto a clump of pillows, and sprint down the three metal steps, following her desperate call. Winding through stables and toward the fenced-in grazing pasture, I squint through the harsh sunlight and spot her up ahead.

The scene that greets me is chaotic. Several horses are galloping around the enclosure, their panicked whinnies echoing all around us, heightening the anxiety. I'm met with a slew of wide and white-rimmed eyes, while frightened hooves kick up clouds of dust and dirt with every step. Natine is in the middle, trying to grasp the reins of one particularly agitated mare, her low, soothing voice doing its best to cut through the havoc.

"Ella." She swings her head toward me when I approach. "We need to get them under control before they hurt themselves or each other."

"I'm on it." I nod, inhaling a deep breath to focus. Swiveling back around, I race to the tack room and snatch a few halters and lead ropes. We need to isolate the most distressed horses first.

When I run back to the scene, I fumble with the padlock to the enclosure, slide inside, then lock it behind me.

"Start with Indigo! She's influencing the others." Natine points to the lead mare, who's pacing erratically near the far end.

I approach Indigo from the side, avoiding direct eye contact to prevent further agitation. Using a gentle, reassuring voice, I murmur, "Easy, girl. Easy. You're okay. You're fine."

Natine does the same with another horse, her body language equally calm and assertive. One by one, using a combination of hushed tones, slow movements, and the familiar touch of our steady hands, we manage to halter the distressed horses and lead them to separate paddocks. With each horse we isolate, the collective panic in the enclosure begins to wane.

Once the last horse is safely corralled, the two of us stand, panting and covered in dirt, in the now-quiet paddock.

"Lord Jesus, that was stressful," Natine says, puffing her cheeks with air, her dark-brown eyes scanning the perimeter. "I wonder what set them off."

Following her gaze, I spot a fallen branch near the edge of the paddock, its leaves rustling in the late-November wind. Beside it lies a torn metallic balloon, the kind children get at fairs and festivals. It must've popped and spooked the horses.

"There," I point. "The balloon next to that branch. I bet it sounded like a predator."

Natine nods, her button nose wrinkling. "Mmm, makes sense. We'll have to do a perimeter check every morning from now on. That holiday market just started in the square."

"Great for my candle collection," I decide. "The horses are notably less enthused."

Chuckling, she sends me a smile, her teeth extra white against dark skin and plum lipstick. Natine readjusts her sage-green headscarf as two golden earrings glint in the sunshine. "I was going to head over there this afternoon. Aside from manure, all I've been smelling this weekend is deep-fried everything. My hips are telling me no, but my heart wants Oreos on a stick."

I giggle as we stroll side by side toward my RV, my knee-high boots sinking into chill-hardened dirt. "Give me twenty minutes to hop in the shower and I'll be your Oreo wing-girl."

"I knew you were good people."

"Of course you did. When you met me, I basically had 'Chosen Little Sister' written all over my face as I ass-planted in the mud."

"Your face was more 'Holy shit, I'm about to ass-plant in the mud,' but, sure, we'll go with that."

I nudge her playfully with my shoulder. "We'll definitely go with that."

It's true that I made a subpar first impression when I drove up to Natine's horse ranch over two years ago, lost, exhausted from months of directionless traveling, and eager to hop on a horse again for the first time in years.

It didn't go well.

Turned out, I wasn't quite the bright-eyed, confident rider I'd once been. The horse sensed my faux self-assurance and decided to play with me, hightailing it into a full-on gallop the moment my feet were in the stirrups. I hunched forward, trying my hardest to stay in the saddle, but it was too much, too soon—I biffed it.

Natine laughed as she ran toward me.

And thus, our friendship began. There I was, floundering in a mud puddle with a bruised tailbone, while Natine, a wise and nurturing presence at the age of thirty-five, stood steadfast by my side, extending a hand to pull me to my feet. She pulled me to my feet in a lot of ways, giving me a temporary job on her ranch as a stable hand while I continue to search for a more lifelong career in the equestrian field. She's also let me live on her property in the rusty old RV Chevy sold to me for $9,500—well under listed value. I used the remaining $40,000 of the inheritance from Grandma Shirley to travel aimlessly before fate landed me at Diamond Acres, one of the few horse farms in the Upper Peninsula of Michigan—making my job hunt difficult—and I still have a lot of that money left over, considering I enjoy living simply. A good portion of it has gone into making my RV sparkle. It doubles as not only my home, but also a small business I started up to sell books and my own bookbinding creations.

I like to call it a modern-day bookmobile. It's served me well, keeping income flowing in, while allowing me to do what I love.

The last two years have been pivotal in my healing process, and regular visits from Mom, Ricardo, Brynn, and Kai have kept me focused on that uphill journey. Excitement has been blooming all week as I gear up for my twenty-first birthday.

Excitement that is only dimmed by one thing.

And that one thing is a constant reminder of what I gave up in order to find my healing.

There are days when I wonder if I made the wrong choice. Those are the dark days. The shadow-fogged, dreary days of wallowing, eating too many carbs, and video-calling Brynn with tears streaming down my face. She tells me he's doing well, visiting with his father in an assisted living center and thriving in a business with Chevy. What began as a side gig in house-flipping has now blossomed into a flourishing career for both of them.

Still, it hurts.

I miss him so much.

There's a hole in my heart, a hole in my entire life. A painful missing piece. And the only thing that comes close to filling it is the Michigan air filling my lungs as I ride my favorite horse, Midnight, through pastures and golden fields, pretending he's galloping by my side.

He is.

I never let him go.

The RV comes into view and I wave a quick goodbye to Natine as she curves toward her small white ranch house. "I'll pop by in a few," I tell her.

"Take your time, Ell. I have some paperwork to finish up." She stops, swivels toward me. "Oh, hey, you still have that interview on Sunday morning? At the new horse farm a bit west of here?"

"Yep," I call out over a gust of wind. "Ten a.m."

"Bummer. I was secretly hoping you'd stay here forever."

"Yeah, right. This RV is an eyesore and you know it."

"But you're not. I'm really going to miss you."

We share a soft look as I readjust my wool hat and waver by my makeshift home on wheels. Part of me wouldn't mind staying here forever, but I know, deep down, Natine and Diamond Acres are just beautiful stepping stones to my final landing place. My ambition to specialize in professional horse training brought the disappointing realization that the Upper Peninsula doesn't offer many opportunities in that field, so I've found myself dragging my mud-spattered feet, reluctant to bid farewell to my dear friend.

To my surprise, Natine got wind of a new farm that just opened up thirty miles west of here. She even helped me secure a job interview on Sunday as a stable manager, which happens to be the day after my birthday. Nailing down a job in my desired field while also staying close to Natine would be the best birthday present ever.

I holler back before traipsing toward the RV. "Nothing is official. You might be stuck with me forever."

"Not mad about it, honey."

Smiling wide, I send her off with a wave and disappear inside before making my way to the tiny bathroom for a shower.

But first, I read one more chapter of *Black Beauty*.

"I'm good, Mom. Stop worrying." I balance the phone between my ear and shoulder as I fumble with a lip-balm cap, my boots sloshing through half-frozen puddles strewn along the small-town sidewalk. "There will be plenty more birthdays you can crash."

Mom is in Cancún with Ricardo.

My birthday is tomorrow.

Therefore, Mom has guilt.

"I feel awful," she moans, despite the music stylings of a mariachi band playing in the background, mingling with laughter and windswept waves. "You're all alone on your birthday."

"I'm not alone. I have Natine, horses, my own sparkling company, and an infinite number of books to read."

"I wish I could be there."

I smile softly. "I love you, but you're full of lies. You're in paradise with your boyfriend, sipping cocktails on the beach. There's nowhere else you'd rather be and you know it."

Her tone is still laced with melancholy. "But you're turning twenty-one. That's a big deal."

"You're moping, Mother. You need to perfect the brood."

A rumble of laughter echoes through the speaker. "You're right. I do have an excellent coach."

"You do," I agree. "And that coach would love for you to visit over Christmas, so we can brood in tandem to gloomy Johnny Mathis songs."

"I can't wait to see you, honey. Please be safe. I'll give you a call tomorrow."

"Love you."

"Love you, too. Happy birthday."

We disconnect the call and I slip my cell phone into my purse as I veer toward the bar entrance. My smile lingers while I think about how far my mother has come in the wake of our catastrophic family upheaval. It hasn't been easy for any of us, but Mom was truly put through the emotional wringer. She dedicated years of her life to getting her son out of prison, only to watch him go right back to a jail cell a few months into freedom.

Thank God for Ricardo.

Kai's father has been the biggest blessing, keeping Mom busy, laughing, hopeful, and growing. They have no plans for marriage and are content being partners, both of them having lived through respective messy divorces. Their dynamic works. They travel often and love hard, and I can't recall a time when my mother was happier.

When I approach two familiar cement steps that lead up to a towering sable door, I reach for the handle and swing it open, a rush of warmth hitting my face as I step inside.

"Ella!" Anderson flips a bottle of tequila in his hand like a pro from behind the bar, sending me a wink as I enter. "Happy birthday, sweetheart."

"My birthday is tomorrow, but thank you," I tell him, pulling off my black beanie and smoothing down my hair. My tresses have grown out to the middle of my back now, after the shorter cut I had due to my surgery. I pull my hair over both shoulders and make my way to a vacant barstool.

"The usual?" Anderson side-eyes me while serving another customer.

I nod. "Yup. Make it a double."

A minute later, two glasses of bubbly Dr Pepper are sitting in front of me. I inhale a big sip of one of the sodas through a straw and almost choke.

Anderson snorts a laugh. "An early birthday treat."

"That tastes like rocket fuel," I mutter through a gag. "Rocket fuel that's been laced with liquid fire."

"It's a Dr Pepper bomb. Shot of rum at the bottom."

"Thanks. I must've missed the warning."

"And miss your reaction? Never."

I glare at him through an amused grin. "I'm not even of legal drinking age yet."

He glances at his invisible watch. "Only two more hours. Worth the risk."

Music spills out of one the vintage jukeboxes, and I glance right, spotting a cluster of twentysomethings browsing through the song list. The dive bar is called Retro Rhythms, a nod to the nostalgia of the past. It's a meshing of aged wood, dim lighting, and a kaleidoscope of colorful vinyl album covers littering the walls. The smell of worn leather and hints of tobacco float through the air, fusing with the laughter and chatter of young and old patrons.

I was never much of a bar girl, but the name caught my attention one day while I was exploring the town's local shops and restaurants.

It's all about the rhythm…

Anderson is my favorite bartender. He's a late-thirties father of two, married to the owner, and he always welcomes me with a smile and a Dr Pepper when I pop in for my usual Friday routine.

I drink a Dr Pepper.

And then I dance.

"You better get a song in before those college kids murder my eardrums with country music," he tells me, mixing a concoction of vodka and lemon juice.

I laugh when he visibly shudders.

"I got you," I say back, drinking down the uncompromised beverage, slapping a twenty-dollar bill on the counter, and hopping off the stool with a salute.

When the country song ends, I wind over to the jukebox and insert my debit card, already knowing my song selection. A moment later, Stevie Nicks fills the room with "Rhiannon."

A bright smile tips my mouth.

I make my way out to the center of the dance floor, hips swaying, the smile sticking to my face, and my hair sashaying all around me. A few regulars cheer me on, clapping and whistling. Sweat slicks along my hairline as I undulate under the lights, and music fills my soul.

Three minutes of restoration.

Three minutes of pure therapy.

Three minutes where I'm with him and he's with me, and we're dancing on a bridge beneath the stars, his arms around me, my cheek pressed to his pine-scented chest.

I feel him more than ever in these moments. I feel his warmth, his strength, his careful fingers stroking back my hair. I inhale his familiar nature-steeped scent and hear a single word whispered against my ear: *"Stay."*

Within these three minutes, I do stay. I never leave Juniper Falls. Tragedy never claws its way through us with black-tipped talons. It doesn't infect us, doesn't contaminate everything precious and good.

There is no Jonah. No McKay. No terror, no bloodshed, no tears.

There are only Max and Ella, swaying on an old bridge over the water with a sun-inspired playlist as our soundtrack.

I slowly lift my arms over my head, then drag my fingers through my hair as my hips twirl, my neck swivels, and my pulse thrums. My eyes remain closed. Images burst to life in full color within my mind's eye and I savor every second in his arms.

And for a moment, I think I *do* feel him.

My skin tingles with a strange familiarity. A pinprick of intuition. Like something is giving my soul a warm hug.

"Souls don't see, Sunny. Souls feel."

I open my eyes and glance around the dance floor, gaze sweeping from face to face, shadow to shadow, while I keep moving, keep swaying in slow motion.

Nothing.

I scold myself for being ridiculous and slam my eyes shut once again, shaking off the feeling.

Three minutes turn into four and the song ends, leaving me cold and alone.

My eyelids flutter back open, my gaze landing on cheerful faces and enthusiastic fist pumps through the air as fellow patrons celebrate my one-person dance performance. I force a smile and take a small bow before traipsing off the dance floor, already craving the next three minutes.

"You make that look cathartic," Anderson notes, refilling my watered-down soda. "When I dance, my wife tells me I look like a malfunctioning Roomba banging against the wall over and over."

My fingers curl around the edge of the bar as I attempt to envision the analogy. I can't. Breathing out a laugh, I offer him a shrug. "I never used to like dancing. I never liked attention on me, or bright lights, or big crowds."

"What changed?"

My smile turns watery. "A boy."

"Ah. Always is." He presses forward on the bar with both palms and tilts his head. "You look like you're entirely somewhere else when you dance," he muses. "Where do you go?"

With a slow exhale, I reach for the glass, finger the straw, then glance back up at him. "Back to that boy."

I make my way home a little after midnight and step inside the RV, flipping on a light and veering toward the miniature bedroom at the far end. After slipping into a pair of cozy pajamas, gulping down a glass of water, and brushing my hair and teeth, I pull my notebook out of a tiny desk drawer and reach for a pen.

Inside the notebook is a list.

It's a list of all the things Max wanted me to do.

Meet new people.
Learn to skip stones.
Watch every sunrise and every sunset.
Find a bridge and toss sticks into streams.
Dance, no matter who's watching.
Read as many books as you can.
Make lists.
Drink Dr Pepper.
Ride horses until you can't catch your breath.

Uncapping the blue pen, I add another checkmark in the columns under "dance" and "drink Dr Pepper." Then, with a melancholic smile, I tuck the notebook back in the drawer and crawl into bed.

Checkmarks #122 and #146.

Chapter 44

ELLA

"AHH, YOU LOOK AMAZING!"

Brynn's chipper voice is music to my ears as I lie back in the grass, my face tipped to the sky and my phone held out in front of me. "Thank you. It was a fun day."

"I hope you had the best birthday ever, bestie! I wish I could have been there with you." Her bright smile droops, momentarily morphing into a pout before beaming again. "Kai had that art show tonight."

"I know, that's so exciting," I say with a grin, watching as Kai comes into view on the phone screen.

He raises his hand with a wave, then sweeps back his bangs. "Happy birthday, Ella."

"Thanks, Kai. Congrats!"

"Thank you. It was pretty cool."

"Don't listen to him." Brynn shoves at his shoulder with hers. "It was *epic*, Ella. A black-tie affair, champagne, important people." A whimsical sigh falls out of her. "His painting was *revered*. Daddio and Pops were bawling. Seriously, their champagne ratio was eighty-five percent tears."

Kai sighs. "She's exaggerating. It only caught people's attention when they mistook it for an accidental paint spill."

The phone shakes through my giggles. "I'm siding with Brynn on this one. I know it was epic."

"I guess it went pretty well," he relents, unable to stifle the proud smile that lights up his face.

"Tell me about your special day," Brynn encourages. Kai waves me off and my best friend takes me with her as she floats around the small apartment they share in southern Florida, after making their relationship official two years ago. Blush-pink walls and girlie knickknacks whiz by while she moves into the kitchen to pour a glass of juice.

"Natine and I started the day watching the sunrise and then we rode horses for a while," I tell her, reminiscing over the feel of the crisp wind nibbling at my cheeks. "We ate lunch in the square, browsed craft vendors, and listened to live music before getting some work in at the stables. Then Natine ordered me to get dressed up, curl my hair, put on makeup, and do absolutely nothing for the rest of the day." I shrug, pleased with my ordinary birthday itinerary. "So I did. It was fabulous."

"Wait, you didn't drink *all* the cocktails? Puke in someone's lap in true birthday-girl fashion?"

My nose scrunches up. "Hard pass."

"For the best," she murmurs, pausing midsip. "You've got that interview in the morning."

"I told you about that?"

She chugs down the rest of her juice. "Sure. You mentioned it last week."

"Right." I nod, my chest fluttering at the thought of becoming a stable manager. It'll open up so many future possibilities in this field. "It's been great working with Natine and relearning everything about the horses," I continue. "But I think it's finally time to spread my wings."

Brynn leans back against the counter. "I have a good feeling about it," she says. "A really good feeling."

"You do?"

"Yup. I definitely think you'll get the job."

"That would be amazing. And I think..." My words drift and my throat starts to burn. "I think Max would be really proud of me."

Her eyes glaze over with tears as a few tense beats roll by. "He's doing good, Ella. Kai talked to him last week. He asked about you."

"Oh yeah?" The fireball in my throat catches with gasoline. "That's nice to hear."

"He always asks about you."

Hot pressure burns behind my eyes.

I took Max's pleas at face value that day in the middle of a gravelly road, rocks pressing into our kneecaps and goodbyes stabbing at our hearts. I made my friends promise that they would never tell him where I was, never give him my new number. They all agreed. Even Mom.

They understood.

And now, even though I'm doing better and have come such a long way, I don't know if anything has changed for us. I don't know if he *wants* to hear from me. Maybe he made me promise him those things for both of our sakes. For his own inner peace.

I've considered reaching out to him more times than I can count.

I've almost buckled under the draw of temptation.

But nearly three years have passed, and so much time has gone by. Max seems happy, settled, successful, free of my trail of tragedy that always seemed to follow us around and attach itself to us like a malignant tumor.

They say that out of sight and out of mind is the only way to truly heal and let go.

Maybe Max finally let go.

Maybe he let me go.

Clearing my throat, I bob my head quickly and force back an embarrassing waterfall of tears. "Well, I'm glad you had a good night at the art show. How's school going?"

Brynn fills me in on her college courses and criminal justice journey, the enthusiasm making its way back into her voice. We spend the next fifteen minutes talking, catching up, and reminiscing about the good times as the dark-blue stretch overhead turns almost black and we say our goodbyes.

It's just me now.

Me and the sky.

Me and my childhood wish.

I lie back and wait, hoping the sky will burst to life above me in streaks of glittering green. It's a clear, cloudless night, the perfect canvas for auroras.

When I was ten years old, Jonah told me about the northern lights. I'd been back in Nashville for a few years and our bond had grown ten times stronger. My wishes became his wishes. His dreams became my dreams. Jonah said that when I was older, we'd take a road trip together up to Porcupine Mountains Wilderness State Park and try to watch the light show when the moon was shrouded and the sky was clear.

I held on to that dream, even after he went to prison.

It became my dream.

So as my mother and I made the drive to Juniper Falls in silence after Jonah's sentencing with our fresh start dangling on a bleak horizon, I made a promise to myself that I would find my way to this park on my twenty-first birthday. I'd spend the night lying underneath the stars, waiting for that first emerald spark.

I'm doing it.

Cold air bites at my nose as my hair halos around me in the grass, spilling out from underneath my wool hat. It's in the low thirties and snow is predicted in the incoming week, a change of season I'm eager to dive into. But tonight, the sky is clear. Tonight, the sky is just for me.

My teeth chatter and my toes curl into my fuzzy socks and fleece-lined boots as I tug my orange scarf a little tighter and fold my arms across my puffy coat.

I wait.

I wait for one hour. Two hours. The cup of hot cocoa I brought is mostly gone, the remaining liquid ice-cold. Frost-tipped grass blades poke the back of my neck, making me itchy. It's nearly 11:00 p.m. when I'm ready to call it quits and give up.

I almost do.

Almost.

But then I hear something.

Frowning, I sit up straight, a strange noise penetrating the silence of nature. At first, I think it's an animal, a white-tailed deer or a curious fox. Hopefully not a coyote.

Only...I think it's something worse.

A person.

Footsteps crunch along leaves and sticks, approaching on my left, and goose bumps prickle the back of my neck. Nerves slither down my spine. All I can imagine is a mountain man leaping from the trees with a rusted ax and hacking away at me until my dreams fade to black beneath an aurora-less sky. It's instinct to immediately conjure up danger, ever since McKay's attack. I've come a long way in my healing journey, but I'm a lot more careful these days.

Truthfully, I shouldn't have come out here alone.

The footsteps approach.

I choke.

I jump to my feet, my gaze scanning the darkened surroundings, senses on high alert.

My heart pounds when a shadowy figure comes into view in my peripheral vision, the face shrouded by the night.

Oh God.

I'm shivering, more from fear than the cold. Icicles bloom in my lungs and sleet rains down inside my chest.

Holding my breath, I clench my gloved hands into fists, gather my courage, and whip around.

And I freeze in place.

A gasp falls out.

But before I can say a word…

A can of Dr Pepper comes flying at me through the wall of darkness.

I catch it.

Chapter 45

ELLA

H EY, SUNNY."
That name.

That voice.

That face.

Familiar features materialize as he steps closer, hands slipping in his pockets, hair fluttering when the wind blows through.

I can't breathe. Can't speak, can't move. I'm frozen to the earth with a can of Dr Pepper squeezed inside my fist so hard, the aluminum threatens to crumple.

My eyes are playing tricks.

The dark is compromising my rational thought.

I start shaking, my knees close to buckling. It can't be him.

He's not here.

I slam my eyes shut and shake my head, my throat stinging. "Max," I croak out.

Maybe I'm still dancing. Maybe I imagined him so hard, I brought him to life.

Before I can spiral, two strong arms are around me, pulling me to a warm chest. The smell hits me first. Pine needles, woods, nature, a trace of mint.

Max.

The Dr Pepper falls from my hand and I fist the front of his coat with white-knuckled fingers and bury my face in the buttons. "Are you real?" I breathe out, tears leaking down my cheeks.

He lets out a long exhale, like he just ran a marathon and finally crossed over the finish line. "I'm real," he whispers, cupping the back of my head, his fingers gloveless as they dip under my hat to graze along my scalp. "I'm real, Sunny Girl."

"How? How…how are you here?" My head swings back and forth, my tears dissolving into the fabric of his coat. "You knew where I'd be. Did Brynn tell you? My mother? Did you—"

"You told me," he says, cradling my face and angling my eyes up to his. "You did. The night I came through your window with a concussion and you bandaged me up. You said you'd be here."

My eyes are wide and glazed as I stare up at his handsome, bristled face, flabbergasted. "You remembered that?"

A smile blooms. "I remember everything you tell me."

I still can't believe it. Nearly three years without his touch and I can't imagine how I ever survived without it.

My head tilts, eyes closing, his thumb brushing along my frozen lower lip. "Max…"

"I took a chance," he tells me, voice hoarse. "I had to. No one would tell me where you were, no matter how many times I begged and pleaded. This was my one shot to see you, even if you didn't want to see me."

"I want to see you," I say, nodding fervently. "Of course I do. I've missed you so much."

He cants my head back up to his, one finger tucked under my chin. "Yeah?"

"Yeah." My eyes dart across his face. His blue, blue eyes, perfect nose, full lips, and mess of rich brown hair. He's beautifully the same and so different, too. Even through the dark night I see a maturity in his gaze. A growth. During our time apart, his charming, boyish glow has transformed into a masculine ruggedness. Bristles line his jaw—not quite a beard, but more than stubble.

I place my fingertips to the side of his cheek, my focus dipping to his mouth before panning back up. His eyes glitter under the milky starlight.

And then he sighs again. That same contented, finish-line sigh.

Max pulls me against him, hugging me tight, holding me like he never plans to leave. I melt into him and let him warm me, let him fill every hole left empty in his absence.

"There's so much I want to tell you, Sunny," he confesses.

I let him hold me for a few more beats before pulling back, a giddiness rising inside me as the shock starts to dwindle. "God, me too. I know it's late…" I bite my lip, watching as a smile hints on his lips. "How long are you in town?"

"A few days," he says, hands sliding back in the pockets of his dark-wash jeans. "Then I'll need to get back to work. I don't want to interrupt your life. I just—"

"A few days." I nod absently, feeling like there's not enough time in the world to keep me from missing him once he's gone. "Okay. A few days."

A few days.

A few days to cherish him. To hug him. To breathe him in, hold his hand, and make new memories.

A few days to add as many check marks to my notebook as possible.

The fire sets his gaze aglow, sprinkling red-orange embers into the blue of his eyes. I'm immediately taken back to a senior-year bonfire over three years ago, where we sat side by side on a log bench and every inch of me burned hotter than the flames, thanks to that mere inch between us.

It's funny how you know your life is going to change. A heavy look, a careful word, a leg brush or a quick touch. An orange flower held in the hand of a little boy.

Somehow, I knew that when Max handed me that rose and then chased after my father's shiny car, he'd reach me one day. He'd find me and I'd find him, and we could finally stop running in opposite directions.

I wonder if that *one day* is finally here.

As wood crackles and smoke rises, our knees touch on the small bench near the firepit, just a few yards from Natine's house, following our return from the park.

I glance up at Max staring down at me. He looks the same way I feel—mesmerized.

"I don't even know what to say," I confess, studying his face, relearning every crease and divot. "God…I feel like I'm dreaming."

He smiles softly. "Feels that way, doesn't it?"

"How are you? I mean…jeez, that sounds so casual, considering our history. But I want to know everything about you. Where you're living, how your dad is doing, your career…"

Do you still love me?

Are we passing ships, or am I anchored in your heart?

Max spins his own Dr Pepper can in his hands as he glances down between his knees with a long sigh. "I'm doing good. Really good," he says. "Chevy and I started up a business after you left. I helped him flip this huge house outside of town and we sold it for a big profit. Then I finally finished the reno on our old house and sold that, too. It kind of snowballed after that. Chevy and I have become close. He's really been a lifeline for me." A smile lifts when he looks my way. "Dad is doing okay. He's in an assisted living center. He has moments of clarity, but…"

I move my hand to his lap and squeeze his knee. "I'm sorry."

"It's okay. He's doing better and the facility takes good care of him. I try to visit him as much as I can. A few times a week, usually. Sometimes he recognizes me, sometimes he doesn't. I've accepted it. Nothing else I can really do." His attention lands on my hand still cupping his knee. "The money you left me… It changed our lives, Ella. I can't thank you enough for that."

Tears blur my vision as I nod. "Of course. I'm so glad I could help," I whisper. "It was the easiest decision I ever had to make. And it came right along with the hardest."

Our gazes hold for a long beat before he glances into the orange flames. "I never resented you for leaving. I hope you know that." The tendons in his neck stretch, his jaw clenching tight through the bevy of emotions funneling between us. "And look at the life you've built for yourself. I'm so proud of you. You're living your dream, riding horses, looking as free as I've ever seen you."

"I've never been free of you," I tell him, needing him to know. It's imperative he knows. "Never. You've been here. I've carried you with me this whole time."

He blinks back at me, his eyes dimming. "You never reached out."

"I know. I wanted to." My bottom lip wobbles as I pull my hand away, wrapping my arms around myself to counter the chill of that truth. "I didn't know if I could, if you wanted me to," I admit, exhaling a frayed breath. "I thought you moved on by now. I figured you created a new life, met someone else…"

"What? No," he says. "There's been nobody else."

This has my chin popping up, eyes flaring. "Really?"

"There's no one else, Ella. It never crossed my mind. Not once."

"Not even…" I swallow hard, grit forming in my throat. "Not even something casual? It's been a long time. I get it if you—"

"No," he answers quickly, frowning. "Not even that."

I'm taken aback.

I never would have guessed he's been celibate, untethered to female companionship. He's a twenty-one-year-old man, after all. Gorgeous. Kindhearted and noble. Perfect in every way.

A tear slips out and I swipe it away, his unwavering devotion filling my chest with something heavy. "But…I left you," I whisper raggedly, my gaze held tightly to his. "We broke up."

Max turns and fully faces me, shaking his head as he lets out a hard breath. Raising his hand, he cups my cheek with a featherlight touch, his thumb stroking away my falling tears. "We didn't break up, Sunny," he murmurs back. "We just broke."

My breath hitches.

An avalanche of heartache rains down on me, burying me alive.

"I wasn't sure if we were fixable," I admit through the knot in my throat. "Everything that happened…with Jonah…"

He looks away, down at the ground, and my chest contracts with grief and sorrow.

I still think about my brother…every day. It's impossible not to.

But it doesn't hurt as much as it once did. In the original case against him, there was always a measure of second-guessing. He never admitted guilt. The evidence had been devastating, but when you love somebody that much—when your whole life is woven and braided with theirs—it's hard to believe they are capable of committing such a grisly crime. I still don't know the truth. I'll probably never know what happened the night Erin Kingston and Tyler Mack lost their lives.

After his original conviction for the double homicide was overturned, Jonah found himself in a legally precarious position. The principle of double jeopardy meant he couldn't be retried for those particular murders. So when faced with the new charge in the death of McKay, Jonah and his counsel decided it was best to avoid another uncertain legal battle.

This time he accepted the plea bargain offered: a reduction of his second-degree murder charge to voluntary manslaughter. In exchange, he was sentenced to fifteen years with the possibility of parole after seven, along with a commitment to attend an anger management therapy program during his incarceration. Given his history and past accusations, many found the sentence lenient.

Even me.

But with the previous trial's complications and its evidence deemed inadmissible, the prosecution felt this was the most strategic way to ensure Jonah faced some measure of justice. And in the end, Mom didn't have to suffer through the heartache of another trial, which was a small silver lining.

Max peers back up at me when the silence lingers, setting down his can. "Have you visited him at all?" he wonders.

I shake my head stiffly. Jonah is at a medium-security correctional complex in Pikeville, roughly an hour and a half east of Tellico Plains. "No, but Mom does. She visits him once a month."

"How do you feel about that?"

I shrug. "I don't blame her. That's her son."

"He's your brother," Max says, tone softening. "He was protecting you."

"He was avenging me," I correct. "There's a difference. And I never asked him to do that. God, that's the last thing I wanted…" More tears threaten when our eyes catch. "How are you doing, Max? With everything?"

His eyes dip to the wood chips beneath our boots. "I'm managing. It's a strange position to be in…grieving someone you loved, while also resenting them for doing something terrible. I know you get it." He swallows. "Some days are better than others."

I do get it. I'm in the exact same position.

The ironic parallel would be funny if it weren't so tragic. And I worried, at first, that if I ever saw Max again, I'd still see his brother's face shining back at me with malice. I'd see dark eyes, instead of crystal blue. Callousness instead of comfort.

But I don't.

All I see is Max.

"I'm so sorry," I breathe out.

And I am sorry.

For everything.

I stand from the bench, holding in a cry. A cry of longing, of despair. Of things we can't change and things we still can. Of unknowns and well-knowns and tragedy and fate.

My legs carry me over to the stretch of woods that border a small creek.

I hear him follow.

I hear his familiar footfalls. Heavy boots against rugged earth.

The water is near-frozen as my feet stall at the edge of the creek, my tears like tiny icicles glued to my cheeks. "I made a list," I murmur softly as Max steps beside me and we're shoulder to shoulder. "I made a list of all the things you wanted me to do. I've kept a running tally." Bending over, I pick up a small stone with my gloved fingers and brush my thumb along the ridges. "But I still haven't figured out how to skip a stone."

Max watches as I arch my arm and toss the stone across the water. It bounces off an ice formation, then disappears into the black abyss.

I sigh, turning toward him with a defeated shrug. "You became my unskipped stone. Forever out of reach."

He stares at me with glazed eyes, the collar of his dark-brown coat tickling his jawline. Then he plucks his own stone from the ground, swings his arm out, and gives it a graceful toss.

Skip, skip, skip.

Plunk.

"Have you found a bridge to toss sticks into?" he wonders, searching for another stone.

"Yes. There's a small bridge a few miles away. I'll drive over there every once in a while."

"Watch the sunrise and sunset?"

"I do. As many as I can."

"Horses are a given," he notes, glancing back at the stables. "Do you dance?" Max tosses another stone with perfect rhythm.

"Yes. Every Friday at a local bar."

"Do you dance alone?"

The underlying question is evident. I nod again, slowly, watching another pebble leave his hand and dance its way across the newly rippling surface. "There hasn't been anyone else for me, either."

Pausing, he glances at me, relief filling his eyes. Then he takes my hand in his, outstretches my fingers, and places a grayish rock in my palm. "Try again."

I sigh. "It's pointless."

"It's not. You'll get it."

Shaking off my jitters, I try to concentrate as I sweep my arm out and whip it forward.

Plop.

I try two more times to no avail.

On the third attempt, Max moves in behind me, until the front of his coat is pressed up against my back. I go still. My breathing feels unsteady, my heart jumping like the stones that refuse to skip. I feel him falter for a moment, his nose dipping to my hair as he inhales a shuddered breath. My eyes close. I lean back on instinct, my balance teetering, my stomach in ropes.

"It's all about the rhythm and the glide," he murmurs against my ear. Max's fingers trail down the length of my arm until his hand is clasped around mine.

I want my gloves to incinerate, to turn to dust. I want no layers between us, no barriers.

Swallowing, I let his fingers tangle with mine briefly before he slowly swings my arm back and forth, assisting with the rhythm. Forward, back, repeat.

It's almost like we're dancing.

"The last time we did this…I think I fell a little bit in love with you," I confess.

A warm plume of his breath hits the shell of my ear. I'm not sure if it's a sigh of relief or a groan, but it sets my insides ablaze. His scent overpowers me, unravels me, as I tremble on two shaky legs. It's freezing outside, but I've never felt more warmth.

"Me too," he says softly. Max's other arm snakes around my middle and holds me tight, while his right hand still sways with mine. "Toss the stone, Sunny."

I close my eyes.

I envision us three years ago at Tellico Lake, the sunset staining the sky in an apricot blush, all of my worries and fears setting with the sun. I recall myself looking forward to dawn, to a new day, to a new beginning. With him. There was a golden glow around my heart, the feeling as unpredictable as the ever-changing weather in our story.

My arm rears back a final time, his fingers still cradling my hand, and I let go of the stone.

A few tiny plunking sounds travel to my ears.

Max hesitates, inhales a quick breath.

Then he leans in to me and whispers gently, "You did it."

A smile pulls at my frozen cheeks. My lashes flutter, my eyes opening, and I stare out at the dark water as I lean against Max, letting him hold me upright. His other arm falls away from my hand to join the one that's circled around my middle. He squeezes me tight, his face dropping to the crook of my neck. I feel his lips graze my skin, followed by a light kiss. Then another.

I shiver.

"You skipped your first stone," he murmurs, sprinkling more kisses along my throat, my ear, his hands skimming the front of my puffy coat.

"I skipped my first stone," I repeat breathily. "And…you're here."

"I'm here."

Spinning in his arms, I reach up and clasp my hands around his neck and lower his face to mine. My lips part when our noses kiss. Max drags his hands up my body in slow motion, then cups my face between his palms.

The feeling never left.

The glow, the shimmer ringed around my heart.

I lift up on my tiptoes and press my lips to his.

His lips are cold, but his tongue is warm when it slips inside. A moan falls out as my hands squeeze the nape of his neck, my eyes hesitant to close as I fully drink him in. Heat blooms everywhere, from my chest to my toes. It's a reunion, a coming home, a feeling of completion.

"You can close your eyes," he whispers, pulling back briefly. "You don't have to look at me if it hurts too much."

I falter, my breath catching. "What?"

Max swallows as our noses brush together. "I just mean…if you still see him."

My heart cracks. Tears pool, and I shake my head back and forth, emotion clogging my words. "No, Max…no," I tell him, holding him tighter. "I only see you."

It's true.

With the weight of our past hanging between us, I see *Max*—the man standing before me now, offering comfort and understanding. The specter of his twin brother's actions may linger in my memory, but in Max's arms, I find a safe space where the wounds of the past can heal, and where the promise of a shared future begins to take shape.

He is not his brother.

Just as I am not mine.

Max lets out a sigh of relief, and I pull him closer, the kiss gaining wings as we soar across a midnight sky, his hair between my fingers, our chests and hearts flush together.

When he pulls back for a breath, his forehead drops to mine. "We're fixable," he says huskily, pushing my hair back and kissing the top of my head. "I never doubted that. Not once. It's always been you, Ella. Since the day I saw you in the schoolyard reading *Winnie the Pooh*, I knew I'd found my best friend."

A small cry leaves me as I yank him back for another kiss.

We stumble, walking backward through the tree line, a clumsy trek toward the property. My hat slides off my head, my boots catch on sticks and branches, but our mouths hardly unlock. Max reaches down to scoop me up, his forearms linking underneath my thighs. I hang on to him as our lips and tongues tangle, our bodies drawing closer to my RV.

He presses me up against the siding, a breath leaving me as my legs circle tighter around him. His eyes pan up briefly, drinking in my decked-out RV that's softly illuminated by an under glow and string lights from the adjacent property. "Wow," he mutters, glancing back at me with a smile. "I'm impressed."

Max stares at my little life on wheels, newly repainted in bright orange with a glossy finish. Large, vibrant decals cover its sides, showcasing iconic book spines that seem to stack upon one another. The title "Sunny's Book Voyage" is emblazoned across the top in whimsical, flowing script. The vehicle has exterior under-glow lights in a soft gold, making it shine.

"The title is lame," I admit. "I couldn't think of anything clever."

He shakes his head, eyes still sparkling and aimed at me. "It suits you."

My heart squeezes as the words wash over me like dawn's first blush. I nibble my lip and nod at the vehicle, an invitation for entry. "I can show you the inside," I offer. "So we can warm up."

He bites his lower lip. "All right."

Max follows me inside and I try not to clam up, knowing what might come next. Max Manning is in Michigan. Standing in my RV. Inches away from me.

His tongue was in my mouth.

And I want it everywhere.

A familiar feeling races down my back as I feel him close in on me in the cramped quarters, and it's the same feeling I had at the bar. That knowing, prickling feeling that revved my pulse and heated my blood. "How long have you been in town?" I wonder, moving to allow him more space.

His focus skips around the interior furnishings. "Not long."

I walk farther inside, my gaze settling on the rumpled bed down the little hallway, spotlighted with a plethora of flickering electric candles and wax warmers. My cheeks burn. The accommodations aren't exactly primed for guests, and there's nowhere else to sit. Just the super romantic-looking bed.

This is terrifying. And magical. And wonderful and scary and surreal. I have no idea what I'm doing.

I wring my hands together and peer up at him through timid lashes.

He's fully lit now, free of shadows and nightfall. The sight of him steals my breath and strangles my lungs.

Max steps toward me with a similar expression, brows bent, eyes full of wonderment. He reaches for me and grabs hold of my coat zipper, sliding it all the way down until the fabric pops open.

I stare at him and wait.

He takes both hands and dips them inside the coat, up to my shoulders, then pushes it off me. It falls down my arms and lands at our feet.

My eyes close and my fingers curl into fists as I wait for more. I hear his own jacket zipper pull down, the rustling of his coat falling away. Warm body heat zaps me when he steps closer, his hands lightly gripping my hips, fingers dipping beneath my rust-colored sweater to graze my skin.

Then he leans forward and whispers, "We don't have to take this any further tonight, Ella. I'm happy just holding you. Kissing you. Watching the sun rise in your arms."

A tear slips out and slides down my cheek.

I think of all the times I made him leave before the sun came up.

The sun was harsh, unforgiving, too bright. It shone light on all of our shattered pieces that I couldn't put back together, so I hid them away in the dark.

Guilt gnaws at me, knowing how much he craved waking up beside me in my bed. How much he yearned to watch that golden light spill in through my open window and bring us a little bit of warmth.

"Max," I choke out, my arms drawing up to link around his shoulder. "Stay."

He smiles as he guides me to the bed, scattering kisses along my hairline as we kick off our boots. I pull him down with me, flipping off the lamp until we're only illuminated by the candles' low light, and I reach for the white stone sitting on my bedside table.

We snuggle up, side by side, his hand resting on the small of my back, under my sweater, and my face pressed to his chest. I inhale deeply, my soul filling with pine needles and fresh mint, with another life and a new life flickering on the horizon in every hue of orange.

Our legs tangle beneath the blankets as my eyes drift closed. Before peace carries me away, I whisper into the silence, "Max?"

He holds me tighter. "Hmm?"

A playful smile hints as I lift my arm slightly and flex my bicep. "We never did have that arm-wrestling match."

I feel his chest rumble against me, a soft laugh teasing the quiet. Max finds my lips for a lingering kiss before he breathes out, "That's because I was never bored when I was with you."

He stays until morning.

He's there when the sun crests and a new day dawns.

We sleep past sunrise, but when my drowsy, dream-kissed eyes flutter open in the glimmering daylight, his face is the first thing I see as I come back to life, wrapped up in his strong arms, while my precious white stone is fisted in my hand.

And it's just as good as every golden sunrise.

It's better.

Chapter 46

MAX

AN ENGINE PURRS OUTSIDE THE FRONT WINDOW AND A NERVOUS LUMP lodges in my throat.

I have Brynn and Kai on speaker phone as I move through the main living area with Klondike zipping around at my feet, his tongue hanging out of his mouth.

My heart jumps between my ribs. "She's here."

"Ahh!" Brynn squeals.

Kai smiles into the screen, his arm around his girlfriend. "How nervous are you?"

"What's the scale?" I shake my head. "Doesn't matter. The scale exploded five seconds ago."

"It's going to be great!" Brynn says, grinning brightly. "Oh my God, Max. It's all coming down to this moment."

She's right about that.

Ella is here for a job interview.

Little does she know, she's pulling up to Sunny Rose Farm for far more than just a job.

Years ago, I recall browsing through Ella's collection of storybooks, novels, and poetry compilations that lined dozens of bookshelves in her cantaloupe bedroom. Those were the days I'd sneak through her window and we'd talk and laugh and let go of every burden weighing us down. That's the best way to describe that year with Ella in the months before darkness rolled in and eclipsed our hard-fought sunlight.

Weightless.

Nothing felt heavy when she looked at me.

Nothing felt like too much when her hand was clasped with mine.

I made a routine of choosing quotes and passages from her books and highlighting the ones that meant something to me—the ones I believed meant something to *her*.

One of those quotes never left me.

"What we call the beginning is often the end. And to make an end is to make a beginning. The end is where we start from."

It's a quote from the poem "Little Gidding" by T. S. Eliot. I carried it with me because I believed in it with every tarnished piece of my heart. Those words kept me going. They allowed the rusted pieces to keep functioning, to keep moving, to keep beating with fine-tuned rhythm.

The end is where we start from.

Once there's an end, you can never go back to the beginning, and that feels permanent. People latch on to the finality of that and overlook the deeper meaning, the hope that resides inside.

No, you can't go back to the beginning…

But you can always create a new one.

You can take those ruptured pieces lying at your feet and glue them back together, knowing you'll never shape them into what they once were, but believing you can create something even better.

That's where healing lies.

That's where overcoming happens.

My new beginning is ten acres, a renovated house, and a little white horse sleeping in the stables. I've been weaving together my fresh start for over a year now and it's only missing one thing. And even if that one thing walks the other way in the end, I've still found my way to the other side. There's been peace in the process. Renewal in the undertaking.

Comfort in the belief that Ella will live out her dream, even if that dream doesn't include me.

Brynn hops up and down, her pigtails bouncing as she stares at me through the phone screen. "I almost gave it away yesterday when I brought up Ella's interview that she never told me about." Her nose wrinkles. "I'm terrible at keeping secrets."

"You did good," I assure her, glancing out the window. "Thank you both. For everything."

Fun fact: Brynn is terrible at keeping secrets.

She told me where Ella was living a week after Ella took up residence on Natine's horse ranch.

But there was no secret in how we still felt about each other, despite everything that happened. Brynn still talked to Ella regularly and told me there wasn't a single conversation where Ella didn't bring up my name, ask how I was doing, or have tears shining in her eyes when she spoke about me.

I was confident our story wasn't over.

And that confidence only gained wings last night when she let me hold her until dawn's light spilled in through the window of her RV.

Brynn is still squealing with anticipation as she bounces next to Kai. "You have to fill us in immediately!"

I heave in a deep, calming breath as I stalk toward the main window. "I will. I'm not sure how she's going to feel about any of this."

"The same way she feels about you," she says assuredly. "I know my best friend, Max. She's still head over heels for you."

"Enough to lay new roots on a little horse farm I named after her?" I internally cringe at the image of her laughing in my face and running in the other direction. "This might be next-level madness."

"Next-level love always comes with a little next-level madness." Brynn and Kai share a soft look. "Okay, go get your girl. We'll be waiting!"

I blow out that breath. "All right. Thanks again."

"Any time," Kai says before disconnecting the video call.

I hesitate before slipping the phone in my pocket.

An orange RV rolls down the long, gravel driveway and comes to a stop halfway in. I watch through cracked curtains as Ella hops out of the driver's side, dressed in a deep-orange, off-the-shoulder sweater and black leggings, her coppery-dark hair swinging all around her. Sunlight glints off her light skin and nervous smile when she peers out at the golden acreage, her eyes bright with promise and hope.

She's hoping for a new job.

I'm offering her a whole new life.

My blue heeler pup dashes to the window and hops up on the couch, his long, silvery tail swishing back and forth with excitement.

I swipe my hair back with one hand, fidgeting in place while I watch Ella assess her surroundings for another minute before she squares her shoulders and traipses toward the front door.

Klondike starts barking.

"Easy, boy," I tell him, ushering him off the couch with a rubber toy and a palmful of dog biscuits. He hops down and takes the treats, then carries the toy to his crate.

Fuck. This is terrifying. I have no idea how Ella is going to react to what I've created, and while I've made peace with a possible rejection, my heart still pounds with pleading hope.

Say yes, Ella.

Stay.

She knocks twice and I move to the doorway.

My palms sweat. My ears ring. My chest hammers with cautious optimism.

I swing the door open and watch as Ella does a double take, glances at me, over to the left, then back at me. Her eyes flare wide and vibrant green.

Her glossy lips part briefly, then snap shut as she stares at me, a startled frown bending her dark brows.

"Hey," I say, a smile stretching. Nerves stomp through me just as Klondike stomps through the living room and pounces on Ella with two happy paws and a wiggling butt. "Shit, sorry…" I take my puppy by the collar and pull him back as she gawks at the both of us, frozen to the porch step.

"What is…?" She starts blinking rapidly, head swinging side to side. "What's going on?"

Scooping Klondike in my arms, I inch away from his tongue slapping at my cheek. "You're here for a job interview."

Ella continues to stare, dumbfounded, glancing behind her at the property sign and then at me. "Okay." She draws out the word. "But that doesn't explain why you're here."

"I'm the one interviewing you."

She gapes at me in shock. "Um…what? This is your farm?"

I nod, as if that answers everything.

"Max…explain."

"Come inside," I urge, moving from the threshold and setting Klondike back down. "Klondike won't hurt you, by the way. He's only seven months old, so he's still learning his manners."

He proves my point by leaping at Ella again.

A huff of a laugh falls out of her as she crouches down in the doorway to pet him between the ears. "I don't understand," she says, peeking up at me. "Please explain. Quickly. My brain is imploding."

"Well, I found him on the side of the road with one of those Klondike bar foil wrappers hanging out of his mouth. That's how he got the name. I took him to the vet and—"

"Max."

Her arms are full of my rascally puppy, her eyes full of questions.

A grin slips. "Yes, this is my farm. For now," I tell her. "And yes…I knew where you were living. I've known for a long time." Those emerald eyes glaze over as her hand absently strokes my pup's short fur. "I bought up these acres over a year ago with my earnings from the house flips, and Chevy and our team helped me with the renovations on the house. Of course, I'm not well versed in the equestrian field, so I reached out to Natine for guidance."

Klondike moves away from Ella and starts circling my feet, allowing her to stand. Ella blinks back tears of disbelief and swipes her palms down the front of her dog-fuzzed leggings. "Natine knew about this?"

"She did." I nod. "We met up for coffee a while back. I told her who I was and asked if she thought this was a good idea or not." Folding in my lips, I shrug. "She said you'd either slap me or kiss me, but she was looking forward to hearing about the outcome."

Ella lifts both hands and drags them through her hair, her cheeks flushed pink. "I…I'm not following. How did you even find me?" Before I can answer, her eyes flare with realization. "Brynn."

"Don't be mad."

"Oh my God. You've known where I've been this whole time?"

My lips purse as I slide my hands in my pockets. "Don't be mad."

"Max…you've been living thirty miles away from me and I didn't know?" Her chest heaves with quickening breaths, her fingers tightening in her hair. "I can't… I'm just…"

"Whoa, hey." I step forward and reach for her, my hands curling around her shoulders. "Ella, listen. I was giving you time and space to heal. That was the whole point of you leaving Tennessee. It wasn't my place to intrude on that. Natine thought it was too soon for me to reach out to you and that you were still finding your way, still vulnerable," I explain. "But I never stopped loving you. Never. I've thought about you every damn day since you drove over that hill in your RV." Squeezing her shoulders, I find her teary eyes and smile softly. "I've carried you with me, all this time. You rise and fall with every sun. You're between the pages of every book I read. You're with me on every bridge, and you're in the verses of every song that plays," I confess. "I never let you go."

Tears trail down her cheeks as her eyes slam shut, lips quivering. "Did you… buy this farm for me?"

The awestruck words fall out on a hitched breath as she leans into my touch. I slide my hands upward and cradle her neck, my thumbs dusting her jaw. "You gave me and my father something I could never repay you for, Sunny Girl. This is nothing compared to that. *Nothing*. I never had a chance to truly thank you, so this is what I decided to do." I press a kiss to her hairline and whisper gently, "So, yes. This farm is for you. It's yours. There's a little horse I adopted in the stables waiting to meet you. There are hundreds of sunrises and sunsets waiting for you to watch them from the open field. There's a life waiting for you here…if you want it."

She collapses against me, her face slamming to my chest. Sobs pour out of her. Her hands latch onto my T-shirt, fisting the gray fabric as her tears soak through to my skin.

I cup the back of her head with my hand and stroke her hair. "This is my *thank-you*, Ella Sunbury. You gave my father a fighting chance at life. You gave us both a fresh start when I had absolutely nothing left to live for," I tell her, emotion catching on each word. "You told me this was your dream, so I'm giving that to you. No strings attached. This is yours."

She shakes in my arms, face smashed against my chest. "I d-don't know what to say…"

"Say you'll take it," I murmur into her hair. "Say you'll stay."

Her face lifts, nose bright red and eyes wet. "Max, I…" Sniffling, she sucks in a breath and swallows. "Is this for both of us?"

I falter, my teeth clenching as my heart teeters with unknowns. "That's not why I did this. A lot of time has passed, so I'm not expecting anything. This is for *you*, Ella." My chest feels strangled because I want to live this life with her more than anything. It's what I've wanted since the day I met her in a sun-soaked school yard. "There's no pressure. Even though it was never over for me, I understand if you don't feel the same way. I've made arrangements if things don't work out between us and I can—"

"Max." Ella's hands raise up to clasp my face. With my cheeks between her palms, she holds my gaze as she whispers back, "It was never over for me, either."

A geyser of hope explodes between my ribs. I drop my forehead to hers, closing my eyes, smiling as a relieved breath falls out. I don't need a direct answer yet. We don't have to move in together straight away and make big plans. With rebirth comes rebuilding, and I will put us back together, brick by brick, even if it takes a lifetime.

I inch away and find her eyes, smile still intact. "I want to show you around. I want to show you everything."

Ella swipes her tears away with two fingers, nodding through an incredulous laugh. "Show me."

Klondike clumsily trots beside us before settling in his crate with a toy, while I take Ella from room to room. The ranch-style house is small but cozy, strewn with new carpet and fresh paint. It's simple yet tasteful, a blank canvas for her own belongings and personality.

The only room I took a chance on is the bedroom.

Grinning wide, Ella studies every furnishing, every decorative splash, every wood beam and high ceiling. When I guide her to the main bedroom, our hands laced together, my heart skips as I bring her through the threshold.

She stops short with a small gasp.

The walls are cantaloupe. Crisp white linens make up the king-sized bed, topped with a collection of bright-orange pillows. In the corner of the room sits a small desk, adorned with bookbinding tools and trinkets. Tall bookshelves are stuffed with her favorite novels and storybooks. On the nightstand, there's a terra-cotta pot with a carrot sticking out from the dirt.

And taking up the entire far wall, directly across from the bed, is a hand-painted mural of a rising sun.

Ella's eyes soak in the room, falling and holding on the sun painting. "Oh my God…" she breathes out, awestruck and mystified.

"Do you like it?" Nerves and insecurity race through me, swirling in the pit of my stomach. "Kai painted that. If it's too much, we can paint over it. I know it's bold, but it made me think of you and—"

Ella throws herself at me, landing in my open arms, just like she did in the middle of the gravel road before an old RV stole her away for almost three painful years.

Our mouths lock together before I can take my next breath.

It's instinct.

I grip her beneath the thighs, her tongue sliding into my mouth, meeting mine. We both moan. Sweet familiarity douses me in warmth as lightning heat streaks through me, head to toe. I walk her backward and press her up against the sun wall as her hands cup my cheeks, our faces angling to taste deeper, my hips pressed between her spread legs wrapped tightly around my waist.

There is no hesitation.

No slow build or soft climb.

No forgetting.

I tug her hair back with one hand and drag my mouth down the expanse of her slender throat, her thighs squeezing me. I harden to steel as she moves one hand to fist my hair, the other gripping my bicep. A whimper falls out of her and I nip her jaw with my teeth, her head dropping backward as her hair blends with the sunny red-orange rays. Ella grinds against me as my tongue laves her throat, tasting her soft skin.

I nip her earlobe, then find her mouth again as we devour each other.

It's like coming fucking home.

Her hands quiver as she lowers them to my belt, fingers fiddling with the buckle, eager for more. "Max..." She croaks out my name with a desperate gasp. "Please."

It's all I need. I spin her around and carry her over to the bed, dropping her on the white linens and watching as she shimmies out of her clothing, her eyes never leaving me. I whip open my belt, unhook the button of my jeans, and tug down the zipper. My pants and boxers hit the floor as I reach for my shirt and yank it over my head, aching to be entwined with her.

Fully bare, Ella doesn't look the least bit shy inching backward on the bed, spreading her knees wide. Sunlight streams in through the lace drapes, bathing her in golden light.

God, the sun suits her. It always has.

Ribbons of coppery red hair spill behind her when she lifts up on her elbows, her big green eyes watching me.

"God," I say on a moan, crawling over her. "I've thought about you every day for twenty-eight months."

Ella pulls her bottom lip between her teeth as I situate myself between her legs and sprinkle kisses along her throat and collarbone. "Did you picture me like this?" she wonders breathily, one leg curling around my lower back, her painted toes grazing the arch.

"Sometimes," I admit. "Sometimes I imagined you just like this." I cup her between the legs, then slip two fingers inside. We both moan, my jaw unhinging as my eyes flutter closed. "I missed you so much."

"Max..." Her head tips backward before she collapses fully onto her back, her arms snaking around my neck. "I need you."

I bite her earlobe again before finding her mouth, our lips slamming together. Our tongues collide, the heat spinning and churning between us as my fingers work her, angling higher, deeper, sluiced with her desire.

Smiling lazily, I waste no time in snatching her by the waist and flipping her over, climbing on top of her until I'm settled between her legs. I slide against her and lower my face to kiss her. Gentle and soft. No rush, no hurry. No inevitable heartbreak looming on the horizon.

The horizon is bright, sunny, and warm.

It's just us and this moment.

Max and Ella.

I reach down to center myself with her entrance, shivering at the contact. I'm drunk on the realization that I'll be sheathed inside her, filling her, wholly connected at last.

"Please," she begs again, grazing her hands up and down the planks of my back. "Make love to me."

I push her knees to her chest, lift up to mine, then glance down and watch as I slide inside her, slowly, an inch at a time. She fists the bedsheets, her head tipped back with pleasure as I disappear inside her all the way, shuddering through the final push.

The only time I had her was on the precipice of goodbye, both of us soaked with rain and regret.

It felt like an ending. A raw finality.

This is a homecoming. A beautiful beginning.

I shift my weight to my forearms as my face hovers a centimeter above hers. Our gazes hold tight. Even through the shocks of pleasure, her whimpers, our low moans tangling as one, our eye contact doesn't sever, doesn't slip. I make sure she's with me as I slowly move inside her, drawing out the moment, the connection.

When she breaks, a tear crawls from the corner of her eye as a gasp sticks in her throat and she trembles beneath me with her hands clutched around my neck. I follow behind, drinking in her flushed cheeks, her parted lips and glossy eyes, as I find my release. Wave and wave of warmth races through me, filling me as I fill her.

When I collapse beside her, pulling her with me as I remain fully sheathed,

I wrap my arms around her and tuck her face underneath my chin. "I love you," I whisper against her hair, kissing the top of her head. "God, Sunny, I never stopped. Not for a single second. I've loved you since the day I laid eyes on you. Seven years old on a school playground, and I knew...I *knew* you were meant to be mine."

Ella cups my cheeks with both hands and lifts up to kiss me. Her tongue flicks against my bottom lip as she murmurs, "I knew it, too. Even as a little kid, I felt it."

I smile, swiping a stray tear from her temple. It's so different this time, the two of us kissed by warm sunlight instead of drowning in rain clouds and cold drizzle. "I don't want this to be over," I admit, tugging her closer. "I never want it to be over."

"I don't either," she says, words hitching on a small cry. "God...but what if we're destined to fail? What if the stars never align?" Terror gleams in her eyes. True fear that we're never going to find our happy ending. "They say all is fair in love and war, but that's bullshit. It's utter bullshit, Max. Nothing is fair about love. Nothing is—"

"You're right, Sunny. It is bullshit," I tell her, cupping her face between my palms and forcing her eyes on mine. "You're right because there is no love and war. Love *is* war. You fight until you win, or you fight until you lose. Imagine the victory after all that pain and struggle, after all those battle wounds." I swallow, pressing our foreheads together, noses touching. "War was never meant for peacemakers. There is no place for white flags and soft hearts. It's loud, feral, and violent. Love is a killer, but not everyone dies bloody. Some stand tall in the end." I squeeze her cheeks between my hands and beg, "Let that be you, Ella. Let that be *us*."

Her soft cry morphs into a sob as she nods, her hands curling around my wrists.

"Fight with me," I plead, slamming my eyes shut. "Win with me."

My heart pounds as she falls back against me, her tears seeping into my skin. I hold her, cherish her, silently beg for her to never surrender, to never give up, no matter what.

It's worth it.

We're worth it.

My gaze lands on the sun mural as she softens in my embrace, a restfulness washing over us both. A quiet hush of ceasefire. And I know. I feel it in that moment, in the next breath she takes in my arms. I feel her surrender…but not to the end.

She surrenders to everything we could be.

To everything we are and always have been.

Our new dawn.

Ella rests her cheek against my chest as our legs tangle atop the bedcovers. "You rarely win," she croaks out, her finger drawing designs over my heart as she glances over at the potted carrot resting on the nightstand. "But sometimes you do."

I smile, pressing my lips to her forehead and closing my eyes as the sun portrait fills my mind and lulls me to pure placidity. "Yeah, Sunny," I murmur. "Sometimes you do."

———————

"Oh, my God, she's adorable!" Ella bounds toward the young mare that afternoon, her boots kicking up clouds of dust. "Is she young?"

The horse's tail swings back and forth as we approach, its dark-brown eyes curious.

"She's a little over two years old," I tell her. "She's docile. Low energy and easily trained."

Ella's face is alight with wonder. "She's perfect. Phoenix was also two when we got him, back when I was just a kid."

I watch as she presses a nurturing palm to the mare's mane, stroking down its nose. "Natine helped me with the adoption process. In mythology, white horses are often associated with the sun chariot," I say, smiling softly. "Made me think of you."

Her eyes pop as she glances at me. "I didn't know that." She returns the smile, her eyes panning back to the horse as it nickers, enjoying the attention.

"She'll be ready to ride in about a year."

"I love her already." Ella spends a few more minutes talking to the horse, whispering kind words, and sprinkling her with loving touches. "Does she have a name?"

I shake my head. "Not yet. I figured I'd let you do the honors."

She nods, then pulls her hand away, turning to face me. "Max…where's your dad? Is he still in Tennessee?"

"No. I transferred him to a facility in Escanaba, where Chevy lives now and where we manage our business. It's about a forty-five minute drive from here so I visit them both regularly," I explain. "Dad's thriving. They take good care of him."

"I'd like to visit him with you some time, if that's okay."

"He'd love that. We both would."

Dad talks about Ella sometimes on his more coherent days. He doesn't remember her name—he simply asks about the pretty girl with red hair who made him brisket, wondering if she's doing all right. I tell him she is. And then he demands I bring her flowers.

We walk side by side out of the stable, the air cool but the sun warm. Ella's brown boots sink into the earth with each slow step as the afternoon glow splashes across her face. "Sunny Rose Farm," she mutters at the sky, her eyes closing against the bright rays. "I like the name."

"It suits you," I say, bumping her shoulder with mine.

Ella leans against me, her head falling to my upper arm. "I can't believe you did this for me. It's too much, Max."

I glance down at her, watching the emotion dance across her features. "It will never be enough. You saved my dad's life. You saved mine. I never would have been able to afford his care…never."

"It was the least I could do," she whispers. "I'm glad I could help."

"It was selfless. Brave. A testament to the amazing girl you are, and always have been."

She takes my hand and squeezes, letting out a long sigh. "There was a time I thought I was a monster," she admits. "Just like him."

Pain bulldozes through my heart as I shake my head at the mere thought.

"No, Sunny." I wrap a strong arm around her and hold her tight, kissing the top of her head. "Neither of us own our brother's mistakes. That's not how it works. Their actions affected us, but that doesn't make us guilty of those sins by proxy, you know?"

"Yeah," she says. "You're right." Sniffling back her emotion, her head still cradled by my bicep, Ella peers out at the low-hanging sun and smiles softly, our fingers interlacing as we stand together in the open field. Then she adds, "I think I want to name her Dawn."

Hours later, Dawn sleeps soundly, curled up in a little ball next to Klondike as he chews on a ham bone. Ella and I are on our backs, shoulder to shoulder, lying upon the vast acreage as we stare up at the twinkling sky. Night has fallen on Sunny Rose Farm and I'm taken back to a moment years ago when Ella and I watched the Taurid meteor shower together after the school dance.

But that's not what holds our attention tonight.

It's not the half-moon or the sparkling starlight, or even the picture-perfect moment of us resting beside a white horse and a young pup.

It's something far more mystical. More magical.

"Look up, Sunny," I say to her, just like I did back then when meteors painted the sky in whimsical brushstrokes.

Her eyelids flutter open.

Her gaze pops.

And she gasps, tears erupting instantly.

Slowly, almost teasingly, ribbons of green and pink begin to streak across the inky sky.

The dance of the northern lights.

Ella's wish.

We don't speak, conversation lost to the light show above. The glimmers stretch and twist across the horizon, moving in waves, each surge of color more enchanting than the last as they illuminate the farm in fleeting blips of brightness.

My own eyes mist.

This moment, this woman, this new dance between us unfolding along with the sky—it's everything.

I suck in a breath, my future so much clearer.

Everything is finally, perfectly right.

As the sky bleeds green like the emeralds in her eyes, I stand up, untangle our clasped palms, and tell her I'll be right back. She watches me jog toward the house and return a moment later, a familiar book tucked inside my palm.

I hand her the novel, the one I snuck from atop her desk before leaving the RV the night before.

Black Beauty.

Ella glances at me, her index finger grazing down the spine, a question in her starry gaze. Her throat rolls with wonder as she blinks slowly, then dips her attention to the front of the book featuring a black horse with a white diamond on its forehead. She starts flipping through, looking, searching, eager for the big reveal. She knows I've left her a little piece of my heart.

When she finds it, she gasps out a tiny cry, bobbing her head up and down as tears well in her eyes.

There, on the very last page, she finds what she's looking for.

The final line is partially highlighted.

A message from me to her.

A message from our past, from our present, from our future, written like it was meant for us as the words glitter under the sky, brightened in neon-orange highlighter:

"My troubles are all over, and I am at home."

Epilogue

ELLA

ONE YEAR LATER

Love conquers all.

That's what Jonah said to me one evening while we were cooking side by side in the kitchen, eager to surprise Mom with a feast of roasted duck and homemade mashed potatoes. I was only fifteen at the time, but Jonah was nineteen, so I figured he knew a lot about love. He had Erin, after all. Love ignited in his eyes when he spoke of her, and love sparkled in her pretty smile when she looked at him. My brother was an expert on love; I was sure of it. He was a maestro.

"Ella, listen to me, and listen good," he said, squeezing my shoulder as he sprinkled rosemary onto the meat. "I don't know much, but I do know this: love conquers all. Love conquers *everything*. If you're ever feeling low—and I mean, rock-bottom *low*—remember that, okay? Remember that I love you. Always. And you'll get through it."

Love conquers all.

And yet, I've always wondered—*at what cost?*

I take a seat at the round table, the room lit with brassy overhead lights beaming down from a sterile drop ceiling.

He hasn't changed much since I last saw him.

His hands and shirt aren't splattered in red, but his eyes still look upon me with that same fierce protectiveness I always saw in them—even on that final fateful afternoon.

"Piglet." Jonah's gaze settles on me, his voice oozing affection. He's seated across from me, uncuffed but fettered in a thousand other ways. "You finally came to see me."

Shoes squeak against linoleum while correctional officers pace the open visitation room, and I stare at Jonah as he sits slouched in a little blue chair. He scratches his thick reddish beard and waits for me to speak, knees spread and bobbing up and down, his green eyes glittering like they've never looked upon grisly horrors and bloodshed designed by his own hand.

There's still anger in my heart.

But more than that...there's peace.

Acceptance.

Love.

Love for *me*—for my own well-being, my bright future, and for all the people who pulled me to my feet and held me steady through the battering of cold winds and the destruction of one too many hurricanes.

Do I love Jonah?

Do I love this man across from me, looking at me as if nothing has changed, as if we're still dreamy-eyed kids whipping up recipes and reading stories by the fireplace?

Yes.

I love him. I love pieces of a long-ago life that still cling to me when my mind wanders and my heart reminisces. I love the man he once was, the man he showed me when innocence reigned and heartache felt like something that only happened in books and movies.

I'm allowed to miss moments and cry tears of loss when the sun hides away and shadows take its place.

I'm allowed to love him.

But the key to healing is when you know what to hold on to...

And what to let go of.

Despite that love.

"I'm getting married tomorrow," I tell Jonah, watching his expression shift into surprise, his eyebrows lifting to his hairline.

"No shit?" he says, sitting up straighter. "Damn, Piglet. My little sister found love. I always wanted that for you, you know."

I tuck in my lips, glancing down at the scratched tabletop. "I'm marrying the brother of the man you murdered."

He goes silent.

Voices chatter around us, loved ones conversing with inmates, correctional officers directing orders.

I look back up.

Jonah presses his tongue against his cheek with a slow nod, the glimmer in his eyes dimming. "Well, that's some twisted irony. I suppose I shouldn't expect an invitation to Christmas dinner once I get out of here, huh?"

I swallow, my heart twisting with barbed knots. "You almost ruined us."

He leans forward on the table, his eyes narrow, forearms flexing as he folds his hands together. "I was protecting you, Piglet. I was saving you from that vile piece of shit who almost murdered *you*," he shoots back, irises darkening like storm clouds. "I'd do it again. I would. In a fucking heartbeat."

My heart hammers like a nail in a coffin.

Jonah is in that coffin. I'm covering him in dirt, lowering him in the ground for good.

I have to.

I have to, even though it hurts. Even though I love him.

"That's why you'll never see me after today," I confess, my voice cracking with pain. "I won't be visiting you again."

Just like that, the storm in his eyes morphs into a sad, slow drizzle as his breath hitches and cracks. "Don't say that."

"I'm not Mom," I whisper back. "I love you, but my love doesn't conquer all. It doesn't override the horrible things you did, the way you dismantled the life I was creating, the one I had just started rebuilding from the ground up. You tore it all down and left me shattered."

"C'mon, Ella," he bites back, pain skittering across his face. "You say it like I'm a fucking monster, when all I was doing was keeping you safe. I swore I'd do anything for you, that I'd protect you until my dying day, and I don't regret keeping that promise. Not one bit." He leans in farther, holding my stare. "And I hope to God that man you marry would do the same."

My bottom lip wobbles. "Max isn't like you. He's good and pure and noble. He fights the *good* fight for me. He protects my honor, but he protects my heart, too." Eyes fixed to the shiny tile floor, I fist my hands together in my lap. "You told me that you'd do anything for me. You swore it."

"You know I would," he confirms. "I think I've proven that, haven't I?"

My teeth grind together as I glance back up at him, watching as his coppery brows furrow while he waits for my request. "I'm going to ask you to do one last thing for me. You have to promise you'll do it."

"I promise," he murmurs, hands curling around the edge of the table, squeezing tighter, waiting, and waiting.

I square my shoulders, heave in a deep breath, and say, "Don't ever come looking for me."

A beat passes.

A tense, silent beat, where my words float to his ears and his features slowly collapse with heartbreak. Jonah deflates, his fight draining, all trace of light flickering from his gaze.

"Please," I beg, tears brimming. "You swore you'd always protect me, and this is how you're going to protect me." My lips quiver, hands tremble. "You're going to protect me…from you."

He shakes his head back and forth, disbelief shadowing the green in his eyes. "Ella, that bastard almost killed you. He could've hurt you again, and I—"

"It's not about him," I say through my agony. "It's about you. It's about the lengths you'll take, the lines you'll cross, no matter the consequences. I can't live my life in fear, wondering what you'll do next or how you might flip my world upside down again. I love you, Jonah, I do…but I need to love you from afar."

Tears well in his eyes as his jaw tics with raw emotion. "No," he whispers. "No, Piglet."

"Yes," I say brokenly. "When you walk out those prison doors in six years, eight years, ten years…you're going to live your life without me. Pretend you don't have a little sister, if that's what it takes. Mom never brought me home from the hospital in a pink swaddle, we never played Pooh sticks on a wooden bridge, and you never shot a man in the chest in the name of brotherly love." I force the words out, breaking down further with each syllable. "I never had an orange backpack that I carried around with me every day, wishing you were there to carry it for me. We didn't have inside jokes, or favorite recipes, or adventures in the Hundred Acre Wood behind the ranch. It was all a dream. A storybook."

Tears slip from his jaded eyes.

Little droplets slide down his cheeks, one by one, as he stares at me in silence, his throat rolling, knuckles going white around the table.

"Promise me," I finish with a small cry. "Promise me you'll do that."

Jonah stares at me for another harrowing second before inhaling a breath and swiping a hand down his face, erasing the evidence of his pain, of the awful pain that he set in motion with the pull of a trigger. He stares, blinks, and his lips part but no words push through them.

All he does is nod.

One nod.

One final promise.

"Thank you," I rasp, nodding back at him, cupping a hand around my mouth to hold in my heartache. "Thank you, Jonah."

Before I inch the chair back to leave, his departing words finally trickle out, landing in my ears and puncturing my heart.

"How lucky I am," he chokes out, throat rolling with sorrow. "To have something that makes saying goodbye so damn hard."

I glance at him one more time. One last look at my big brother.

Then I pull my eyes from his, stand from the chair, and run from the room.

Goodbye, Pooh Bear.

———

Instead of lighting candles or filling vases with sand, we toss sticks over a bridge. The branches slip from our fingers before we race to the other side of the rail, and I hold up the hem of my orange dress—the same one I snagged off a thrift store rack and wore to the Fall Fling. Max is beside me, his hand in mine, and together we lean over the railing and watch both sticks glide down the stream and appear below us.

Neck and neck.

Side by side.

As always, mine takes the lead and inches ahead by a centimeter.

A smile blooms as I celebrate my victory and Max gifts me with a teasing glare. "One day the universe will take pity on you," I tease.

"Maybe this is just the universe's way of trying to even things out," he replies.

"How so?"

Before we turn back around to face our friends and family, Max bends to whisper something in my ear. "You win every round of Pooh sticks," he murmurs. "But I win you."

The late-June breeze rolls off the water and my hair takes flight, right along with my heart.

Chevy has his hands folded in front of him as he waits for us to reapproach, prepared to officially give us the title of husband and wife. Max always said Chevy was a jack of all trades, and he wasn't wrong. The guy does everything. He dabbles in dog training and runs a kennel out of his house, plays the harmonica like a seasoned blues musician in a smoke-laden jazz club, and on clear nights, he sets up a telescope in his backyard and invites us over for stargazing underneath a milky moon.

When Max asked him to marry us on this old Michigan bridge we've come to love just as much as our Tennessee bridge, Chevy wasted no time in getting ordained.

Max twines our fingers together and leads me back toward Chevy as we finish the simple vow ceremony, sealing every perfect promise with a kiss under the summer sun. I laugh when he dips me, almost dropping me, my hands clinging to his father's hand-me-down suit as my hair spills down my back and my bouquet of vibrant orange roses lifts toward the sky.

Everyone cheers.

"Woo!" Brynn lights up from behind us, her flower bouquet also heaving skyward, the pink petals matching her bubble-gum lipstick. "You did it!"

Matty and Pete have their arms around each other, Matty's head on Pete's shoulder as he dabs a handkerchief to his eyes.

"Hell, yes!" Natine shouts, fist-pumping the air, her giant gold earrings catching on a sunbeam. "That's my girl!"

Max hauls me back up and plants a sweet kiss on my forehead.

The moment I leave my husband's arms, I run into my mother's. Mom lets go of Ricardo's hand and wraps me in a warm, hard-earned hug, her face falling to the curve of my neck. Tears wet my eyes as her familiar gardenia scent washes over me and fills me with nostalgia-spun memories.

"I love you," I say against her permed hair. "So much."

"Love you most, sweetheart."

I no longer question if she loves me most—more than the countless challenges life slung our way, or more than the faded memories of our past.

More than Jonah.

The warmth in her voice, the tender touch of her embrace, and the years of sacrifices and silent battles she fought for our family all affirm her love for me. Jonah may have stood at the forefront of her efforts at one time, as her way of clinging to control in a seemingly powerless situation, but in this moment, wrapped up in her arms, I feel the clarity in my mother's words.

Ricardo hugs me next, telling me how proud he is, and Kai steals me away to spin me around and squeeze me hard, thanking me for seeing him all those years ago when no one else had.

Brynn had, though.

Brynn sees everyone, no matter how small, no matter how quiet, no matter how shadowed and obscured.

It's her Christopher Robin eyes.

And I see her, too—she's unmissable, skipping toward me, a vision of hot-pink happiness.

"Ella!" she chirps, leaping at me with one of the luminous grins that have brightened my heart for years. "I'm so happy for you. Gah! Do you know what this means?"

I pull back from her hug, my cheeks streaked with tears. My eyes pan to her glittering engagement ring, showcasing a pear-shaped diamond, ringed with pale-pink stones. "What does it mean?"

"We're basically sisters!" she squeals. "Just like I always knew we would be."

I breathe out a charmed laugh.

In a way, she's right.

Mom and Ricardo said "screw it" a few months ago and eloped to a private beach in Mexico to officialize their love. And by this time next year, Kai and Brynn will be married—making us, in a roundabout way, sisters.

Not that we need the title.

I recall standing on a similar bridge once, telling Max about a passage that's often taken out of context: "The blood of the covenant is thicker than the water of the womb."

As I look around at my chosen loved ones, I know the quote rings loud and true.

Max's father sits in his wheelchair near the edge of the bridge with a nurse beside him, his eyes glazed and whimsical as he stares into the joyful chaos, his peppery-thin hair fluttering in the breeze. I jog toward him, hiking up my dress as my sneakers slap across the bridge planks.

"Mr. Manning," I call out, watching as he blinks slowly before his focus falls to me. "I'm so glad you could be here today."

The nurse smiles pleasantly, stepping aside to allow us a moment.

"Hello, there," Chuck says, a wide smile stretching as something like recognition fills his eyes. "Look at you. You remind me of my late love, Vivian."

"Vivian?" I'm positive Max's mother's name was not Vivian. "Your wife?"

"Oh, no," he murmurs, that glaze settling back into his gaze for a beat. "My wife left me willingly. Vivian never did."

I move in closer, letting down my dress and squeezing the flower stems. "I've never heard you talk about her before."

"Haven't I?"

"I don't think so," I say.

He smiles fondly, lost in unseen reveries. "I only had her for one summer before the lake stole her away from me," he says. "She had red hair, the color of cherries in late summer. She promised me we'd always be together…and I can't help but wonder if she's still waiting for me."

Blinking slowly, I stare down at him, unsure of what to say. I don't know if Vivian was real, or if she's just a figment of his ailing mind…a hopeful promise of better days.

Either way, I don't think it matters.

I stretch a warm smile and crouch down in front of him. Inside the pocket of my orange dress is a familiar white stone. I slip my hand inside and pull it out, weighing it in my palm before handing it to Max's father. "I want you to have this," I tell him. "It means a lot to me. It's kept me grounded for years, whenever my thoughts were dark and my mind was restless. Maybe it will do the same for you." I reach for his sun-spotted hand and stretch out his fingers, pressing the little stone in his palm. "Maybe it will bring you closer to Vivian."

He glances at it with cloudy eyes, his thumb grazing along the smooth ridges. "Thank you," he whispers, clutching it tight. "This is very kind of you. I wish I had something to give you in return."

Max comes up behind me then, pressing his palm to my lower back.

I glance up at Max before my focus floats back to Chuck. "You have given me something," I say softly. "You've given me more than you know."

Pulling to a stand, I watch as the two men clasp hands, Max's father holding his son's palm with both of his and tugging him forward for a long hug. I don't hear the words said, but I feel the palpable love between them, the devotion. Max never gave up on his father. Not once.

And I will never give up on them.

We end the ceremony on two horses, me riding Dawn, and Max galloping atop our newest family member, Phoenix II, with a "Just Married" ribbon dangling from each tail as we wave goodbye to our friends and family who are cheering us on in the distance. And an hour later, we are back on Sunny Rose Farm, guiding our beloved horses to the grazing pen as we share an intimate dance beneath the shimmering sky.

Max turns on a familiar playlist, and "Surefire" by Wilderado fills the air while the same emotions I felt in Max's truck on a crisp fall afternoon sweep me up in a tearful, emotional swirl.

Living.

Pure, wholesome *living*.

I've come to realize that some people have a way of making you feel as if living is more than just being alive. Being alive is a privilege, sure, but it's basic biology. Existing is the automatic rhythm of breathing in and out. But when your lungs breathe rapture, and your heart pumps with passion, and you find yourself fully present in every precious moment?

That's where you find life's true rhythm.

And living, I've learned, is a priceless gift.

The song fades into another sun-kissed melody as I wrap my arms around my husband and bury my nose against his chest, closing my eyes and letting him thaw the remainder of my frozen pieces.

We stay like that for a handful of blissful beats before Max glances down at me with a smile. "I'll get the horses put away, then meet you inside so we can...*consummate* this eternal commitment." He kisses the tip of my nose and adds, "Wife."

I lift up on my tiptoes and kiss him right back. "I'll be waiting with a Dr Pepper."

Moments later, I'm stepping inside our bedroom for the first time as Ella Manning, the sun mural lighting up the far wall and making me beam just as bright. Heading toward my work desk, I pull out the leather-bound book Max gave to me on a Christmas long ago—the book he created that predicted our happily-ever-after within pages of sweet words and vibrant sketches.

I graze my fingers down the front, smiling at the title.

Eeyore's Happy Ending.

As I set it back down on top of the desk, I shift my gaze to the right and discover an old, tattered notebook resting out in the open, put there for me to find. Max must've uncovered it from one of the unpacked boxes still stored in our bedroom closet.

A frown furrows. I haven't opened this notebook in years. Not since the day at the clearing when I was just a moody seventeen-year-old.

With a knot in my throat, I flip through the old notebook, memories coloring my mind and warming me up, head to toe. Doodles, drawings, notes, and wishes. Everything feels like a lifetime ago as a reminiscent sigh leaves me on a shaky breath, reminding me of how far I've come.

But before I return the notebook to the desk, I stop when something catches my eye.

I go back, reread.

My eyes glaze over, my heart skipping like a smooth stone across a lake.

My unfinished letter to Jonah stares back at me, the one I'd started in the clearing that sunny afternoon when Max wandered through the trees and changed my whole life.

I still never finished that letter. I never intended to.

But…

Someone did.

My eyes slide down the page, skimming over the sparkly pink ink scribbled onto wrinkled paper from years past.

A sharp breath leaves me.

Tingles ripple down my spine, tears filling my eyes.

And love stabs me right in the heart as I read over Max's handwriting scrawled at the bottom:

Dear Jonah,

Today I fell in love with a boy who

finally caught the sun.
And he never let her go.

THE END

ACKNOWLEDGMENTS

A lot of love went into this story, and where there is love, there are people.

Thank you to my husband, Jake, for keeping me driven, focused, and inspired. This story took a few unexpected turns throughout the writing process, and you were always there, reminding me to trust my intuition, as well as helping me navigate through the unknowns.

You see, this idea came to me out of the blue while I was writing a completely different book. The song "Thrown Down" by Fleetwood Mac came on, and thus a story bloomed—vividly, tragically. There were tears, a notable aha moment, and then there was the subsequent panic when I wondered if I had time to start from scratch with a totally un-outlined story and still meet my deadline.

Thank you, Jake, for believing that I could. And for always cheering me up and making me smile when my inner Eeyore threatened to take over. I love you more than Brynn! loves glitter.

As always, thank you to my ride-or-die, Chelley St. Clair, for being my sounding board and outlet every step of the way. From bombing you with chapters titled "CHAOS GRENADE!" to giggle-fests till midnight, I know that your friendship makes all the difference for my sanity when I'm drowning in angsty words. Thank you for your selfless hours of brainstorming, direction, and honesty. Forever and always.

Huge thanks to my incredible PA, Kate Kelly, for being my behind-the-scenes maestro when I'm flailing in the writing cave (and in life). You keep everything around me from imploding, and I appreciate that more than you know.

Thank you to my kind and brilliant editor, Christa, for your belief in me and my words. Your guidance has been invaluable, shaping my author journey into something I never could have imagined. Thank you, Letty, for your fabulous suggestions and overall enthusiasm for this book. And thank you, Dee, my sensitivity reader, for your wonderful feedback, as well as everyone who had a hand in bringing my words to life.

To the entire Bloom family: my heart is so full. My gratitude is endless. And to my agent, Nicole, I appreciate all that you do for me.

Last, but never least: thank you, lovely readers. Every single one of you holds a special place in my heart. Your curiosity, passion, and dedication to the worlds I create make this journey incredibly rewarding. As you turn the pages, please know that you are the fuel behind the stories, the reason for the late nights and early mornings.

Here's to the stories we've shared and the ones yet to come. Until the next heartbreak-filled adventure unfolds—XOXO!